Mercury At Risk

Steve Rzasa

Mercury At Risk by Steve Rzasa
www.steverzasa.com

Cover illustration and design: Kirk DouPonce
Layout and design: Steve Rzasa

International Standard Book Number: 9781733585125

Books

Urban Fantasy

Mercury On Guard
Mercury For Hire
Mercury At Risk

Space Opera

The Word Reclaimed: The Face of the Deep 1.0
The Word Unleashed: The Face of the Deep 2.0
Broken Sight: The Face of the Deep 2.5
The Word Endangered: The Face of the Deep 3.0
Severed Signals
Cryptic Commands
Failed Frequencies
Mixed Messages
Empire's Rift: A Takamo Universe Novel
Strife's Cost: A Takamo Universe Novel

Science-Fiction

Man Behind the Wheel
Multiverse
For Us Humans
The Echo Watch

Superhero

Airfoil: Origins

Fantasy

The Bloodheart
The Lightningfall
Just Dumb Enough (contributor & editor)

Steampunk

Crosswind: The First Sark Brothers Tale
Sandstorm: The Second Sark Brothers Tale

CHAPTER ONE

September

I was pining for my couch as the astral fiends ripped the trees of an ancient forest to shreds.

Seriously, it had been way too long since I'd kicked back with a cold brew and a warm slice of pepperoni pizza just in time to binge my favorite series on Netflix. Don't get me wrong. My brother, Teget, and our extended family in the world of Meda put on great meals and our accommodations, though spare by 21st Century Earth standards, were comfy.

Did I forget to mention that part? How I'd spent a month and a half living in a different dimension from home? Then again, Meda was my birthplace, so, "home" was variable.

Let me back up.

The trees towered as tall as any skyscraper I'd seen in San Camillo, and trust me, there were some doozies. Branches as thick around as my torso crisscrossed in haphazard patterns, forming a spiderweb of pasty gray bark streaked with iridescent blue and speckled with brown. I could have used the leaves for blankets, albeit dark-green, dew-covered ones.

A fiend slashed one slimy, mottled black and purple tentacle across my field of vision. The branch above exploded in damp splinters, its innards steaming in the cool night air.

"This forest is a thousand years old." Teget, my younger brother, landed on a branch beside me. The guy moved with a mountain lion's lithe gait, except he was a young man armed with a silver, triple-bladed ax. He smashed the tentacle with said ax. Blue ooze spattered us. "The sooner we cleanse if of this infernal filth, the more at ease will be my soul."

"I'll be happy with not dying." I flopped onto my back as two more tentacles aimed for my midsection. They gouged the branch, tearing off thick chunks of bark.

I wasn't about to let them drain my life in a wave of freezing agony. My weapon of choice? The pulsar stave, a long cylinder etched with runes. Think of it as a metal fighting staff. It was separated into its twin components, both crackling with yellow-white energy. Each one's end sputtered sparks, forming wavering blades.

They made it easier to slice through tentacles like I was cutting melted butter with a chainsaw.

The fiend's shriek set my teeth grinding. I'd have bet the people of Meda's city could hear it, even though we were a couple miles away. Its wide-open maw let loose a torrent of fetid air.

That gave Teget the opportunity to shove the ax deep into its gullet.

Light exploded with the color and brilliance of a morning sun. And, you know, that sucks when it happens in your esophagus, because the astral fiend also exploded, its hide bursting like a balloon. I shielded my face from the worst of it. Still left shreds of dripping, clammy fiend skin draped on my body. At least it was already sublimating. It'd be gone in a minute, leaving behind a steaming stain.

Kinda what I'd wished would happen to his buddies.

"Five more approach." Teget aimed the ax skyward. He wiped blue ooze from his face. It soaked into his neatly trimmed beard and moustache. At least he was shaved bald. No worries about showering it out of his hair afterward.

Me? Well, I was a mess. Living for a month away from the modern conveniences of urban San Camillo meant I had developed a patchy scruff on my chin which, I'm sure, made me look equal parts manly and unkempt. My hair should have been brown but under the streaks of ichor from our astral fiend buddies looked more like sodden mud. On the plus side, the baggy trousers and leather vest paired with a gray linen tunic made us twins—even though he was, at the moment, the better looking one.

That was me. Mercury Hale, monster slayer, paid vigilante, and hero of a mystical realm.

I wished Loredana could see me.

"Yeah. Great." I squinted as the fiends broke through the canopy. Branches snapped in a peal of thunder. They brushed by, leafy spears that would have at the very least inflicted concussions had they hit us. I made the mistake. You know. The one where you're not supposed to look down from a great height?

The ground was a sea of black six hundred feet below.

I swore and rolled off the branch into freefall.

"Mercury!" There was a *whoosh,* and when I glanced up, there was Teget following right down the trunk, like the maniac he was. Guy looked like he'd been born skydiving.

Me? I did a fair bit of flailing until I landed in a crouch on a new branch fifty feet down.

The move had the desired effect, though, because, the astral fiends came shrieking after us. They caromed off the trees like they were pinballs in a sloppy version of the game, played by drunken college students.

I waited until they were close enough that I could see the saliva dripping from their fangs, then launched myself back up into the canopy.

The first fiend didn't bother to get out of the way. He spread his tentacles with the obvious plan of giving me the world's biggest and deadliest hug.

I spread my arms, too, my jump aided by the staves' power coursing through my body. It felt like someone had attached jet turbines to my legs. The tentacles stabbed in at me. I lopped one off, spun around, taking two more in a streak of light. I flipped end over end, my boots on target with the fiend's underside.

The fiend reversed himself in midair. By reversed, I mean one second, he was facing *down*, and the next, he was facing *up*. The speed at which he could do that astonished me, like it did every time I'd seen it live and in person, but that didn't mean I was unprepared. A tentacle's spikes glanced off my vest, leaving a slash dripping with ooze.

Too late for him, though.

I reunited the pulsar stave into a single staff and jammed it into what on a human would have been the king of all beer bellies.

The stave's energy purged itself into the monster. A golden scythe ripped through its hide, exiting on the opposite side in ragged bolts.

The fiend screamed at me until my head felt like it was going to explode. Fortunately, he burst first.

All those aerobatics, though, put me in a bad spot. That is, mid-jump, with more astral fiends surrounding me. A tentacle wrapped around my left leg.

The pain was immediate. It felt like I'd put the bare

appendage into a freezer full of ice cubes in the middle of the Antarctic. In winter. I gasped. Swore I could see my breath, even though Meda's night was a pleasant springtime temperature.

That's because astral fiends have a thing for human life energy. And when I say thing, I mean a ravenous hunger, like me and pepperoni. I tried not to think about me being their favorite snack food.

I swung the stave at my captor's tentacle. I nicked the flesh. All that did was tick the monster off and he responded by slamming me back-first into the nearest tree trunk. The impact crushed all the air from my lungs. If it weren't for the power of the pulsar stave giving me superhuman strength and rapid healing, I'd have broken my spine, no question.

Idiot. Why'd I throw myself into the middle of these goons like that? My brain usually employed more strategy than savagery. Engage one fiend at a time, but never, ever, when they show up in one big group, ready to party.

Funny the things you berate yourself for while a monster is draining the life from your cells. I struggled to breathe. My heart slowed. Someone had replaced my blood with ice water. Yet, amid dying—because that's what was happening, make no mistake—my anger bloomed.

You die, you'll never see Loredana again.

Get up, Mercury!

A bloodcurdling war cry interrupted my combo mope-fest and rage session. Teget's ax severed the tentacle holding me. Warmth rolled over me like a tidal wave. My vision cleared and, thankfully, so did my brain.

First thing I could focus on was Teget hopping from fiend to fiend like a berserker locust, tearing hides apart, truncating tentacles, and putting big ugly monster eyes out.

The screams reverberated throughout the forest, drowning out his outraged shouts.

Of course, by cutting me free, Teget had made me start falling again, so I had to address that first. Because gravity sucked.

I snagged a branch with one arm. Something popped in my shoulder. I really hoped it wasn't bone. The sharp pain spurred me on, though, forcing me to concentrate on dragging myself up to solid footing. I wished it was the saggy cushion of my couch beneath my butt, instead of yet another unyielding surface. I sat there a second, exhausted, until I could recover and stand up. Which I did in time to see an astral fiend rush up from *beneath* me.

Huh. They're pretty predictable, but even hideous interdimensional monsters must get bored of the same old tactics.

Tentacles lashed at my branch, cleaving off bark and pulp. This plan of his wasn't without flaws, though, because he had to squirm around the branch to bring his mouth full of fangs to bear.

Didn't matter, though, because as soon as that clump of spideresque eyes peeked over the top, I stabbed the pulsar stave deep into their midst.

The eyes popped and sizzled. The stench made me glad I hadn't eaten anything, as hungry as I was. Didn't make the fiend any happier, though, and he resorted to a frenzied attack that slapped me against the trunk.

I ducked another incoming blow and cut the tentacle off. I backed off far enough to get out of his reach, and held the stave at the ready, business end aimed like a shotgun's muzzle. Instead of leaping into the fray again, doing my signature slash, I willed the stave to accumulate energy, even going so far as to drain some off myself. Which might have been a bad idea, at the outset, because my wrecked shoulder started moaning for attention instead of fixing itself.

A few seconds more.

The fiend flopped onto the branch. Watching a monster with the girth of a grizzly bear balancing itself on a round column of wood as broad as a sidewalk brought a smirk to my face. Funny? Absolutely. But more so because of what I had in mind.

The shriek from deep in the fiend's gullet signaled his displeasure with his ruined eyeballs.

"You said it, not me," I muttered.

I fired.

Yeah, that's right. Fired. I picked up that trick when I made a trip through the Interstice months back. You see, in that nexus between dimensions, that nightmare wasteland that was home to the astral fiends, the pulsar stave's abilities were amplified. As in, I could use the thing to blast energy in prodigious amounts. Not something it could do well on Earth, but after some experimentation on Meda, I realized I could charge the thing up for a single, fiend-shredding blast.

White-hot energy tinged with yellow, writhing sparks shot from the stave. A lightning bolt looked anemic by comparison. The blast struck the fiend clean its face—or the ruined parts thereof. It burned a trough just above the mouth, cauterizing whatever was left of his damaged eyeballs, and exiting eight feet out his backside.

The fiend slumped, its body suddenly limp, and started a slurping slide off the branch.

Not that I was going to let the beast have even the slightest chance at recovery. I had no idea if an astral fiend could heal that devastating of a wound, but hey, I'd seen them merge with each other to make *bigger* fiends, and that was not at the top of my to-do list.

I covered the twenty feet between us with a single burst of speed, courtesy the pulsar stave, and drove the shimmering blade of light clean through his back. One puddle of astral fiend goo, coming right up.

That one was out of the way. I glanced up, to see how Teget was doing.

Oh. He was tangling with the last two fiends on a branch forty feet up and a couple hundred yards away. Man. He'd taken out that many on his own? Made sense once I thought about it. Here I was, slashing and slapping like a crazy person, while his attacks and parries had a cold calculus to them. How he managed to inflict blows on one fiend while blocking the tentacles of another, without getting himself killed, was a major miracle.

I figured he could use a hand.

The tree branch supporting Teget and the astral fiends broke. It sounded like a car being torn in half which, trust me, is a noise I'm way too familiar with. The whole thing, about fifty feet long, start a plummet toward the ground that was gonna end in 400 feet with someone or something very dead.

Teget slipped.

I ran, every muscle burning, especially the bruised and battered ones holding my shoulder together. The branch ahead of me broadened, becoming flat like the aforementioned sidewalk, eventually merging with several other branches. When Teget had first showed me these avenues that formed within two hundred to three hundred feet of the ground, I'd gotten a little teary-eyed at the sight of something Meda's environment had produced.

Right then, I was just glad I could sprint without falling to my death.

Meanwhile, Teget's branch continued its fall, tipping like a seesaw. He buried the ax in the bark, arresting his slide, but that left him defenseless from the fiends. On the plus side, they were so busy hanging on for dear life that all they could do was slash at him with the couple of tentacles not wrapped around the branch.

Which gave me an opening.

I followed the branching avenues until one path ended on a huge clearing. We're talking straight drop to the forest floor, unimpeded. Time for the pulsar stave to do its trick. I willed power from the weapon into me, pulling everything I could for the jump, right up until my boots left the edge.

I felt like I was flying.

I leapt a hundred yards. Halfway through, the wind whipping at my face, I separated the stave and let them regain their energy, because my landing wasn't going to require as much as I was going to need to kill two fiends.

They saw me coming, sadly.

I caught a tentacle to the same shoulder, this one sharp enough to cut skin. Blood splashed the side of my face.

I landed atop the same fiend and hacked into him like I was never gonna get another chance to fight these beasts.

Teget wrenched his ax free and blocked the second fiend. He battered the thing to the end of its perch, severing limb after limb, until it fell. A couple seconds later, it burst, tattered hide disintegrating as the pieces dropped.

Me? The fight had taken its toll. I missed what should have been an easy block, letting a tentacle strike me again on the shoulder. Astral fiends must be able to sense wounds, because this guy would not go after another part of my body, no matter how he oriented.

The thought only stoked my fury. I went nuts. Straight crazy. I ignored the hits the fiend dealt, making cut after cut, until I realized I was slicing into the branch itself, because the fiend was dead. Dead and sublimating.

A cold tentacle touched my shoulder.

I spun around, pulsar staves humming. They struck solid metal instead of slimy skin. Teget's ax.

There was astonishment on his face, and a flicker of fear.

We didn't have time for a brotherly chat just then. "Come on!" I ordered.

Together we jumped.

It was a stretch. A dozen feet later, and we'd have missed entirely, and no amount of interdimensional weapon healing could have saved us. But we landed on an even broader avenue a hundred feet from the ground. The tumble sent searing pain through my shoulder.

The tree branch impacted on an expanse of moss-covered rocks. It broke into five parts, sending up a spray of splinters that I swore I could smell.

I collapsed on my side, panting.

Teget slumped beside me.

"Hey," I croaked. "We did it."

He glared at me.

CHAPTER TWO

The forest was silent after the echoes of the fight faded away.

Sure, there were the ambient sounds—the chirp of insects, the rustle of leaves in the wind, the calls of winged lizards. But without the rampage of the astral fiend battle, it was downright sepulchral.

And yes, I said winged lizards. Every time I'd seen them, I'd thought they were geese, until my brain worked out that they lacked enough feathers and had scales instead. Plus, the sharp teeth were a giveaway.

I sat on a slab of weathered sandstone, feet immersed in the burbling waters of a stream that wound among the tree trunks. The pulsar stave was propped against the rock, inert. Could have been rebar. It wouldn't unlock unless a person descended from the original warriors for whom the weapons were created were to touch it. That included me, and Teget. Our family, really.

But it also included the man-slash-monster responsible for my current problem.

Teget bound my shoulder with straps. I guess he was

rigging up a harness, so I didn't strain it further. "You should be using the pulsar stave to heal. Without it, this will take a great deal longer to return to full mobility."

"At least I've got that good old Medan physiology. Better than regular human."

"That does not make you invincible." He tightened a strap. I winced. Pretty sure he wasn't going easy on me.

"Stick with the monster-slaying," I muttered. "Your bedside manner makes you a lousy nurse."

"I would not have to exhibit any bedside manner if you had exhibited caution instead of insanity."

"Pretty sure I didn't ask the astral fiends to put in an appearance. They're the ones infiltrating Meda for the first time ever."

"Do not change the subject, as you'd say, Mercury."

"Okay, I'll bite." I slid off the rock and stood in the stream. The cold soothed my ankles and shins, which were as beaten up as the rest of me. "Teach on, Professor."

"You are becoming reckless. I fear one day soon you will choose the wrong path, fall off, and no amount of my healing will save you from your wounds."

Wow. Talk about blunt. Apparently, relaxation time was over. I got out of the water and pulled on my boots. Have to hand it to the Medans. They made a comfortable pair of footwear. "Quit whining. We stopped the fiends. Everybody's happy."

"Do not walk away from me. This is a vital matter."

His voice was already diminishing, because I really was walking away from him. Why not? I didn't have time for his obnoxious brand of introspection. I needed a partner in battle, not a therapist.

"Mercury!"

"What's your problem? We're keeping the fiends good and dead, and Meda safe." The limb of a small, stunted tree brushed the top of my head. It grazed my scalp. Didn't hurt, but I was fed up with getting wounded. I sneered at it like it was an attacking astral fiend, then lopped it off with the pulsar stave. It smoked like a lit cigarette. "Happy and holy in Medaville."

"Stop it!" Teget seized my arm.

"You'd better let go."

"What of it? Will you dismember your younger brother like we did the foul monsters—and a terrifying branch?"

He'd been working on his sarcasm. I gave him a B-minus. "I'm considering it."

Teget shook his head. "This is foolish. You have been blinded by hate. Led astray by vengeance."

"Yeah, well, when the man who's trying to create a couple apocalypses kills hundreds of innocent people in your city and opens a portal that sucks in your—" The words stick behind my teeth.

"Loved ones."

"Yeah. Those." I'm resisting the memory of their faces. Lieutenant Gabriel Ramos, for one. Perpetually grimacing, but beneath the scowl he had a heart for everyone, especially his family. And me. If there were adoption papers involved, he'd have signed them years ago, regardless of—or maybe because of—the fact that my parents died defending Earth from the same astral fiends I hunt. I recognized that love too late.

And Loredana.

Loredana Lark. My handler at Procyon Foundation, the organization that secretly kept tabs on interdimensional incursions while supporting community initiatives as its cover. She was the one who made sure I carried out their century-and-a-half-old mission of slaying astral fiends. She'd become a friend, and we were on the verge of more.

Were.

Then Alexander Arkwright upended my life. All three of them had been tossed through an interdimensional rift. No clue where they'd landed, until Teget dragged me here. Home. Sort of.

I pulled the tracking device from my pocket. It looked like a smartphone on steroids, and had accumulated scratches, dents, and one cracked screen in the past seventy-some days. I ran the scan for the eight thousandth time.

Loredana was in Meda. That knowledge brought me from Earth. But I couldn't pinpoint where.

"Your machine will show us what we need, in time." Teget released my arm. I'd fallen so deep into my reverie that I'd forgotten both his grip and my accompanying threat. The screen's glare bathed his face in green light. "We will find her. Even as we speak, Grandfather's scouts are due to return—"

"Which is what you said a week ago. And week before that, and so on and et cetera." I shoved the scanner into my pocket. "I don't know whether the tachyon link between the earring Loredana gave me and the one she kept is weakening or if this thing is on the fritz. I can't stand holding it for longer than 30 seconds, because every time I touch it or look at it, I'm reminded that Syndax made it—Arkwright's personal research firm and experimenters on astral fiends. The ones who reanimated corpses to breach a portal between worlds. The ones who made this whole mess, that I only made worse by not killing more of them!"

I separated the staves and lashed out with a wordless shout. A ten-foot tree toppled. Flame flickered from its charred stump.

Teget, who was wearing fingerless gloves, tamped the fire without even looking at it. His gaze bored into me, instead. But he shut up and let us walk on in peace. Since we had a couple miles to go until we returned to the city, I was okay with that.

I mean, I can't blame him. I was worried about me, too. There wasn't a day that passed I didn't wake up feeling sick with anger. Guilt was worse, though—guilt at the realization I'd failed my friends. Failed San Camillo. Sure, we'd stopped the bad guys, but the cost was too high. Too many people had died before we'd gotten our act together. All because one lunatic from another dimension had decided to play God and try to mutate astral fiends into a new form of life.

The experiment had worked, too.

I should be back in San Camillo. Defending my city. Because Meda wasn't the only place hit by astral fiends. The rips had started opening again. And unlike Meda, San Camillo didn't have a race of people who possessed powerful weapons not only attuned to interdimensional weapons but also perfect for fighting fiends.

Teget and I followed the stream to where the forest thinned out into a smaller, shorter version of the ancient glade. I could feel something different, like the air itself was pulsating.

"Hold." He stepped ahead of me, ax at the ready. "This juncture is active."

Juncture was a good word for it. The small clearing housed a point where Meda and the Interstice overlapped. This was how Teget both left and re-entered his world. Heck, as far as we knew, it was the only way in and out. At least, that's what we thought until astral fiends started popping up within a few miles' radius.

My guess? Another consequence of that catastrophic showdown in San Camillo's Cavill Cemetery. We'd unsettled the natural barriers between worlds.

Now something else was coming through that wasn't supposed to.

The brilliant light made it daytime for a few seconds, and I thought I was finally gonna get another chance at killing Arkwright, but when the afterimage faded, what I got was a slim man of Middle Eastern descent, dressed like he'd just come home from a 9 to 5 in an architect's office.

Which, I guessed, he had.

Dominic Zein had on a blue button-down shirt, black slacks, and shiny Oxfords. I half expected him to have a briefcase, too, but instead, he wore twin armbands, each one shimmering with latent energies similar to those of the pulsar stave. The bands slowed from a frenetic spin, clusters of fragments coalescing into a static shape. Pretty dramatic. Echo Watches, he called them.

"Mercury. Teget." Dominic nodded. "Good to see you both."

"Likewise." I offered a hand.

He shook. A frown deepened. "Are you all right? You look—awful."

"It's the lighting."

Dominic snorted. "I'll leave it be, then."

"What brings you through the Interstice? My regular early morning traffic update?"

"You're the one who wanted regular reports from home. I'm providing those." Dominic rolled down his sleeves, covering the Echo Watches. "And in case you've forgotten, I have my own missions for Procyon that babysitting you is interrupting."

I chuckled. Nice to see he could dish it out as well as he could take it. "So?"

"So, fiend incursions have risen. Liz is doing her best to keep them tracked, but support from the rest of Procyon's offices has been limited. It doesn't help that Homeland Security's been breathing down our necks, quite literally, sometimes."

I rapped the pulsar stave against my leg. "If fiend incursions are up, I can't stick around here for long."

"You should return to your city, and help your people," Teget said. "I will continue the search for your friends."

"No way. I'm not leaving here without Loredana and Ramos. Wherever they're at." I ran a hand through my hair. "But with fiends running amok again—"

"We're handling it," Dominic said.

I rolled my eyes. "What, you find an extra pulsar stave in the closet?"

"No. Liz is modifying experimental Procyon technologies, using data we—you, I should say—appropriated from Syndax."

Translate: info we stole from Procyon's rivals. That was partial good news. The other part, though … "And who's doing the fighting? You?"

Dominic seemed abruptly bashful. He scuffed his shoe in the grass, like a kid called on the literal carpet of the principal's office. "There's … a measure in place. I can't talk about it. Manager Alvarez has classified the details to Liz, himself, and some in Procyon Security."

"So, a bunch of people, except for me." Alvarez. Condescending didn't even begin to cover his attitude. At least he hadn't turned me over to the feds when they'd come knocking.

"Get over yourself, Mercury. We all have a job to do. When you're done here, Procyon wants you back on yours."

"Oh, that's good to know. Once I'm done here. You mean, when I'm done searching for one of their most valuable employees? The operations handler who has the inside scoop on a boatload of their secrets?" I poked Dominic in the chest with the pulsar stave. "Namely, you and me, Teleporting Man."

Dominic tried not to smirk, but he did a terrible job masking the expression. "I'll be back in three days. That's the earliest I can manage. I have my hands full as it is tracking down a ... person of interest from Arkwright's world."

"I'll bet."

Teget glanced between us. "There is another world?"

"Like Earth, with some major changes. Arkwright was from there. He killed off his counterpart and took his place, insinuated himself in Syndax, remade it to serve his purposes, all so ..." Dominic waved his hands. "Well, here we are."

"Yeah." It occurred to me Dominic didn't have to keep feeding me intel from home. In fact, if it was interfering with his Procyon orders, it might be costing him something. Just like it was probably costing Teget his sanity to keep me from taking increasingly unstable actions. "Hey, uh, thanks. It's killing me no knowing what's going in back there, but I can't walk away from Meda, either. I can't leave. Not yet."

"I know. I understand." Dominic showed me his left hand. There was a silver-gold wedding band on his ring finger. "Trust me. I'll keep my eye on the city. But it is being protected. They're doing their best, until you return."

Great. Pronoun game. But if Alvarez wanted to keep a secret, Dominic was the guy who'd enforce it. He was the

Boy Scout version of me.

A bell clanged in the distance. Teget turned. His expression was one of utter shock. I'd seen him worried, and tense, in the middle of a fight with rampaging monsters and facing the end of the world. Right then, he was scared.

"That sounds like the temple bells," I said.

"A signal for prayer?" Dominic asked.

Teget took off running.

I waved at Dominic. "Go on, I'll catch him!"

"Be careful." He stepped back into the nexus and, with the Echo Watches glowing, vanished in a burst of light.

It was a testament to fifty days' worth of training and fighting in Teget's world, the world of my birthright, that I was able to catch up with him after less than a minute. "Hey! Stop!"

"We cannot. There is no time."

"Sure, we can! What's with those bells?"

Teget slowed, enough so we could both catch our breaths. "It is not a call to worship. It is an alarm, one that is rung only when the temple is under attack. I have never heard it before, except when Grandfather rang it as a test of recognition—and only he may initiate the sounding."

An alarm. A signal for attack? And Naos was the only one who rang it?

That meant someone was raiding Meda's storehouse of powerful relics, and our grandfather was smack in the middle of it.

I started running.

CHAPTER THREE

We broke from the forest in a full-on sprint. Every peal of the distant bells made me wish I'd been a distance runner in high school but really, I was the nerdy type who kept to himself. Par for the course when you're an orphan who's bounced between more foster families than customers at Carlito's pizza place on a busy Saturday night.

Terrible comparison, I know.

The extent of the alarm was immediately obvious. The sky was rusty, Meda's domes and slanted roofs silhouetted against a flickering reddish sky. Smoke drifted north, pushed by the breeze. Ash drifted across our path. The scent of burnt wood stung my nose.

"Been here enough times to know you guys don't have a fire department," I said between gasps. "Any chance you've got people dousing the blaze?"

"We have volunteers. They will pump water from the canals." Teget needed to sweat more, if he didn't want me to smack him for being as fit as he was. "One assumes there are enough people not involved in the defense of the temple."

"Yeah. I thought about that."

A shrill cry reached us. The sound had nothing to do with astral fiends. It was from people.

I was all set to slice and dice the former, so the first sight of our adversaries. A pair of children, dressed in loose tunics and leather breeches, came running over the stone bridge. Tiny boots tapped a frantic rhythm on the bricks. Tears cut clean paths down soot-smudged faces.

In that instant, I was a crying kid, alone in Carlito's, because my parents were dead and there was no one in the world who knew who I was.

Their mother, I assume, was on the opposite bank. Three corpse-fiends surrounded her.

Wait, corpse-fiends? Reanimated dead bodies, here?

Great. Last thing I wanted to tackle after a smackdown with astral fiends at high velocity and a long way off the ground was a herd—horde?—of desiccated beings fueled by the dark powers of the Interstice.

"Teget!" The little black-haired girl slammed into him, her arms latching to his waist. "Mother told us to run from them! They chased us from our house! She's hurt!"

"Stay near, Alaia. Protect your brother. Remain quiet and pray. Mercury and I will slay them." He got the girl and the littler boy tucked behind a hedgerow, then joined me as we advanced on the corpse-fiends. "What new manner of evil is this? Arkwright now desecrates the fallen among our people?"

"Short answer? Yes. He pulled the same trick on Earth, like I said, and he's not real picky about recruits," I muttered. "Listen. Killing these guys won't be like cutting up astral fiends. Move quick and strike fast. Give your weapon the chance to melt them. That's the only way to prevent infection."

"Infection. The dead are ... sick?"

"No, they're not sick. If you kill them with a regular blade or gun, they're gone, all right, but they can spread particles to live people and turn them into corpse-fiends. After killing them."

"Astral fiends would be easier to use."

"Yeah, well, I didn't get to advise Arkwright on the best army-building techniques!"

Teget nodded and, kicking off the bridge wall, launched himself at the corpse-fiends.

"Wait up!" I ran, again, because who doesn't love more running? I skidded up behind them right as Teget landed. The corpses had the woman cornered against a house, their hands outstretched just like in the zombie movies, except these walking dead trailed purple sparks. She scrabbled backward along the cobblestones.

All three shifted their attention to us, which was good for the woman, but I prefer having the element of surprise. Something about the tachyon emissions from the pulsar stave and Teget's ax made them magnetic to these guys.

I planted the stave into the nearest one's chest. The latent energies immolated his form, melting him like a candle in a time-lapse video.

Teget severed the head from the second, then slammed the decapitated body into his buddy's. They ricocheted off the wall of a house across the street, which gave me the opening to stab both of them until they were charred stains on the road.

Way easier than tangling with astral fiends. I blew out a breath.

"Mariel." Teget helped the woman up. "Your children—"

"Did you find them? I sent them ahead of me. It was the only way to get them free of those things." She wasn't crying. If anything, she looked irate.

Speaking of cries, there was a greater clamor up the road. I gripped the pulsar stave tight, watching the side streets of the neighborhood for anymore hungry zombies.

"They are safe. Go to them. Then take shelter in the catacombs. Have you seen others?"

"The guards went to the temple. They summoned as many men as they could find, those who weren't hunting or weren't sent out to scout the countryside as Naos commanded."

I winced. Yeah. Guess what those scouts were out doing? Looking for Loredana and Ramos. While I was running around dealing with monster after monster, all because the stupid tracking device wasn't working.

Easy, Mercury. One thing at a time.

First, the temple.

The woman rejoined her children. I spotted them joining another family, this one with a couple of teenage boys carrying what looked like flintlock muskets. I figured they were all good for protection, as long as no one got too close to a corpse-fiend.

"Come," Teget said. "The temple."

The deeper we got into the city, the larger and more imposing the structures. First time I was here, I'd run my hands over the moss growing in patches and sheets. The stone was ancient. The styles, mixed. Any archaeologist would have tripped his partner to get a gander at these. I wish I could remember my childhood here, what it was like to grow up among the long alleys and broad avenues of what should have been a city long buried on Earth but was instead a living, breathing community.

Except tonight, when it seemed dead.

The temple wasn't the tallest building in the city, but it was the biggest, the most sprawling, a step pyramid that looked like the Mayans or some other long-lost culture had just finished carving it. It was, however, the source of the fire, because the massive wooden doors that allowed access at the top of the steps were burnt to a crisp.

So were several men.

Ten of them, by my count. Most were dressed in the charred remains of Medan temple guards, but one wore patchy armor—slabs of metal linked with a twisted version of chainmail. He had a mask, too, with only eye slits to allow a clue as to who was behind it.

The eyes were bloodshot, and dead, but still had a hint of a purple glow.

"Looks like Arkwright brought new friends." I stepped around the bodies, pulsar staves ready. The clash of metal echoed from inside the temple. Fighting up ahead. I willed my heart to slow down. Guess what? Unlike the stave, it didn't listen.

"I do not recognize their attire," Teget murmured. "Could they be from Earth?"

"Doubt it. He preferred guys who wanted to play special forces. I don't think he had a bunch left after the showdown at the cemetery. But the purple eyes—yeah, that's what rings a bell. They were using astral fiend leftovers as a way to boost their strength, enable covert communication ..."

"Stop. Please." Teget's harsh whisper shook his throat. "Speak no more of his foul practices."

"Maybe I want you good and outraged when we face him."

"Fear not. I will rest only when the ax is bathed in his

blood, to atone for the atrocities he's committed."

Sounded good to me.

The hallway was darker than it should have been. Golden yellow stones lit uneven patches, while the rest were pale fragments, like broken lightbulbs. And someone had done worse damage to the paintings lining the stone walls. Some were streaked with ash; others, completely obliterated, as if a grenade had blown them apart. I'd say a good third were ruined. There wasn't even a rhyme or reason to the destruction—the scenes depicting the paradise Meda promised were the prime targets, but some of the paintings that showed how terrifying astral fiends could be were also scarred.

I got the feeling it didn't matter to Arkwright what he ruined. If it was Meda, it was fair game.

We entered the Atrium, the massive central room of the temple, complete with a cavernous ceiling that rose four more floors. Steps led up the sides, to balconies and catwalks surrounding the space. Archways were cut into the walls. Tiny channels crisscrossed the stone throughout the room, draining away from a square pool. A marble platform stood a couple feet above the water, with an onyx pedestal four feet tall at its center.

But the water was dark with blood.

Medan guards and regular locals traded shots with more of the armored guys in a lopsided battle that had nothing to do with numbers and everything to do with skill. I counted eleven Medans still standing, and that same number dead. Nine bad guys were doing the bulk of the fighting, with just a couple of their companions lying on the stone.

My mind was trying to assess the tactical mess even as one of the armored goons cut down two Medans with a short, blunt version of a musket, its gears whirring relentlessly above the trigger mechanism. Smoke made it hard to see exactly what was going on, shrouding the action in a thick mist.

But I could see to the fourth-floor walkways.

Arkwright was up there, exactly where he shouldn't be.

He stood in front of a doorway built of a thick crystalline material that was riven with cracks. The metal frame was corroded, and worse, shaking. Bits sloughed off. Red light rippled throughout the crystal, sympathetic to the vibrations.

It was hard to pay attention, because of the blood rushing to my head. You know how they talk about people developing tunnel vision in stressful situations? Yeah. All I could focus on was Arkwright.

He'd started out a handsome, well-built man with brown hair. The model of a wealthy, fit, playboy entrepreneur. Thanks to sucking tachyons out of one too many corpse-fiends—and killing some of his own soldiers in the process—Alexander Arkwright, Chief of Logistics for Syndax Multinational, was now a mutated monster freak. Eight feet tall, tentacles writhing from oozing protrusions on his chest and back, ripped like John Cena in his bodybuilding prime—he was literally a beast. The handful of glistening purple orbs that he had for eyeballs didn't improve his looks. But I was kinda envious of the obsidian scales that covered his arms, chest, and legs, poking through gaps in a very Medan set of leather tunics.

"Hold them off until I can complete the sequence!" His voice thundered above the fight, a hideous, warped chorus of overlapping tones.

"Hey, fellas!" I shouted.

Teget gaped at me. So much for surprise, I know, and

I didn't have anything better in my arsenal for a dramatic battle cry.

With that preamble, I threw myself at Arkwright's latest recruits.

Could be they were expecting the typical Medan temple guard. You know, the ones with muskets and swords who were losing the fight. So, the first one I augured toward did the normal thing—he raised his big gun and fired.

Too bad for him I was already standing almost toe to toe with him, close enough to read the surprise in a pair of wide, purple-glazed eyes. You'd better believe the surprise was still there when I stabbed him clean through the armor with the blazing, sparking end of the pulsar stave.

When I was prowling the streets of San Camillo in search of criminals to trounce—to pay the bills, you know—I was worried about how people would react if I killed one, either on purpose or by accident. Most of them weren't murderers. The worst a lot of them did was smack people around. Who was I to decide which crimes were punishable by death?

Things were different here on Meda. These scum had invaded a sacred place, a sanctuary not only for people but for my memories. Arkwright and his men—both the soldiers on Earth and whoever his new groupies were—had demonstrated they didn't care about the innocent.

Fine. I could play that game.

The next guy got wise. He and his buddy came at me with swords. Even managed to put some gashes in my leather vest which, let's face it, was never intended as armor. More like, slightly prevent death.

I blocked one sword with a stave that was so powered up, the blade melted immediately. Its owner screamed as molten metal splashed on his hands and through the slits of his helmet.

Teget was right behind me, and then beside me, dropping as many of these intruders as he could. It helped that the surviving Medan guards—the ones not dragging their injured friends to safety—showed renewed vigor by the appearance of everyone's favorite interdimensional-weapon-wielding brothers.

Before long, we'd slain or knocked out eight guys.

The last one was another story.

Teget advanced on him and found himself fighting his equal. No joke. Things didn't improve when I lopsided the odds in our favor, either. The guy battled us with every move we knew, and a bunch we didn't. His weapon was part of the problem. It was a sword, similar to a *katana* or *ninjato*—Liz back at Procyon was our resident sword expert and would have to fill me in, I'm sure. But the blade was a deep, dark black, like it was made of those nanotube filaments you hear about. Whatever its origins, it took hits from the ax like a champ, and the blazing energy of the pulsar stave didn't faze it.

I pushed my attack, hacking at him until sweat drenched my face and I had him backed against the wall. That's when I slipped. Whether it was blood or water didn't matter. My foot went out from under me, and the flat of the blade hit my face. I thought my neck would snap.

Suddenly, I was on my side, rolling, the walls and floor of the Atrium a blur of worn carvings. I saw Teget fall, too, flat on his back, eyes wide, face glazed with pain.

The masked warrior stood over us, chest heaving, the black sword poised to kill.

No. Not before I could find Loredana.

But he did a backflip instead, landing neatly the next

floor up, on the walkway with Arkwright—who was smiling down on us, the big jerk.

"It's been a while, Mercury. Sorry I can't stay for a tour. I managed to find my way around." He struck the crystalline door without looking back.

It exploded in a hail of glittering red shards.

Hundreds of metal shapes shot into the center of the atrium, whirling inside an expanding cyclone of water. The spray coated us, even as the rectangles and triangles and circles spun closer and closer together. They glowed, first a dull blue, then brightening to a silvery white that was probably gonna burn my retina. With a flash and a sonic boom, they struck each other all at once.

A bizarre, warped triangle floated in their place. It had even absorbed the water. It seemed to have three sides, yet was three-dimensional, an impossible triangle that shouldn't exist. I couldn't focus on it, no matter how I stared.

Teget groaned. He sputtered the word "hedron" before passing out.

The object drifted into Arkwright's outstretched arms, like a baby come to its father's embrace.

"I never thought it possible," he said. "But thanks to the Whisperer for showing me the way, and Marigold herself for guiding us. Oh, and Mercury? I'll tell Ms. Lark you send your greetings—since you can't seem to find her yourself."

Purple lightning skittered across the platform. I pushed up onto an elbow, my limbs shaking, and aimed the pulsar stave. If I could will enough power to it—just a single burst—I could end him. Right then.

Nothing but sputtering sparks.

Arkwright's masked companion saluted, and the two of them vanished in a violet flare.

I shouted at the dark, empty ceiling of the Atrium until my throat was raw.

CHAPTER FOUR

Morning was worse than that awful night, because the death and destruction was even more apparent. Painfully so.

I stopped counting bodies draped in white shrouds when I got to thirty-five. Most were men, yeah, from the local guards, but a few were women. Some were child sized.

Guilt was easily overtaking fury at that point.

I sat on the bank of the canal nearest our family home. It was a single-story cottage, made of white blocks with sandstone-colored columns at each corner. Hexagonal, with a copper dome that gleamed in the early sun. I fiddled with a strand of ivy I'd torn from around the brass hinges of the front door.

"Mercury?" Teget sat down beside me. He winced, his hand pressed to his forehead. A bloodstained bandage covered his brow.

"I think you need a fresh one." I tossed an ivy leaf into the unhurried current.

"I will mend." Teget smiled. "Or as the healer says, only if I stay still long enough for the salve to take effect."

"Probably you should listen to her. I'm good here."

"Let me save us both time by not listing the many reasons you are not 'good.' The men who died—they were brave souls who defended their homeland."

"I know that." Another leaf drifted away.

"Then since you know already, wise one, you are well aware their deaths are not your fault."

"No? Pretty sure I'm the reason Arkwright ended up here. I mucked up his portal, which dropped him into Meda's dimension."

"Yes, but it is not the first time we have been attacked. And what of it? Would you have stood by and let him achieve his goals? What would have become of many worlds if he had gained access to all of them? To how many would the scourge of the astral fiends have bled over from the Interstice had you not intervened?"

He had a point, but this whole self-pity thing was reinforcing for a guy like me. You know, somebody overly impressed with his self-importance. I recalibrated my thoughts toward the men who'd died protecting Meda. I hadn't made them do that. They were like me—ready to fight against encroaching darkness, to protect the people and places they loved.

But who let the darkness encroach? Your rash behavior has consequences, Mercury. It always has. One's nature is not subject to change. It's a terminal sickness.

There it was. The voice. It dug out of the back of my brain, right to the forefront of my thoughts. It wasn't my conscience, though. This was from an external source.

The Whisperer.

I hadn't figured out a way yet to deflect his insidious urgings, even though I'd noticed the pattern—defeat.

Always. It was bad enough that shadowy denizen of the Interstice could project himself into my thoughts. Worse that, on occasion, his voice took on the singsong, musical tones of Marigold Yen, the woman hailing from a genetic line obsessed with permanently opening a massive breach between Earth and the Interstice. They just wanted a freeway through which all the astral fiends and who knew what other horrors could pour into the "normal" world. No big deal.

I ground my teeth and focused on something else. Anything else. Like Aerosmith. Or the Stones. Classical music, in other words. Instead of drowning out the Whisperer's voice, it mingled, creating an insane buzzing.

"Mercury." Teget jostled my shoulder. The still-damaged one.

Sharp pain did the trick. My head cleared of the Whisperer's nonsense and the lyrics to "Walk This Way." "Thanks. I think."

"You were far from here."

"Not far enough."

Teget raised an eyebrow. "It was him?"

"Yeah. The Whisperer."

Teget sucked in a breath. "His connection to you is—unfortunate."

"You think? Give me some good news for a change."

"Very well. The corpse-fiends, as you call them, are no more. We counted five dozen, most of whom were not citizens of the city."

I felt more relief from that statement than I'd had in weeks. "So, most of them were Arkwright's imports."

"It would seem so. Yet ..." Teget frowned. "Our healers and physicians agreed upon one thing: they were not from your world, either. Their clothing and physique are Medan."

"Okay. Did you check among the dead? See if anyone's missing?"

"Of course. Our census is accurate."

I ran a hand through my hair. Might as well have been petting a sweaty dog. Nasty. I resisted the urge to dive into the canal. "Medan, but not from the city. There's outlying settlements, right? I mean, you've never taken me to any of them."

"There are. We have sent messengers to ascertain if they have fallen under attack, but we have also received no warning within the past several days. Usually the smaller towns stay in close contact with the city." Teget shook his head. "I am puzzled."

"You and me both. What about the relics from the temple?"

Teget plucked ivy from my hand. He examined a leaf, twirling it in the sunlight so it was a pale, translucent green. "The night's blade is accounted for. Neither Arkwright nor his men took it. The rest are safe."

"Yeah, right."

"I beg your pardon?"

I tossed the rest of the leaves into the canal, then snatched back the one he'd appropriated. "Look, Teget, I might not be a local, but I'm not blind. How hard did you get hit in the face? Arkwright took the swirly mess of metal pieces from behind the big No-No door in the Atrium. He combined them into a … thing. You said 'Hedron' before you played Sleeping Beauty."

Teget made a face like he'd eaten the sourest fruit from a dinner plate. "It is … that is what Grandfather wants to discuss with you."

"He's awake?" I shot up from the bank. "That's what

you should have led with."

"Hold fast." Teget intercepted me before I could reach the door of our house. "I cannot provide the answers. He can. But remember: You might not want to hear them. I am concerned it may further destabilize you."

"Destabilize?" I folded my arms. "Arkwright let a bunch of jacked-up Medan warriors into the Atrium and stole something you don't want to tell me about—and worse, he *left* the night's blade. You remember that, right? The weapon that combines with mine and yours to create a huge, gaping open portal between the Interstice and Earth? For someone who kisses the feet of Marigold and her matriarchy of wanting to destroy the world, he sure seems like he's got a new goal in mind. So, move."

Teget sighed but got out of my way.

The house's truncated vestibule opened onto a smaller hexagon, a sort of communal room. There were six doors and arches leading into the side compartments. I took off my boots before treading over the antique rugs that covered the tile floor.

Naos, my father's father, lay on a bed in the room opposite the front door. He was definitely the man from whom Teget and I were descended—black hair, like my brothers, even though most of it had long ago turned gray. The smile that creased a weary, lined face was mine. "Mercury. Ah. I should have known better that to conceal my injury from you."

The room was small, with just enough space for the narrow bed and a couple of chairs. Sunlight bled through a thick, stained glass window high on the wall. Rows of musty leather-bound tomes filled a floor to ceiling shelf. Spiky red plants lined the other.

A middle-aged blond woman sat by his side. She wore a

white cloak and poured a thick, noxious concoction into a glass. Naos gagged when she made him drink it. No wonder. I could smell it from eight feet away.

"Every last bit," she said. "If you do not, the wound's infection may spread."

"Infection?" I knelt with them. "Was he stabbed? Shot?"

The woman lifted a corner of the covers, revealing a thick bandage. Whatever had happened to him, it had left a black and brown gash that oozed through the white wrappings.

The ooze was streaked purple.

"She has arrested its spread quite well." Naos tried to sit up but grimaced and clutched at his side.

"No!" The healer slapped his hand away. "It is sure to spread if you touch it!"

"Easy guys." I helped Naos settle against the cushions. "Nobody wants that to happen. Corpse-fiend?"

Naos and the healer looked at each other. "A curious term, but accurate. I received this in defense of the temple, but not before I dispatched the last of the infernal creatures."

He gestured to the corner of the bedroom.

Yikes. No wonder Teget said the night's blade was accounted for. It was propped like a walking stick, its broad, shining edge still slick with blue-violet ooze from the corpse-fiends.

That's my grandpa.

"Please give us time alone," Naos said to the healer.

She glared at both of us. "He needs rest and needs to keep his hands off the wound." She poked a finger at my chest. "Hands. Off."

"Yes, ma'am." I grinned and mock saluted.

The woman left, muttering sharp phrases in what I was pretty sure was German, or something close.

"She means well, Mercury." Naos coughed. "Her manner is—stern but caring."

"Yeah, that's great, but I don't really care about her manner. We've got a bigger issue."

"You are here about the relic."

"Bingo. And don't pile it on about it not being a problem, because Teget just lied to me about it. You know, Teget, who I'm pretty sure couldn't lie about what he'd had for breakfast. As soon as I brought up 'Hedron,' though, he got as cagey as a kid who's been caught with pot out behind the football field bleachers."

That last line must have confused Naos, because he stared at me for a moment with the same befuddled expression I'd caught a few times in my bathroom mirror. Back when I had a mirror. And a bathroom. In my apartment.

Man, how I wanted a couch and some pizza.

"It was wrong of him to do so, but his actions were in line with the temple code. The item in question is called the Hedron of Orbits. It is not to be trifled with."

"Pretty sure Arkwright's got some trifling in mind, Grandfather. And besides, it was more than one thing. It was about a hundred of them."

"Yes. It is one made of many, each as potent as the next, yet when they are combined, they compose the greatest threat to the worlds than any could imagine."

Uh-oh. I didn't like the way he said "worlds," because my last count, I knew of four. "What is it?"

"We do not know. I do not know." He shifted position, prompting another round of coughs. Those sounded rough, like he had sandpaper stuck in his throat, but at least his color had improved. I peeked under the blanket. The oozing had lessened, too. "You recall your first visit to the temple, do you not?"

"Sure. It's burned into my brain. Finding out you were born in a different dimension from the normal one—the one that has San Camillo and California and the United States—is memorable. As in, forever."

"Good. Then you recall also what I told you of our people's history. Many important records were lost in the schism between those who sought to preserve the ancient relics and those who wanted to exploit them. They wanted power for power's sake. The worst came for the Hedron, and it was only through grace our ancestors—yours and mine, Mercury—were able to defeat them. Thus, the Hedron was disassembled."

"How?"

"Again, that is unknown to us, thanks to the destruction of our records." Naos looked like he wanted to spit, which was the same face I made whenever the Internet went out. "What we do know is the Hedron has yearned for this day."

I thought he'd misspoken, or I'd misheard. "Um, yearned? It's a weird metal triangle."

"It is much more than that. The Hedron does not merely fulfill the will of the possessor. It supplies its own, complements desires, works to its full potential."

I shifted my weight. The pulsar stave, secure and compact in a leather holster strapped to my belt, pressed against my leg. I tried not to think about this weapon, with its ability to vanquish astral fiends and act as part of a key to portals between worlds, having a mind of its own. "Can it be used to get Arkwright back to his home dimension? That's all he wanted—well, not all. First, he wanted to get home, and once he did that, he wanted to bring about the 'breaking of the wall.' Flooding Earth with astral fiends, as per Marigold

Yen's ancestral goals."

"I am not surprised, but if that were his aim, he would have simply stolen the night's blade, and then killed you and your brother."

I grimaced. "Gee, thanks, Grandfather."

Naos smirked. "Do not sulk, Mercury. You know it to be true: the sons of Sabik possess the pulsar stave and the ax. Once, you paired against evil and usurped the blade, combining the weapons into the protective trinity they were meant to become. No, this Arkwright has other ends in mind. I fear they can only be destructive."

"Wouldn't be as much fun if they weren't," I muttered. "Okay, so, he's gone. How do I find him?"

"Use the ax to divine the Hedron's whereabouts. Teget uses it to determine when a portal leads to the Interstice, or vice versa, and you spoke of using it for the same purpose when hunting the location of the night's blade on Earth. So it shall be with the Hedron."

"There is another way, Grandfather."

When Teget had snuck in the front door, and then crept across the living room, I had no clue, because I about jumped out of my boots. "Okay, don't ever. Do that. Again."

Teget smiled, but only for a moment. He was somber when he took the healer's chair and touched Naos' hand. "Grandfather, you must tell us about the attackers. I found one of the temple guard captains. He says you issued the order for their bodies to be burned."

Burned? I frowned. Cremation wasn't a big deal back home. Of course, I didn't know where the Medan cemetery was, so maybe ...

"We would never burn one of our own," Teget said. "And those men ... they are of Meda."

"No." Naos snapped the word. "They are not. Traitors and deceivers, the lot of them. They deserve only fire, not a burial in peace."

"How can that be? Are they from the other settlements? If so, they still are heirs to the same end we are."

"They—" Naos coughed, but it didn't sound as ragged as before. If anything, I would have guessed he intentionally prolonged it.

"Hey." I stood. "Let me clue you two in on a secret: I hate them. Secrets, that is. The bigger they are, the bigger mess they cause when they come out. And they always do. Save everyone involved the heartache and tell me who those guys were, Grandfather, and why you're not their biggest fan."

Naos seemed sickly again, though I'd put money on it having nothing to do with his wound. "Very well. They are Kutsatuta. The befouled, unclean, infected."

You know the stereotypical drop in temperature you experience when you hear something creepy? I got one of those. "Sounds like you're talking about the corpse-fiends."

"Far worse, Mercury. They are descendants of those we cast out during the schism of centuries past. No one knows of their whereabouts, save that they inhabit the northern wastelands, beyond the mountain shield. But ..." Naos sighed. "That does not explain their knowledge of the Atrium and the temple's layout. Such infiltration can only be achieved firsthand."

Teget's eyes widened. "There are recent Kutsatuta. From the city."

Naos nodded. "When our citizens fail to treat the relics with reverence, and attempt to corrupt them to dangerous means, we banish them from the city and the settlements."

"North. You banish them north." I shook my head.

Naos's silence was plenty of confirmation.

"Great. Just great." I stormed for the door. "Come on, Teget. Looks like Arkwright found a bunch of traitors to do his dirty work."

CHAPTER FIVE

I checked the tracker again while Teget loaded our gear.

Sure, there were blips. But they were blurred, random. I'd be staring at a set of coordinates and then, in the next second, they'd shift by dozens of miles. I scowled. It didn't help matters that the tracker had been originally programmed by Syndax on Earth, so Global Positioning System wasn't much help. I mean, wrong globe, and all that.

Teget had loaded a couple of big rucksacks with dried fruits and the local equivalent of jerky. Those flying lizards were tasty when you roasted them on a spit, turned out. He stowed the packs in a long, flat-bottomed barge tucked into a corner of the canal, seven blocks north of the house. Stone steps descended to the water level at an old dock encrusted with algae. A steam engine that looked like a cross between something I'd find in my Subaru and the old-time train boilers chugged softly at the back, sending up a constant stream of white mist.

"Do not be so hard on Grandfather," Teget said. "He is burdened with the care of our people and great many secrets."

"Did you catch the part where I don't like those? Also, I'm not mad at him." I smacked the tracker. It glitched again.

Teget rolled his eyes, in me-fashion. "Of course you are not upset with him. How could I have been so mistaken? You have such subtle emotions."

I snorted. "Okay, you get the sarcasm badge for the day."

"I shall treasure it always." Teget pulled on a rope, making sure our packs were secure. "Take heart, Mercury. I am just as displeased with his revelation, but that does not mean our goal is any less in doubt. Think of it this way: we have a chance to not only stop Arkwright, but finally find your friends."

I had already considered that. If Arkwright really did zap himself back to a new headquarters in the north, wherever his Kutsatuta buddies lived, odds were good that was where he'd stashed Loredana and Ramos.

I'm coming for you guys. I promise. It felt better to say that, again, because I worried if I forgot, it would never come true.

Naos hadn't completely spaced on the old stories about Kutsatuta. He'd furnished us a map of the northern wastelands. Not that there was much to see on said map. It was a lot of dry gulches, barren plateaus, and broken ridgelines. Reminded me of the Interstice terrain, except not as ugly. Hopefully.

There were also a ton of features that lacked labels, which didn't inspire much confidence in our navigation of that region. Fortunately, we had an edge.

Like Naos had suggested, we headed for the temple to get the ax calibrated with a tracking vision as close to our departure as possible. To say the Medans had beefed up security was an understatement. Eight guys in armor, bearing muskets and spears, lined the last stretch of the causeway. Four more waited on the steps. And six more bracketed the entry. I heard hammers and smelled sawdust nearby.

"The door is being rebuilt," Teget explained. "It will be more than equal to its predecessor. Our blacksmiths have devised iron reinforcements for each panel. And the temple wardens have … other measures that can be adapted from the relics inside."

I had a sudden fantasy of ex-Medan Kutsatuta attacking the new front door, only to have it zap them with bolts of lightning, giant sized death rays ala the pulsar stave's energy. "Sounds like a plan to me. I'll bring the popcorn."

"Popcorn?"

"To watch the show if someone tries a repeat attack."

"I do not understand what popcorn has to do with this. It is a snack food on Earth, yes?"

"Sure, but … there's these GIFs that show up when you want to show a fight between two …" I shook my head. "Never mind."

We boarded the platform in the middle of the atrium, its glossy marble surface swaying under our footsteps. He inserted the ax into the pedestal at the platform's center.

Teget had us wait at the edge of the pool as he went upstairs for the ax. I stared at my wiggling reflection. Looked confident, bold. Which was not how I was feeling. If it was possible to have third, fourth, and fifth thoughts after your second ones, I'd lined them all up after each other.

"Prepare yourself for possible disorientation," he said. "If you remember."

"Hold onto your butts," I muttered.

He twisted the ax 90 degrees counterclockwise. Metal rumbled underneath. The platform and everything attached to it—plus us—rose smoothly through the air. Dripping water echoed in the silence of the Atrium.

The green glow from the crystals that, I assumed but no one had bothered to explain, were holding us aloft provided plenty of illumination inside the dark confines. That became moot when the ceiling opened like a giant mouth was spitting us out into the gorgeous turquoise sky, the sun highlighting its greenish tinge.

We finally halted twenty feet from the roof. If the local chamber of commerce—assuming they had such a thing—wanted a place for a panoramic photo, this was the place to take it from. The city of Meda was an octagon reaching for all points of the compass. There was our tiny toy of a boat, way down in one of the canals branching out of the city to the north and south, where they formed a much larger channel that stretched far into the horizon. The landscape south and southeast was divvied up into rectangular farmland. The forest was a thick carpet strewn across the western landscape, and the trees got gigantic the farther one's eyes traced.

I was more interested in the massive mountains of sandy pink rock capped with gleaming white snows that loomed to the north, rising above long, rolling hills. That was our destination.

Only one road north, a skinny path that followed the canal.

The platform hovered, like it was waiting. I clenched my fists and waited for the next part, the one that might make me pass out. Fair warning.

The ax dumped warm light all over us, but man, was it frigid. Even Teget's teeth chattered. The world around us went monochrome, and purple lightning cut the sky.

Hundreds upon hundreds of possible portals appeared, ghostly indicators of where they *might* show up. I tried not to count, because they hurtled by so fast, I thought I was the one who was gonna slam into a very unyielding surface in a moment.

I shoved a hand into my pocket, where frozen fingers clutched two sharp-edged objects—a sapphire earing and a gold crucifix. Even with my senses overwhelmed, the cacophony of light and sound threatening to drive me insane, I could feel every facet of the jewel, every tiny feature on the face of the miniature Jesus.

Come on. Please. I just want to save them.

Over and over I thought it. Begged it.

Then, the portals mashed into one—one long, jagged tear in the landscape. There was a pine forest on the other end, dark trees bristling with needles, and in the middle, a structure that looked like a Mesopotamian ziggurat from an old history book. It was akin to Meda's temples, but—newer. It lacked smooth edges and mossy growths.

The vision thrust me through stone, through its very walls, until I was face to face with the mind-bending impossibility of the Hedron's warped shape.

I caught a glimpse of red hair out of the corner of my eye, the only splash of color in this washed-out trip.

Loredana?

Everything snapped into reality with such abruptness that I gagged. Don't vomit. Seriously. Took several deep breaths to keep myself from doing so. When I opened my eyes, it was a normal, sunny morning in downtown Meda.

Teget rested his hands on his knees. His face was pale, but he had that grin on his face, the grin that promised he'd found what he was looking for and now he was ready to charge into battle. "I know the way which we must go."

"Terrific," I croaked, "Because that sucked."

Naos was out of bed and waiting for us at the boat. His healer was two steps behind him, arms folded, glaring as if she could make us burst into flame. I stayed out of her line of sight.

"Forgive me for not giving you the whole truth," he said. "Such secrets of our past are kept for a reason, Mercury. They are not so kept out of a desire to do harm, but to alleviate our people of an historic burden that can be too great to bear."

"I don't blame you, but it is their history. Generally speaking, it's better when people know the facts. All of them. That's how they make decisions." I clapped his shoulder and winked. "But you guys probably aren't much into elections around here."

Naos's smile froze in place. Yeah, too much, probably. I hugged him close, not ready to part with him but more determined than ever to end the misery Arkwright had put me through

He was the reason I was still here.

"Do not forget yourself, Mercury," Naos whispered. "Do not give in to dark hiding in your heart even as you fight it without. We all harbor the same potential for evil, to lesser and greater degrees. Be wary of that lion."

I nodded. Not sure what he meant in all of that, besides a generic pep talk about not becoming a bad guy, but I figured the lion was metaphorical. I knew I had to be careful not to cross too far over the line. Because if I did, Loredana and Ramos wouldn't recognize me—and then what was the point to saving them?

Huh. Probably that was why Teget kept lecturing me.

We left the city without fanfare, only Naos and his healer as our audience. Teget guided the boat expertly up the canal, following the branches until we merged into the largest of the waterways leading north. The big sprawling buildings gave way to more homes, then a few houses with barns and broad fields, until we were alone among a very pastoral landscape. I leaned against the gunwales, letting the sun bake me as I gazed out over the farmland. Aside from the chugging of the super steam engine, birds and flying lizards provided the only other sounds.

"Two days," Teget said. "The canal terminates at Lake Azaron. From there, we continue on foot into the mountains."

"That's not so bad."

"Two days *on foot*, Mercury. We should reach Azaron by nightfall. It is the nearest settlement to Meda."

"Oh." I adjusted my lounging place, using a rucksack as a pillow. There had to be a better way to ease my aching shoulder. Of course, when I shifted, a twinge passed through my leg.

"Does it hurt again?"

"Off and on. You'd think getting it snapped by Arkwright would be the worst thing ever. But it's healed well. Didn't bother me any during our treetop fight or inside the temple." I rubbed at the muscle. "So, I relax."

"No mean feat, I am sure."

I watched the clouds pass. Teget hummed a tune I couldn't place, but it was a jaunty hymn, something that would go well with a brass band. "Question for you."

"Yes?"

"The exiles. Unclean people, as Grandfather called them.

"Kutsatuta."

"Yeah. Those guys. Is that still a thing?"

"What do you mean?"

"Come on, Teget. I might be oblivious to some stuff, but I've lived in your city—our home—for more than a month. You don't have a jail."

"We have the cells in which offenders are held if corporal punishment is not warranted, or not enough."

"Okay, not jail, then. Prison. Long-term incarceration for terrible crimes."

Teget stiffened. "If you speak of murderers, or those who have committed a salacious attack on a woman, their execution is guaranteed."

No doubt about that. I'd seen someone shot for killing a child in cold blood. "What about the crimes like Grandfather mentioned? There have to be people who've tried to steal the relics, or at least harnessed their powers for some really bad stuff."

"I do not know if they have. The rulers keep such proceedings quiet, so as not to alarm the people."

"Grandfather was telling the truth, then. There's been recent banishments."

"Again, they are not—"

"I know, I know, they keep those things quiet." I sighed and rubbed my face. Some more sleep would be nice. "It'd be helpful to know who they were, why exactly they were banished, so we could figure out how they're connected to the temple. He said it himself. They knew where to go, which room to hit."

"There are always rumors of disappearances, but I am not aware of any in recent years. Such talk has not been as rampant as when I was little." Teget stroked his beard. "Many families were in an uproar back then—perhaps four years after we knew Mother and Father were dead, and you were assumed lost. In short, I do not know who had such knowledge. Nor had I ever seen the sword which our attacker wielded."

"It was strong, whatever it was," I said. "Deflected not just your ax but the pulsar stave's energy. I didn't know anything could."

"Nor did I."

"Too many questions." I missed Ramos and his penchant for digging to the bottom of a mystery. Heck, he was a police lieutenant, after all. How many times had I watched him work his way through a puzzle, looking for the right witness to confirm a crime? WWRD, right?

The mountains ahead didn't seem nearly as inviting as they did when I spotted their peaks from the temple summit. They seemed like they were hiding something. Which they were.

A fortress home to our enemy, plus generations worth of disgruntled Kutsatuta who would, most likely, be not happy to see us.

"Rest, Mercury." Teget took a break in his whistling. "Obsessing over a future you cannot foresee, or control will do you no good."

"Thanks, Dr. Phil. I suppose you've got your own method for staying calm."

Teget didn't answer. I craned my neck. I could see his white-knuckled grip on the boat's tiller.

"You're scared." I leaned my head back and reconsidered the clouds.

"Does that surprise you?"

"Kind of. Never saw you bat an eyelash, so to speak, when we were surgically dismantling astral fiends."

"A man who is not afraid is a fool." Teget sounded like he'd eaten a rotten lemon. "How the fear is corralled and harnessed, though, that is what makes the difference."

"Between winning and losing."

"Between dying and staying alive. I am not concerned about the state of my soul, nor about its final destination, but I am in no hurry to make that last journey."

"Amen to that." It was oddly comforting to know Teget was as freaked out by the prospect of wandering into this foreign place—or maybe not freaked out, but at least mildly concerned. Sometimes he seemed way too good at his job, but then again, coming from an urban lifestyle in California, nothing about his state of being matched up with my experiences.

I doubted he thought about reuniting with his worn out, comfortable couch in the middle of a fierce battle, for example.

The map Naos gave us was unfolded in the center of the boat. Teget had anchored it with his boots. "I don't like the idea of sailing upstream into an unexplored land, without a clue about what kind of bad guys are waiting for us."

"It seems dire, but you forget one thing."

"Enlighten me, o bringer of sunshine."

Teget smirked. "We are traveling *down*stream."

CHAPTER SIX

Teget's estimate was right on. We left the canal behind for the broad, curving shores of Lake Azaron. The sun dipped below the horizon, splashing pinks and reds onto the horizon that quickly dimmed to purple. Stars spilled across the sky.

The city was far behind us, without so much as a glow from its lamps, but the lakeshore town of Azaron was our lighthouse. Not that it was much of a burg. Couldn't have had more than fifty houses, a couple small temples, and assorted other structures. It did have one feature the city lacked: a wooden palisade, nine feet tall, ringing the entire town.

Teget didn't bother heading for the gates. He had a hushed conversation with a pair of musketeers stationed on the pier outside the palisades. I made sure the boat was tied tight, in case we were headed back this way.

"Come." Teget handed me a pale-yellow crystal. It let off a pleasant glow, like one of those sticks you crack and shake. Had a good heft, too, and sharp edges. He showed me how to tuck it into my belt for illumination. "The sentries report the path is clear of predators."

Until then, I hadn't paid much attention to Meda's fauna, besides the small, edible kind. Concentrating on astral fiends, I guess. "That's good news. I'll hang onto the pulsar stave for my flashlight, thanks."

We trekked on through the night, up winding passes and through valleys with such steep sides I really hoped we weren't gonna try to scale them. It must have been local 10 or 11 o'clock when we camped out under the stars, taking turns on watch every few hours. As soon as daybreak started banishing the night cold from the valley, we trudged on.

Man, I hated camping.

All I could think about was Saito-on-Sky, the ritziest sushi restaurant in San Camillo, site of my one and only date with Loredana. Well, I guess the brief dance we had at Procyon Foundation's Rampart office was the second date, even if tracking down Syndax was the motive behind our attendance. I mean, it was still a great night. Minus the monsters.

But tromping through the woods, out onto open rock, and over steep trails that led deeper into an arid landscape devoid of all but the hardiest shrubs was no fun.

I kept my grumping to myself, though, because the next time I checked the Syndax tracking device, the indicator dot for Loredana's tachyon-laced earring pulsed stronger than I'd ever seen it.

"We're on the right trail!" I slapped Teget's arm. Could have kissed him, too, but for the beard. Too scratchy.

"I had hoped as much. The ax should have given us an accurate vision, with the Hedron as its target, but independent verification is good, too." Teget stepped through a thicket of scraggly bushes.

"No need to feel threatened because my tech's working better," I said, grinning.

The next twenty-four hours were a blur interspersed with periodic updates from the tracker. Loredana was somewhere nearby, and I wanted to run the remaining distance, except the tracker's rangefinder was hazy on that number. So, we kept going until we slumped into our next camp at the base a plateau with steep sides. It was one of a dozen equally huge plateaus with equally steep sides.

Teget swigged water from a canteen. He wiped dirt from his face with a wet palm. "Tomorrow, we climb."

I groaned and rolled over on the hard ground. He could take first watch.

It wasn't until we were halfway up the face in the early morning sun that I remembered, Dominic Zein was gonna show up outside Meda sometime that day, ready to update me on the state of San Camillo. And I didn't leave a forwarding address.

Oh, well. Hopefully the guy was smart enough to go find Naos. He knew the drill.

We crested the top of the plateau, and bam, there it was—the dark, ragged forest with the new fortress sticking out of the middle, just like we'd seen in the ax vision. I say new because, up close, it had even sharper lines than I'd first seen. You could tell it was built way after the temples in Meda. The stones hadn't faded, and there was no moss or rust staining its sides.

And if it had been originally intended as a house of worship, the current occupants had given it a high-security makeover.

The front doors were wooden, but half of that structure was covered with thick iron bars. The few windows I could see from our perch were also sealed with a metal lattice.

"No sentries." Teget crouched behind a boulder, the ax already in his grip.

"Don't know why they'd need them. I can't find a single entry point, can you?"

"None easily accessible."

"Unless we had blowtorches," I muttered.

Teget frowned. "If you blew upon a torch, that would hardly be enough to douse the flame."

"That's not … Forget it." I squinted. Could be movement. Shadows behind the windows on one of the upper levels, maybe? It passed. "What's the plan?"

"Nightfall will provide us the greatest cover."

"I don't want to wait that long."

"It has been seventy-four days, Mercury. One would think you could be patient for another twelve hours." Teget gestured to my clothes. "If you were in possession of your suit …"

"Hey, you saw the thing. My fight with Arkwright left it tattered." Which was a bummer, because the suit had been designed by Procyon Foundation's Winston Yen, a technological genius who concocted a way to harness tachyons emitted by the pulsar stave, turning the jumpsuit-slash-superhero costume into an advanced active camouflage system. Handy for sneaking around in.

But with the suit beyond my ability to repair, or anyone in Meda's ability for that matter, and its maker locked up in Bulwark State Prison for trying to destroy San Camillo, it was civvies for me for a while.

"If Loredana's in there, I'm not waiting five seconds longer. We go in now." I skulked behind the boulders strewn across the plateau. Teget's muffled curse followed, though he stepped so lightly I had trouble following his movements without looking back.

Getting through the forest was a snap. No traps, no guards, no energy blasts or bullets or even arrows. Teget caught up with me a hundred feet from the base of the ziggurat. "What have I told you about your reckless behavior?"

"Something about me getting killed." I crept between the trees. Somewhere up there were the windows. Ah. Bingo. "I don't know the full text. I was ignoring you."

Teget sighed. "You will be the death of me yet, let alone yourself."

"Lighten up." I socked his shoulder and drew the pulsar stave from its holster. A quick twist brought it to life. "You'd be bored without me."

"Yes, the occasional foray into the Interstice for purposes of slaying astral fiends was 'ho-hum,' as I believe the phrase goes."

I snorted at the dose of heavy sarcasm and started climbing.

Hanging out with my brother had rubbed off on me as much as he'd absorbed my sarcasm. I couldn't even hear *me* clambering up the sides of the fortress. I found a window five floors up that was the right size for us to squeeze through. Jokes about stealth aside, didn't want to blow a hole in the wall, so I pressed the pulsar stave to the grating and willed it to slowly increase its energy discharge and, along with that, its temperature.

The metal went red, then orange, to a blazing yellow, before melting. The bars dripped away like melted cheese, leaving a puddle that clicked as it cooled and hardened. Man. I must've been hard up for Carlito's pizza if the destruction of an enemy's barred windows made me hungry.

As far as stealth, we were golden. I grabbed the lip of the window, tucked my legs and slid in, Dukes of Hazzard style. Teget's slide was equally catlike.

"You should have surveilled your surroundings before we entered." Teget's whisper was as sharp as the edges of his ax. He crouched by the wall, weapon ready, watching both ends of the corridor.

"Okay, well, I didn't so, shut up," I hissed between clenched teeth.

But we were okay, and no guards came running. Which was weird, because the ax had shown us this was the place. No stomping boots, no voices, no sounds of alarm. Only the distant, soft drip of water on rock, and a subtle vibration underfoot. I knelt and placed my palm on the nearest carved block. The tremor intensified. It was like holding hands with a subwoofer. Or soaking up the beat from my Subaru's speakers, which I have to say, were pretty kickin'. At least until an astral fiend ripped the car in half. And then ripped its replacement in half.

Best not to dwell on that.

We made our way through the halls, taking sharp turns, aiming for the center of the structure. The vibrations grew, and the tracking device gave me the clearest signal yet from Loredana's earring.

Then the pulsar stave started shaking, too.

"Weird." I held it aloft, watching its sides shiver.

"Indeed. The ax has the same response." Teget didn't sound pleased by the development.

A corner brought us to a broad archway lined with white stones. Each one bore a black letter in script I'd never seen before—or if I had, I couldn't translate. "You know this?"

Teget shook his head. “It is similar to the alphabet used in the temple, based on our ancient language, but outside of the wardens and Grandfather, I have never seen anyone read it. It was certainly never taught to me.”

“No hopes for Google Translate, then, even if I could get a signal,” I muttered.

The arch opened into an octagonal chamber, with walls leading straight down several floors. There was another archway on the opposite side. A pair of stairs led from each balcony down to the main floor.

Arkwright was there.

He and his partner stood surrounded by twenty-four soldiers in similar Medanesque armor, hands on their swords. The blades shimmered under the flickering flames of torches ensconced in the walls—all except for the partner’s. His weapon was still black as midnight.

Arkwright’s tentacles encircled the Hedron. He was murmuring something, over and over, but nothing was happening, save for pulses that rippled the air like heat waves.

“Whatever he’s doing, it can’t be good,” I murmured.

“Our priority is to retrieve the Hedron.”

“How about lopping Arkwright’s head off?”

“If the opportunity presents itself, I will take it.”

“Glad to hear it.” I checked the tracker yet again. It showed Loredana nearby, but even with the room doused in shadow, I could tell she wasn’t down there with Arkwright and his cuckoo cult. Which meant … “I think the prisoners are either directly over this floor, or beneath.”

Teget nodded. “Searching separately will help us achieve our goals quickly.”

Splitting up seemed like a terrible idea, but I was okay

with it if it meant saving my friends. We headed back into the corridor. "I'll go down, you go up. Watch your back, got it?"

Teget saluted with his ax and disappeared around the bend. I hoped he knew how to navigate this place. If anyone could do it without modern tech, though, it would be him.

I kept the tracker running as I circled the floor, checking every corner and alcove for a staircase. Finally found one about thirty feet in the opposite direction from the window we'd broken through. It seemed too narrow to be a main stairwell; if anyone came up while I was padding down the winding steps, we'd have a collision.

The tracker's indicator was getting brighter and more solid. I kept descending, until the stairs ended in a musty alcove. I saw a reflection of my boots on the ground but wasn't fast enough to avoid splashing in the puddle.

"Ricos? Have you come for the prisoners, you lazy beast?"

The rumbling voice echoed down the hall. My brain went blank. Who's Ricos? A big guy or a little guy? Should I say anything? Backtrack? Stay put?

Footsteps grew louder. "Tell Arkwright I will bring him fresh meat if he is truly desperate, but only if he asks nicely." The voice chuckled.

And I caught a whiff of bad breath. Like, sticking my nose in a bag of crushed garlic bad.

He was right around the corner.

I swung into view, the pulsar stave lit up like downtown San Camillo on Christmas. The guy was a head taller than me, but no less trim, with lanky arms and ropy muscle unhindered by his tunic and chainmail. He had a surprisingly round, doughy face, and stubble that made my unshaven mess look as well-groomed as Teget's beard. He had a couple seconds to give me a look that was equal parts quizzical and irritated before the pulsar stave smashed him in the nose. His neck snapped back and hit the floor so hard he bounced.

I landed on his chest, on the off chance he wasn't knocked out. He was. I paused there, feeling the rise and fall of his breathing. If he raised an alarm, Teget and I were toast, and worse, we were apart. I lifted the pulsar stave and let its energy condense into a spear over the guy's heart. Too bad his last thoughts would be, "Where's Ricos?"

My palms went sweaty. What was I doing? Was I really gonna murder this guard, who as far I know didn't have anything to do with the attack, and even if Ramos and Loredana were here, had anything to do with their treatment?

On the other hand, this band of Medan traitors raided the city temple and killed a bunch of people, good people protecting what they held sacred.

Yeah. But he should answer to the law of the land. Was I the judge, jury, or executioner?

"Ah, screw it." I powered down the stave. Then I stood and kicked him in the ribs for good measure, so he remembered how agitated off I was.

Six cells lined the wall. The tracker was going nuts, red indicators leaping all over the place. Two cells were empty, which was good news, because they were dripping with condensation and smeared with muck.

The third one held a body.

I snagged a ring of keys from the beaten guard's belt and opened the rusty bars. The corpse was chained to the wall, upright, and the clothes were shredded beyond recognition. I couldn't even determine male or female from its decayed state. The smell turned my stomach.

There was a glint of blue at its feet.

I sank to my knees, not caring about the sludge that squished underneath. My fingers shook so bad I almost couldn't touch it.

It was blue, all right. A sapphire earring.

I wiped it clean, then dug into my pocket. A perfect match. The tracker's insistent pulses became a steady hum, a single brilliant scarlet light.

Loredana's earring.

Tears stung my eyes. I couldn't breathe. The cell disappeared around me. All I could see was her face. That sly smile.

It wasn't fair. How could I come this way and be late, so late, that she'd probably been dead for weeks?

The crucifix fell into the muck. I wanted to tear it into atoms. I lit the pulsar stave, letting its power bake the mud around me.

"Loredana," I said. "I'm sorry. I'm so sorry."

A haggard cough exploded from the cell next door. Chains rattled. Something scraped against stone. And a *whisper—*

"Rescátanos y presérvanos para que no nos perdamos para siempre, sino que te sigamos, regocijándonos en el camino que nos lleva a la vida eterna ..."

Spanish.

I leapt up, then scratched at the mud, pulling the soiled crucifix free. As I did, the stave smacked the skeleton. Its head tore free of the last dried ligaments and it bounced off my boot.

God, no.

But there was hair smeared on my boots. Curly black hair. Short curly black hair.

Not red.

Wild hope kicked me in the chest. I tore around the corner. Couldn't get the key into the lock. I fumbled with the bars until they banged opened, crashing like a cymbal against the stone frame.

A man was slumped in the far corner. He wore the last dregs of what had been a pale-green dress shirt, every button gone save one. A single shoe remained on his right foot. The socks were stained and rumpled. His hair was a thick, unruly mop peppered with gray at the temples. A scruffy beard obscured the lower half of his face, but his lips moved ceaselessly, as he pressed gold to his face.

Not gold. Gold-colored. A badge. "Ramos?"

Gabriel Ramos's eyes snapped open. They were bloodshot, but they knew me. He stared, mouth hanging open. "M-Mercury? It-it was you. I heard you. Called your name. I prayed for this, for you to come. Only you could make it. Rescue us and preserve us, so we do not lose ourselves forever."

I sank next to him and held his shoulders. There was no stopping the tears now. Yep, full on blubbering fool, that was me. I grinned. "Ramos, it's good to see you."

"Son. Thank you." He smiled, his lips chapped and scabbed.

"Loredana. You have to tell me—"

"He took her. Arkwright. Not long ago. Or a while ago. I-I can't remember."

"She's not dead."

"No! No. I protected her as best I could but ..." He wept. *Ramos* wept. "I couldn't. Too weak. Too tired."

"It isn't your fault, you hear me? Come on. I've got to get you free and find—"

The entire dungeon shook. Dust filtered through the

stones. Everything seemed suddenly still. That's when I realized the vibrations had stopped.

And Teget's war cry filtered through the fortress walls.

CHAPTER SEVEN

Every instinct told me to rush upstairs and leap to Teget's defense. Except Ramos wasn't traveling at top speed. More like gimping along.

We stopped at the second landing up from the dungeon when Ramos stumbled, nearly bringing us both down. "Let me rest. I'm too tired to be any help."

"If I leave you here, they'll find you and lock you back up." I wiped sweat from my forehead. Ramos wasn't a big guy, but I don't do a lot of weight training up multiple flights of steps. "And then you'll wind up like your gross neighbor. I'm not gonna go back to Olivia and explain how I left you behind to die because we both needed to take a breather."

"Olivia." Ramos's face could've been carved from the stone surrounding us. He dug his fingertips into the seams between the blocks and dragged himself upright. He squared his shoulders. Now, if he only had a gun. "Get me back there."

"I know. We're gonna go home." Better leave the part about how it was a two-day hike down a plateau and valleys to the boat that would motor us to Meda. If I could get him there more quickly—

Quickly.

I shook my head. What a moron.

"Hang on." I looped my right arm around Ramos's waist. I held the pulsar stave in the other and willed its energy to drain into me. Man. It was like I'd drank six cups of coffee at once.

Ramos grabbed my arm and hooked his grip around my shoulder. He must have had some inkling about what I was thinking, because he squeezed his eyes shut and grumbled, "Please be better at this than you are at driving."

I just grinned and took off.

I made an Olympic sprinter look like he was limping along with a cast on both legs. I was *fast.* The stairwell blurred by, but I kept focus on each step, counting alcoves out of the corner of my eye. At the turn to the fifth floor, I banked into the corridor. My elbow brushed a stone block and threw me so far off balance I was sure we'd paste ourselves along the walls. I adjusted my trajectory, still running.

My boots skidded so hard they threw off smoke. We were back on the same balcony from which Teget and I had discovered Arkwright's bizarre Hedron-plus-muttering ceremony.

Except it had devolved into a full-on melee.

Four men were strewn across the floor. Another six were pressed into a corner, guarding a robed figure. Six more formed a phalanx around Arkwright, who kept on chanting.

Teget was fighting the other eight, solo.

"Stay on the steps." I helped Ramos settle halfway down, against the railing. "I'll be right back."

"You're going to fight them all?" He made a face that

indicated he thought I was the world's biggest idiot.

Ah, yes. That familiar Ramos scorn. It warmed my heart even as I wanted to smack him. "Relax," I said. "I'm always up for a good melee."

I backflipped, separated the pulsar stave in midair, and landed between two of the men nearest Teget. A couple surprise swipes with blazing yellow-white energy slapped them into the walls like swatting flies.

"Hey," I said. "What's up?"

"Mercury!" Teget ducked a flashing blade. He brought the tail end of the ax up into the guy's jaw, and once he was fallen, kicked him in the gut. "You found one of your compatriots!"

"Yeah, and I also found my brother being about twenty times more reckless than I ever was while you were lecturing me!" I blocked an incoming sword, the stave blazing with such power the blade melted clean off its hilt. The soldier wielding it gaped for a half second before I broke his nose. I was getting good at that. "Come on, Teget! You got bored searching for my people and decided you needed to break up this party?"

"I discovered their armory and destroyed it." Teget grinned. He reached into his belt and held up something. A gun.

After weeks living in a dimension in which all the weapons were either bladed or patterned after antique gear-based flintlocks, seeing a modern semi-automatic pistol was a shocker. Until I realized who it belonged to.

I snatched it and yelled, "Ramos!"

It spun end over end and, thankfully, he was still with it enough he caught it. I heard the familiar crusty click of the slide being racked and a round being chambered.

"Um, Teget?" I said. "Duck."

We hit the floor at the same time, as the room echoed with gunfire.

Ramos leaned over the stone railing, his stance as perfect as if he'd shown up at San Camillo Police Department's firing range. I can't imagine what he'd gone through in all the time I'd been searching for him, but the stoic cast of his face and the speed with which he emptied the magazine told me it hadn't been pretty.

Let the guy have a little revenge.

His shots weren't perfect. I heard a few *ping* off the stone blocks, chips of rock spraying. They didn't have to be great, as packed together as the soldiers were. When the shooting stopped, the rest of the men Teget and I had been fighting were down. Four were dead, with bloody wounds to their heads, necks, and chests. The others were wounded. They moaned and writhed as they grasped wounds had to be agonizing.

I was past caring about these guys.

Arkwright turned from the Hedron. He'd given up chanting, and despite his hideous new appearance, he wore the expression of a parent trying to make a phone call while the kids are hollering for attention. I also noticed, somewhat worryingly, that the Hedron of Orbits was floating in midair and emitting hair-thin streamers of purple light. Hey, at least the whole building wasn't vibrating any more.

"Mercury Hale." Arkwright sighed. "You're dogged, you know that? I offered you an alliance once. Well, I suppose it was more of a job back then, since I was still concerned with the earthly trappings of my former life."

"Yeah. I bet getting through Syndax's front door with that face is gonna be challenging," I snapped.

He chuckled. "That's part of what you bring to the table. Unrelenting humor to match the determination. My new compatriots aren't very funny. Seems to be part and parcel of the exile experience. What's your plan now? I still have a dozen men to guard me—and, as the saying goes, an ace up my sleeve."

One of the six guarding the robed figure stepped forward. It was the masked soldier carrying the black blade.

Great. I glanced at Teget, who shrugged, looking downright exhausted. Likewise. Last time, we'd gotten the beatdown from this joker. I was not yearning for a repeat.

Instead of launching yet another fight, though, the soldier pulled the hood of the robed figure down.

I was waiting to see an old, wizened priest, maybe a wrinkly dude who was a ragged, snarly, evil version of Naos. Seemed fitting, since we were inside their dark temple fortress.

Instead, a flash of red brought a much-needed splash of color to the drab interior.

Loredana Lark.

Her face was bruised, but otherwise in far better shape than I'd anticipated. Her lip was puffy, like she'd been struck there, too. Seeing her in front of me—alive!—sent a surge throughout my body that had nothing to do with the pulsar stave's harnessed energies. I was ready to take on these dozen goons and Arkwright with a spork if that was the only weapon available.

She gazed at the floor, listless.

"Loredana?" I headed for her. Black Sword Guy put that blade up in my face and shook his head. "Listen, pal, you might want to step aside unless you're sure you don't ever want to have kids again."

"Let him by," Arkwright said. "It's worth it to see the disappointment."

I tried to shut out his needling as I approached Loredana. "Hey. I ... Are you okay?"

Talk about lame ways to greet the woman you love—yeah, love. I'd come to terms with that. Can you blame me? There was no one else who had my back other than her. Except Ramos. And she was prettier.

Instead of a joyous hug, I got a slap.

The palm strike stung for long seconds as the sound hung in the air. Teget sucked in a breath.

Worst part of it? She didn't say a word. Just glared at me.

"What?" I rubbed my cheek. "I came to rescue you!"

"Seventy. Six. Days." Her voice was raw. She'd either been screaming or yelling or crying. Or all of the above. Her eyes were read from—lack of sleep? Crying?

Worse?

I zapped myself right past the guards, halting a foot from Arkwright. Shocked outbursts sounded from the soldiers. Ha. They didn't know about my tachyon-enhanced speed trick. Suckers. I grabbed Arkwright by his shirt and yanked his face down—way down—to mine. "What did you do to her?"

"It didn't take much. Physical torture's such a waste of resources." Arkwright sneered. "Of course, her defiant attitude earned her a handful of beatings. Can't let defiance go unpunished. But solitary confinement for long, long stretches, in a room devoid of light and sound, does wonders for cracking someone's psyche."

I snarled and swung the pulsar stave in his face.

He caught the weapon inches from his bulging spidery eyes, black talons scraping on the metal. Sparks arced up and down the length of the stave as it tried to figure which master it should obey. Arkwright had found a way to merge himself with not only the Whisperer from the Interstice, but via him, the essence or spirit or whatever of Marigold Yen. She'd been destroyed, sort of, and combined with the Whisperer when Teget and I killed her in defense of Meda. When this trio got together, Arkwright gained access to the genetic code that allowed activation of the interdimensional weapons, like the night's blade, Teget's ax, and my pulsar stave.

And, therefore, the Hedron of Orbits.

"You're too late. Again." Arkwright smirked. "Your friends are wounded. Your temple's guardians are dead. Your city is desecrated. And before long, nothing else you do will matter, because I will tear the very planet from your grasp."

"How about you skip to the part where you tell me your diabolical plan, so I can foil it," I snapped as I struggled against his grip. The stave inched closer to his face.

Arkwright put on a good front, but his arm was trembling. "That would take far too much time, and I'm on a schedule. I'll see you around, I hope."

The Hedron exploded.

Not a real explosion. It wasn't destroyed. Everyone in the room was thrown aside by an undulating wave of pale green light. Streaks of shimmering gold washed over the stone blocks, giving the chamber a heavenly appearance. I dug the pulsar stave into a seam in the floor arresting my backwards slide.

Good thing, too, because the Hedron reversed its actions.

A portal split the center of the room. It was a perfect sphere of white, with a center of the deepest black. Purple lighting swirled around it, sending out occasional bolts that cracked rocks where it struck. Wind whipped us at hurricane force.

Arkwright somehow remained upright throughout it all, his tentacles anchoring him to the floor. "Go! Now!"

Black Blade let go of the wall, where he'd apparently clung, and dove straight into the middle of the portal. His buddies followed him in twos and threes.

The portal sucked in the dead bodies next. Weapons too.

Arkwright seemed unruffled by the chaos, like he'd stepped outside into the balmiest spring afternoon ever. He simply unhooked his tentacles from the floor and fell backwards into the portal.

If he got himself to his home dimension, we were gonna have some serious problems—never mind the inhabitants of said home.

I squinted at the outline. Those metal shapes I'd seen inside the Atrium of Meda's temple—squares and circles and triangles—they spun in rings around the portal, forming its boundary. Naos had said the thing was a weapon, and was thinking, like a person, so what was the deal with it being a portal?

Loredana slid along the floor, Teget beside her, both drawn inexorably toward the void. I rolled over, careful not to lose my grip in the stave that held me in place, and blocked Loredana with my arm. The impact about wrenched my shoulder from its socket. Guess what? Same injured shoulder. Fun.

Teget snagged my boot with one arm and jammed the ax into the floor with the other.

The vibrations from before had resumed in earnest. The whole room shuddered. My first instinct was to run outside, away from the dust trickling down from the ceiling, because it sure felt like we were trapped in an earthquake. "We've got to shut the thing down!"

"If we can reach the Hedron, perhaps we can issue it a command!"

"Hold onto her!" I repositioned myself, so my head was closer to Loredana. "Hey. Hey! I'm gonna let you go! Teget's got you!"

She clung to my arm, eyes wide and frantic. "Don't! Not again!"

Again?

We'd lost our grip when she'd been pulled into another portal, more than two months ago. Now here I was, intentionally releasing her.

A stone plummeted from the ceiling. It shattered not four feet away, pelting us with dirt, dust, and shards of rock.

I had to do it.

I let go and broke the stave free.

Loredana's angry shout followed me all the way to the portal. I stretched out my hand for the rim, where the pieces of the Hedron abruptly stopped spinning, even as the portal itself built strength like the aforementioned hurricane.

I could feel something. Like when I willed the stave to action. There was a sensation of a response in those cases, not a mind, you know, but like when a computer responds to your input. This was clearer, stronger. It *knew*.

Shut down, I thought. *Stabilize. Close the portal.*

Instead of the automatic response, or a surge of energy, I heard—a voice.

No.

The pieces snapped into the center of the portal, and in an instant, the Hedron had reformed into its mind-bending triangle. Then it blinked out. Gone.

And the portal went nuts.

Lightning shot all over the place. It was ten times worse than a rip, those portals that I'd seen countless times on Earth when they dumped astral fiends in my backyard. Except his one started blasting holes in the pyramid.

From somewhere way too close to us, I heard a great roar like an ocean wave, except the grinding, crunching sound that accompanied it told me it was probably a wave made of rocks, which would suck.

There was only one way out of this, before we were all smashed like bugs on a windshield at freeway speeds. "Ramos! Let go of the railing!"

He listened, without argument, which is how I knew he was in rough shape. The portal's winds sucked him over the edge, tumbling through the air.

I caught his foot. Just a few more seconds ... "Teget! Get Loredana and let's get out of here!"

Teget scooped her up, oblivious to the kicking and punching she unleashed on him and launched himself from the ground.

I let the pulsar stave loose from where it anchored me at the same time.

Nothing made sense. Time ran forward and backward simultaneously. I could see from my perspective and from outside, like I was watching the four of us in a movie. Teget screamed and laughed—except maybe I imagined those. Loredana was seated across from me, a coffee cradled in her hands, wisps of steam rising in front of sapphire eyes. She smiled.

I could have let myself freeze right there for eternity.

Instead I landed face down in a puddle.

There was grass stuck in my teeth. My feet were stuck in something wet and bristly. A stick scraped my shin.

The pain and nausea and disorientation cleared, slowly. I raised myself in the world's most awful pushup, and looked up into a gray, rainy sky.

We were surrounded by trees, and there were lopsided, ruined walls nearby. So, we'd managed to wind up elsewhere on Meda?

A car horn honked.

Cars streamed by on the other side of a hedge. Cabs, buses, SUVS, all streamed through the rain along a street lined by brownstone apartments. Two guys with sandwich carts struggled to close their stands and cover their goods.

"Rosa Roja," Ramos gasped. "The park."

We were home. Finally, home! I whooped and snagged Ramos in a one-armed hug.

Teget stared at me. "You do realize what this means."

Wait. If we got here, then so did Arkwright.

"Well, great," I said.

CHAPTER EIGHT

First order of business: I checked to see if I had cell phone reception.

I'm kidding. That thing was dead as a brick, because I'd lost battery power weeks ago.

The tracker, though, had an advanced power source. Liz Stojan thought it had something to do with absorbing the very tachyons it tracked. Whatever. Point is, I used it to send a message to Procyon.

Two silver SUVs picked us up five minutes later and whisked us to the waterfront office.

I almost cried at the sight of the triplet towers, with their familiar walkways linking the fourth and seventh floors. My vision blurred as big guys in black "Procyon Security" shirts hustled us inside and up to the top of Tower Three. It was a shock to the system, all right, seeing nothing but glass and steel and concrete, after living a lifestyle that was more appropriate to Earth a handful of centuries ago.

Our quartet wound up in the infirmary, where two familiar faces were waiting.

Elizabeth Stojan had been crying. Easy to tell, because it

had ruined the dark-blue mascara she wore. I caught a flash of spiky pink hair as she slammed me with a hug. "Mercury! Oh, Mercury, I thought you were dead! I thought everybody was dead but look, you brought them all back and they're all okay, I mean you're okay! The tracker worked, didn't it? I didn't think it would—I mean, I *knew* it had to, it just had to, but if it didn't—"

I hugged her back, even with the searing pain in my shoulder demanding attention. "It's good to see you, too, Liz."

She sniffed and wiped her nose on her sleeve. At least it wasn't on *my* sleeve. Then she blew it clean on a handkerchief decorated with silver medieval helmets. "You came back through a portal! I got readings on all of it, so we can—"

"Everyone except the patients clear out!" Dr. Arne Becker started shoving security men to the infirmary door. He was dressed exactly the same way he'd been the last time I saw him: blue T-shirt and gray pants under a rumpled white lab coat. The waxed handlebar moustache and perfect beard didn't fit; he looked like he should have been playing in a jazz band at a coffee house downtown. But the attitude would have made him a terrible performer. "I don't want any interruptions until I've examined everyone beginning with Ms. Lark and Lieutenant Ramos."

Dr. Arne had a few Procyon medical types helping him. Loredana and Ramos were taken to separate areas of the infirmary, each one shielded from view by foldable white partitions. Teget and I got beds near the front. And I take back what I said about modern conveniences versus Meda living—my bunk in the canal-side cottage was infinitely more comfortable than the lousy medical mattress.

"Your blood pressure's high, but it's coming down." Arne

listened to my heartbeat, lungs, and poked and prodded me in every way imaginable as he muttered. He took more notes in that exam than I swear I ever managed in school.

"Yeah, well, I hear interdimensional travel does that to you."

"What can you tell me about their conditions?" He glanced back at the partitions.

"Likely tortured and starved." I ground my teeth. "You want details, you'd better ask them."

"It's a miracle neither of you are dead." He frowned at Teget. "Speaking of which, I don't think we've been introduced."

"My brother, Teget. Also, from not here." I leaned against the pillow. A nap would be great. After pizza. "Check his blood and DNA against mine. You'll see what I mean."

"Right." Arne tugged at his moustache. "Fine. You two stay near your devices. There's little I can do that will be an improvement on your advanced physiologies and the healing properties accelerated by them, so I'll go check on my real patients."

"Hey." I grabbed his arm. "Let me see her."

"Loredana? Out of the question. She's undergone tremendous trauma. Besides, you had your chance to talk on the ride over."

"She was in the other vehicle."

"Your oversight, not mine."

I got toe to toe with him. Bad idea. My head swam, but I grimaced through it. "Look, Doc, I've killed a lot of nasty nightmare creatures to get back to her, and I just brought her home, so give me five minutes with here."

Arne glared. "You *look*. She's in need of medical care, and she's not going anywhere. So, sit yourself *down* before

I shoot you so full of sedatives, you'll be sipping coffee through a feeding tube."

Then he pushed me back down on the bed and stormed off. He snapped orders at his med techs and boy, did they hop-to.

I glanced at Teget. "Forget what I said about your bedside manner. Arne makes you look like Mother Teresa."

"Of whom was she the mother?" Teget asked.

I shook my head. "So. Arkwright."

He winced. "I would recommend we discuss the matter with whoever has the same tracking capabilities in the facility as your module. The sooner we can locate him, the sooner we can discern his purpose and retrieve the Hedron."

"Yeah, about that—when I tried to shut it down, it told me off."

"How so?"

"It literally said, 'No.'"

He stared at me.

"That's about the reaction I had."

"First, we rest. Then, sustenance."

"You're absolutely right 'sustenance.'" I grinned at the ceiling. "Man, wait until you try Carlito's. Funny—it's the place I got dropped when Mom and Dad died, and yet, it's the place I almost always go back to."

"This is the home of the pizza which you endlessly mentioned." Teget smiled. "How could I resist such a chance to finally sample the mythical dish?"

"Mythical dish." I snorted. "Mythical deep dish. They should put it on the menu."

We both laughed. Laughing felt good.

Even if my cheek still stung from where Loredana slapped me. I'd have to figure that one out later. Right then, I chalked it up to PTSD.

Best case scenario, right?

"The only kind of pizza anyone's getting will have to be delivered."

Hector Alvarez stood in the doorway of the infirmary. For someone who was a foot shorter than the security men bracketing the entrance, he seemed way more intimidating. I chalked it up to the silver-gray suit, black shirt underneath, and white tie. Otherwise, Alvarez was short, thickset but not tubby, with wavy black hair and a goatee-moustache combo. Not handsome, but not unfortunate, either.

"Interim Manager Alvarez." I propped myself up on my elbows. "I'd shake your hand, sir, but doctor's orders: no respecting authority."

Alvarez scowled. "It's Manager without the Interim, Mr. Hale."

"Oh? Congrats. You get a raise with the permanent title?"

"What I got was a nasty surprise when you returned unannounced and in a very public fashion. That last word I'd received from Gemini via coded call was that you failed to make your scheduled rendezvous."

Gemini? Right. I was gonna have to ask him about that goofy code name. Maybe someone liked the space program. "How is Dominic? Tell him I'll buy him a slice."

"Please maintain the fiction that you care about our operations and respect the titles we assign."

"Whatever, Alvarez. I respect my people, and I carry out Procyon's mission because no one else can."

He smirked, like he'd found something exceptionally amusing. "When you're up to it, join Ms. Stojan and me in Tracking. Your arrival back on Earth wasn't the only one detected."

I was already on my feet. "Ready to roll."

"No, you're not. I'm serious. Rest first. And we will get you pizza."

"I'd rather take a break and show my brother my favorite local haunt."

"Mercury, the Department of Homeland Security has been dogging our steps for weeks, and hounding every move made by our employees." Alvarez jabbed a finger at me. "You are not leaving this facility yet—and yes, I realize the irony, given that I never wanted to you to step foot back inside not that long ago."

Teget covered his mouth.

"What?" I asked.

"Your effect upon people with whom you disagree is universal." He tried and failed to keep a straight face.

I rolled my eyes, but Alvarez didn't appear to be budging. "Fine, but you'd better make sure the pies have pepperoni on them, or I'm sending them back."

Alvarez left, trailing the two security men. He launched into a rapid and muffled conversation on his cell phone. The snatches I could hear were in Spanish.

I spared another glance at the partitions. Doc Arne's voice, much softer and kinder than it had been when directed at me, filtered through. Someone sobbed. A woman.

Teget must have seen my miserable expression. "Let your healers heal. Only then will she be ready to speak of what transpired."

"Yeah." I rubbed my face. "It just might not be to me."

I took Teget up to Tracking later, a slice of pepperoni pizza from Carlito's in each of our hands.

Teget had some trouble with the cheese. We'd left a trail leading from the infirmary to Tracking that Hansel and Gretel would have envied, unless they were lactose intolerant. But he did make me proud by peeling the pepperoni off and devouring each one before starting in on the slice.

I, on the other hand, was deft enough to gulp down pizza with one hand while scrolling through the newsfeed on a tablet I'd liberated from the infirmary. Crime, politics, celebrity nonsense. Didn't sounds like I'd missed much—until, that is, I got to the news from Drake City a couple weeks back. Man. The jury was still out on whether a freak earthquake had struck that East Coast metropolis, or a guy named Domitian had tried to make it his personal kingdom.

Either way, Airfoil saved the city and ended the mess.

I shook my head. It'd be more fascinating if I didn't have a huge disaster of my own to clean up, but hey, I had to give the guy credit, his supersuit was slick. I could use some armor.

Tracking was a dark space yet comforting in its own gloomy way. The only light came from the myriad monitors and computer screens scattered around. Liz's station was in the middle. One of its three monitors had been folded down, so it worked like a giant tablet. She was hunched over it, murmuring about particles and field density. The dim lighting made her hair into a neon beacon.

First thing I noticed was Procyon's staff must have come back off their hiatus, because there were five others seated at terminals. I gazed at the sprawling maps of San Camillo, California, the United States, and the world. "What's new, Liz?"

She spun in her chair. "Oh! You're up. Good. Yes, so,

well, your return was the biggest tachyon anomaly we've had in a long time—since the incident at the cemetery, that is."

Right. Where Arkwright's portal game had gone too far. "What about the rips?"

"We've only had a few. They're at normal levels, when compared with past activity. They're handled. Okay, so this …" She expanded a map of the city, then zoomed into Rosa Roja Park. "This is what it looked like right before you came back."

I didn't know what the bright colors meant, but the numbers attached to them were big. Bigger than I'd read in this room before. "Arkwright?"

"That's what we figure. We were about to dispatch drones when we read the second arrival, which was yours. Okay, that was bad, you see, because when you arrived the fluctuation in tachyons so flooded the area it made it impossible to track the remnants from the first arrival, and by the time we *did* get drones overhead, which was while you were driving to Procyon, they'd dispersed so much we had no idea—"

"Deep breath." I touched her shoulder.

"Um, yes. I know." She exhaled. "Basically, we're going to have to watch for him. Okay, but my theory is, if we can keep tracking the regular rips, Arkwright could very well seek them out."

"I like that idea. There's another problem, though: he brought a new toy back."

"An artifact? Like the pulsar stave?" Liz's eyes widened. "Ooh. Fun!"

"Not really. It opened that portal all on its own and destroyed a building from the inside out. Also, it might talk."

"Like, it's sentient?" Her hand went to her mouth. "That

is so cool!"

"A little less cool and more terrifying." I clapped Teget on the shoulder. He was wiping crumbs from his beard. "But if you can point us in the right direction, we can get it back."

"If it's as powerful as you say, then that will help us find it." Liz turned in her chair. "Leon? Re-task Drones, oh, let's use Six and Eight. They're the least glitchy. I want their sensors hunting for low-level tachyon leaks, like the kind you'd see from the pulsar stave."

"On it."

I couldn't see who in the shadows Leon was, but he was hammering at his keyboard. Something bugged me worse than that, though. "Liz."

"Yeah?"

"You said the rips were happening again."

"Well, sure. Something about the anomaly at the cemetery and its interaction with the pulsar stave reset the breaches. Which is too bad, really, because we thought that after the North Beach Battle they were done and over with—"

"Liz! I know. I saw fiends trying to get out, during that fight with Procyon before everyone got sucked away from this Earth."

"Okay." She shrugged. "So, what's your question?"

I rolled my eyes. "If the rips are forming, that means we're getting astral fiend incursions again. Here. In San Camillo."

She chewed her lip, but I didn't get an answer, or any other reaction.

"Astral fiends? They have returned to your world?" Teget touched the ax. "It seems we are destined to slay them no matter the place, brother."

"Yeah. I figured." I folded my arms. "Liz?"

"Um, yes. Okay. There have been astral fiends reported."

"And?"

"And, thankfully, no one's been hurt yet. After the first incursion failed, we took steps."

"Liz."

"I thought Dom—um, Gemini told you," she blurted.

"Classified."

"Oh. Right."

I sat on the edge of her desk, so she couldn't ignore me. "Liz. Back up. If fiends are coming through, are the police handling them?"

She giggled. "No, of course not."

"Then how are you killing them?" I snapped. "It's not like you can advertise on Upcycle for a monster slayer, especially not when the interdimensional weapons are out of your reach!"

"She doesn't need one!" Liz countered. "And she even knew you'd get like this."

"She."

"Yes." Liz took a long sigh. "Wilhelmina says hello."

CHAPTER NINE

She had to be kidding.

Instead of spending a relaxing night at home—on the couch!—I was on my way across San Camillo's seedier industrial district, on foot, heading for a potential rip that was forming, hoping my old mentor didn't get herself killed.

Look, it's not that I doubted Wilhelmina's fighting ability. She was, after all, right in the thick of the battle when the three of us had shut down Marigold's attempt to permanently link Earth with the Interstice. I'd seen her perform amazing acrobatic and martial feats—but those were all conducted with the aid of one half of the pulsar stave. Of which I currently had both. With Teget in possession of the ax, and the night's blade still locked up in Meda on the other side of an interdimensional portal, she was left with zero weapons. None. Nada.

Unless, of course, Procyon had dug one up out of their Historic Vault.

I grumbled under my breath. Secrets and more secrets. If I had my way, the presence of astral fiends would be broadcast from every TV station and uploaded to YouTube for the world to see. Those slimy tentacled monsters would think twice about popping into our world if there were armies and, oh, I don't know, cruise missiles aimed at their ugly faces, right?

Maybe.

Maybe Teget and Naos were right about the need to shield people from certain uncomfortable truths.

Maybe I just wanted Loredana to get better so things could get back to the way they'd been, before this mess: her in the office directing my missions, me sneaking around San Camillo at night, slaying monsters. At the end, we go out for dinner. Happy ending.

Instead, I stepped over a ripped open trash bag and a pile of human excrement.

"We are not far, according to the map." There was Teget, dressed in something other than his Medan warrior outfit—a white T-shirt, lightweight gray jacket, blue jeans, and, for the one exception, his homespun boots. Me? I'd reverted to my favorite black polo and khakis.

Yeah, the map. He was carrying around one of those fold out deals issued by the chamber of commerce. Fit the bill for a tourist out for a stroll, except we were in a part of the city where two guys dressed like us were likely to get jumped for their wallets.

Let someone try. I'd spent enough time fighting crime on these streets that they'd get a cracked skull before they could say, "Stick 'em up!" Which, to be fair, no one after the '50s did. "That's great, Teget. You want to stop by the more scenic sights on the way? Or maybe we should pick up a T-shirt that says, 'I Heart San Camillo.'"

"I would suggest you clear your mind for battle instead

of cluttering it with your usual wit."

"I would suggest you shut up."

"Indeed? You are the one who initiated the conversation."

"Whatever." Okay, so I was being a jerk. Perhaps intentionally. But there was a lot on my mind.

I considered laying off a bit.

The rip was scheduled to appear inside a dilapidated warehouse, one that was abandoned and without power, because why not? Astral fiends were proven darkness junkies. They liked using rips this way, which was odd, because they were drawn to humans in order to feast on our body's energy. You'd think appearing in a crowded street event would be a better bet.

On the other hand, we still didn't know how much of a hand the Whisperer had in directing these rips and astral fiends' incursions. He could be orchestrating them for maximum psychological effort—the fiends emerging from dark corners of the city when least expected.

Seemed to be working.

The rip was already spitting sparks when we snuck inside the warehouse. It was a dark slash rippling with purple energy.

And there was an astral fiend forcing his way into our world.

This was more like it—one slimy, tentacled brute, shrieking into a dark building. I could take him out, no sweat, and was kind of bummed I didn't have my earbuds with me. Or a phone that worked.

Problem was, someone was already taking him out.

Wilhelmina sidestepped an incoming tentacle as easily as stepping over litter. She swung a very familiar dagger down. It lopped the tentacle off like she was cutting Play-

Doh with a steak knife. Not bad for a gray-haired lady who was probably in her seventies.

"My dagger," Teget murmured. "She handles it well. Where is its companion?"

"Lost in another dimension," I said. "Be thankful Procyon scooped up this one."

Wilhelmina had been, a long time ago, Sherry Jean Crown—Procyon's operative, same as me. That explained a great deal about how she evaded the astral fiend as it slammed into a rusty metal support post. Even so, she shouldn't be moving *that* fast. Okay, so she wasn't at a Medan level of combat skill. But, come on—the dagger wasn't the same kind of weapon as the pulsar stave. It wasn't a source of tachyon energy fields. As far as I knew it was plain old metal, albeit of the stronger Medan variety.

She definitely had more get up and go than when she was in normal old lady mode.

"Child, if you're waiting for an invitation, it ain't coming!" she hollered.

For a moment, I thought she'd seen me, but she must've been talking to the guy who stepped out of the shadows. That was Garvey, a huge specimen of Procyon's security force. John Cena could have been his brother, if John Cena had a thick brown beard. Buzz cut matched, though. He had on a ragged green sweatshirt and stained blue jeans. Not the typical security uniform.

Of course, he was in public with an old woman fighting a monster, so, wardrobe considerations were key.

I was more interested the device he cradled in his hands. It looked like a police radar gun on steroids, three times as large, and someone had extended the stock, I guess, so it could be braced like a rifle. There were huge blocks suspended from the underside. Batteries? I'd last seen it at Cavill Cemetery, in the hands of Gary DeBarthe, the Procyon tech who'd gone to great lengths to help us stop Arkwright's initial plan to kill a lot of people and destroy more than one world.

Gary died that night. Left a daughter, and an ex-wife.

"Back away, Ma'am!" Garvey lifted the device and slid a switch on its left side. The entire apparatus glowed a sickly purple.

"Don't you 'ma'am' me, boy! Shoot him!"

Bolts of energy, wild as a summer's thunderstorm, lanced out. They struck the astral fiend, lassoing him.

Did that ever infuriate. The fiend writhed in the grip of this energy burst, slashing through the air. It battered a huge chunk of the corrugated metal wall, right behind us.

Oops.

"Mercury!" Garvey stared. "Mr. Hale! Sir, it's good to see you!"

"Hey guys." I lit up the pulsar stave. "How about you let the A-Team take this one over?"

Wilhelmina snorted. "As happy as I am to see you haven't got yourself killed, you sit a spell and let your elder show you how things are done. Go on. Sit!"

Teget sat down on a nearby box.

I was about to ignore her and jump into the fight because, hey, that's what I do, when a beam of light zapped the fiend. It shriveled, moaning and mewling like giant wounded puppy. Garvey slowly turned the weapon, pulling the fiend at the end of a long, intangible leash, inching ever closer to the rip.

"Hold him steady, so I can bid him a decent good-bye, you hear?" Wilhelmina strode into the midst of those thrashing tentacles like she was gonna hug the astral fiend. I really hoped she knew what she was doing, but so far, so good.

"Understood, Mrs. Crown!" Garvey shuffled backward, teeth gritted.

The rip nibbled at the fiend's backside, and then, with a brief, guttural cry, Wilhelmina rushed it. She inflicted a dozen or more slashing wounds with the dagger, each one potent enough to force the fiend deeper into the rip.

When it was halfway in, Garvey flipped another switch.

A second, brilliant pulse surged along the length of the beam. The rip absorbed the full force, contracting into a dazzling white pinpoint.

It closed.

How about that. Procyon figured out how to *close* a rip.

The equally important part was that the astral fiend had been halfway into the rip when it closed, so the remaining half—the tentacled, toothy front half—collapsed in a sodden mess of blue ooze and slick black hide onto the warehouse floor.

Wilhelmina kicked aside a limp tentacle and stabbed the dagger into the cluster of eyes, so deep she wound up with slime all over her hands. "Back to hell with you now, you hear?"

The astral fiend sublimated into a large steaming stain and that was that.

I applauded, a slow, somber clap. "I'd call for an encore, but you seem to be fresh out of monsters."

Wilhelmina positively beamed. She limped over to a crate, where there sat a cane and a handknitted bag emblazoned with a brown and white stripped kitten whose creepy green eyes were on the wrong side of adorable. "Lordy, but it's good to see you, child. Glad you're still among the living."

"In the flesh, as they say." I hugged her. "You're not looking too bad yourself, Sherry. Drake City agreed with you?"

She poked me in the side. "Sherry's gonna take a while to make a return. I realized I shouldn't be ashamed of Wilhelmina. Lord knows I've kept the name this long. Family was the thing I needed, even though I'd spent decades trying to escape them. It was a nice time, yes, but when I heard about what all happened here, there was no question what I had to do."

"Okay, then. Wilhelmina it is. So, Procyon didn't drag you back from the other side of the country."

"Pfft. Them kids wouldn't know what they needed if it were a pair of knitting needles they sat their hind ends on." She considered the blue slime on the dagger's blade. "I walked up to their front door and offered my services. They happily accepted, seeing as how they'd misplaced their operative."

"My bad." I pointed to the dagger. "What's the deal?"

"It's been modified." Garvey had the pulse rifle-thing slung over his shoulder, looking like a vagrant who'd signed up to fight aliens. He handed Wilhelmina a rag. "Ma'am."

"Thank you." She patted his cheek. "This young fellow's been taking good care of me, so don't you fret, Mercury."

"And I'm glad for that, really. But spill, Garvey—modified?"

"Miss Stojan consulted the specifications drawn up by Gary DeBarthe, based on old designs confiscated from Winston Yen's archives. She designed and installed a device that, as far as I know, sucks up ambient tachyons and redirects them."

I could see it now—the dagger's handle was double its original girth, with a module attached below the hilt. Tiny LED lights blinked. "Into the weapon, or the person?"

"Little of both." Wilhelmina sucked in a breath. "Can still feel it, matter of fact, now that the battle's done. A bit like the aftereffects of adrenaline."

"Ingenious." Teget leaned over the bag. "Such a clever melding of the technologies known to both our worlds."

"Well, now, there's another face I'd not thought to lay eyes on." Wilhelmina touched Teget's hand.

"A pleasure, fellow warrior." Teget clasped her hand in his. Hers was dark-skinned and vanished beneath long fingers. "I am happy to see time has preserved your grace."

"Don't he know how to be a gentleman." Wilhelmina winked at me. "Take notes."

"Oh, trust me, I will."

"What news, child? If you're here, I hope it's good."

"I brought back Loredana and Ramos."

Wilhelmina put both hands to her mouth so fast she dropped her cane. She wrapped her arms around my neck for a second, and more intense, hug. "Thank God," she whispered in my ear. "Thank God for all of you."

"Yes!" Garvey pumped his fist. "I knew you could do it! Sir."

My face was burning, and it had nothing to do with exertion, because I didn't fight anything. "Yeah, okay, you're welcome. Teget helped too."

That earned him a kiss on the cheek from Wilhelmina and a slap on the back from Garvey. "If that don't beat all," Wilhelmina said. "Why the long face then, Mercury? Don't tell me you lost your car again."

"Actually, I did, but that was before ..." I shook my

head. "Forget that. There's bad news with the good. Liz is trying to track down what came back with us—Arkwright, a new army of rogue Medan soldiers called Kutsatuta, and something powerful."

"The Hedron of Orbits." Teget was solemn.

Sounded way worse coming out of his mouth, with his accented inflection.

"My word," Wilhelmina murmured. "Something tells me this is going to take more than our fancy leftover dagger and Garvey's special gun."

"It is. Teget and I can handle it."

"With my help."

"Look, it's not like thrashing astral fiends. These guys aren't brainless, instinct-driven monsters. They make the last bunch of soldiers Arkwright employed about as scary as a pack of cubicle jockeys playing paintball on the weekend."

"Don't you give me that." Wilhelmina waggled a finger in my face. You seen what I can do. What we all can do, together. Get me ahold of a part of the pulsar stave."

"She can wield it to great effect," Teget said. "After all, she did use it and the night's blade against our enemies. I would gladly have her fight at our side."

"Um, no, we're not enlisting someone's grandma!" I snapped. "We'd be better off limiting the damage to the two of us."

"Beg your pardon, sir, but you don't get to make that call." Garvey stood at attention, like he was an Army recruiter. "We're a team, and we've been protecting San Camillo from these kind of threats while you were gone, so if anyone's going to need permission, you'll need it to join us."

Wilhelmina smiled and patted his arm.

I was impressed, too. It was probably the most words I'd

ever heard Garvey string together.

Teget leaned in. "This is where the democratic processes of your adopted land influence decisions, is it not?"

"Something like that." I scratched the back of my neck. "Okay, fine. It's stupid, but when it comes down to it, we'll all four go after Arkwright. Deal?"

"Attaboy," Wilhelmina said. "Now, let's get on back to Procyon before the local law enforcement takes interest in our handiwork."

"Handiwork?" Oh, right. Two huge chunks of the warehouse wall were down. They'd crushed a chain-link fence belonging to the adjacent business.

"Car's parked around back." Garvey led us into the shadows. "Used Buick. Mr. Alvarez suggested we, ah, not take a company ride."

"Good tactic." As we walked, I sidled up to Wilhelmina. "So, um, Drake City. Nice place for the smelly, crowded East Coast?"

"You'd like it. Very urban. On the water. Got enough old New England charm for us seasoned folks."

"Good. That's cool."

Wilhelmina smiled slyly. "Go ahead and ask, child."

"Did you see him? As in, in person?"

"Oh, surely did." She produced a flip phone, one that was apparently advanced enough to record video. It was a shaky recorded image of a man in white body armor, face shielded behind a sleek visor, lifting a boat from the water. He carried it, water streaming from a huge gash on its keel, to the beach. Firemen and EMTs rushed off a nearby boardwalk as a crowd of cheering onlookers aimed their phones skyward. The man gave them a wave and shot off so fast it blew sand and water into the air.

"Airfoil," I said. "That's ... awesome. I thought he was urban legend."

"As real as you are, Mr. Monster Slayer Man."

"But you didn't get hurt, right? When all that craziness happened with the quake and the gunmen attacking all around Drake City?"

"My relatives are all south of town, outside Cape Ashwin. I wasn't paying much attention to the news at that point." She patted my cheek and smiled. "Does warm the heart to know you were that worried about me, though."

I had a thousand more questions with her, but they were forestalled by Garvey holding up his hand. We all stopped. He had his fingers pressed to an ear. "News from HQ?"

Garvey nodded. "Doc Arne had Ms. Lark sedated. She's awake now and wants to see you."

I snatched the keys from his belt loop. "I'm driving."

CHAPTER TEN

The lights were out in the infirmary when we got back, except for a couple soft yellow ones at Dr. Arne's desk. He was scribbling notes onto a tablet. Good thing the computer could translate his untidy scrawl into legible text.

Ramos was behind his partition, asleep. He looked way better. The IV drip into his arm must have restored some of his fluids. He'd gotten a shave, and smelled like he'd showered, too. His hands were clasped atop his sheet as he dozed, his breathing light.

"Glad you're here," I murmured. "It hasn't been the same, talking with Teget. He's great and all, but—too brotherly. Treating me like I'm the kid because I'm 'new' to Meda. Not like when you steered me back on course."

Ramos didn't say anything, true, but it didn't matter. What was important was he was lying in a bed, in Procyon, safe. He snored softly.

I rubbed at my eye. "So, yeah, anyway. Sleep well."

The crucifix was in my pocket. Still had mud on its edges. I eased his fingers apart and tucked the cross itself into his palm. His hand tightened around it, probably out of reflex.

I didn't get it. But I'd never seen anyone with quite the backbone and integrity as that man, so if it served him well, more the better.

Of course, if you asked Ramos, he'd tell you he was the one doing the serving.

Loredana was in the recovery room, a separate compartment off to the side. I peeked in the door. The curtains to the hallway window were closed. She was seated upright in bed, reading from a tablet.

I touched the door handle, and that's as far as I got.

"It isn't locked," Arne said from his desk.

How long had I stood there? I retreated to where he sat. "Is she okay?"

"As 'okay' as someone who's been through what she has could be. Malnutrition, dehydration, signs of physical abuse—all those will heal. Give her time. But the psychological strain ..." He frowned. "That's far beyond my area of expertise. I'm recommending time with a therapist."

I raised an eyebrow at the thought of Loredana on some shrink's couch, baring her soul. "How's that gonna work?"

"Probably not at all," Arne muttered. "It's the only recourse I have. Lieutenant Ramos has confirmed she was locked in solitary confinement for most of her incarceration, and there were beatings. No evidence of other forms of physical abuse, so that's in her favor. Still. She was a prisoner in a foreign dimension, Mercury. How can we have any idea how that affected her? I don't even know what the days and nights there are like! How did that affect circadian rhythm? Did she pick up contaminants? Diseases? Too many questions and not enough protocols in place to handle them."

"But it's okay if I see her."

"That's what I told Garvey. She requested you, after all."

Arne made a shooing motion with his hands. "Go see her."

"Because she wants to see me." I was repeating it for my benefit, not his.

"Probably. But more importantly, because I'm tired of talking to you and I have work to do." With that, he resumed scribbling on his tablet.

What a pal. I propelled myself across the floor through sheer willpower, like I was telling the pulsar stave to power up and get ready to fight. Seriously. What was I afraid of? This was a regular woman, and a friend, and a ... someone more, I hoped. You'd think I was about to step into the ring with another astral fiend.

I think that would have been preferable.

Her eyes snapped from her reading as soon as the door handle clicked. Red splashed across her cheeks, filling in the gaps between freckles. "Oh. Hello."

"Hi." I closed the door behind me. There was a chair off to one side. I gestured. "Can I?"

"Yes. Of course."

I dragged it closer, until I was near enough, I caught a hint of perfume. She'd cleaned up, too, and if not for the lingering bruises—and how I'd found her in the exiles' fortress—I would have thought she was in the hospital after a car accident. "So, um, we should probably talk."

She shut off the tablet and set it aside. "Yes. You're right."

I was having trouble finding words. My heart was pounding away. If it got worse, Doc Arne was going to rush in here and sedate me. But that wouldn't work. I had to say it.

"Mercury." She said my name, and that's all it took.

"I searched for you for weeks," I blurted. "Day after day,

checking the tracker and hoping, praying, it would fix itself. Scouts came and went, without any word, and I thought I was going crazy. I threw myself into more fights with astral fiends, because they kept trying to attack Meda. Maybe I was convinced that the more of them I stopped, somehow I'd get closer to finding you. And then, just like that, we were there, and … I saw a body. I thought it was yours."

She had tears in her eyes. Okay, so did I. She held out her hand.

I pulled the chair in until it bumped the bed and took ahold of her fingers. "It doesn't matter. It's done with. You're safe, and I won't let anything like that happen ever again."

"Mercury, please." The tears were on her cheeks now. "When you found me—"

"You slapped me." I gave her a half smile, thinking she'd see the humor in that reaction compared to now.

Wrong move. Her sorrowful expression only deepened. "You don't understand. In that moment, I had no hope left. I'd given up long before. I thought—I *knew* you would never come for me."

I stared at her. No words.

"I talked myself into it. Perhaps you were dead, or Procyon recalled you, or the federal agents watching us had you locked away. It didn't matter the reason. There was no way out of that dark place, and I don't just mean my cell." She touched her head. "Here. This was the other cell. The one that was inescapable."

"But you're free now. We're back. I did come back for you."

"I never thought it would happen."

"How could you think I'd abandoned you? After all we'd been through together. I …"

"You what, Mercury?"

Say it, you dope. "I love you, Loredana. Probably I have for a long time. Others smarter than me saw it. And I pushed it away. But that's why I never gave up. That's why I wouldn't come back without you."

"I know you do." She leaned over and kissed me.

I wanted to leave right then, with her, forgetting all about relics and weapons and monsters and Procyon. I'd even leave Ramos to be with his family. The two of us could get out of the city, or the country.

Then she pulled back. "I hit you because I'd given up hope, Mercury, and I knew to survive, I had to cut all ties to here."

"What does that mean?"

"All of this." She indicated the room. "The secrets. The plans. The strategies. The bloody, unending war against forces that want to consume us. Procyon itself—and everything associated with it."

"Everything."

Loredana wiped her eyes. "Everything. It has to be done."

"Ah, yeah, no it doesn't." I stood from the chair and jerked a thumb at my chest. My head was spinning and if you could have taken an x-ray, you would have seen my ribs cracking, because someone was ripping my heart clean from my chest. "I'm right here. You want to quit Procyon? Super! Let's go. This second. I'll pack us bags and we can get lost. No one will find us."

"Please. This is difficult enough." She looked me square in the eye.

"It shouldn't be."

"Don't presume to tell me. You have no idea what I've been through." She pressed her hands to the sides of her head. "The things I've withstood. And then there you were, out of nowhere, like an answer to prayer, and you didn't ..."

She shut down the sentence, but there was an accusation hiding back there. I could feel it. I flashed back to when the final showdown happened inside the exile fortress. The fight with Arkwright's men, and their subsequent escape.

"You could have ended it," she murmured.

"I didn't." The realization hit me in the face way harder than Loredana slapped. "I didn't kill Arkwright."

"And now he's loose. Again. And we'll have to fight. Again." She picked up the tablet and threw it across the room. It crashed off the wall, shedding plastic bits. "I'm sick of it! Sick of giving everything I have for a cause that is never acknowledged, saving the world and having to hide what we do! We deserve more than this, all of us. And what happens instead? Gary DeBarthe is dead, and so is Jack Jackson, and so is Marigold Yen. Wilhelmina's family. Countless of our people. So much sacrifice."

"To save everyone. To stop the evil that's gonna consume us if we do nothing, Loredana."

"You sound like me, when I was blind and stupid." She turned on her side and hugged her middle.

"What's wrong with you?" The pain of loss, even though she was sitting there in front of me, was rapidly transforming into anger. The fact that she was close to being right didn't help matters. "You can't turn your back on everything. On everyone. We depend on you. Think of the actions you've taken that have saved lives!"

"They're outweighed by those I've taken that have resulted in the deaths of innocents. We're both guilty of that."

"Loredana, please."

"Go, Mercury. I wanted you to understand, but it's clear you don't."

I touched her shoulder. "That doesn't matter. I'm still here for you. Let me help."

"You can't. And you couldn't. Everything you've done is too little, too late." She shrugged me off.

I couldn't feel my legs. Too numb. A cold, sickly sensation washed over me. After all I'd done, all I said, that was how it was going to be.

I walked out without saying another word.

Her sobs echoed through the door.

Procyon's waterfront walkway was one of the more beautiful aspects of the city. I sat at the end of a public pier that branched off into San Camillo Bay. Just me, and my good buddy Sam Adams in the form of a six pack.

I finished off Number Three, belched, and flung the bottle as far as I could. Before it hit the water, I blasted it into smoking shards with the pulsar stave.

"That's the stupidest thing I've ever seen you do," Ramos said. "And when you consider the list, that's saying a lot."

My chuckle was distinctly devoid of mirth. "What'd you do? Shoot Doc Arne and stage a breakout?"

Ramos leaned heavily on a cane. I'd heard him thumping down the dock—duh—but assumed it was some homeless guy. Hadn't figured an explanation for my actions, especially the whole shooting bottles with energy beams part. "Are you sharing?"

I held up Bottle Number Four.

"That swill? It will have to do."

I helped him sit, then cracked open the bottle. He drank

deeply and smiled.

"You missed that."

"Beer? It's more the moment. Do you know what it's like to never relax for more than a month?"

"Gee, no, I don't." I grabbed Number Five—or, I guess, my Number Four, even if it was fifth in the case. Whatever. I took a swig. "Maybe I'll go ask Ms. Lark. I'm sure she'd explain it."

"Sounds like you already did."

"She blames me, Ramos. She's ready to throw this life away and me with it."

Ramos nodded. "I'm not surprised. Things were hard in that place. The fact that we're alive is a miracle, and a testament to your loyalty."

I was terrified to the point of my guts churning to ask, because if the answer came out the way I feared, I couldn't take the consequences. "Do you blame me?"

"No." Ramos took another drink. "I was close to that, at the beginning, because I missed my family. But I thought about how you must feel—the guilt, the pain, the uncertainty. With that out of the way, all I could do was trust in God."

"Like always."

"Like always." Ramos clinked his wedding ring against the bottle. "Mercury, all these events that have happened, that have led up to this moment and are carrying us toward whatever the outcome will be, they're not random. We may have no clue what's going on in the stream of time as it flows, but the one who stands outside time knows the beginning and the end."

"That's pretty deep, even for you." I didn't want to hear it. Just keep drinking.

"Shrug it off if you like, but it's what got me through

those days." Ramos wiped his mouth with the back of his hand and gazed up at the few stars that could been seen through the haze of San Camillo's lights. "Give her time. She needs to recover."

"You think she'll change her mind?"

"No idea. But you need to be prepared for either possibility. I'll remember you both in my prayers."

"Thanks."

"Meantime, do you think you should stop shooting your secret weapon at beer bottles out here?"

I snickered. That was funny. Really funny, four beers in. "Good thing I'm drinking most of these. You don't need to be hung over tomorrow."

"What's happening tomorrow?"

"I'm taking you home, Lieutenant, to see your wife and kids." I drained that bottle until it was empty. "Somebody ought to get a happy reunion."

CHAPTER ELEVEN

I finally got another car.

That seems like a petty thing to consider, what with rescuing my friends and considering the breakup of a relationship that had barely started. Oh, and waiting for Procyon to track down a potentially world-ending device.

But what can I say? I missed my Subarus. Thankfully, Procyon kept a stash of "loaners," as Garvey called them, for emergency situations in which they didn't want to draw official attention. Hence the old Buick Garvey drove last night.

For me, they had a Honda Civic.

Talk about the most generic car ever. I wasn't going to complain—too much—as Ramos and I made it through traffic unhindered by police or federal agents, the latter of whom were apparently on the prowl for me.

I drummed the steering wheel as we pulled up outside Ramos's house. The radio churned out tunes that, for Ramos's benefit, I kept at a low roar. "Okay. Here you are."

"No charge?" Ramos watched the front porch of the bungalow as if he expected it to explode.

"I'm not giving up superheroing to become an Uber driver, if that's what you mean." I shut off the engine. "Come on, let's do this."

"They think I'm dead."

I shook my head. "Not Olivia. You didn't see her—look, Ramos. She was the one who told me you weren't a goner. No one else was there to tell me everything was going to be okay. Do yourself a favor: get out of the car and go say hello to your wife and kids."

He opened the car door and propped his cane on the asphalt. That's as far as he got. I rolled my eyes and met him around the passenger side. He made like he needed help getting out, but I'd seen him navigate the uneven surface of a pier in the middle of the night. Something held him back, and I wasn't talking about his seatbelt.

We'd made it halfway up the concrete walk to the porch steps when the front door banged open.

Twin girls barreled across the deck, flinging themselves onto him at the last moment. If I hadn't been holding him, Ramos would have been bowled over—and after a half minute of their joyous screams and teary hugs, he winked at me.

I let go.

They tumbled onto the lawn, laughing and crying, with Ramos doing most of the latter. Two boys joined them, a lanky teen and a stout middle-schooler. Ramos disentangled himself enough to hug both boys. He saved a strong handshake and secret, whispered words for the oldest, who grinned and straightened up like he'd been awarded the Medal of Honor.

Then Olivia came down the steps. She was a short lady, with curly black hair and a smile that was meant only for one SCPD Lieutenant Gabriel Ramos. He was so enthralled with his kids he hadn't even spotted her. She took both my hands in hers.

"A little worse for wear, but I got him," I said. "Thanks."

"Thank me?" Her voice sounded like it could shatter. "You brought him home, Mercury. I'll never forget that. I should be thanking you."

"Maybe, but you knew I could do it from the start. I needed someone in my corner. Let's call it a joint effort and leave it at that."

"Olivia!" Ramos pushed past his children and pulled his wife in for the deepest, longest kiss to which I'd ever been in close proximity. It warmed the heart, sure, but after a few minutes I started whistling to myself and checking out the clouds. Turning into another hot day, yessir.

Finally, the middle school boy made mock vomiting sounds. That earned him a glare from his father, though Ramos softened the warning look with a smile. "Alejandro, what have you been told about interrupting your mom and me?"

"Chores as punishment." The kid's voice morphed into that of a robotic monotone. "Affirmative. Kissing does not compute."

Ramos sighed, in what I assumed was loving exasperation, then glanced at me. I paid no attention whatsoever to the miniature version of Mercury Hale who was apparently living in his house.

"Everyone back inside, let's go." Olivia alternately pointed and snapped her fingers at the stragglers. "Hector, help the girls with their breakfasts, please."

"You got it." The tall teen scooped up the twin girls, who squealed with delight. "Camila! Lucina! Now boarding for the flight to the kitchen!"

The midget quartet blasted back into the house, full of laughter and horseplay. It stung, a little, only because my memories of those ages were full of conniving, brawling foster siblings and temporary parents who ranged from incompetent to borderline abusive. Actually, the best *family* recollection I could muster was meeting my huge extended band of relatives when Teget first took me to Meda.

"Thanks for the lift." Ramos had his arm around Olivia's waist. "Are you hungry?"

"That's a dumb question. Always, yes."

"We can feed the poor boy. Though I assume you two will have to get to the precinct." She touched Ramos' face. "I still can't believe you're here."

"Neither can I. But you're right. I need to report in."

"You didn't call anyone?"

I cleared my throat. "That'd be one heck of a phone conversation. 'Hey, guys, I'm not dead, I was stranded in a different dimension.' But I suppose having monsters downtown and reanimated corpses might make them more openminded."

"I doubt it," Ramos muttered. "Bureaucracy thrives no matter what. Right now, I need to be with my family again."

Yeah, he did. I watched them head inside, speaking softly in Spanish. Lucky for Ramos we got him back home on a Saturday.

Really? It was Saturday? I checked my phone—a new one, programmed with basic contacts for use by Procyon personnel. Yeah, Saturday. I'd lost track during seventy-six days in Meda, where the specific days of the week weren't so important.

I was so lost in the realization that I almost missed the

dark sedan parked behind my Honda.

When had that gotten there? Probably when I was in the midst of the Ramos reunion. My first thought was, this was Garvey or someone else from Procyon Security. But they should have called me, if they needed to check in.

The guy who got out was big enough I thought he'd pop free of his black blazer. He wore it over a pale-blue shirt, sans tie, which he'd paired with blue jeans. Cowboy boots clomped on the sidewalk. He was tanned, not like a beach bum or someone who spent too much time on the UV bed, but more like a guy who spent time in the field. As in, a literal farm field. There was a swagger to his step. Totally unhurried. He had thick, curly blond hair and a big beard. Broad, crooked nose and a thick neck. Made me think of a college version of Santa Claus.

"There's the man I need to see." He grinned, blue eyes locking onto me as he approached.

"If you're, uh, looking for the homeowner, he's occupied." You know, after seeing his family following more than a month in captivity. Plus, I guessed he and his wife were going to find a way to kick the kids out of the house pronto, so they could get reacquainted, if you catch my drift. "I'm just visiting."

"Lieutenant Ramos is really returned, is he? That's good news. No, friend, I'm here for you." He extended a beefy hand.

I shook it. Rough and leathery. "I don't think we've met, even if you do know Ramos."

"I know his reputation. Solid lawman, no nonsense, loyal to a fault." He kept that grin in place. "Maybe I should call you 'fault' instead of Mercury Hale."

I froze mid-handshake.

"Yeah, I suppose that's not fair of me." He lifted the corner of his jacket, so I could see the shiny badge. "Hudson Bowe, Homeland Security."

Part of my brain calculated if I could arm the pulsar stave and flatten this goofball before he could alert anyone. The other part told me to watch my back and the adjacent yards for a team of federal agents who wanted to arrest me. "Oh. Hey." So much for a snappy response.

"Hey is right." He jerked a thumb over his shoulder. "That your ride? Wouldn't last half the winter on I-90 between Billings and Bozeman. I'm a Ford man myself, F-250, three-quarter ton."

"Loaner."

"I'd have pegged you for an Uber kid, being a Millennial and all."

Oh, definitely wasn't gonna like this guy. "Yeah? Maybe I'm in the market for a new car."

"Bet you are, since monsters destroyed the last two."

That time, I couldn't restrain the reflex. My hand whipped to my right side, where the pulsar stave was tucked in a holster under my shirt.

"Easy, kid." Bowe's hand rested on the top of a holstered pistol. Big, shiny, and silver. He was still smiling, but there was a predatory feel to his body language. Like he was daring me to attack. "No need for a brawl."

"Only if you're here to take me in. I've got work to do and I can't get it done luxuriating inside a Supermax. Plus, I'm kinda important to the whole monsters not destroying this city."

"That much is certain. I've seen the YouTube videos. Read the police reports. San Camillo's finest has a soft spot for you, don't they? Considering how many messes you've been a part of—"

"None of which I caused."

"That's debatable."

"Then I assume you've got a warrant for my arrest. If you do, try taking me in. If not, you can leave."

Bowe shook his head. "You've got this all wrong, Mercury—"

"Mark Hale."

"Sure. Mark. I'll bet you've got a lot more than your driver's license that says that, too. Now, I wonder what Procyon's records would give us if we went huntin'?"

"Try 'huntin' and call me when you come back with a big fat nothing." I folded my arms. "Warrant?"

"Not yet. All I have is the need for conversation." He shrugged. "Whatever deal your Procyon friends have with the federal government is apparently above my pay grade. Fine. I can snoop around as well as the next agent. I tried the direct route a month or so ago, when the massacre downtown took place. Word was terrorists with ties to Syndax Multinational killed a bunch of people."

"Word sounds right to me."

"Sure. Then it gets strange. We hear about people turning into zombies, and a group of armed assailants shooting it out with those terrorists. Assailants who may or may not be employees of Procyon Foundation." Bowe cocked his head, as if he were a dog considering which side of the bone he'd like to gnaw on first. "It's bizarre enough, but when it comes on the heels of the U.S. National Guard being called in to stop a threat of unknown origin, we take such things as potential threats to the national security of the United States. Especially when half the city would swear on a stack of Bibles that giant space octopuses nearly destroyed a couple blocks."

He walked around me. "What do you think happened to all those people your enemies have enlisted? The mercenaries who helped out Calvin Hodges and the Yens were from the same crew that Arkwright employed. Only a few survived, and those who cracked gave us a boatload of answers. Syndax is coming apart, the remnants that we've arrested and that haven't fled underground."

I don't know whether he expected me to confess to my involvement with all that, but if he thought I'd roll over and tell him every secret Procyon kept—no matter how much they irked me—he was an idiot. "Look, Agent Bowe, I've got things to do and a bad guy to track down. You want to stand around and ask dumb questions, be my guest. I'd rather have you go after said bad guy, too, but that's just me."

"You and your crises have got to be stopped."

"I'm not causing them. I'm the only defense."

"Says you. Uncle Sam has other ideas in mind." He poked me in the chest. "As far as we're concerned, the threats are all linked—you, Arkwright, the monsters, Procyon, Syndax. We'll take care of them one at a time, or all at once, whichever's more convenient. I'm a patient man, Mercury. I've got time. You, on the other hand, do not."

That was enough. I drew the pulsar stave and willed it to life. It was worth him pulling his gun in response to that, so I could see the moment of panic on his face. "I'm leaving. Follow me if you want, but if you do, know that I'll treat you the way I treat every enemy I've faced."

Bowe had his finger over the trigger, but he wasn't in any rush to aim at me. "You're talking treason."

"I'm talking preventing the end of the world, and if that means I break your rules, I'll do it over and over again until

I get it right." I took a step toward him. "Leave Ramos alone."

"That a threat?"

"A request. He's not part of this."

"He's in just as deep."

I shrugged. "If he is, then he's my ally, and if you come after him, well ..."

"I've had about enough of your lip." Bowe dialed a number on his cell phone. "It's time I push back against whoever—"

The rumble came out of nowhere, building steadily beneath our feet. Car alarms went off up and down the street. Windows rattled in their panes. Shingles cracked and sloughed off roofs.

Really? An earthquake, now? I glanced at Bowe. He seemed to be just as worried as I was about this turn of events. "You better dial someone else other than your buddies."

Bowe was staring past me, not even remotely interested in me or the pulsar stave. "This isn't an earthquake."

What? Of course it was. This was California. There wasn't a month that goes by without at least a tremor. Even if this one was more localized ...

Wait. It was too local.

A terrible crunching noise echoed down the street. I couldn't look away as three houses ripped free of their foundations, trailing water pipes and gas lines as they wobbled into the air. They slowed between fifty to a hundred feet in the air, drifting apart from each other.

Then they fell.

Walls splintered. Gas lines ignited. Fireballs tore the remaining structures apart. In seconds, six houses were in flames. People ran for cover. Screams brought others to the rescue.

"Fire and EMS to this address!" Bowe ran for the street, shoving his gun into his holster. "Every unit you can muster! Don't worry about that now, get them here, pronto!"

Ramos burst from his house. He was at my side in an instant. "What is it? What happened?"

I was rooted to the spot. "I think Arkwright's finding a use for the Hedron of Orbits."

CHAPTER TWELVE

I'd never felt so helpless. Give me a monster to kill or super-soldiers to spar with, and I was good.

I had no idea what to do in a disaster, natural or otherwise.

Agent Bowe took charge of the relief efforts, at least until local PD showed up. He was in the midst of the rubble, pulling people free. He didn't even notice I was right next to him, helping to pull an elderly couple out from the wreckage of what used to be their living room.

The wife wept over shattered pictured frames. The images were warped and bubbled beyond recognition. How many decades' worth of photos had she lost? Her husband took her toward the ambulances lined up in the middle of the street.

Firefighters shouted at each other along the entire block as they hosed down the blaze. Whoever was on the other end of utilities in this part of San Camillo was quick on the switch, because nothing else had blown up, as far as the gas lines were concerned.

The pulsar stave wasn't much use to me when I couldn't

find something to hit with it, but it did give me an advantage with speed and strength—which I put to use as subtly as possible. It was bad enough Bowe knew way too much about me; I didn't need to flaunt my abilities in broad daylight. Not with eight cell phones already taking video from all angles of the disaster.

Ramos pulled me away from the house Bowe and I cleared out. No more people inside; just the elderly couple. "The damage is widespread. I'm going to have to head back in soon."

"I bet your buddies are already asking questions." There were a knot of SCPD officers—those not hurrying to help victims—talking amongst themselves. Whatever they were saying, there was disagreement on how to handle it, because one young rookie kept reaching for his radio and the senior officers slapped his hand away every time. "I bet Detective Bradley's gonna kiss you."

"One can hope not. You better get back to Procyon and figure this out."

"Yeah. Earthquakes are one thing. Houses dropping *Wizard of Oz* style are another." I elbowed him. "Don't fall into a fire, okay?"

Ramos shook his head and limped toward the SCPD contingent.

I slipped away from the crowd, hoping Bowe remained too busy to continue hounding me. Ramos was right. If anyone had any clue about what had just happened, it was Procyon, and hanging around here wasn't going to solve—

My phone buzzed. "Hey."

"Mercury! Are you hurt? I saw you were near the epicenter of one of the quakes and I just knew you might be in danger and it would be totally unfair if you'd made it all the way back to Earth only to—"

"Whoa, hey, Liz, slow down." I held the phone at arm's length to limit the auditory assault. Once she stopped—or at least got quieter—I asked, "What're you talking about, one of the quakes?"

"There's reports coming in from across San Camillo." She still sounded breathless, but she'd reduced her speed and volume. "I have seven locations on the map."

"No way the city got hit by seven small but powerful earthquakes at the same time."

"Not if we're assuming they're natural, which they're not, and that's the most exciting part!"

An EMT wheeled a gurney by. The man atop it was crying. Blood had soaked the sheet, about where his right leg was. I winced. "Poor choice of words, Liz. Nothing's exciting about innocent people getting hurt."

"Oh, sorry. I didn't mean that." She sniffled.

"Don't get upset. Tell me what you found." I walked back to my car. En route, I glanced over my shoulder. Huh. No sign of Bowe. That could be good or bad.

"Okay. Procyon's got lots of equipment watching the area for anomalies, except those are primarily geared for detecting tachyons."

"Sure. That's what Winston had made the drones for." The memory of the bleach-blond tech genius evoked mixed emotions. On the one hand, a warm, fuzzy feeling about sharing the fight against monsters, occasional dinners, and infrequent beers with him and his wife. On the other, visiting him in prison after he was locked up for his role in a plan to flood the world with the same monsters. "It's how he could get his readings on the rips."

"Right. Yes! Oh, so, that's what the detectors detected.

I guess you could say they're massive tachyon outbursts."

"What, at the earthquake sites?"

"No, not in them. I only found residuals there. The real epicenter was, well, in the center. Of the earthquake sites, I mean." She sighed. I hoped she was exasperated with herself as I was with her. "I'm sending you the directions. Could you please go catch up with them?"

"Catch up with who?" I hopped into my car. Whoops. Bowe was on his way out of the circle of emergency vehicles, snapping orders into his phone.

Headed right for me.

"Um. Your brother. He left with Wilhelmina and Garvey a couple minutes ago."

"Yeah, great, thanks." I hung up the phone and started the car. C'mon, Liz. Send me the address.

There. Corner of 29th and DeLeon, not far from the waterfront.

Not far from Procyon, actually. No wonder they picked it up.

"Hale!" Bowe was twenty feet from my car. "Don't you go anywhere!"

I gunned the engine and flipped him the bird. Very satisfying to watch him fume in the rear-view mirror as I raced off.

The phone buzzed again. "What?"

"Mercury! I forgot to tell you! It's underground. The tachyon burst, I mean. Garvey's got the schematics. I'm pretty sure it's down in the sewers."

"Of course it is," I muttered.

The intersection of 29th and DeLeon was five blocks from

the bay's edge, with the ghetto-fabulous Court Street neighborhood the ragged corner. One of these days the city was gonna have to address the rampant poverty plaguing it, because from where I parked, you could see the broken windows, the abandoned cars, and the homeless people. Not the best advertisement for San Camillo's main drag, because it was the most direct route to the booming renaissance on Bay Avenue—Procyon's home.

I parked in an alley, right behind the ugliest Buick I'd ever seen: a maroon, 1990s LeSabre. And I knew it immediately, because it was the same terrible choice of a ride in which Garvey had transported us last night.

Suddenly, having Procyon saddle me with a Honda Civic didn't seem so bad.

I found Teget prying a metal panel off the asphalt. He stopped with it halfway raised, Garvey holding the edge. "Ah. Mercury. You were contacted by Miss Stojan, no doubt."

"No doubt. Don't let me stop you two from your criminal trespassing."

"Rest easy. We posted a scout to alert us of trouble."

I snickered. "Great job. I drove in here unbothered."

Something sharp and metal pressed against my lower ribcage, perfectly positioned to disembowel me if the bearer was so inclined. "I told you he'd open that mouth of his, soon as he got here."

That would be Wilhelmina. Who better to have as your lookout in the middle of the morning, then an old lady dressed like she was out to buy groceries? The massive Medan dagger ruined the image, however. "I stand corrected."

She smiled and patted my cheek. "Your sass ain't always needed, child. Worth a laugh, sure, but not every five seconds."

Garvey broke into a coughing fit that I decided was disguised laughter. I rolled my eyes but decided it was better to help them with their stupid plan than risk further embarrassment.

We climbed down into what was apparently part of the adjacent building's basement. I splashed into a slimy puddle of—stuff. Didn't want to examine it, so I'll leave it at that. Garvey led us down a short tunnel to a second drop, which required us to clamber down ladders so encrusted with filth I wished I'd brought gloves.

The sewer drain was a long pipe with a slight downward slope. Garvey had a Maglite attached under the muzzle of his semi-automatic pistol, providing a brilliant white cone that did its best to cut the fetid gloom. Wilhelmina followed, her souped-up dagger at the ready, while Teget and I brought up the rear. The pulsar stave and his ax provided extra illumination, which was great, because I was not keen on running into astral fiends or corpse-fiends or whatever-else-fiends in a cramped, suffocating, confined space.

Give me a wide-open warehouse any night.

"The distortion's three hundred yards ahead." Garvey's whisper still echoed, like we were visiting a cemetery. Bad comparison. A really dirty museum? "Or should be. I'm getting the residuals, I think."

He had a Procyon version of Syndax's tracking device clipped to his belt. Must be how he knew where to go.

"For the record, this is a bad idea," I said.

"I agree, sir," Garvey muttered.

"This is the likeliest location in which Arkwright has tested the Hedron." Teget's hushed voice had the combined impatience of every adult I'd ever dealt with as a teenager.

"A direct assault is our best chance to stop him."

"Okay, Mr. Tactics, but did you consult the ax first? To make sure we're not, you know, wrong?"

"Of course. It was the first thing I did when Miss Stojan informed us of this location."

"Because I wouldn't object to you double-checking."

"I believe I just said that I—"

"Hush, boys!" Wilhelmina glared at us. She waved the dagger inches from the ends of our noses. "If them folks get a drop on us because you won't shut your traps, I'll let 'em get to you first!"

Teget and I glanced at each other and nodded to demonstrate we understood.

We pressed on, creeping in silence along the wide, sloshing current of waste that was headed downhill to the bay. San Camillo's wastewater treatment plant was southwest of here, past the Court Street neighborhood, and I was hoping we'd find Arkwright before that, because the ideal of two opposing forces smashing into each other within the walls of a sewage center was gross.

The pipe bent left and we found him.

Not him, though, but one of his guys. Only one. A soldier in modified Medan armor and a blank metal mask, with only two eyeholes as an indicator of who we were facing.

I ignored the purple-tinted brown eyes and focused on the black blade he held before us.

"Oh, great," I muttered.

"Smells like a trap." Wilhelmina tightened her grip on the dagger.

I glared at Teget, only to find he was already rushing past me, his outrage reverberating off the curved concrete walls.

Garvey took that as his cue. He opened fire. The sound

set my ears ringing and promised to grant a massive headache as an encore.

The warrior didn't care much for bullets, dodging the shots as he rushed headlong to meet Teget. Since Garvey had to shift his aim, avoiding killing Teget, the warrior only got nicked in the shoulder, from what I saw.

The two collided in a flare of sparks from the ax. They parried in close quarters, blades scraping off the sides of the tunnel when they got to close to the edge.

I channeled power from the pulsar stave and flung myself forward, marveling as everything slowed down while I simultaneously sped up.

The impact blew the warrior off his feet and threw the sword from his hands. Of course, it carried me along with him. I caromed off the tunnel wall. My splashdown was as graceful as a baby duck's first time out of the nest—which is to say, not.

Covered with filth, my head spinning, I could only watch as the guy scrabbled about for his sword six feet away. His gaze met mine.

Teget got the ax handle around the warrior's throat, using both arms and the weapon to put him in a chokehold, which seemed like a great way to get him to pass out—because I wanted answers, not another dead body. But the warrior let out a savage cry, and his eyes glowed an intense, dark violet. He leapt toward the ceiling, with Teget on his back.

Concrete cracked, and so did bone. When Teget landed in a heap beside me, I didn't think he was getting back up. But he was still breathing, thankfully. I snarled and lashed out with the pulsar stave.

Warrior Guy blocked the blow, because you know, he'd managed to find his sword, which I had really hoped wouldn't happen.

He suddenly cried out. A blade stuck through his armor, dark with his own blood. Wilhelmina's expression was fierce and determined in the flickering light from Garvey's gun.

Speaking of Garvey, he had the guy covered from the back. The pistol was a foot from the base of his neck. "Put the sword down, sir. Don't move, or you're dead."

"Dead? I've never been more alive." His voice was raspy, like he'd swallowed razor blades, found them appetizing, and went back for more.

He didn't drop the sword. Instead, he withdrew, holding it close to his chest. The blade dazzled us with a brilliant, white light tinged with purple. I saw spots.

I also saw him stretch his arms to either side and bolts of lightning thrash Wilhelmina and Garvey.

"Enough of that!" Half-blind, hard of hearing, and with a throbbing headache, I lunged for him with the pulsar stave.

He jerked his head away, but the stave caught the tip of his mask, shattering it.

And his wild swipe with the sword tugged at my chest.

I cried out at the fiery streak. I collapsed, soaking my knees in the sludge. My lungs burned for breath.

Even the warrior was kneeling. Garvey and Wilhelmina moaned, yeah, but they were moving. Teget reached for the edge of the channel. His arms and chest shuddered as he pulled himself out of the water.

"I should have known you would not be an opponent easily vanquished." The warrior's voice was easier to distinguish, with half the mask gone. He turned toward me.

No way. The remaining half of the mask glowed like a dying ember where the pulsar stave's power had shorn it, but the partial face I could see …

It was like looking at a younger Naos.

"Crux?" Teget's voice was reedy, and it shook.

"As I said, very much alive." This Crux guy wrenched the dagger free of his side, wheezing in pain, and then planted the sword deep in the muck surrounding us.

A whirlpool of purple sparks that churned with a deep, dark malevolence sucked him into the waters and he vanished, leaving behind four badly beaten people.

Including two furious relatives, apparently.

CHAPTER THIRTEEN

Hearing about our disaster downtown was enough to bring Loredana out of the infirmary and back to Tracking. She folded her arms, examining all of us crossly.

"Your cousin." Her tone was full of ice.

I'd never seen Teget look so ashamed. His head was so low his chin rested on his chest. A curt nod was the only confirmation.

"This complicates matters." Loredana studied the map on the main monitor, hands clasped behind her back.

"You think?" I sat on the edge of Liz's desk, tapping the pulsar stave on its surface. *Clunk. Clunk.* The rhythm helped me think about our predicament and focus on anything but my last conversation with Loredana. "The guy is Arkwright's chief lackey. He was left behind after Arkwright tested out the Hedron, so we would walk right into a trap. Which almost worked."

"Yes. It would seem having the four of you operate as a team was the prudent course of action."

"Gee, thanks." I rolled my eyes. "Does this mean you're

not filing the retirement paperwork yet?"

She glanced over her shoulder. Let her. Here we were, in the middle of yet another crisis, and one of the people key to our past successes was all set to throw in the proverbial towel. Maybe she was right. Maybe this was too much to handle. But guess what? Everyone else was handling it. So I figured I didn't have to like her decision, if that's what you could call it.

"Your cooperation is the only thing that didn't get you killed," Loredana said smoothly. "One would think among the four of you—considering your combined experience—someone would be able to formulate a plan of action that didn't involve wanton recklessness."

Teget shifted in his chair, like he'd sat on a cactus. Yeah, served him right, lecturing me about being reckless when *he's* the one who charged into the fight down there.

"What more can you tell me about this new adversary?" Loredana kept her back to us and her eyes on the map, like she was busy searching for something.

"Crux was—is the son of our uncle," Teget said. "Edasich and Sabik were among three brothers and a sister, children of our grandfather, Naos. Crux is the third and youngest son of Edasich. We played together when I was young, running the canals, climbing the temple steps, following caravans to and from Meda. He was always the cautious one, a very studious young man, whom I assumed would surpass the rest of us in our devotions and rise to the post of a temple warden."

Liz cleared her throat. "Um, I downloaded everything from Garvey's tracking device, Ms. Lark."

"On this screen, please, Elizabeth."

A blurry image of Crux in full armor appeared, inset over the map. His sword was tinged with purple, as were the eye slits of his mask. Funny. With him frozen up there, and me having the time to inspect him, I could see echoes of Teget's battle stance in the way he wielded his weapon. The guy had to have been trained in Meda. Trained to fight.

No wonder he had nearly taken all four of us on his own.

"It would seem this Crux did not follow in the footsteps you expected," Loredana said.

"No. He did not." Teget sighed. "One day, he went missing. There was a great uproar at the temple, and that same night, raiders came from the north. It was the only time they visited in my lifetime, until Arkwright's attack. A house on the edge of the city burned. I was told Crux perished in the inferno. Grandfather wept."

Loredana turned around. She held a up hand, indicating the frozen image of Crux, and raised an eyebrow in that questioning fashion she did so well.

"I can plainly see that was not the truth," Teget snapped.

"Indeed. It would seem someone lied to your grandfather." Loredana looked at me. "Or …"

"Naos lied." *Clunk. Clunk.* So much for the rhythm keeping me centered. "Yeah. I considered that."

"I do not understand," Teget said. "Why would Grandfather—?"

"Lie about his grandson dying in a fire?" I snorted. "C'mon, Teget. Maybe I'm the only one in this room who gets lied to on a regular basis, but everyone has secrets."

"They're often kept for a reason." Wilhelmina sat opposite us, in a chair tucked between computer monitors. Garvey was so silent and statuesque behind her, I'd forgotten he was still in the room. Nothing about his stolid expression indicated he wanted to weigh in on this conversation. "Lord knows I've had my fair share."

"This is different, and you know it." I strode to the monitor and smacked the stave against Crux's image. Multicolored lights rippled across the surface.

"Easy!" Liz yelped.

"Sorry." I made a face at Wilhelmina and tried to ignore the fact that Loredana was standing only a couple feet away. "We told Grandfather who we fought inside the temple. For all we know, he saw him! If Crux wasn't dead, Naos probably knew all about it. Think—the kid was obsessed with the temple from a young age, and then he supposedly 'dies,' and the next thing anyone sees of him, he's leading Arkwright into the Atrium to retrieve a powerful, forbidden artifact! He got himself banished from Meda, ladies and gentlemen, and since everyone was so ashamed of the disgraced outcasts hiding way up north, no one ever did what should have been done."

"What's that mean, child?" Wilhelmina asked.

"They should have marched an army up there and burned the place to the ground," I snarled. "And hauled the outcasts back in chains. Locked them up. Or killed them."

That brought Teget to his feet. The ax clanked against his chair. "You would advocate the execution of our kin?"

"Why not? That's the punishment you mete out for way less dangerous crimes. These guys are tampering with artifacts that shouldn't *exist*, let alone be stored in one place where any idiot with the right knowledge could go get them! The reason we're in this mess is because the great and powerful temple guys of Meda—Naos included—didn't take the necessary steps to contain the evil they should have known would come back to get them!"

I don't know whether I expected a chorus of voices raised in opposition, or a slap from Teget, but I got nothing except stunned silence. My chest heaved. I gripped the pulsar stave so tightly I could feel its carved edges leaving imprints in my palm.

Teget was staring at me, his mouth hanging open, like he couldn't find the words he needed to argue. Liz picked at her keyboard, not making eye contact with anyone. Garvey stayed at attention, while Loredana ...

She nodded. "You're right, of course, but debating what should have been done will make no difference to what must be done now."

Wilhelmina snorted. "Please, girl. Make no difference? It makes all the difference in the attitude here." She pressed both hands to her chest. "The heart, Mercury. You got the rage bad, and believe you me, I know what all I'm talking about, so don't you give me none of your lip, you hear?"

I pursed my lips, ready to drop a salvo of choice profanities, but who was I kidding—this was Wilhelmina. I'd rather go up against a platoon of nuns in a ruler fight. I shrugged instead.

"Good. Best if you mind your elders." Wilhelmina grimaced as she got out of her seat, accepting Garvey's arm as she did so she could maintain her balance. Once she stopped tottering, she patted his hand and joined me and Loredana at the monitor. "Killing this boy up there isn't going to change a thing about the past. You'd better get used to the alternative."

"What's that?"

"Our keeping him alive. He's right now the best link we have to Arkwright and whatever plan he's got cooking. Which, by the by, we still haven't figured out, and instead of sniping at each other like little ones who got their noses bloodied in a playground scrap, we ought to get to it." She poked me in the chest. "Granddaddy may have lied to you. So, have others. Deal with it."

Teget was her second target. "And you, son? You take Naos down off his pedestal. Ain't going to do anyone any good, you worshipping him like he's infallible and can see all outcomes of every action. He's a flawed man, like the rest. Only one who isn't."

"I see wisdom in your words." Teget sure didn't *sound* like he did, but he scuffed his boot on the floor and offered no argument.

"And you, missy." Wilhelmina squinted up into Loredana's face. "I only got to know one thing—word is you're dropping this life, and us, for good. That a fact? You going to walk away in the middle of a fight?"

I stared, my turn to be astonished. Who the heck told her? I hadn't spoken about my conversation with Loredana to anyone except Ramos. But watching Loredana's cheeks go red and hearing her blurt a few inarticulate sounds was worth the security breach.

"I … that is, I am weighing my options." She cleared her throat, and when she resumed speaking, her voice had lost its constant steady edge. "You don't understand. This life with Procyon is costly."

She seemed to understand her error right before Wilhelmina got even more up in her face, which I didn't think was possible. "Don't you say that to me again," Wilhelmina snapped. "Like I haven't given Procyon everything I loved in this life. Like they didn't wish I'd disappear into the gutter when I did. Like I didn't rescue this boy and keep him here, where he was destined to be, when no one else thought it the right move. Speak to me about cost again, I'll slap you so hard your daddy'll feel it back in England."

Wow.

Loredana's mask of control slipped back into place. "Yes. Of course. I apologize. I will stand with all of you until we can end this crisis."

Left unspoken is what she'd do once it was over, but hey, that was better than nothing. I'd take it. With everyone struck dumb by Wilhelmina's tirade—probably because that was the biggest chastening we'd ever gotten in our lives—I blew out a breath. "Okay, guys. She's right. We're not gonna stop Arkwright this way. That's where you come in, Liz. What've you got?"

"Oh. Okay, my turn." She patted the hard drive of her computer. "Cyril's been crunching away at the data Garvey brought us, so it was a great thing I could cobble that tracker together from the Syndax tech we brought back from Rampart. The quakes weren't natural, we've established that. And there's no doubt that whatever caused them was right where you guys found Crux, so the Hedron of Orbits must have been there."

"Any way to track where it's gone?"

"You said Crux disappeared, and that got me thinking—it sounded a lot like what the fiend-hound was doing when it was terrorizing San Camillo." Liz typed feverishly. A new series of numbers and readouts flooded the main screen, pushing the map and Crux to the left. Red figures overlapped green ones. "See? This is a comparison of tachyon pulses from Crux's disappearance and the many instances we had of the fiend-hound teleporting. They're near identical—okay, with a few variances but not enough to make a difference."

Wilhelmina frowned. "Fiend-hound? Teleporting? I been gone for too long, it seems."

"You didn't miss much," I said. "Syndax merged leftover

bits of an astral fiend with an animal and got a Frankenstein beast that was draining life from people. But unlike the astral fiends, it never left our dimension—right, Liz?"

"Uh-huh. It created a breach between two points of space in this dimension and bridged them." She snapped her fingers. "It could hop from one place to the next."

"Like Crux did." A thought flashed on in my head. I faced Loredana. "And Dominic."

"Gemini's use of the Echo Watches hinges on the position and temperament of a specific tear in space-time that bridges the Interstice to connect with the same location in an alternate version of this dimension," Loredana said. "I am sure Elizabeth has already compared the data Procyon has available on that phenomenon."

Wilhelmina's eyes were wide. "Don't that beat all."

"Yeah." I rubbed my forehead. "Okay, Liz, so can you back track or forward track or whatever with where Crux went?"

"Um, sorry, no. The tachyon trace petered out not long after he vanished. I got a vague direction—east by northeast—but that doesn't narrow it down for you guys. I've got a couple of drones up and running, and by tonight I should have a few more ready. We'll be able to cover a lot more square mileage that way."

"Sounds like a plan."

"Indeed, it does, but ..." Teget made a face. "I am perplexed. Arkwright has the Hedron. Whatever his aims, I do not understand why he delays. Surely he can wreak whatever devastation he desires."

"Maybe the poor boy don't have the instructions for it," Wilhelmina quipped.

"Seriously?" I asked. "That's kinda far-fetched."

"Why not? He ain't from Meda, and far as you know, the only one of your people who's got close-up knowledge of whatever that relic is happens to have left town when he was but a boy. You telling me your granddaddy gave him the details on how to use a forbidden object?"

"No," Teget murmured. "Naos would not have. No one would have."

She had a point. How did we even know if the temple wardens knew what to do with the Hedron? There had to be legends. Somewhere. And Naos hadn't been forthcoming. "Looks like we need to have a chat with good old Grandfather. More like an interrogation."

Loredana put her hands on her hips. "You're returning to Meda?"

"Why not? Might be better if I lay low. Especially with the feds around, and Bowe making his veiled threats—"

"Bowe, who?"

Oh. Right. In the haste of our pursuit, after the earthquakes, I kinda left that part out. I scratched the back of my neck. "I may or may not have been visited by one Homeland Security Agent Hudson Bowe, when I dropped Ramos at his house. A bit more on the 'may' side, actually."

Loredana sighed and shook her head. "And he's watching for you, I take it."

I pantomimed shooting. "Bingo."

"Then you must remain here. Where he can do precisely that."

"Are you nuts? Alvarez had Dominic zap me to Colorado rather than be questioned by the feds. Now you want me to stay in town instead of conveniently hopping to another dimension where Bowe can't find me?"

Something about Loredana's expression made her seem

terribly troubled, like she'd experienced a spike of fear, but she smoothed that worry from her face. It was like watching an actor take on a new role. "If you disappear again, DHS will lean all the harder on Procyon itself, and I—and I suspect Manager Alvarez—would rather avoid increased scrutiny."

Fair point. "Fine. I'll stay here. Sorry, Teget, looks like you're making this trip solo."

He patted my shoulder. "Worry not, brother. You have lusted long after pizza and your couch. It would be well if you sated that lust, so I never have to hear of it again."

"Har har. You're hysterical."

"I have a fine mentor in that regard."

"Well, you better get going, because the sooner we get answers from Grandfather, the sooner we can put the intel to good use figuring out what Arkwright's doing with the Hedron—besides the very generic 'tearing the very planet from you grasp' threat."

Loredana headed for the door. "Everyone should resume normal activity, so as not to cause undue suspicion on the part of federal authorities. Ms. Crown may remain here, if she so chooses."

"I think my time would be best spent making sure this boy don't get himself into all manner of danger." She prodded me with her cane. "'Cause we all know he needs supervision."

"Hey!"

Loredana nodded. "I concur."

I rolled my eyes. Plus side, though, is I'd get to go home. Finally.

Teget peered over Liz's shoulder at the computer. "Would it be too great a trouble for you to indicate where a rip may next open, so I can return to Meda?"

A breeze brushed my skin and ruffled my hair. Weird. I wasn't standing under a vent, I don't think.

"Um, okay, sure, I can do that." She giggled. "I mean it's not like we don't have a way of watching for them, even without someone dreaming dreams over in Forecasting, which was a really easy way to do it but since the last person in charge of that department turned out to be one of the villains I guess—"

The air in the middle of the room bulged. Don't ask me how. I'm hazy on the physics or magic or combination of the two that fed into this kind of mess. All I know is, it looked like we were standing on one side of an invisible wall and someone put a giant fist against the other side, pushing a bubble toward us.

"Everyone please take a step back." Loredana could have been announcing we'd need umbrellas outside because it was raining.

White light exploded from the center of the bulge. It mashed into a ball no bigger than a marble, a marble with the same brilliant intensity as the entire sun. This time I was smart enough to shield my eyes so I didn't, you know, fry a retina or two. The dot widened, pulling itself into an oval that a hazy image filled in.

Dominic stepped free, dressed like he usually did, in business casual attire. His was a bit more rumpled than Ramos'. I wondered if the latter would give the former some ironing tips.

"Ah." Teget clapped his hands together. "That will do nicely!"

Dominic didn't come empty handed. Even as the Echo Watches on his wrists stopped their spins and reassembled into solid armbands, their internal light fading, he handed me a rumpled bundle of cloth that sported some awful gashes. My poor supersuit. Guess it needed more than a dry clean. "I figured if you were coming back to Earth, you could use this. Also, you missed our rendezvous."

"Yeah. About that …"

"Naos filled me in on some details. But only some. He's tight-lipped, as I'm sure you know. So, I decided to check in with the boss." He blinked, and turned slowly, as if suddenly realizing how many people were currently crammed into Tracking. "But I guess I'd better start with, what did I miss?"

CHAPTER FOURTEEN

Finally.

First thing I did when I got home was flop face-first onto my couch. The cushions absorbed the impact of my body like a mama bear hugging her cub.

Okay, other than what I'd seen in cartoons, I had no idea if female bears actually did that. But it fit with my imagination. Granted, I banged up my nose a bit.

Wilhelmina's cane clicked on the floor. "Ain't the Ritz-Carlton, but it's an improvement from Court Street underpass."

"Glad my apartment is a step up from being homeless in San Camillo's worst neighborhood," I muttered.

"Y'all got anything worth eating in a place like this?"

"Fridge." I pointed, aimlessly, my voice muffled by the cushions.

She was into the kitchen before I realized my terrible mistake. I pushed off the couch and intercepted her as she put her hand on the refrigerator handle. "No! Wait."

Wilhelmina raised an eyebrow with such disdain she gave Loredana a run for her money in that department. "Might want to remove that, unless there's an astral fiend hiding behind your ketchup bottle."

I held my hands up in a gesture of surrender. "Um, I'm more worried about the fact that no one's seen the inside of my fridge since late August."

She ran the mental math and made a face like she'd eaten a bag of limes. "Child, if your momma was still kicking, she'd reach across the dimensional barrier and smack you in the back of your head."

"I bet." I opened the door with as much caution as a nuclear physicist taking a peek at a reactor's core. Okay. The smell was funky, sure, but not toxic. Downside? There wasn't much to offer, besides old pickles, half a six pack of beer, very flat soda, assorted condiments, and a plastic container of salad that looked like it was trying to take root and grow a new garden.

"Well?" Wilhelmina rapped on the door.

"There's a sandwich shop down the street. Check the end table. I think there's a menu there."

Which, there was, buried under the small mountain of mail that had come for "Mark Hale" in the past few months. Even with Procyon setting me up a new identity that could withstand scrutiny—except Homeland Security's, it seemed—I didn't get that much. No magazine subscriptions. No catalogs. Mostly bills.

I puttered around the apartment, picking up, well, everything while she perused her choices. Shorts here, a newspaper there, an empty cup that should have been washed of its soda dregs a long time ago. Sink, recycling, and bedroom laundry bag, in reverse order. I sniffed my sleeve. Yeah, that wasn't the fridge, that was my shirt. It carried the aroma of sewage. I stripped out of it and found a red long-sleeved shirt hanging over the end of my bed. "What's your pick?"

Instead of her sandwich order, I got a very official announcement instead from the televised talking heads. "We're outside San Camillo Police Department's Ninth Precinct, where officers are celebrating the return of one of their own who has been missing since the tragic events of the Cavill Cemetery Massacre."

Yikes. Massacre? Alvarez was gonna hate that one. They weren't wrong, though. More than a hundred people had died when the corpse-fiends invaded that area of Thirteenth Street and DeLeon.

Wilhelmina sat on the edge of her couch cushion, ramrod straight, her cane propped under her chin. The TV on the wall opposite her, right next to the door, was running local news. Yep, there was Ramos, dressed up in work clothes—pale blue shirt, dark slacks, a gold tie, and his signature mirrored shades tucked neatly in his chest pocket. He was freshly shaved and, besides a couple bruises here and there, he looked fit as ever, if a little on the gaunt side. He still leaned on the cane, yeah, but come on, he'd barely been back in our world for a day.

"Lieutenant Gabriel Ramos has been SCPD's go-to officer when it comes to things strange and troubling," the rather jaunty voiceover pronounced. "He showed up at the scene of a small but powerful earthquake near his home, one of several that unexpectedly shook San Camillo early this morning. His disappearance in August raised questions surrounding the department's handling of the massacre, though city officials have credited Ramos and his officers with preventing even greater loss of life. Questions of a pending federal investigation have been deflected to the mayor's office, which has refused to comment ..."

"Land's sakes." Wilhelmina shook her head. "Was it as bad as they say?"

I grabbed my tablet from the kitchen counter and swiped dust off the screen before turning it on. "Pretty much. We had our hands full closing the rift and let me tell you, there's a lot of pressure to not screw up when the Air National Guard has fighters ready to flatten downtown if you fail."

"Hold on." She turned up the volume.

" ...persistent stories on social media, accompanied by video that's best categorized as 'unconfirmed,' tell of zombies terrorizing the cemetery and its adjacent neighborhood. Lieutenant Ramos had no comment when asked about these matters, nor did he provide any insight as to where he's been since the incident took place."

They weren't kidding. I didn't have any accounts on social media, because keeping a low profile meant staying offline, but man, was my newsfeed clogged with stories about the weird stuff happening in San Camillo—most of which I knew about firsthand. Astral fiend sightings, the rampage of the fiend-hound and its abrupt ending, the defeat of the corpse-fiends, all accompanied by shaky-cam video and fuzzy images that looked like some high school kid cooked them up in his tech class. The city was split between two mindsets: the majority in a major state of denial; and the fringe who knew, just knew there was something terrible and supernatural going on. Of course, the city was telling everyone that it was all tied together with a terrorist plot concocted by Alexander Arkwright and Syndax Multinational, which was technically true.

They just did their best to leave out the part about monsters.

And then there was me.

Yeah, people had taken way better images of yours truly, decked out in the stealth suit, slugging it out with criminals during my brief stint as a neighborhood vigilante. Pretty good footage, too. I downloaded one particular shot, from a long way off, of me planting a would-be mugger into the asphalt with a swipe from the astral stave.

But those blog posts and articles culminated in an analysis posted by the *Bayside Breeze* last week. Seems that in my absence, not only had crime spiked, it had exceeded the levels it was at *before* I started smacking criminals around. Something about them being emboldened by my absence. Like they figured I was gone for good.

Community Asks: 'Where is Mercury?'

Complete with a shot of my business card, in the hand of an elderly man laid on an ambulance gurney. He'd been shot for the thirty bucks in his wallet.

I slammed the tablet down on the counter.

"Hey, now." Wilhelmina muted the TV news. "There a problem?"

"What do you think?" I shoved the tablet into her hands and stormed for the fridge. Beer? Why not. I popped the cap and took a swig. It didn't help the headache, which, I recalled, was due to my binge the night before. And possibly getting my butt handed to me by a long-lost cousin who was in the city as one of Arkwright's warriors. "It's obvious I'm not having a lot of luck at this superhero thing."

Wilhelmina read the post, then set the device aside. She came over and gently removed the bottle from my hand. She wrinkled her nose as she set it back inside the refrigerator and closed the door, her back to it. "You're putting too much weight on yourself. Destiny came a 'calling, and you acted.

That's all you've got to concern yourself with."

"I should have been here to help people out, especially in the aftermath of the cemetery mess." I rubbed my face. "Instead I went on a wild goose chase."

"For your friends. To save them. And it was at great peril to your own life, Mercury. Ain't no greater love than that."

"I can't be everywhere at once. How could I be? That's why this whole superhero business is never gonna work out. That's also why I only feel like I'm getting things done when I'm dismantling an astral fiend at close range."

"I figured as much. Things could be worse, though."

"I seriously doubt it."

"Oh? Hang on a spell." She retrieved the remote and switched channels, surfing like a couch potato pro until she found what she was looking for—construction work. Not just any construction work but clean up and rebuilding efforts of rubble in the heart of Drake City. "All those government folks are calling it terrorism. People on the street, though, they got their own ideas about what went down—about a man with too much power who tried to create a personal kingdom and another man, a nobody, by all accounts, who rose up and stopped him."

The newscast had some amateur video to accompany the story, bouncing around like it'd been taken by a kid on a skateboard, which, who knew? It might have been. For a moment, it looked like the white-armored Airfoil and another guy were tussling with … Was that a container ship? In midair. The video cut out. Great. Another reminder that there might be a real superhero out there, and meanwhile, I was a guy with a glowing stick, cleaning up the dirt he couldn't be bothered with.

"If that's your pep talk, it sucks," I said.

She squinted, eyes closed to blue slits. "That really all that ails you?"

"What, it's not enough?"

Her scowl deepened.

"Okay, fine. Loredana."

"Don't be harsh on her, child. You got no idea what she's suffered."

"That's not what she heard from you when you brought up the same thing."

"I won't deny, she hit a nerve, and yes, I slapped her down for it. She should've minded her tongue. But who're you to tell her when she can be done with Procyon? Wasn't a soul who understood what I'd gone through back in the day. She's got to make her own call, and if you love her—which you do, child, it's plain as day—you'll be there by her side for as long as she's got."

"Then what? I let her walk off?"

"Maybe you do, if that's what she needs."

"Maybe." I shook my head. "You know, for sage advice, that's pretty noncommittal."

"If I told you what to do, it wouldn't be your decision, now would it?"

I leaned against the counter, its edge cutting into my backside. How was it possible a conversation could wear me out in a minute's time worse than tangling with rogue warriors? "It's just ..."

"Just, what?"

"I don't want her to leave."

"Because you love her."

I nodded.

"Then tell her that, son." She touched my arm, that grandmotherly gesture that broke through every wall surrounding me.

"Already tried it. I think—maybe she's too hurt for any of it right now. Me. Us. Procyon."

"Oh, I got no doubt of that. Things touch you deeply, you lock them away, and lock everyone else out, until it's you and only you inside a steel box. One that locks from the inside, and the only person with the key is the one sealed inside."

My phone buzzed. I about hopped off the counter. Loredana? Could be she'd snapped out of her funk.

Nope. It was Liz, texting.

Hey we're watching the tachyon scans for more activity I got an app on this link for you to install. You can get the same info so I don't have to bug you every five seconds we get something of course if it's a really big deal I'll probably bug you anyway :) Rest up!

The app was easy enough to install, and in a couple seconds, I had the means to get updates directly from Procyon. The map that showed up had the seven locations of the prior earthquakes, plus the epicenter at which we'd faced Crux.

It was a matter of waiting. I hated waiting.

"That girl's got all manner of skills, doesn't she?" Wilhelmina smiled.

I nodded. "Thanks for the talk, by the way. You got anything else?"

"Sure do." She slapped something paper against my chest. "Pastrami on rye. Mustard and mayo. Lettuce. No tomatoes."

"No tomatoes? You are messed up."

She swatted at my head as I left.

I'd made it a couple of apartments down the hall when

Isaiah, the old black guy who lived across from me and down on, cracked open his door. “Mark! Man, where you been?”

“Out of town, man.”

“You didn’t miss much. AC broke again.”

I made a face. For what I was paying in rent, the super was gonna have to step up his game if he didn’t want the pulsar stave shoved up his … nose. I was *that* close. “You told him to fix mine first, right?”

Isaiah shook his head but gave me a toothy grin. “Age before beauty. Hey, speaking of beauty, you catch up with the blond?”

“Blond woman?”

“She wasn’t no man, that’s for sure. I hoped she wanted to talk to me. Asked if you were back in yet, oh, maybe an hour ago.”

“You sure she wasn’t a redhead?” That’d be weird of Loredana to not call first.

“I’m old, not blind.” He pointed down the hall. “Get your rear in gear and go find her number, ‘cause if you ain’t interested, I am.”

I snorted and kept on walking. Typical Isaiah. Just once I’d like a phantom beautiful woman to actually be on the lookout for me. I mean really, who wouldn’t?

The late morning sun took some of the autumn chill off, putting the weather in the upper sixties. I headed over to the corner of 25st and DeLeon, then up the road to Katsaros Deli. It was easy to spot, even two blocks away, because it was the only business with a line of ten people snaking out of the front door. I’d seen worse.

Daydreaming about whether I should text Loredana while I was waiting in line meant that I missed the sedan that pulled up to the curb as I crossed the Street. And I missed the guy getting out of said car, until he stepped in front of me. Hudson Bowe.

"Wow." I shook my head. "Homeland Security must be really bored if following me to lunch is top priority. You want me to get you something? I'm not paying, though."

"You sure skipped out of Lieutenant Ramos' neighborhood quickly this morning."

"I'm not a first responder. I'd get in the way." I gestured past his formidable set of shoulders. "Speaking of in the way …"

"The sandwiches can wait. You're going to make some time to talk with us right now."

I rolled my eyes. "I've had about enough of you and seriously, since I've only talked with you for a combined total of five minutes, that's saying something about your attitude. Arrest me or take me in for questioning if you want, but the only person you'll hear from is Procyon's attorney. Or Loredana Lark, who, by the way, is way worse than a lawyer."

"Maybe. Or maybe I'll have my boys bring in the old lady for questioning." Bowe smiled. "Homeless, right? Nobody'd miss her."

"Touch her and I'll—"

"Gentlemen, this is silly."

The voice belonged to a blond woman who got out of the passenger side of the sedan. She was dressed in a dark jacket and slacks, heels that could stab an astral fiend's eye out, and a pale blue blouse that was mostly buttoned. It was the DHS badge that was more eye-catching, though. She was a head shorter than me, blond hair tied in a ponytail, with brown eyes and the slightest quirk to her lips. "Agent Bowe has better things he could be doing. Isn't that correct?"

"We could haul him out of the city, and no one would care." Bowe was still smirking at me. "If we did it right, no one would even notice. He's got a lot of answer for."

"And if his superiors didn't have close ties to officials far above our heads, I'd be inclined to agree, but your approach isn't helping matters."

"And also, he's standing right here." I crossed my arms. "I already told Agent Bowe, Miss ..."

"Agent Serena Cyr. Bowe's partner. *Senior* partner."

We shook hands because I wanted to be polite and it seemed to irk Bowe. Anything other than me in handcuffs irked Bowe, however.

"Agent Bowe, wait with the car." Agent Cyr checked her cell phone. "I'll be back in thirty. Tell the rest of the squad I'm off comms."

Bowe blew out a breath. "You sure about this?"

"Don't worry about me. I'm sure Mercury Hale's a perfect gentleman." She hooked her arm through mine and winked. "C'mon. That line's not getting any shorter, and I'm starved."

CHAPTER FIFTEEN

Agent Cyr was being awfully familiar for some federal officer I'd just met. But I have to admit, it was a nice feeling walking up DeLeon in the sunshine with a pretty lady holding my arm. Other guys took notice, which only enhanced the ego boost.

"Gotta say, you guys at Homeland Security play things a little bipolar. First Bowe shows up and glowers at me, like I'm gonna break down and sob out all my secrets to him while begging for his mercy, then you … what, take me on a date, Agent Cyr?"

She laughed, a bright, cheerful sound. As surly as everyone around me had been lately, it was a welcome change. "You can call me Serena. I insist."

"That's great. What do you want?"

"A chance to offer an olive branch. I know Hudson can be intimidating."

"Hey, I never said I was intimidated."

"Of course you weren't. He's a good agent, fair, dogged in his pursuit of justice. They don't make many men like him. I knew he was going to be an excellent partner when I recruited him out of Montana Highway Patrol. You, though, are an enigma."

"Not much to me. I enjoy a lot of the same things most guys do."

"Up to and including the destruction of monsters?"

I shrugged.

"There's no sense hiding that fact, Mercury. We might not know much about what goes on behind Procyon's doors—besides the philanthropic work—but I have confirmed enough from my sources to know what you really do. I know it was you who saved San Camillo when the Yens threatened its destruction. I know you prevented something even worse when you banished Alexander Arkwright from this world, at great personal cost."

"Yeah, okay, I'm gonna give you the standard 'I can neither confirm nor deny' line on all that." I was glad we were still half a block from Katsaros. This was not the information I wanted bandied about the city streets, not when there could be criminals in earshot who had friends I'd captured. Or maybe crimefighting victims were here in the flesh. "Any other rumors you'd like me to not address?"

"Only what your plans are for Arkwright."

"Whoever he is."

"Mercury, let's be honest." The smile didn't slip. Neither did the relaxed posture. "I don't care that you sneak around killing those things. I'd rather you did a lot more of it. Homeland is worried about everything that's transpired, but frankly, can you blame them? Events of this sort are becoming more public. The government can only cover up so much in this age of omnipresent video cameras, when everyone has a phone in her pocket that takes pictures. These attacks, coming on the heels of the terrorist strike in Drake

City, have people on Capitol Hill upset—upset for waning public confidence. They want to get re-elected. Letting panic spread about strange and costly disasters doesn't get that done."

"Your point?"

"My point is, I want a win. I want Arkwright dead, preferably in messy, public fashion, so I can parade his carcass on CNN and Fox News. That'll keep both parties and my bosses happy."

I blinked. Somehow, we'd shifted the focus from detaining me to defeating my prime enemy. "That sounds good to me. Like I told Bowe: stay out of my way and I'll make it happen. He's got a lot to answer for."

"And the best way to get that answer is if you let me bring the resources of the Department of Homeland Security and the U.S. government to bear. We want this done right. I want to be the one to put a bullet in Arkwright's head."

The smell from Katsaros, spicy and enticing, wafted over us, but all this talk of killing had soured my appetite. Only somewhat. I was down to wanting half a sandwich. And what had Wilhelmina wanted, anyway? "Don't tell me he threw friends of yours down a portal."

"Nothing so dramatic. It's plain old betrayal." Serena's expression tightened, like she was trying to keep emotions other than her cheery outward nature locked up. "Our families knew each other, the Arkwrights and the Cyrs. Alex used to babysit me. I probably harbored a crush on him, when I was a middle-schooler and he'd gone off to college. It was a relief when my parents told me of the remarkable change he'd undergone, from party animal to top of his class and budding entrepreneur."

She squinted at the skyscrapers looming downtown.

"Then came the car accident. He'd returned home for Christmas. Everyone was impressed with what a fine, respectful young man he'd become. And I was a newly minted driver, hurrying out onto the icy roads to get more eggnog for our family party. That's when I hit a slick corner and rolled the Taurus."

I could almost hear the sirens, feel the metal crunching. I'd seen worse, watched as an astral fiend ripped a car—my car—apart, twice, and heard the cries of injured in that earthquake.

Serena took a shaky breath. "Alex found me. He pulled me out of the car, while it caught fire, dragging me up a snowy embankment. He comforted me until help arrived. I owed him my life."

"Owed him."

"Yes. Until Cavill Cemetery." Serena's smile returned, but it was harder, without the cheer she'd shown before. "That's when everyone saw who he was."

I thought about what I could do to ameliorate the hurt. Wilhelmina would say I should tell the truth. Which sucks, but sometimes, it's the best thing to hear. "I wish I could say he became someone else after that, but the switch had already happened. Alex—the other Alexander Arkwright—killed and replaced his counterpart sometime before that."

"I know. Or at least, that's one bit of relevance Procyon saw fit to share. All it did was make me more resolute to stop him, knowing that the young man who saved me was already a liar, a person who was steeped in deceit and remained that way for the next twenty years. Maybe it made it worse—the same man who so selflessly rescued me had killed dozens and made himself into a devilish creature. That's why I have to stop him. That's why I won't rest until I put him down like the rabid animal he is. What I want, Mercury, is your cooperation and your assurance you won't oppose me."

"This isn't your regular suspect, Serena. We're talking otherworldly forces, the kind you're ill-equipped to tangle with. I'll pay you the compliment of assuming you've done your homework, so you know all about North Beach Battle. Ask Lieutenant Ramos how that went for the conventional forces, once you're done stalking me at his house."

"We're prepared." She smirked. "But I'm not stupid. You're the one with the powerful weaponry—weaponry that, rumor has it, only works for a select few. I'll let you lead the charge. Just make sure I'm there to put on the cuffs."

"Or to put the bullet in his head. Your words."

She shrugged.

I blew out a breath. The last thing I needed was a fed dogging my steps. But I guess it was worse to have them dogged by a man who wanted me locked up instead of a woman who wanted to join the team. Or at least provide fire support.

"What do you think, Mercury?" We were in line behind a trio of young women laughing about whatever was on one or all of their phones. They were oblivious to the details about our conversation. Which they should be. Really, who wanted to deal with all that? I'd rather not.

"I think," I said to Serena, "I'm buying you lunch."

Pastrami on rye. Mustard and mayo. Lettuce. No tomatoes.

Weirdo.

Plus side? I remembered Wilhelmina's sandwich order without having to write it down. Can't remember much of what else we talked about the rest of the afternoon, because my conversation with Serena took up all available space.

Agent Bowe wasn't happy when I left Serena at their car. Whatever. I had her promise that she'd keep him and the rest of Homeland Security at bay—or at least keep him from hauling me off to a Supermax prison.

So, why did I trust her? Was it her connection to Arkwright? I knew what it was like to experience betrayal. Procyon pulled the rug out from under me, with the revelation that I wasn't from Earth, that I was brought into their service with them hoarding a whole bunch of ulterior motives, and they didn't see fit to clue me in until they had no option. They left me no one to trust.

No one, except Loredana.

I glanced at my phone for about the hundredth time that afternoon. Seriously, if I'd kept it up, I would have had to schedule an appointment with my chiropractor. Nothing from her. Don't know what I was expecting.

You could always text her, dummy.

Thanks for nothing, brain.

There was a new text from an unidentified number, though. All it said was, "Standing by."

Subtle, right? I saved the number in my contacts, unnamed. When Serena said she wanted to keep in touch, she wasn't kidding.

"You ain't said hardly a thing since lunch." Wilhelmina's knitting needles were a blur. Someone was getting a pair of black socks with orange stripes. Going for a Halloween gift? Judging by their size, I'd put money on them being knit for Garvey.

"Maybe I ran out of things to say."

She shook her head.

Okay.

The window behind the couch was cracked open to air out the apartment, just enough to allow a fresh breeze entry. The sun had turned the clouds pink and purple in anticipation of sunset. They were like neon signs against the cyan sky.

I gave it only a cursory glance before getting back to the work at hand—namely, my latest sketchbook project. I'd left it at Procyon months ago. It was full of dream-induced visions of Marigold Yen, the Whisperer, astral fiends, the fiend-hound, corpse-fiends—notice the pattern. I'd slipped in a few happier images. Meda. Teget. Ramos. Loredana.

It was Serena's face taking shape on the paper. Didn't know if her smile counted as comforting or unsettling, but it was interesting. I erased a line and swiped shavings onto the floor.

"You. Out of words?" Wilhelmina clucked her tongue. "I'd sooner believe the bay had turned upside down. You been closed-mouthed since that nice stroll you had. Thought you'd come up with a way to starve an old lady, you took so long."

"I needed time to think. My brain's been packed full."

"With Loredana."

"And, you know, other stuff. Like Arkwright."

"That man's got us all on edge, I don't argue."

"Uh-huh." I scowled at my drawing. What was intended to be a faithful portrait of an enigmatic woman had turned into a clown rendering. I slashed a line through the drawing and flipped the page.

"Trouble?"

I sighed and set the pad aside. "If we're gonna do this whole interrogation thing, how about you get on with it? You have a specific question about me and Loredana, or are you fishing?"

She just smiled.

I shifted, suddenly uncomfortable. How was she zeroing in on me without missing a stitch? "I took your advice. I'll let her figure things out and, you know, be there for her and all that, in the meantime."

"Mm-hmm."

"Okay, listen. Different topic, apropos of my walk. What if we found ourselves some outside help for this upcoming fight?"

"You talking about Meda? Thought we had your brother for that."

"No. And I'm not talking the cops. Ramos has that angle covered and, frankly, I think SCPD's gonna steer as clear of us as they can."

"All right. How's about that other young man working for Procyon? The boy who can pop in and out of any which where?"

"Dominic's handy for fast transport." I frowned. "But he seems distracted. I'd bet Loredana's got him busy doing whatever it is he does when he's not providing a teleporting Uber for me. No, I'm talking law enforcement, but, um, higher than cops."

"The feds?" It was her turn to make a face.

"Bingo."

"Wasn't they going to arrest you and throw away the key? And that's why you went off on your quest?"

"Yeah, but I've renegotiated my standing with Homeland Security. I think."

"Best take care with that. It don't matter what that agent you met at Ramos' house tells you, they'll try to find some way to leverage control. You don't think they'd love to get their hands on something as powerful as the pulsar stave?"

I rolled my eyes. "I know what I'm doing. It's not like Procyon's had a clean track record keeping their own plans out in the open, so it's nothing new for me."

"True. But who took care of you? Even that new Alvarez fellow—"

"Condescending prick." I thought it bore repeating.

"—Even he covered for you, got you out of the city when he could have stripped you of the pulsar stave." She wagged a needle at me. "Wouldn't be the first time the weapon took precedence over the operative. Don't make the mistake of thinking those folks with Homeland Security got your best interests at heart, just because they might share your goals."

"Whatever you say, Obi-wan." Don't know what I expected besides a sermon from her. Still, it was nice to have someone who I could talk to who wasn't a cop or a relative or my boss. I pushed off the couch and stretched. "You want something to drink?"

"Tea would be nice."

"I was thinking something cold and carbonated, but let's see what's stashed in the cabinets."

I was digging behind half-empty snack boxes when my phone buzzed. In my pocket? First thought, Loredana. Nope. Serena? Double-nope.

Ah. Ramos. "This work-related or you miss me that bad?"

"Nice to see your ego's undamaged," Ramos muttered. "I've got something you might be interested in. Public Works reported a strange piece of metal stuck in a pipe at one of the earthquake sites. Fifteenth Street, up by Santos. You should take a look at it."

Well, now. "Oh yeah? What kind of metal?"

"The kind inscribed with markings I think you're familiar with. I'll text the directions."

I rubbed at my face. What I really wanted was to turn in early and sleep for a really, really long time. "Can it wait until morning?"

"That's possibly the stupidest thing you've said since we got back. No, Mercury, it can't wait until morning, because if I don't remove it from the scene, how long do you think it's going to take for Homeland Security to get wind and dig it out themselves? I'm taking it on faith that Procyon's the only one's suited to handle—whatever this is. So, get yourself up here right now."

He hung up. I grimaced. Fair point. Made me look lousy when the guy who I'd rescued from months of torture and solitude was right back in the game, while I came up with excuses.

"Problem?" Wilhelmina stashed her knitting needles in her bag, the project paused.

"Ramos found an object. He thinks it's related to the earthquakes." I shrugged. "Want to go for a ride?"

Before she could answer, my phone buzzed again. Liz, this time. "Hey, if you're calling to tell me about the metal thingy Ramos found—"

"Oh, good, Mercury, you're not asleep! That's great because I need you to be quiet and pay attention, okay? There's a rip forming, and we've got a decent window of warning, but you have to get moving now or else—"

"Whoa, hey, Liz, slow down." I mouthed *Astral fiend!* to Wilhelmina, who grabbed her bag and found her dagger. "Gimme the address. We're on our way." Ramos would have to wait.

"Right. Sure. It's a park closed for renovations, around

Fifteenth and Santos, and get this! It's one of the epicenters of the quake—"

I'd already hung up and was running out the front door.

CHAPTER SIXTEEN

A Honda Civic doesn't have the awesomest engine in the world. That said, it could sure move if I was in a hurry.

I drove through San Camillo's streets like I was playing *Grand Theft Auto* after tossing back a case of Red Bulls. Between Wilhelmina's admonitions, the constant buzzing of my phone, and the flurry of honking car horns every time I pulled what I thought was a sweet slide through an intersection, my heart was racing.

No sirens. That was a nice surprise.

"You best mind the road," Wilhelmina snapped. "We won't be any use to Ramos if we're smeared across the pavement."

"Hey, have some faith in my abilities." I slipped us into the right lane to avoid a slow-moving minivan, then raced up alongside it before weaving back and forth between two more cars that were plodding along. And by plodding, I mean traveling at 10 mph over the speed limit.

"Land sakes!"

"Look, if you want to do something useful besides

worrying and praying, answer the phone so Liz will stop bothering us!"

She scowled at me but did as I requested. "Hello, this is Wilhelmina, sitting in Mercury's seat of death."

Everybody's a comedian.

Whatever Liz said in response was urgent and loud, because Wilhelmina held the phone so far from her head, I thought she was priming to throw it out the window. "That girl talks too much and too fast."

"Put it on speaker so we can both enjoy."

One press of the button and the interior of the car filled with, "—trying to match the tachyon emissions with the spike we saw associated with the Hedron test, but this isn't it! It's a standard rip, stable as they've ever been, and I had Cyril compare against every known recording from the past five years. It's shaping up to be a nice big one, too, so I wouldn't be surprised if you get a larger than usual fiend or even more than one!"

"Hey, that's great." Which it was not. Not great. Not by a long shot. "Where's Garvey?"

"He's on his way with the repulsor but I don't know if he can make it in time. There's a lot of crosstown traffic."

I cut off a San Camillo Bay Transit Authority bus and ran a red light at Journeyman Street. Car horns barraged us. I didn't care. Santos was four blocks away. If there was a flicker of purple lightning before we got there … "Any chance of contacting Dominic?"

"Gemini went on assignment right after he took Teget back to Meda. I sent him a text, but I don't know if he'll get it in time. Or at all. Ms. Lark says he's pursuing some leads—"

"Liz, I'm trying hard not to be rude, but I really don't

care. Let me know when something changes." My gaze flicked from car to car. She wasn't kidding about the traffic. "Is there anything you can do to clear things up in this neighborhood?"

"You mean, like, rerouting traffic? Or messing with the lights?" She whooped, like her baseball team had won the pennant. "Sure! Yeah, I can do that. It'll be fun! Oh, but won't I get in trouble."

"I assure you, the risks will be ameliorated." Loredana's voice cut across the open line. "Mercury?"

"Oh, hey. How's it going?" Ever try to play it cool and suave in a phone conversation with the woman you love while speeding through crosstown traffic in a loaner car you've only driven once before while an old lady literally clucks her tongue at you? Me neither.

"A fair sight calmer than whatever you're doing." I could hear the bemusement plain as day. "I will have Elizabeth clear the streets as best she can. The park in question is unnamed, and may not appear on your navigation maps, since work began two weeks ago. It is set back from the corner, half a block up from Fifteenth."

"Got it. Ramos sent me the address. But the visual's helpful."

"There is still damage in the vicinity—a collapsed storefront, several crushed cars. Also, and this is most pertinent, the street itself caved in eight feet."

"So, there's a gaping sinkhole in front of the park?"

"Yes."

Wilhelmina and I glanced at each other. "Never hurts to know the terrain," she murmured. "That'll give us the edge over the fiend."

"Or fiends." I blew out a breath. "Loredana, if you've

got drones incoming, I could use any and all feedback."

"Understood. Check your earbud. I'll talk you through it."

Earbud? I patted my pockets—which was poor planning, because I swerved and clipped the left rearview mirror against an SUV. Good-bye, mirror. Hello, property damage.

"Mercury!"

"Relax! We're fine." I tucked the earbud in place.

"What was that?" Loredana's voice, softer and more insistent, filled my hearing.

"Nothing. Fine. We're good. I'll check in when we arrive." I gestured to Wilhelmina to hang up.

"*If* we arrive," she said.

I couldn't resist a smirk. You know, it was probably better I skipped learning how to drive with my real parents. "Try Ramos again."

Wilhelmina dialed. All I got in the earbud was the voicemail recording. Great. I didn't have any doubts Wilhelmina and I could take out an astral fiend, or maybe two. But Ramos would get himself freeze-dried and mummified in true fiend feeding form, even if he'd brought a rifle with him.

I glanced in the rear view as we sped through yet another red light. It stayed red behind us. So did the cross street's light. Nice work, Liz.

No sign of police cars in pursuit. I wondered if any of those headlights glaring at us in the distance belonged to a sedan driven by one overzealous fed and his pretty supervisor.

By the time we reached Santos a couple blocks later, the roads were deserted except for whatever cars were already parked. I flipped a U-turn in the middle of the street, so we faced the opposite direction, a few buildings away from the intersection.

"Bad enough you try to scare a soul with your terrible driving." Wilhelmina stretched her back as we exited into the cool evening air. "Now you'd have an old lady cross the street by herself in the middle of the night?"

"Look." I powered up the pulsar stave and kept to the shadows as we ducked between cars. "Three things: A, you can fight as well as I can when you've got a tachyon-powered weapon in your hands. B, I'm crossing the street with you, so get me my Senior Citizen Assistance Badge. C., it's barely past 7. And D ..."

"Four things, child."

I sighed. There was no winning with her. "D, I am *not* losing another car, even if it's not technically mine."

Century Park. That was the name. Took me forever to remember. I'd seen a mention while scrolling the *Breeze*'s newsfeed since returning from Meda. The city had torn down three abandoned buildings between Santos and Derringer, east of Fifteenth, resulting in a barren, L-shaped parcel. A community coalition raised the funds needed for its renovation through concerts and cookouts to reclaim what had been an eyesore and a drug den.

Before the local renaissance could get a ribbon-cutting, though, the rough ground was littered with construction equipment. A bulldozer and two backhoes sat tipsy on mounds of dirt, looking like three tired workers hanging out at the bar after a long day. A chain link fence surrounded the property, with a plastic banner heralding, **Century Park: Our Home, Our Neighborhood**, with cutesy cartoon children and playground equipment inviting a better future. The sun had disappeared behind the buildings, lowering a shroud of shadows over the nascent park. Gave it creepy vibe.

The massive, eight-foot-deep hole in the middle of Santos Street didn't help.

Middle of? More like, spanning it from crumbling curb to crumbling curb. The collapse had ripped out a couple sidewalks. Four trees had faceplanted, roots ripped free, leaves discarded.

Ramos' black Dodge Charger was parked at a haphazard angle on the lip of the crater. His cane lay discarded in the front seat. Had a rifle in there, too, which was great, but it'd better already be in his hands.

"Mercury!" Ramos waved from where he crouched, at the treads of the bulldozer.

Thank God. The nightmare fantasy of finding his shriveled corpse, after all the weeks I'd spent searching for him in a foreign dimension, weren't fading any time soon. "Hey, Ramos, instead of skulking in the dark waiting to get your life drained, how about we get out of here?"

He scowled. Ah, like the good old days. "How about you stop whining about the dark and cut this free?"

Purple sparks skittered across the ground, emanating from the center of the triangle formed by the construction equipment.

"Mighty nice night for a walk, y'all." Wilhelmina twisted the attachment at the base of the Medan dagger. The hum was barely perceptible, like a mosquito at the edge of my hearing.

"She's not wrong, Ramos." I crouched with him. He had a flashlight shining on the bulldozer tread. "Tracking's got a rip incoming, at this location—"

"I know. Liz called me."

I tossed the rest of my sentence back and went fishing for a new one. "Then why are you here instead of running away? Or grabbing your long gun?"

"Because I didn't want anyone or anything taking this piece of evidence away," he snapped. "If you're going to find Arkwright, you need every clue we can take away, and since Procyon's hunkered down, I did what I do best—my job."

And risking your skin. I kept that part in my head. But he wasn't kidding about evidence. The flashlight pointed out a jagged shard, as long as my thumb, two fingers wide. It appeared to have broken off from something. Else. And, yeah, it did have carvings that kinda looked like those on the pulsar stave. I was more interested in the pieces jutting from one side that looked like a computer circuit board, except they were worn down by ... age? Exposure? The whole thing seemed extremely old. I was hesitant to touch it.

Lightning exploded from the center of the playground. Blackness ripped apart the air.

"Okay, back up." I lit the sparking end of the pulsar stave and sliced off the chunk of the bulldozer tread containing the fragment.

"Mercury! The rip's expanding and the tachyon readings have spiked!" Liz's interruption caught me by such surprise I about took my foot off with the stave.

"We noticed! Where's Garvey?"

"Still on his way!"

Wilhelmina stood between us and the interdimensional maelstrom. "Ain't gonna be soon enough, boys and girls."

I reached for the chunk of tread, but Ramos slapped my hand away. "Fingerprints!"

He was wearing gloves, I realized. He snagged the chunk and slipped it into his jacket.

Right as an astral fiend burst from the rip.

It was an ugly one. Okay, they're *all* ugly, but this guy

was particularly gross. His eyes were clumped so closely they overlapped. The fangs were misshapen and, I suppose, slimier? And he was a big fella, with a twenty-foot body and tentacles that could extend to at least that length.

I didn't have a ruler, but I guessed at their length when two slammed into the dirt where Ramos and I were hunkered.

I'd already kicked him aside and rolled myself out of the way. Dirt showered my face.

Ramos dragged himself up the side of the bulldozer. Once steadied, he unlimbered his Sig Sauer pistol and let the astral fiend have the entire magazine by way of the muzzle. I don't think he missed with a single bullet, judging by the blue ooze that splattered the fiend's hide.

Wilhelmina swept in, and I do mean swept, because she moved with the sudden grace of a gymnast. She slashed through one tentacle with her dagger and kicked the other aside, leaving an opening for me to impale that second offender with the pulsar stave.

The astral fiend's shriek rattled every bone in my body. It went nuts, slapping at everything within reach as it barged through the darkness toward us. The windows of a backhoe's cab shattered under the fusillade, spraying glass overhead. Ramos ducked behind the bulldozer as he dug into a pocket for a spare magazine for his pistol.

I did a backflip over the bulldozer and landed atop its engine compartment. A quick twist separated the pulsar stave into its components, and I launched myself at the fiend, corkscrewing through the air as spiky tentacles whipped all around me.

The fiend bellowed a challenge at Wilhelmina, which was funny, because I was the one aiming for his eyeballs. Then it flipped the backhoe end over end, ten feet up.

Well, perfect.

I shifted my trajectory and, yes, let one of the tentacles slap me. Try being hit with a tree trunk covered with glistening black spikes. Not fun, but thankfully the stave's energy soaking my body meant that it hurt a lot less and would probably leave bruises rather than snapping my spine and tearing flesh.

The slap also meant I headed right for the backhoe.

I landed, feet first, on its top, as it somersaulted toward its rendezvous with the ground and Wilhelmina. I reunited the pulsar stave and willed it to maximum power—which, incidentally, I had no idea what that meant. It's not like it comes with a battery gauge.

Yellow-white light blazed from the stave, like a welder's torch the size of a sword. I cut through the backhoe, forcing through the metal, until I was halfway between. Then I pulled the stave apart once more and blasted either side.

The flash broke the vehicle in half. The pieces landed a couple feet to either side of Wilhelmina, splashing hydraulic fluid and scattering bits of plastic and metal. But she wasn't hurt.

I hit the ground hard, a jolt of pain shooting up my right leg. I'd need Ramos' cane at this point. "You okay?" I gasped.

"Better'n you are." Her eyes went wide, and she shoved me down to my knees. The dagger's blade whistled inches from my hair. In fact, she might have given me a trim a few days ahead of when I wanted to go to the barber's.

The blade connected with a tentacle, which was great, because the attacking appendage flopped into the dirt instead of clawing off the top of my head. Downside was, the blue ooze slopped all over me.

It would sublimate, like the fiend, when we finally killed it. Speaking of which ...

The astral fiend barreled into the bulldozer, its hide twisting the frame and smashing the lift cylinder. Ramos cried out, but he was on the other side, sprawled on his backside. The impact must have knocked him over.

Tentacles rasped over the top of the cab, pulling the fiend toward its intended meal. As soon as the gaping mouth full of gnarled fangs drooled over the edge, Ramos opened fire, muzzle flashes from his gun lighting up the night.

Wilhelmina and I leapt onto its backside and stabbed as deep as our weapons would allow.

Bits of astral fiend splattered onto the bulldozer. It screamed and writhed, trying to buck us off, but I dug deep with one half of the pulsar stave while fending off flailing tentacles with the other. Wilhelmina cut a long gouge, opening up the fiend's pale, gooey insides, which gave me the opening I needed to finish this.

One strike with the combined stave sent bolts of yellow-white light shooting from its body, tearing off hide and burning tentacles, until it exploded.

We slid down the ooze-slicked face of the bulldozer, ending up at Ramos' feet. He helped Wilhelmina stand.

"Lordy," she wheezed. "I don't know about you boys, but I'm ready for bed."

"I think we'd better secure the scene and take this object to Procyon before anyone turns in for the night," Ramos said.

Sirens wailed in the distance. I could hear traffic moving, which indicated Liz's temporary jam was ended. "Hey, Liz?"

"Are you hurt? I lost track with the drones when the rip surged and folded in on itself!"

“We’re good but tell Garvey to turn around.” I took the fragment, still embedded in bulldozer tread, from Ramos and tugged Wilhelmina’s hand. “And if you can give our rides a clear shot to Procyon with no stops, I’d be a happy camper.”

CHAPTER SEVENTEEN

Liz was a genius. She got us to Bay Avenue without a single red light, which I'm sure made a whole bunch of other drivers super happy. It was going to make the rest of my commutes a pain by comparison.

We regrouped in the lab located on the sixth floor of Procyon's Tower Three. Same place where they'd run countless experiments on the pulsar stave and a few tests on Teget's ax, back when he'd been briefly incarcerated. Also, home to any and all equipment manufactured by the techs. The place had more computer monitors than a gaming center. Everything hummed, and between the pale blue lighting and the white and silver décor, Apple would have sworn the foundation copyright infringed their Genius Bar.

A couple guys were actually working on my poor, tattered supersuit when we came in bearing a new gift. Whatever they were using resembled a sewing machine that had watched way too many episodes of *Star Trek*, rigged out with lights and readout screens and ... Was that a laser?

I breezed past them to the table at the center of the room, in the midst of all kinds of microscopes, test equipment, and centrifuges. Liz was waiting, her arms outstretched. She wore a pair of examination gloves. "Good to see you, too."

She wrinkled her nose. "You smell awful, and I mean, really bad, like garbage and that's one of those smells that doesn't come out easily no matter how much you—"

I sighed and handed her the hunk of bulldozer tread.

"Hello, there." She set it inside a container with a wide-open top. "Let's see what news you can share, okay?"

Liz beckoned one of the lab techs, a young Indian guy, over to the table. Their hushed voices didn't give me much of a clue as to what was going on, but they were sure intent on the toy we'd recovered from the playground.

Ramos leaned against a table and wiped sweat from his face. "I should get back. SCPD's going to be crawling all over that site. I'm assuming every neighbor within a block radius called in a disturbance."

"What, from the rip itself or the astral fiend shrieking?"

Ramos snorted. "Either one." He placed his hand on my shoulder. "You did good. Thank you for keeping an eye out for me."

I scratched the back of my neck as heat suffused my face. Wasn't used to this warm and cuddly version of Ramos, yet. I guess the time spent in captivity had a different effect on him, after all. "Yeah, uh, no problem. And likewise, Tex. Good shooting."

Ramos smiled and shook his head. He nodded to Wilhelmina as he left.

"There goes one happy cop," I said.

"You'd rather he was growlin' at you more often?" she asked.

"Kind of? It's funny how you get used to someone's personality. You don't notice until it's changed, and then it's too late to do anything about it."

"If you say so." Wilhelmina glanced over her shoulder. "Oh, and speaking of personalities ..."

Dr. Arne barged into the lab. "Am I the only one in this building who's not notified when there's a medical emergency? People are injured and you're all standing around here like there isn't an infirmary one floor up!"

"Hey, Doc, relax. Nothing worse than bumps and bruises." I grinned and rolled up my sleeve. "See? Already healing?"

Arne scowled, and reached for Wilhelmina's wrist instead. He checked his watch. "I'm more concerned about elderly patients. Your pulse is steady. I'd like to check your blood pressure and vitals."

"Sakes, child, I'm not ready for the senior home yet." She patted his check. "Though I don't mind being doted over."

"Ma'am, with all due respect, you're not one of—them." Arne jerked a thumb at me.

"Thanks, I think." I rolled my eyes.

"What I mean is, she doesn't possess a DNA structure capable of rapid healing because she hails from another dimension," Arne snapped. "She's regular human."

"Not 'regular' as you think, but I appreciate the concern," Wilhelmina said. "I'll tell you what—let me hear about what all we found out there tonight and then I'll be glad to visit your infirmary."

"Okay. I appreciate that." Arne crossed his arms, apparently perplexed by her sudden acquiescence. "I would have appreciated it more if someone had told me Lieutenant Ramos was here, too, because he definitely needs further observation."

"I think SCPD's got that handled, Doc."

"Good news!" Liz chirped. "It's not a bomb."

The three of us turned around. "Sorry," I said, "Not a what now?"

"Bomb. I thought maybe it was a trap Arkwright left for you. I mean, I would have done that. Maybe. If I were a villain." Her cheeks went dark, which only made her pink hair appear more brilliant. "Sorry, um, what I mean is, it wasn't a trap. I don't think this object was left intentionally."

"Its elemental structure is similar to that of the pulsar stave and its companion ax," the Indian guy said. Narang, that was his name. "Not identical but bearing enough similarity we can say it was manufactured using metals of the same atomic structure."

"What all is it, then?" Wilhelmina asked.

"Um, I don't know, because it won't do anything," Liz said. "It isn't responding to external stimuli. In that regard, it's a lot like the stave. Could be it's activated by the same DNA triggers."

"Could be, huh?" I joined them at the table. The silvery fragment was free of its bulldozer tread, shimmering under the intense overhead light. I squinted. Easier to make out the circuitry patterns, but the carvings weren't any clearer. They were, if anything, fuzzier. "Hang on. Is this thing vibrating?"

Liz nodded and pressed her hands together. "Neat, right? It is vibrating, so fast that it's almost imperceptible. That's what makes this part even more interesting."

Narang was holding a tracking device, like the one Garvey had used in the sewers as we went after Crux. Whatever it was picking up made jagged red lines leap to the top of the screen.

"Tachyon spikes like you wouldn't believe, in intermittent bursts, though they're tiny and super-compressed." Liz was near whispering. "That's not even the best part. It's the gravitational distortion."

"Gravitational distortion."

"Yeah! This." She reached under the edge of the table and pressed a lever. The table's top lowered, bringing everything on its surface—including the box—down six inches.

The shard stayed where it was, with a slight wobble.

"That's … Wow," I muttered.

"Right?" Liz grabbed my shoulder, so hard her nails dug in, and heaven help me, bounced on her tiptoes. "I think this is a piece of the Hedron you guys saw. You found it at the location of one of the quakes, it shows the same artifact properties, and if it can manipulate gravity, that would explain the origin of the quakes, if, you know, that's what the Hedron can do."

"A Hedron shard," I said. "The thing's shedding?"

"Can't say that sounds like a positive development." Wilhelmina peered over the table.

"Oh, it's probably bad, but the important thing is to find out why it's breaking up. I think our original theory is gaining merit."

"You mean, Arkwright doesn't have a clue how to use the thing and this is a test run." I stared at the shard. Wonder if it would work for someone else with a similar DNA trigger. My fingers twitched.

Liz nodded. "I think so. But give me more time to run a full analysis. I bet we can look for more of these shards if I know their composition and the unique particle signature they emit—which could lead us straight to the Hedron. In the meantime, there's only one way to know what this object does."

She must have read my mind.

"Everybody stand back." I stretched out my hand.

"Hold on, now," Wilhelmina balked. "Why'd you say that?"

I shrugged. "Everything else we'd messed with, it seemed a reasonable request."

She took a couple steps back, along with Doc Arne, who'd been glaring in silence the whole time.

My fingertips brushed the shard. Man, that was *cold.* Like reaching deep inside a freezer after working outside in the hot summer sun.

"Stop."

Loredana? Her heels *pock pocked* as she arrowed for our conclave around the table. There was curious mix of emotion on her face—anger, for sure, but possibly fear. "Do not touch that item."

"Um, it's the only way we'll figure out how it works so—" I ignored her and reached again.

She caught my wrist. I looked up, right into her eyes, and however stern her voice was, the pleading there was evident. When you work with someone for years the way we did and got as close as we had over the past few months, you just knew. "Mercury. Please. You could bring the entire building down."

Yikes. I hadn't considered that. But, of course, I should have. I backed up, after reclaiming my wrist. "No harm done."

"Not yet." Loredana smoothed the waist of her suit jacket. "Elizabeth, conduct whatever analyses you must, but take the necessary precautions."

"Sure. I mean, yeah, that's what we'll do." She raised the table, returning the shard to its container. She and her techies carefully moved it deeper into the lab.

Wilhelmina nudged me. "I best get upstairs with the good doctor for that exam."

"About time," Arne muttered. "Ma'am."

He guided her from the lab, leaving me with Loredana. I caught a glimpse of Wilhelmina's impish smile and knowing wink before she disappeared out the door. "All part of her master plan," I murmured.

"Sorry?" Loredana said.

"Nothing." I squared my shoulders. "So. Any repercussions from our sundown party? We had a blast."

"I suppose we shall hear from the city about the destroyed bulldozer," she said dryly. "Lieutenant Ramos kindly kept me informed of the property damage which, for a change, was kept to a minimum."

"You're welcome."

She joined me leaning against the same table. "Are you hurt?"

"Me? No more than usual." I showed of the same bruised arm. "Like I told Arne."

She brushed her hand along the skin. "If there were another way to do this, I would send someone else every time."

Wow. Sparks ran up my arm. Not literal sparks, but hey, with everything else I'd seen in this job, that wouldn't surprise me in the least. I caught her hand with mine and held it. "I'm fine. Really. And this is what I was meant to do. Besides, as willing as Garvey and Wilhelmina are, we both know they'd get slaughtered out there."

"They did well enough in our absence, from what I understand."

"Okay but shoving a couple astral fiends back through their rips is not the same as the hordes we faced."

Loredana nodded. "North Beach Battle."

"Cavill Cemetery Massacre. Not a fan of that one."

"As well you shouldn't me. These are matters that try even the hardiest souls." She pursed her lips. "Yet you remain unperturbed. You, and Lieutenant Ramos."

Ramos? I thought we were having a moment here. "Ramos has his faith. That's got to be what sustains him—his belief that his soul's eternally protected and he's got a home away from this one when he dies. Otherwise he'd just be crazy."

"And what does that say of you?"

I snorted. "The crazy. But hold up. Why's this bugging you?"

She gripped the edge of the table. "I should have withstood our ordeal. I should have been stronger than I was. But now ... Do you know, I haven't gone home since we returned?"

"Why? Get evicted?"

She smirked. "Hardly. And focus, please."

"Just trying to make you smile."

"Which I appreciate." Loredana rubbed her face. She suddenly looked exhausted, more worn down than I'd ever seen her. "I haven't gone home, Mercury, because I can't. The idea of closing the door behind me induces fear. The fear of being alone."

"You were never alone. Ramos was there."

"Gabriel did what he could, both by his presence and his prayer," she whispered. "But all those days and nights spent in darkness, until I couldn't tell one from the other, the cruelty and hardship and pain. You have no idea."

She broke off. Tears swamped her eyes. Her knuckles turned white and every breath was a ragged gasp, like she was struggling to the surface of San Camillo's bay.

I put my arm around her shoulder. A gentle nudge was all it took to guide her head against mine. "Whatever you need, ask. Okay? I'll take you home, if you want. Not like that. I mean, I can camp outside in the hallway if it makes you feel better. Probably your buildings' HOA has rules about vagrant monster slayers but ..."

She laughed through the tears. Shaky, but laughter, nonetheless. "Thank you. I do appreciate it. After all we've been through."

"Sure. No problem." A question gnawed at me, though, until I couldn't keep it stuffed inside any longer. "So, when this is over, when we get Arkwright and find the Hedron, are you still done?"

"Yes. I think. I am. There's only so much I can take."

"Ah. Well, I guess it'll be easier to drop by and see you if you're not on Procyon's payroll."

"That may be difficult. I'm, ah, considering other options. The primary of which does not involve San Camillo."

Whoa, wait a minute. My arm slipped. "Seriously? Are you headed off to Drake City on the other side of the country like Wilhelmina did?"

Loredana cocked an eyebrow. "Perhaps farther."

Garvey came to the door. "Excuse me. Mr. Hale, glad you're okay, sir."

"Yeah, thanks. Sorry you missed the fireworks." At the playground, that is. "What's up?"

"I'm here for Ms. Lark, actually. Ma'am, your guest is here."

"I'd wondered. He said his flight had arrived early, miracle of miracles." Loredana stood, fixed her jacket. "I'll be right down."

I walked with her, Garvey ahead of us by a few steps. "You know, you've got the whole Picard Maneuver down. Kinda hot."

"Hot that I remind you of a balding starship captain in his fifties?" Loredana smiled. "If so, perhaps I should get a haircut."

"That's not what I—never mind." Man. If I could regain my wits around her, that'd be great, instead of sounding like a rambling idiot.

Our trio rode the elevator in silence to the lobby. Right as the chime sounded and the door opened onto the first floor, Loredana reached out and gave my hand a desperate squeeze. What was she so worried about? Another fed visit? Oh. Maybe it was someone from Procyon's board, come calling after the latest in our string of disasters.

Whoever I was expecting, it wasn't the debonair older man waiting with hands clasped behind his back. His chin was lifted slightly, giving me a great view of a bushy silver moustache, the same color as thinning hair slicked to perfection off a right-hand part north of his widow's peak. His attire was similarly neat—tan slacks, brown shoes so reflective I could have bounced a laser off them, pale blue shirt, navy vest, white tie. Every piece seemed brand new, like he'd finished shopping somewhere hideously expensive and walked out wearing his purchases.

"Ah. There you are, Lori. It's nice to see you looking so lovely." All this with a British accent, each syllable clipped as precisely as his haircut.

"Keeping to the regimen you taught me." Loredana touched his side gently and leaned into his chest. "You appear equally fit."

He kissed her forehead. "Made my laps around Heathrow

before the departure. Dreadful time among the pedestrians, but I made do."

"I'm sure you did." Loredana smiled. "Let me introduce—"

"I can manage." Old dude squared his jaw, and in that moment, I was reminded of a weird combo of Teget's warrior stance and Loredana's poise. Or maybe I should call her "Lori." No wedding band on this guy. "You must be Mark Hale."

Who was Mark?

Oh, right. "That's me. In the flesh." I shook his hand. He squeezed back, no sign of a smile, and for a couple seconds, we were in one of those grip-testing contests. I called it a tie.

"Archibald Kenneth Lark, Her Majesty's Special Air Service, retired," he said.

I stared.

"Mark, this is my father," Loredana said softly.

CHAPTER EIGHTEEN

She had to be kidding me.

There I was, in Loredana's office, standing by the door with my hands behind my back like a good soldier while she got her dad a cup of tea. Her dad. All the way from jolly old England. Her ex-SAS dad, from the decades-old branch of the British military that made the Navy Seals seem like an after-school chess club.

Why couldn't he be an accountant?

"I must say, Mark, I have heard stories from Lori regarding your sense of humor and your agreeable nature, yet there's little attention paid to your employment." He cocked an eyebrow, and there was no mistaking the Lark family gesture. That's when I noticed the freckles hidden in the wrinkles on his face, and the pale orange hair among the silver. "You are employed, are you not?"

"Last time I checked," I said. "How about you?"

"Dad, let's not do this at the moment." Loredana handed him a steaming mug. "It's not your usual but there is a nice store downtown that stocks an acceptable selection."

Archibald Lark sniffed the contents. "Hibiscus? Passable.

Thank you, Lori. As to your inquiry, Mr. Hale, I am retired from military service, though I do manage accounts for several clients who are otherwise incapable of handling their own finances."

Huh. Ex-military *and* accountant. "Sounds like a cushy job. Set your own hours?"

"As every man should. What of your work for Procyon Foundation?"

"Mark is on my operations staff. He handles tasks no one else in our organization can, and does so with considerable skill and aplomb," Loredana said.

Skill *and* aplomb? I stood a little straighter.

Archibald glanced at her, those pale hazel eyes searching for something. "Does he indeed? I imagine that will make it easier for him to move up the ranks when you resign."

I must have looked irritable, because Loredana quickly said, "Talk of my resignation is premature, Dad."

"Is it? I assumed you'd be returning to England with me. That is why I've come."

"You said it was to check on my well-being."

"Your well-being? Lori, you have been out of touch for months, and then you initiated contact with the most hysterical of e-mails. I did not put three clients on hold and take a trans-Atlantic flight at great expense because I felt you needed a chat. One can accomplish the same via Skype."

I guessed by "hysterical" he didn't mean super funny. Loredana's cheeks reddened, and for a moment, she seemed to be at a loss for words.

Fortunately, that's rarely a problem for me. "As far as I know, Loredana has a project she's working on that needs her full attention until it's done, Archie. Can I call you Archie?"

"You can and will address me as Mr. Lark."

"Whatever you say, Archie. She's been through a lot lately and I don't think dragging her back to England's going to do her any good."

"No one is dragging anyone anywhere, young man, but if you think I will leave my daughter's well-being to the likes of you—"

"Likes of me. What's that mean, exactly?"

He stepped nearer, the steam from his tea wafting up between us. I thought for sure he was gonna pull some X-men antics and freeze the vapor with that look he was giving me. "It means young, brash, aimless, *American*. Shall I go into greater detail, or does the description suffice?"

"Enough." Loredana slashed the word across our conversation like she had a verbal version of the pulsar stave. And if that wasn't enough, she put her arm between us. "Dad, whether or not I return home with you is not yet determined, but Mark is right—matters here require my attention."

"Then why on God's green Earth did you summon me?" Archie, still glaring at me, blew steam off the tea and sipped from his mug.

"I thought perhaps we could talk. Of our lives. I've encountered challenges recently that have left me uneven."

"Indeed. Then you've forgotten your training. All the more reason you should return home and work for me, as we discussed."

Loredana rolled her eyes. I couldn't have been prouder. "That was never my intent, no matter how much it was yours."

"What of it? Surely it's a far more fulfilling and profitable enterprise than however you're wasting your time and talents begging for money that goes to the dregs of American society."

Every time he spit "American" like it was something he'd stepped in, I wanted to punch the pulsar stave through his face. Then drink his tea, and spit in *that*. "Without Loredana, Procyon—never mind this city—would be in worse shape than you and your limited imagination could conceive."

"My imagination turns to dark things when your name comes up in conversation, Mr. Hale." Archie set aside his tea. "My things are waiting in the cab. Shall I have the driver take us to the airport?"

"Dad! What have I just said?"

"Very well. Then shall we retire to your home, or am I to sleep on a cot in your commissary?" Archie gestured vaguely at his surrounding, which I always thought were posh. "If you won't accept my offer now, I'll obviously need time to convince you."

Tension tightened Loredana's face when he mentioned her home, but she nodded, nonetheless. She wasn't about to head back to her condo. Not alone. Still wasn't healthy, though, and I seriously doubted ol' Archie was gonna let her sort-of boyfriend tag along for their family reunion.

"Well?" Archie indicated the door, which he did by pointing past me like I wasn't right there in front of his face.

"Tell you what—I can keep an eye on things here, for tonight. Wilhelmina needs some help, and I need to make sure Liz has her, um, project under control. For the board's review. That stuff." I smiled at Loredana. "Let your dad take you home, okay? It'll be fine."

"You're sure."

I'd rather it was me taking her home. I wanted to make sure she was safe and no longer in pain. That wasn't going to happen overnight. "Yeah, no problem. I've got this."

She walked past Archie and touched my hand. Gave me a smile, too. "Thank you."

I gave her a chipper, fake salute, partially because I was striving to be light-hearted and partially because I calculated it would anger Archie—and, bingo, I didn't like the guy. His neck went red like those cartoons where the character literally blows his top, steam and all. "At your service."

She left the room, Archie following behind, while I stared at the wall and wondered whether Liz needed help with her lab work. Hanging out in Loredana's office wasn't going to accomplish much, that's for sure.

I turned and there was Archie, blocking the doorway. "Mr. Hale."

"Still my name. Hasn't changed in—" I checked my watch. "Nine seconds. What's up?"

"My blood pressure, I suppose, but I'm due to take medication in the morning." Funny, but said without a hint of humor. "Put assumptions that Loredana will turn her back on her family aside. She will return home with me. It is what's best for her. This dalliance with Procyon Foundation may have assuaged her guilt, but it was never more than a—"

"Lark?" I grinned. See what I did there?

Archie sneered. "Treasure your cunning wit. It will be all that remains when she leaves you."

I've never wished so badly for an astral fiend to maul someone as I did right then.

Procyon kept staff bunks on second floor of Tower One prepped at all times, in case a weary operative needed a safe space in which to recover, especially if said operative had had his apartment trashed by a monster. The rooms were windowless, with cinder block walls, cheap but clean carpeting, and assorted potted plants. My favorite room had a watercolor of a harbor hung over the bed.

I'd like to say it was a night well-spent, but I was awake six or seven times. Nightmares about fighting a masked man with Crux's body plagued me. Didn't help that each time I defeated him, and removed the mask, the face was different.

Naos.

Archie.

Agent Bowe.

Me.

The next morning, as I let the hot spray from the showerhead batter my skull, I wished Marigold was still around. She'd have made sense of the dreams. Or lied to me about them.

Her husband was still around. Winston was biding time in a maximum-security prison up the coast. I doubt he'd be available for a friendly chat. My list of allies and enemies was muddled.

Forget that. I'd had enough of people telling me one thing and doing another. In my most frustrated moments, I wished I was face to ugly cavernous maw with an astral fiend again. At least they don't fudge the truth or refuse to follow through on what they say they're going to do—or, at worse, betray you in the worst possible moment.

My phone buzzed as I finished drying off. Liz again. "Yeah."

"Oh, hey, Mercury, I'm glad you're up."

"I was gonna head for the gym and smack around a robotic sparring partner, but if you've got a target for me who'll bleed, I'll push it to the top of my list."

"Come on up to Tracking." She hung up.

I made a face at the phone. Two short sentences, that I didn't have to cut off? Not like her at all. I grabbed a fresh t-shirt and the pulsar stave before hurrying out the door.

If anyone else in Procyon was wondering what I was doing or where I was going, they didn't make like it was important. I passed Garvey as I exited the elevator on the seventh floor of Tower Three. "Hey, you seen Wilhelmina around?"

"Yes, sir. Dr. Becker asked her to stay overnight, for observation. I think she's still in the infirmary."

That set off alarm bells. "Observation? For anything in particular?"

"He didn't say, but he didn't seem upset. Only abrupt."

Ah. Typical Dr. Arne, then. Probably irritated his supposed patients weren't taking his health and welfare recommendations seriously.

I let myself into Tracking, without waiting for Liz's acknowledgement. She was the only one in there, which was weird. What, was everyone off for the day?

Oh. It was Sunday, wasn't it? Maybe the weird part was the sheer number of people still working.

"Hey, Liz." I rapped on the top of her computer monitor when she didn't look up. "What's the big news?"

"Not now!" She popped out of her chair and grabbed me by the shoulders. I was more amused than startled, so I let her guide me about six feet away from where I'd been standing. "We've only got ten seconds."

I glanced over my shoulder at the room, empty and dark save for the glare of the constantly lit giant monitors. "Okay."

She was staring at a set of green numbers spinning down

to hundredths of a second, dead center of her screen. "And … go!"

Wind whipped the interior of Tracking. I held up an arm, shielding my face from the sudden tempest, complete with blinding light. When it cleared, three men were standing in middle of those obnoxious afterimage blobs blocking my vision.

Dominic, with Teget and Naos.

"Mercury." Naos took a step but immediately collapsed. He would have faceplanted if I hadn't caught his arms, and Teget hadn't grabbed him from behind. "I am sorry. The sickness is holding on stronger than I expected."

Sickness? He meant the wound the corpse-fiend had inflicted. I'd hoped it would have healed by now. But even though the bandages were new, the damage underneath turned my stomach. "The healer was supposed to take care of this."

"There is only so much she could do." Teget clipped each word. His tone was sullen, and I realized he wasn't meeting my eyes or Naos'. "Grandfather was insistent we return, though, so he could speak to you."

"I needed to explain … why I …" Naos' eyes rolled up.

"Come on, Teget, let's get him to the infirmary." I nodded at Dominic. "Thanks for bringing them back."

"It seems to be my side job these days," he said dryly. "Liz, you have my number. I've got to get back to Rampart for a meeting this morning. If anything comes up, I can get to where I need to be, but some notice would be appreciated."

"Got it!" Liz grinned. "Thanks, Dominic … er, Mr. Gemini. Just Gemini. Whichever."

Dominic's bands activated, and he disappeared in an eye-watering flash, but I was already heading out the door with

Naos supported between me and Teget.

Fortunately, the infirmary wasn't far, and Dr. Arne was in more of a curious mood than cranky one when we brought our grandfather. "Who is this?"

"A patient. One of us. I need you to fix him." We helped him lay on an exam table.

"With manners like that, how can I say no?" Arne muttered, reaching for his stethoscope.

"Wait." Naos grabbed my arm. "Mercury. There is no amount of healing which will reverse the infection process. We are beyond that, as I have told your brother. Let me say what I must about Crux."

Well. Funny how fast your feelings for someone can change in an instant. I dropped his hand, cold sweeping throughout my body. "Our cousin, you mean? The guy who tried to kill us—twice—after slaughtering a temple full of guards and helping Arkwright steal your most powerful artifact? That one?"

"I failed him, as I failed you. I was arrogant—I recognize that now. There was no wisdom I did not possess, or so I thought. That was why I perpetrated the ruse of his death, because I assumed by banishing him from the city of Meda, he would be chastised to the point of redemption."

"If he survived the wild lands." Teget's face was a steel mask. "Surely you considered he might die—truly die, yes?"

Naos grimaced, either from the pain of his wound or the harsh memories. "Perhaps. It was a possibility. But my duty was to protect the artifacts, to make certain no one—*no one*—could abuse them. Not even my own flesh and blood."

"And what if it were I who showed too much curiosity? Or our father?"

Naos sighed and stared at the ceiling.

"What a piece of work," I muttered. "All three of us, I mean. I am seriously tempted to follow Loredana out the front door."

"Do not." Naos grabbed my arm. "You must not give up hope. I made that mistake, when I should have dealt honestly with your cousin rather than forcing him onto a dark path from which he could not return. Please, Mercury, Teget, do not make the same mistake I did."

"Would you have us extend the olive branch to Crux?" Teget snapped. "Risk our lives to save one who has already killed so many? The one who led you to this bed, facing death?"

"I mean for you to end the threat to Meda and Earth, as I should have." Naos seemed genuinely puzzled. "You must, of course, kill him."

The trembling spread from my arms to my core and into my shoes, until every cell in my body was quaking.

Check that. I wasn't the only thing quaking. Medical instruments rattled on metal trays. Rolling chairs scooted across the floor. Dr. Arne clutched his tablet, watching in horror as lights flickered overhead.

"Tarnation." Wilhelmina braced herself on the door to the recovery room. "You boys better get a move on."

"She's right." I slapped Teget on the shoulder and ran for the door. "Feels like Arkwright's practicing again!"

CHAPTER NINETEEN

Liz was in full-blown panic mode.

"The tremors are building past Richter Five point One!" she yelped. "I'm picking up a second epicenter twelve blocks northeast of here. The tachyon pulses built to this one much more quickly than the first quake, so much so the drones barely had time to send me emergency notice with the accompanying data!"

"Relax, we've got it now." I let power surge through the pulsar stave. "Soon as you can get us a fix, we'll nail Crux with the Hedron."

"Arkwright, as well, if he is the one activating its abilities," Teget said.

"Okay, with the second quake ramping up, I should be able to get a fix on the center, because there's tachyon surges building in five other locations again." She tapped five pulsing red dots on her monitor, all of which joined the bigger indicators up on the main screen. "I shouldn't have any problem figuring it out if you guys want to get going."

"I'm driving," I told Teget.

I pushed the car to its limits, watching the RPM needle flip as the engine revved its way up DeLeon. No cracks in the streets, no fires or broken water mains—yet—so that was a plus, but police cars zipped across several intersections.

"With seven locations in danger, it will be difficult for the wardens of your city to maintain law and order while helping those citizens in danger," Teget said.

"Yeah, I think that's part of Arkwright's plan," I muttered. "Doesn't matter how long it takes him to get through his equivalent of a YouTube tutorial on using the Hedron, he's gonna take every chance to sow some chaos as he can. Because, you know, he doesn't strike me as the kind of guy who lets go of a grudge."

"Nor should we be, if we are to believe Grandfather."

I glanced at him. "Hey, whatever avenging headspace you're in, step out of it. We're not hired killers, and we sure aren't assassins. I for one am not about to carve Crux up, now that we know he's family."

"Are you certain? His being kin makes his treason all the more detestable. And he would not be the first you killed."

"Cheap shot, Teget. Yeah, I killed, both Syndax soldiers and Kutsatuta, but that's to protect others. Every time. And it doesn't mean I liked it."

"No one should savor killing, but there are times it is necessary."

"That's great. Let's have the murder debate later, got it?" I risked taking one hand off the wheel to jab a finger square in his face. "Let's try this: you don't kill him unless I say so, because this is my world and that makes me in charge of you. Plus, I'm the older brother, so …"

"So, what?"

"In your face." I blew out a breath and goosed the Honda

for more acceleration. It whined.

"Good news!" Liz's yelp was scratchy from my phone, which was sitting on the armrest between me and Teget. "Got a location for you! Texting the coordinates."

"Atta girl. Teget, give me the address."

He squinted at my phone's screen. "Your device indicates it is in the location where we made our initial return, the park named Rosa Roja."

"Out in public? In broad daylight?" I snorted. "Someone's getting ballsy."

Teget gave me a quizzical look but I ignored it as I skidded around a corner, cutting between a half dozen cars, and sped for the park.

By the time we got there, people were already running away, screaming, which I counted as in our favor because the more people escaping, the fewer people in danger. We pushed past them, and no one seemed the least bit interested in two part-Asian dudes with glowing, archaic weapons hustling *toward* the bad stuff they were fleeing.

And the bad stuff was out in force today. No Crux hiding in the shadows of a sewer, solo. Nope, he was there, guarding Arkwright, as the latter delivered his unrepeatable chants in a deep monotone. They were surrounded by the rest of the Kutsatuta gang, but it was only six guys. None were wearing masks; in fact, they'd forgone their otherworldly armor for tan Kevlar, padding, fatigues, and long-sleeved shirts. Not quite as special forces as the Syndax soldiers, but not casual San Camillo, either.

Even Arkwright had gotten the memo about dress code—or perhaps delivered it. He looked just like I remembered him from our first meeting in Syndax, a handsome brown-haired guy, this time in a thin black jacket and khakis. The glowing purple eyes were the only indicator something was seriously messed up about this dude.

That, and the spinning, glowing Hedron of Orbits floating over the center of the park.

The ground swayed beneath us, making every step toward our enemies a chore, compounded by huge tree limbs that snapped off and landed in our path. Teget gave me a hard shove, which was gonna leave a bruise but one I didn't mind because it kept me from getting brained by a six-foot branch. The shaking intensified the nearer we got.

I touched the earbud, making sure it wasn't gonna fall out of my head. "Liz? Liz, do you have drones getting all this?"

"Sure do! They're circling the park and the neighboring blocks, and Cyril's collating the data as fast as it comes in! We'll be poring over it for weeks, there's so much here!"

"That's great! All I have to do now is figure out how to shut the Hedron off," I muttered.

"Something of this nature does not respond to removal of a power source, or anything as mundane as the flipping of a switch." Teget staggered against a tree, taking a break from our long slog. We could have been trudging through snow, we were making so little progress.

"Yeah, well, there has to be a way to kill its power."

"Unless it is a power source!" Liz chirped. "That could be a problem."

I rolled my eyes and pressed on.

Suddenly the shaking stopped. I tripped, like there was a rock or a tree root in my way, but nope, nothing I could see.

"What happened? What did you do?" Teget let go of the tree; he was still staggering like a drunken frat boy.

I checked my hands. Not trembling. Of course, neither

were any of the Kutsatuta. Or anything else in their immediate surroundings. It was like we were inside a hundred-foot bubble, protected from the Hedron's strenuous efforts to open up another San Andreas fault line.

Crux saw me then. Didn't seem in a hurry to fight. He beckoned two of his men, the gesture plain enough: *Intercept these fools.*

Intercept away, boys.

I let them get fifty feet from me before I willed the pulsar stave's energy into my body, for a good old-fashioned surge of speed.

Except nothing happened.

Oh, sure, I ran, but a normal run, like I was late for lunch with Loredana. Nothing stave-assisted.

Wonderful.

Footfalls behind me indicated Teget was closing fast, because he'd have no problem closing the distance even without the aid of his weapon. Weird. The stave was still coursing with power, seeping yellow and white light, and had extended to its multiple segments separated by crackling energy. I gave it a quick twist, ready to separate it so I had two weapons, one for each of the soldiers only a dozen feet away now.

Nada.

No. It is forbidden.

Voices again? What a time for the Whisperer and/or Marigold to start yapping inside my skull.

Except, I knew it wasn't either of them. I recognized the strange, ringing tones. The Hedron. It was blocking the weapon's full capacity, keeping the energy pent-up.

I swung it like a quarterstaff, a move I probably telegraphed a mile away, because both guys dodged it. They came at me with swords, which reminded me of the Medan dagger Wilhelmina had been using, only with longer, broader blades. Parrying both their blows was tricky, but nowhere near as bad as an astral fiend's flurry of tentacles.

Teget leapt at one of the men, his battle cry echoing off the stone ruins of Rosa Roja. The ax clashed against a sword in a burst of sparks, and the initial surprise drove Teget's adversary back, but that was it. His momentary advantage devolved into a stalemate, with the two of them circling each other, sweating, battering at each other's defenses in desperate search for a weakness.

Me? I fought dirty.

After a few minutes of back and forth sword-versus-stave slashing, I waited until my opponent came back for another slash and ducked. I put the pulsar stave into his crotch. That produced a delightful howl, and with a grin, I bashed his jaw with the stave. His sword cut my left arm, not deep, but enough of a long, hot line of pain that I whirled around and hit him so hard I could hear his shoulder *crack*.

That left me open to lend Teget a hand, which I did by body checking the tall, dark-haired warrior. As in, my elbow jabbed into his spine.

He flailed. It was enough of a surprise that Teget cut the Kevlar vest with his ax and hit the man square in the face with the pommel.

"Two down." I panted, hands on my knees.

"This … used to be simpler." Teget was similarly short on breath.

Crux had taken notice of our success, because he led two more guards our way in a triangle formation that promised a lot more pain. Meanwhile, I heard glass shatter, and stone crumble. As calm as it was inside the Hedron's sphere of influence, outside San Camillo was weathering a quake at least as bad as the first collection.

"Topping out at Richter Seven point Five!" Liz said. "There's a ten-story apartment near Court Street on the verge of collapse and I don't think anyone's been evacuated!"

I slapped Teget's back and gestured at the oncoming warriors. "Hang on, Liz! We've run into a problem! The weapons aren't working. I mean, yeah, we can fight, but they're not lending a hand to our bodies. Try being Superman without the super, if you catch my drift."

"Wow. Oh, wow. No wonder the drones are giving me weird readings. It's as if the normal tachyon surge is amplified around the center of the park, but inside there's—nothing. Like, I can't even tell you guys are there, if you weren't on the phone!"

Teget must have been watching my scowl deepen, because as we headed for our enemies, he murmured, "I suspect she does not bear good tidings."

"I'd take really bad tidings at this point," I snapped. "We're fresh out of any."

It wasn't until we engaged Crux and his trio that I realized the bad guys were just as hampered as we were, thanks to their boss. Not a purple eye among them, nor any evidence of enhanced abilities. Five guys, all trained to fight, duking it out.

And our weapons were more powerful.

Check that. Crux's black sword could deal with the pulsar stave easily, so it must be leaking tachyons all over the place. I pressed home my attack, battering him toward a tree, until I put enough space between us that I could kick him in the knee. He cried out, staggered, and backed off.

"The fight goes well for you, even without your crutch,"

he snarled. "Would you set it aside, and fight me like a man?"

"If it means upping my chances of losing, uh, no." I vaulted away—no, literally, using the pulsar stave like a pole vault—and landed not all that far off, where Teget was tackling the other two goons. Together we battered one of the men until he had a broken arm and something I'd never thought I'd see: a Medan weapon, snapped in half.

That left the other guy, who was as astonished as I was. Teget planted the ax square in his chest, above the line of the Kevlar vest. The spray of blood and the way he crumpled told me he was dead, instantly.

"What are you doing?" Teget shoved me. "You have your opponent cornered! Now is not the time for mercy."

"How's about you worry about your warrior skills and I'll figure out how to apply the Geneva Conventions to our evil cousin," I snapped. "Maybe we should ask Grandfather again—oh, wait, he wants to kill him, too."

Crux used the tree as his crutch, until he was back on his feet. Each step he took toward us contained less and less of a limp. Either he had enough of Arkwright's tachyon infusion left in his body, or he could heal faster than either me or Teget without it. Neither was good news for us. "Listen to you two. Squabbling over your roles, blindly taking orders from that old fool. He would have you bow down to him, and keep the Hedron locked away gathering dust, instead of using it for its true purpose."

"Great, here we go," I muttered. "Can I buy the flash version of this speech? Let me guess, world domination? That seems to be what all the cool kids want."

"What good is that sort of power? Telling people what to do, giving orders. I speak of reshaping *worlds*." He looked way too happy about that. "Only then does political control mean anything. Only then do we of Meda take our rightful place as rulers over lesser humanity."

"There we go, see? Crazy guy wants to take over the world. Called it." I brandished the pulsar stave. "Give up, and we'll find you a nice cozy dungeon in Meda for your home. Maybe the same one you locked my friends in."

"No." Teget leveled the ax at Crux, like he was daring him to approach and yet warning him to stay back, all at once. "There is no imprisonment for traitors to our blood. I will carry out your sentence, as Grandfather would have me."

"I see the blood runs hot in your side of the family tree," Crux said. "You would execute me only because I have the vision to change the world, to want to see it bettered. Have you not perceived its vile state, when compared to the near paradise that is Meda? Even in exile, my brethren enjoyed better lives than the starving, diseased, and war-torn of this mud pit Earth. I want to purify it, to make it better for everyone."

"Breaking the wall," I said. "Arkwright spews the same garbage."

Tires squealed from the edge of the park. I could see SCPD squad cars and a black Charger disgorging San Camillo's finest and one Lieutenant Gabriel Ramos, in his Kevlar labeled "POLICE", M4 rifle ready. Another set of vehicles approached from the south—nondescript sedans and a hulking black van. These brought the feds, including Serena, Agent Bowe, and a bunch of DHS guys in full tactical garb, black from head to toe.

I sneered. "See that? The people who disagree with your plans for a so-called 'better life' are on their way to kick you off the 'mud pit.' Surrender and you won't be shot to pieces."

"I will not surrender to you." He spit. As in, on my shoes. That's just gross. "You call yourself a Medan? You and your bloodthirsty brother? Lining up to imprison or kill your kin, while these feeble people would do the same thing without hesitation. Arkwright has shown them the error of their ways. But I see they need further education."

What more education we needed besides man-made earthquakes, I didn't get to ask, because the tremors suddenly tossed us off our feet. The tranquil environment in our immediate vicinity shook everyone and everything mercilessly. Even Crux had to use the sword as an anchor, but the shaking still forced him to his knees.

"You've got to get out of there!" Liz's yelp in my earbud didn't help soothe my psyche, or my blood pressure, for that matter. "Whatever Arkwright is doing with the Hedron is seriously fouling up tachyon levels and all kinds of background radiation! The drones can't get a clear read because it's overwhelming their sensors!"

Wouldn't be doing any good for the tracker in my pocket, either. I dug into the dirt, tearing up a handful of grass so I could anchor myself and at least get a good look around.

Purple lightning skittered across the park. Four, count 'em, *four* rips opened, spewing mini-maelstroms, several hundred yards apart. Astral fiends clambered out of each one, thirty-foot bruisers that screamed in such a ghastly way I had a hard time believing it was still a bright, sunny morning downtown.

Arkwright swiveled, facing us, the Hedron in his hands. Sort of. It was there, but then it wasn't, and then it was right in front of me.

Mercury …

That sing-song tone—Marigold.

Such brazen disregard for truth, Mercury. After all the lies you've been told, one would think you would walk away to preserve your sanity.

I gritted my teeth. Last thing I needed was the Whisperer infiltrating my mind on the verge of—

All around us, the ruins of old San Camillo that have gathered moss for a couple centuries or more vibrated and tore free of the ground. Huge stones, whole walls, entire foundations of villas and churches floated thirty feet up and kept going, until the skeletal remains of a dozen structures hovered overhead.

And the moronic police were already charging into the fray, swarming Arkwright and his monsters.

"Great," I muttered. "Just great."

CHAPTER TWENTY

Bullets flew immediately.

Whoever among the law enforcement types had the bright idea to open fire on a monster horde inside a park full of gravity errors was, well, lacking brains.

Ramos hollered to no avail, mouth wide open but nothing coming out as far as I could tell—nothing I could hear over the thunderous barrage.

Meanwhile, not wanting to get shot by trigger-happy idiots after successfully surviving multiple astral fiends, I flattened myself against the ground, with a tree trunk shielding my head. Bullets intended for the astral fiends went into corkscrewing gyrations. Go home bullets, you're drunk. They ripped up tufts of grass, filling the air with shredded green blades and gouts of dirt.

Teget and Crux put aside their mutual loathing long enough for them each to dive for cover behind stone walls—the ones not floating way overhead. Guess Arkwright couldn't juggle everything, even with the newfound powers of the Hedron seriously increasing his muscle. Speaking of Arkwright, the fusillade didn't seem to faze him. He stood with his hands thrust toward the police, fingers still cradling the Hedron.

The ruins of Rosa Roja Park flung themselves at the police, not quickly, more like a leisurely bike-riding pace. But when it's multi-ton stones instead of a Schwinn or a BMX, the result's bound to be worse.

"Cease fire! Cease fire and take cover!" The fact I could hear Ramos' exasperated orders meant the gunfire had slackened. The cops scurried from the incoming projectiles. Their cars didn't have the same reflexes. A piece of a hacienda wall smashed two cruisers flat. Huge blocks crumpled the roofs and hoods of several DHS sedans. One jagged chunk ripped through the black van, leaving only a misshapen cab with a twisted chassis protruding from the back.

How many cops got hit, I couldn't see, but judging by the shouts for help and cries of pain, it was a fair few. There were still plenty to swarm deeper into the park, guns aimed but refraining from shooting again. Smart.

"Kill them!" Arkwright demanded.

Wasn't sure whether he was talking to Crux or the remaining two Kutsatuta soldiers, so my stomach did a sickly flip when the astral fiends charged from the rips whipping up wind and tree branches.

"Uh, Teget?" I pointed.

"Yes, I see them." He spat grass. "I am open to suggestions."

"Why not simply lie here and accept your inevitable death?" Crux held his side. Blood seeped from between his fingers. Must've got struck by a stray shot.

"Got a better idea." I offered my hand.

Crux, bewildered, reached for it, maybe thinking I was losing my mind or extending the greatest grace ever known.

Nah. I just needed him distracted. I bashed him across the forehead with the pulsar stave. The blow put him down, unconscious but breathing.

"I really just wanted him to shut up," I muttered.

I spun toward the nearest fiend, wondering how I was going to fight the thing with the Hedron blocking the stave from going all sharp and slashy, when I twisted the halves in desperation yet again.

They split. Yellow-white energy stabbed out from each one.

"This is a pleasant development." Teget stared at the shimmering lines of his ax.

I grinned. Arkwright must have guessed or felt what happened. Either way, he had let go of the Hedron and taken a step back, scowling.

The fiend went bonkers as soon as the stave activated at full strength and shifted his trajectory, so he came straight for us.

I planted a sharp, blazing end into the tentacle that lashed at my feet and pole-vaulted over his face, landing with a squishy impact on his hide. The fiend slapped frantically at me, but Teget had him occupied from the front. Dividing his attention between two attackers stopped him in his tracks, as he cracked a tree trunk and slammed into a stone wall.

Spikes ripped through the air, striking my ribcage. I'd backed off without a second to spare, meaning I didn't get my innards pulled free and scattered across the park. I was going to have a nice set of nasty bruises the next morning.

Teget barreled in from the side—which must have confused the fiend thoroughly, seeing as how he was right in front of its teeth a second ago. With the stave and the ax restored to their full power, we could take full advantage of the benefits they offered. Like superspeed.

Riding that fiend like a bull, though, I didn't need to be that fast.

A tentacle stabbed right for my nose. A swipe severed it, and I dodged the remnants as they flew past my head. I had to block incoming blue ooze with my forearm, because as unlikely as I was to go blind from contact, I didn't want to dwell on what the fiend's biochemistry would do to my immune system. Not that I'd ever thought about it in great detail before.

My gyrations atop the fiend did their job, though, because as annoying as I was and as many injuries as I'd inflicted, Teget was the one doing the real damage. He cut through the thick hide, ignoring the half dozen hits the fiend scored on his back, midsection, and shoulders, until the ax drove deep into its core. The explosion sprayed thick, black chunks like car tire over a forty-foot radius and coated the grass in ooze, which started sublimating and steaming before most had even hit the ground.

One down, three to go.

"Mercury, whatever Arkwright is doing has seriously messed with dimensional barriers and if he keeps it up I don't how bad the breach will be when it's all said and done. I mean it won't be as rough as when they tried to—"

"Liz!" I sprinted for the second astral fiend, which was busy tearing an SCPD car in half. Man. Here's hoping the city had a line for new vehicles in the next budget, because they were gonna need it. "Unless you've got good news for me, quit shouting in my ear! I'm busy!"

"Okay, that's what I was getting to! Garvey should be there any second!"

Garvey? One more gun wasn't going to make a big

difference, not with SCPD resuming their attack—or defense. Whatever you wanted to call it. Ramos led officers in a reinvigorated shootout, now that they realized the bizarre gravity distortion around the center of the park had dissipated. Eight or nine officers got an astral fiend backed against a stand of trees, so it couldn't decide whether to sample the tasty human morsels whose bullets were cutting up its thick hide or tear apart the innocent flora.

But then again, Garvey might bring the portal gun. Happy thought.

I leapt at the fiend, managing to come in at the same angle as the gunfire, which meant I didn't get shot in the process of trying to save lives. Always a plus. My path took me straight for the fiend's mouth, at which point I entertained the possibility of getting eaten. But the poor beast had taken so much damage from the police, he was already rolling onto his side, blue slime turning the surrounding landscape into a soggy mess.

He gave up the rest of the fight when I stabbed him in his glistening, glaring compound eyes.

"This is a disaster." Ramos cleared a magazine from his M4 and inserted a fresh one. Give the guy credit—if he was scared, he hid it well, unlike the other young officers with him. Most were wide-eyed and pale. One doubled over and vomited. "You had better have a handle on this."

I wiped ooze from the side of my mouth. Did *not* want to risk tasting it. "Thanks for the confidence, Ramos. Two out of four's a good start."

"What about the man you were fighting? Arkwright's warrior with the sword."

"He's—" I glanced back. Crux? Where was he?

Standing between the other two astral fiends, woozy, but

upright. He held the side of his head as he gestured with his sword, like a general giving commands. And the astral fiends responded by rushing towards.

"He's not unconscious," I muttered. "Great."

"Here they come!" Ramos shouted to his officers. "Fall back to defensive positions."

"Not gonna help much." I couldn't see Teget. Where was he hiding?

Never mind. I had more pressing concerns. Like the feds swarming into our midst, men barking orders as they readied automatic weapons. And the fact that two more rips opened, disgorging two more astral fiends.

"*Dios.*" Ramos made the sign of the cross. He looked at the DHS guys. "Never thought I'd be thankful to see federal agents horning in on our territory."

"If it's a problem, I can always send them out for lunch." Serena was there, with her own M4 and Agent Bowe. "Hello, boys."

"Hey, Serena." That earned me a bemused stare from Ramos, which deflected faster than an astral fiend's tentacle. "And Agent Bowe, since we're not on first name speaking terms, buddy."

"Screw you, Hale." Bowe gestured to the Homeland Security officers. "Light 'em up!"

The barrage that ensued made London's anti-aircraft defense during the Blitz seem like a kid's backyard firecracker display. The astral fiends slowed their charge to a crawl, but didn't stop, even as they were slowly torn to bits. It took the combined might of SCPD and Homeland to reduce one of the fiends to a quivering mass, incapable of movement—well, almost. It moaned, trying to drag itself on one ragged stump of a tentacle. I walked toward it.

"Hold fire!" Serena ordered.

That gave me the window to plant the pulsar stave deep in its face, destroying what was left.

Screeching tires cut across the rumble of the battle and even the shrieking of the astral fiends. A maroon Buick LeSabre careened through bushes, dragging torn branches around its wheels. It skidded up beside us, which was both good and bad—good, because Wilhelmina and Garvey got out, the latter hefting his portal-closer gun, and bad, because the DHS agents were about five seconds from shooting holes in both of them. And the LeSabre.

"Y'all should put those down," Wilhelmina said sweetly. "I'm not near as frightening as those monsters."

"Never seen you fight, have they?" I muttered. "Garvey, now'd be the time to do your thing. I'm going after Crux."

"Crux. That's the guy you were fighting with—and talking to." Ramos was near enough he could keep his voice low, which was great, because I really didn't want to answer Crux-related questions with Serena and Bowe eavesdropping.

"Yeah. He's a Medan exile. A Kutsatuta. One of Arkwright's lieutenants." I scratched the back of my head. "And my cousin."

Ramos stared. "Cousin."

"On Dad's side."

"Mercury!"

That was Teget, hollering from the center of the clearing, where he was face to face with the aforementioned Crux, again. He was hollering because he'd gone to his knees, with a gash along his right arm.

And Crux had his sword raised over his head.

I didn't think. Wasn't time to. I soaked every bit of power from the pulsar stave that I could in the time it took my heart to beat. My skin buzzed. Vibrations rattled my brain inside my skull. It was like the worst caffeine kick known to mankind, magnified by a thousand.

I hurtled across the clearing. Everyone and everything else around me was stuck in the air—even bullets, as they traipsed toward one of the astral fiends. Something smacked me above my eyebrow, like an errant branch or a rock. Took me a bit to realize I'd run into a fly at who knew how many miles per hour.

Had to get there.

Faster.

Crux's sword descended in slow motion. I stretched out with the stave, reaching, hoping …

Made it.

His blade hit the stave with a tremendous *clang*, like it was a gong the size of a car. Its sharp edge skidded along the stave, spraying sparks, away from my brother.

Thank God.

But when the weapons separated, a tremendous burst of light sent us all tumbling.

My ears were ringing, so much so I could hear only muffled words. Thankfully, Crux had been knocked clear, so he couldn't do me or Teget any more damage. And Teget? He was knocked out.

Arkwright stood over me.

I thrust upward with the stave, but he was ready, and whatever he did with the Hedron flattened me on my back. I was suffocating, with a huge, invisible force shoving me into the dirt. My muscles ached, then hurt, then screamed. It felt like they were being slowly, intentionally ripped from their mountings.

"There was a time I wanted you to join my side,

Mercury," he said. "There was another time I wanted you left as a witness to the greatness I'll achieve. But given how much of a challenge you've been of late I'm going to settle for torturing you. Slowly. While your friends and family watch, because frankly, I'm furious with you for your interference. I thought you deserved that explanation."

He wasn't kidding. With more astral fiends emerging, none of my allies were in any shape to help. Ramos and the police kept losing ground to the fiends, their gunfire more and more sporadic, even with Homeland bolstering their ranks. There were bodies in between—shriveled remains of police and DHS agents, drained of life, husks serving as warnings to those still breathing. Wilhelmina was with them, battling back an astral fiend as the beam of light form Garvey's portal device forced it back into a rip.

I was on my own.

No matter how much I willed the pulsar stave to respond to my commands, it remained a pent-up source of power, unwilling—or unable—to strike at Arkwright. It was barely enough to keep me from being crushed, but I was on the losing end. Spots appeared in my vision. Breaths wouldn't come. Come on, let's go! Break free.

No. It will respond only to me.

The Hedron. It was talking again. I directed a simple thought its way. Could it read minds? I pictured giving Arkwright the finger.

He is inconsequential. You are inconsequential. All are inconsequential. There is only power, and it is mine.

Not ominous at all.

Arkwright grit his teeth. Sweat trickled down his nose. The Hedron must be as taxing on him as my resistance, or so I hoped. It didn't matter. Darkness ate up all but a blurry version of my sight. The worst thing? The bleakness. The feeling I'd failed everyone. I'd never get to talk to Naos again.

I'd never see Loredana.

The pulse of energy and light that interrupted my desponding was about as big a surprised to my addled brain as it was to Arkwright, judging by his startled expression. Even better was seeing Dominic emerge from the spherical display, the bands on his wrists glowing like the sun.

He shot Arkwright.

Shot him with—lightning? Or energy like from the pulsar stave? It was powerful enough to knock Arkwright down, but not free the Hedron from his grasp.

Couldn't believe he was crazy enough to battle in broad daylight, until I realized he wore a black compression shirt and military-style pants, black shoes, and had a mask covering the lower half of his face. With his hair the same color, all you could see of Dominic Zein was copper skin and brown eyes. He might as well have been a ninja.

"Mercury, are you hurt?" Dominic knelt, his hand pressed to my chest.

"Augh ... working on ... talking." I couldn't suck in air fast enough.

"Stand down, then. I'll do what I can." He pivoted, facing Arkwright.

Crux was there. I swear, the guy could move like a ghost, but he wasn't on the offensive. Instead, he looped an arm under Arkwright's shoulders.

Arkwright's eyes took on their familiar purple blaze and a rip opened, the same kind that the fiend-hound used to vanish himself, and the same that Crux employed to escape us in the sewers. They were getting away. Again.

No way.

"Help." I grabbed for Dominic's arm. "Got to—go after—"

Something about the suggestion pinched Dominic's face. Like he was arguing with himself. After a second, as Crux dragged Arkwright through the rip, his posture changed, and his expression hardened. He pulled me to my feet. "I'll try."

I coughed. "You know what Yoda would say."

Dominic smirked but instead of arguing, aimed his armband at the rip.

The world around us streaked, like ruined paints running on a canvas, and threw us after our enemies.

In an instant, I could see a bunch of places at once—a sewer drain, Procyon's parking lot, my apartment, SCPD's Ninth Precinct, the Shattered Mug coffee shop, Carlito's, stores and parks and rooms. All at the same time. Merged and messy.

Then we burst into sunlight, slammed onto hard-packed dirt covered with pine needles. Weathered walls rose above us, reaching to a tilted, sagging roof. A crumbling cross leaned precariously off the top. Birdsong filled the air, instead of astral fiends' screeching.

I collapsed onto my side, my stomach heaving. Dominic was better, just kneeling, with his hand pressed against a wall for balance.

Movement, out of the corner of my eye. A slender, black shape slashing through blue sky.

"Mercury!" Dominic launched himself into its path.

Metal clanged on metal, someone cursed, and then there was a sickening, fleshy noise. I thought I had cut into an astral fiend.

Rough hands yanked my hair. Crux's spit clung to my

face. "You dared to wound me? Follow me again, cousin, and it will be your blood on this blade."

Silence.

Dominic lay on his back, panting. His skin had lost color, going a sickly tan. Blood pooled crimson under him, and from the cut to his midsection.

"Hey. Hang on. Hang on, okay?" I reached for the wound, put as much pressure as I could. Blood seeped from between my fingers. "Hang on."

Dominic stared at the sky, eyes wide, but he was breathing. "I tried ... I tried."

I looked around. Had to be someone to help. But I finally recognized our location—the old Domingo monastery, dating to the foundations of San Camillo, up the hill from Lilac Ridge Cemetery. We were miles north of downtown and Rosa Roja Park, without a soul around, all the sounds of modern life absent.

Except for one.

A buzzing intensified. Something approached, the noise growing louder. I steeled myself for yet another attack and knew there was no way to protect myself, let alone help Dominic.

A tiny drone hopped over the tree line and hovered in place.

I waved frantically and pressed harder on Dominic's wound. He had to stop bleeding. "Hang on, okay? Just hang on."

Beeping. My phone? I had it set to vibrate, not any sounds.

The beeping grew louder. Then I saw it—a timer, red numbers at 0:08 and counting down, attached to a black box riddled with wires.

I did the only thing I could do. I shielded Dominic and aimed the pulsar stave at the wall holding the device.

The world disappeared in a thunderous blast.

CHAPTER TWENTY-ONE

I don't remember anything from the explosion but the flash. When Procyon security dug me out of the rubble, Dominic and I were unscathed except for bruises. I'd blasted the bomb through several walls of the dilapidated monastery, which had collapsed in on themselves, so when the explosive triggered, it was a hundred feet farther away.

Still left me with an aching body.

Dr. Arne was there, mending the cut to Dominic's midsection. He'd ripped open a packet covered in military lingo and poured in its contents. Dominic shouted. "Hold still!" Arne snapped. "It's clotting the wound. If you quit squirming, I can keep you stable until we get back to the infirmary. Load him into the truck!"

Security guys lifted Dominic onto a stretcher, a model more compact that what'd I'd seen come out of an ambulance and propped open the back doors of an SUV. It was just like the one Procyon had stashed a massive laser inside, used against a corpse-fiend horde, except it was rigged with medical equipment. A covert ambulance, I guess.

They got everything packaged up and ready to roll so

fast my head was spinning. Could have been vertigo from the fight and the portal trip and the explosion.

Dr. Arne frowned over me, arms crossed. "Are you sure you won't go?"

"Nothing short of sedating me will get me off this hill, Doc." I rested my head on my knees. "Cops will be here soon. Ramos is gonna need me."

"I'd stick the needle in your eyeball if I thought you'd hold still," Arne grumbled. "Fine. If you pass out from a repeat concussion and die out here, I'm not responsible, because you refused care."

And that was that. The SUV rumbled off down the hill, following a dirt road.

A police helicopter thundered over the treetops a minute later and squad cars kicked up dust outside the monastery thirty seconds after that. The place went from idyllic and vacant to swarming with cops, two of whom spotted me slumped outside the walls.

"Hands up! Drop the weapon." The younger of the two made sure I could see straight down the barrel of his pistol.

"Already did." The pulsar stave tipped across my shin. I rolled it down to my shoe.

"That's the guy." The female officer was older and shorter, not to mention a whole lot calmer. She was a black woman with a short, curly haircut, who touched the radio clipped to her shoulder. "Lieutenant, we got him."

"I said, drop the weapon."

"Give it a rest, Hornsby." The lady cop holstered her gun. "Ramos has this one."

"He's—" The kid stared at me like I'd turned into an astral fiend. "That's Mercury? Really?"

"In the bruised flesh. Sorry, no autographs."

Ramos stormed through the horde of officers. "All right, quit sightseeing. Secure the area. If you find anyone, detain and disarm."

"Sir, what if they're monsters?"

I blinked, waiting for the lady cop to smile, the punch line to her own joke. Nothing doing.

"Then he'll deal with it, Capstone. You stay out of its way. We didn't bring enough firepower up here for that kind of response."

"Yes, sir." She jerked her chin. "C'mon, Hornsby."

The kid followed his partner into the trees, whispering and craning his neck until neither of us could see the other. "How about that, Ramos? Even when I get whipped, I keep my fanbase."

Ramos made sure the rest of his officers were scattered throughout the ruins before helping me to my feet. "Shut up. You need a doctor, not a publicist."

"Already sent the first aid off to Procyon with the worse-off patient."

"The other guy? The one who popped out of nowhere? Ramos frowned. "Like your brother. He was dressed native for around here, though, so I assume he's not another cousin."

"Nope. Works for Procyon. One of their assets from out of town."

"Okay. So, you decided it was a great idea for the two of you to follow Arkwright and his warrior friend—"

"Crux."

"Crux. Your cousin, who was armed with a sword and I could have told God to his face was talking with monsters. You followed them here, without backup, without reconnaissance ..."

"They didn't leave directions, Ramos," I snapped. "We had an opportunity, and I took it. And we've had zero luck finding Arkwright's base of operations. Our last foray led us into a trap."

Ramos gestured at the blast site. "And this doesn't resemble a trap to you?"

"Look, my bet is, this is—was—his base. It can't be a random exit."

"Of course it could. Nothing says it wasn't a safe waypoint, a pre-set location to which he intended to retreat if things got out of hand. Judging by the trouble encountered, I'd imagine a retreat was exactly what he needed."

"I made him bring me here. Dominic, I mean." I wiped my hands on my shirt. The blood came off, but my palms and fingers remained stained. "Yeah, that was a great idea, wasn't it? Crux stabbed Dominic and we almost got blown up."

Ramos surveyed the wreckage—for what, I had no idea. Footsteps crunched over dirt. Police shouted to each other far off, but I didn't hear any excited responses. None of that interrupted Ramos' search. "We'll check for bomb fragments. Those should give us a manufacturer, which should lead us back to Arkwright. Evil as he is, I don't peg him as a weapons expert, and his new non-Syndax partners seem too much like Teget and that other guy you recruited a couple months back to be up on modern technology, at least as it pertains to this dimension."

Other guy. He meant Skipper, a stranger from a yet-to-be-identified Realm who'd showed up during my hunt for the fiend-hound. I'd fought alongside him at Cavill Cemetery against corpse-fiends, even as Arkwright tried to use a more stable portal to return home, with Skipper as the jump-start.

That was where I'd lost Ramos and Loredana, for way too long.

Lots of people died there, too, which was why my muscles tensed and my blood pressure spiked with Ramos' suggestion. "You're seriously gonna try to nail Arkwright on a bombing, like he's ISIS, after what we just saw? Come on, Ramos, he was tossing walls! He lifted a couple of houses, and that might have been by accident!"

"I saw." Ramos fingered his crucifix. "Believing it is another matter entirely, but I'm working on it."

"We're outclassed. Man, I can't believe we threw everything at Arkwright—me and Teget, Wilhelmina and Garvey's portal gun, your cops plus the feds—and he still got free!"

"We'll get another chance."

"Um, yeah, and what do we do if the Hedron doesn't freak out again? Because so far, the only thing keeping Arkwright from flattening us all is his inability to control the artifact." Never mind whether the Hedron *could* be controlled. Its steely, uncaring voice haunted me, alongside images of Dominic bleeding out and Arkwright's furious face as he crushed me into the earth. "I don't know what I'm going to do."

"Listen, Mercury: we're going to do our jobs." Ramos put a hand on my shoulder. "I believe there's a reason we've all been brought together, and I won't discount what's beyond our understanding."

"That's because you're crazy."

"I'd say, 'faithful,' because there's plans I'll never understand. Plans higher than mine."

"Like I said, crazy."

Ramos smirked. "I've read that what everyone considers

people like me. Come. Let's find some bomb pieces."

I glanced at him. What I wouldn't give to walk around with his confidence, not worried about a thing, even with the threat of our imminent destruction literally hanging over our head. Made my concerns about getting home to my couch and missing pizza while I was looking for my friends in another dimension petty. "Are you gonna tell me Dominic's injury wasn't my fault, then? Because this seems like the right time."

"No. It was your fault. You're right. If you hadn't encouraged him to join you, he'd probably be unhurt."

I opened my mouth but couldn't decide if I should argue the point or agree.

"That's not what's important. Dominic chose to go with you. He could have said no, but he didn't. Your encouraging him to make what I'd say was a bad decision doesn't make you also bad, or even incompetent. It makes you a fallible man, like everyone else—including your opponent. All you can do now is go after forgiveness and make it right. If Dominic works for Procyon, then he must know the risks people like you face. Accept that and move on."

Move on. Easy for him to say. He seemed free of lingering effects of his imprisonment, except for the limp—and a tendency to wax philosophical. At least he was honest. He didn't shy away from his opinions or try to mislead me when I was searching for a direction.

I needed a lot of direction right them.

More of his words stuck with me. People like you, among them. There were more and more people like me, the ones gifted or cursed to face dark threats. Dominic—what was his deal? Teleporting around for Procyon, sure, but that couldn't be all they wanted him for. Interdimensional Uber, like I said.

Loredana would know. Assuming she'd tell me.

Ramos held up his hand so fast I ran into it, chest first. "What's up?"

He pointed. "Not up. Down."

I rolled my eyes, but he was right. There was a black smudge near his shoe. How he'd spotted it among the charred stones and sooty blocks, I have no idea, because it wasn't like the monastery floor was clean *before* the blast. The debris was mixed in with tattered vines and a carpet of burnt pine needles. Smelled like a campfire. "Useful?"

"Maybe." He bent, pulling on a pair of gloves. He took care to wipe dust off his shoes, restoring their shine. "Or it could be litter."

"Hold up." Metal gleamed in an otherwise dark corner. I bent forward. "That looks like wire."

"Let me get that."

"Sure. I left my evidence gathering kit in my other pants."

Ramos scowled, but the expression morphed into one of surprise at the sound of more footsteps. Those belonged to a single person, broad shouldered black man built like the stone pillars holding the monastery remnants up. He wore a shirt and tie, like Ramos, but the clothing had apparently been left on his floor for days, as rumpled as it was. "Stan?"

"Hey, L.T. I've got to kick you off the scene." Detective Stan Bradley said it like he was apologizing. "You know how it is. Captain says you're too close to the case."

"If she means the only one who has the best knowledge of the horrors we're dealing with and the most experience in these matters, then she's right." Ramos brushed aside rocks with a pen, revealing more of the shard he was after.

"Probably you're right. Doesn't matter, though." Bradley folded his arms, which reminded me of the giant tree limbs in the forest outside Meda. "She's insisting. That's why I'm here."

"To do my job."

"After I make sure you leave the scene. I've got orders to get all evidence back to the lab ASAP. So, if you've got anything interesting in your pockets, now's the time to hand it over."

"I'm good, Stan, but I'm not that good. I've just gotten started." Ramos glanced up at me, a subtle look, hinting I should—do something. But what, I hadn't the foggiest. ESP was not one of my talents. "I wouldn't want to interfere."

Ah. Check. He wanted *me* to interfere. I grinned at Bradley and tapped the pulsar stave against my leg. "Hey, Detective, how's about I show you where the bad guys planted the bomb? It was very bomb-like."

"I don't need your help, Hale. Keep out of this, unless you want me to drag you in for obstructing an investigation."

"Who's obstructing? I'm helping." I stepped around him and pointed back the way we'd walked. "The bomb was attached right under that windowsill. Well, where the windowsill used to be."

"Hey!" Bradley grabbed my arm. He turned me back, so we were facing opposite of the way we'd been standing. Which was great, because then I could see Ramos and he couldn't. "Which part of stay out of this are you not getting through your thick skull? I don't need any more screw-ups by you after that mess in the park. There's three officers dead because of you, and a few more who won't walk any time soon. If ever."

I stomped down the sickness in my gut that accompanied the surge of sympathy. "Yeah, that does suck, especially when you weren't there to lend a helping hand. Did they get a donut delivery at the precinct? You volunteer for quality control while your officers were out there dying?"

Bradley shoved me against a wall. Dust shook free of rotting rafters. "Keep talking, punk, and I'll lock you up and forget where I stuck the key."

Ramos picked up a few objects in rapid succession and tucked them in his jacket.

Hurry up! "I've got a great suggestion as to where you can put it, Bradley," I said.

He drew back his fist, ready for a punch, which I found hysterical to consider. Wonder how many bones he'd break when his knuckles hit a fully charged pulsar stave. Which, incidentally, I held up between us, the energy cracking with the intensity of a live wire.

Fingers seized Bradley's arm. "That's enough, Detective," Ramos snapped. "Remember which one of you is the officer of the law and which is the vigilante. Tell the captain I'll check in with her later, if she doesn't mind—and if she doesn't have anything pressing for me to do."

Bradley shook his arm free. He straightened his tie, scowling as he watched me put the pulsar stave away. "Sure thing, L.T. Where should I say you're headed?"

"Around." Ramos tapped my shoulder. "You're with me, Hale."

I made sure to blow Bradley a kiss as we left. He flipped me the bird. Good times.

We kept our mouths shut until we wound up inside Ramos' Charger. "Was it worth me picking a fight?" I asked. "Because I gotta say, that was fun."

"I figured you'd enjoy the opportunity to make him mad. Can't say I disapproved, either." Ramos drummed his fingers on the steering wheel. "*Tonto del culo.* Taking me off the case. Unbelievable. As if there's anyone with the knowledge and experience to work this case."

"Easy, Kojak. I bet your captain figures with the feds around, she can risk not having your expertise. Either that or she doesn't like you."

"Likely both." Ramos plucked a pair of small plastic bags from his pocket. "These could change her mind."

One contained the shard he'd located. The other held wiring attached to melted plastic and what looked like a ruined circuit board. I grinned. "She'll have no choice but to let your back on, once you toss those on her desk."

"Eventually. But we're taking them to Procyon first."

"Right now?"

"Of course. Your friend Dominic is injured, and no doubt everyone on your team has regrouped there."

"Yeah, I know that. But what about your case?"

"This is bigger than a case."

I wasn't about to argue with him, but I didn't want him jeopardizing his career, which he'd only gotten back a couple days ago. There were several good points I wanted to make. My phone's insistent buzzing froze them all.

Serena Cyr. "Yello."

"Tell me you got something." Wherever she was, lots of people were yelling. Radios crackled. Sirens blared.

"I got something."

"Good. Let's meet."

"Hang on. We're getting this stuff analyzed. If it's anything useful, or something we can't figure out, then I'll call you back."

"That wasn't our agreement, Mercury."

"Oh yeah? I thought our agreement was you helping me. Also, it wasn't written down, so I wouldn't worry too hard on the legality of a Homeland Security supervising agent quietly working a deal with a vigilante."

Ramos' eyes widened. He mouthed, *Homeland?*

I shrugged.

"Okay, fair point." Serena blew out a breath. "We're lending a hand with the mess down here. Nothing left of the monsters—the ones that weren't destroyed disappeared, pulled back into wherever that was. I'll get in touch when I know more. And you should do likewise, so I can track Arkwright down."

"Check with SCPD. I'm sure Ramos's captain will be glad to help. I got to go."

"Take care of yourself. You're too valuable to risk losing."

I hung up. Nice to hear that, for once.

Ramos cleared his throat.

"Yeah?"

"Are you going to tell me why a Homeland Security agent is calling you on the phone like you two are partners?"

I winced. "Don't get all jealous. It's a long story."

Ramos gunned the engine. "And we've got a fifteen-minute drive. Talk."

CHAPTER TWENTY-TWO

Ramos wasn't happy about it, and, admittedly I wasn't sure I was pleased, either.

He stood off to one side in Tracking, arms folded, head shaking. Brought back memories of the start of every lecture I'd ever gotten from a disapproving adult.

"Not now, okay?" I rubbed the end of the pulsar stave against my forehead. If it could zap headaches into oblivion, I'd pay extra for the feature. "Liz is gonna interrupt, anyway."

She was busy whispering with Alvarez, who'd decided to come down from his office and badger us for a while. This time, I couldn't blame him, because we hadn't taken part in a half-concealed, nighttime hit-and-run against a solo astral fiend, or even a fight under the city's streets. Nope. We're talking broad daylight, which meant lots of witnesses and even worse than that. Video.

"This is exactly what I'd hoped to avoid." Alvarez aimed his coffee cup like a weapon at the monitors. They were filled with images of our battle, filmed inexpertly and in terrible quality, but from a bazillion different angles. You couldn't get a good glimpse of people beyond the police line, until Arkwright threw the ruins at the cops, at which point pandemonium took over. Someone snuck close enough to get a decent shot of me and Teget in the final showdown before flashes of light blotted out the finale.

"We're supposed to operate with discretion. It's not as if Homeland Security didn't have enough reason to push for an investigation. Handing them this is a complication we don't need. The board's already screaming through the phone and flooding my inbox." Alvarez came up for air. "And you have nothing to say?"

"Other than, 'We won,' and 'You're welcome,' no, not really." I tipped my head toward the same screens he was watching. "You caught that part, right? What do you think would have happened if we stayed home and watched it on the news?"

"I understand you saved lives and prevented a greater disaster. I'm allowed to voice my concerns about the way in which the operation was handled." Alvarez cocked an eyebrow. "I am the one in charge, last I checked."

"Too bad," I muttered.

Loredana entered the room, as dapper as ever, and thankfully did not have Daddy Dearest in tow. I was *not* in the mood for a rehash of that conversation. "If you gentlemen are quite through critiquing each other's performances, I am sure Ms. Stojan can provide a more enlightening analysis. Without blame."

"Right. Okay." Liz sat up straighter. Her keyboard rattled. The video disappeared—which was too bad, I enjoyed one of the slow-mo playbacks of me slicing a tentacle—replaced by a map of San Camillo. It was the earthquake tracker she'd set up the other day. "If we overlay today's seismic and tachyon activity, you'll see that seven different spots were affected, each with a greater radius than those of the last incident. Easy to see the tachyon intensity building, right? Okay, so that's a bad thing, but what's worse is the stability of those pulses."

"I take it they're degrading," Alvarez said.

"Um, that could be worse, yeah, but only because it could lead to subcrustal fractures reaching to the Earth's core, leading to the detonation of the entire planet."

"It's official—two words I never want to hear in the same sentence again are 'detonation' and 'planet.'" I joined Loredana at Liz's computer. "But I'm guessing the pulses are stabilizing."

"Right, so there won't be the catastrophe."

"But it's still bad?"

"Bad, because if the pulses are stabilizing, that means their source is also stabilizing."

"Arkwright is learning to control the Hedron," Loredana murmured.

"Maybe." I glanced at her, unsure how much I should say. But really, if I couldn't tell her or Ramos, who else was left? "This is probably a good time to mention that the Hedron of Orbits has talked to me."

Ramos made an inarticulate sound that could have been surprise. Alvarez choked on his coffee, mid-sip, dribbling brown liquid down his shirt front. Loredana grabbed my collar, which was the equivalent of anyone else screaming in my face. "You've withheld this from us, why?"

"I withheld it because I didn't want everyone in Procyon assuming the guy with the superweapon was losing his mind." I pulled my collar free and smoothed it. "Which I'll bet is what you're all thinking but look—I did bring it up as a possibility. Liz wondered if the artifact or device or whatever was sentient."

All eyes targeted Liz. She hunched her shoulders, as if hoping to hide inside her keyboard. "He maybe mentioned in passing once when he was in here with Teget."

"See?"

Loredana folded her arms. "Very well. Let us assume that's a possibility. What did it say?"

"It's—not happy with us. Humans in general. Whether or not Arkwright knows, I haven't a clue. But it also can exercise command and control over our weapons, again, sometimes. That part seems to be up to Arkwright." I rapped my knuckles on Liz's monitor. "What're the odds we can find us another fragment like the one Ramos found at the playground?"

"Oh! I'm glad you brought that up." She smacked at a touchscreen. A photograph of the shard appeared inset on the San Camillo map, next to a 3-D rendering. The latter spun slowly, its exterior fading to reveal an interior so packed with complex pathways and carvings, I got dizzy just from looking at it. "The shard's been—rewiring itself. I guess that's the best word. When the second quake attack happened, its power levels spiked. The shelving it was stored on tried floating up to the ceiling. And we tracked a tachyon tether, if you will, directed at or sent from Rosa Roja Park."

"The Hedron sought it," Loredana said. "Or it was trying to return home."

"Either way." Liz grinned. "The best part is, Cyril put together a pattern analysis that shows the shard is still active. It's still working on trying to find its way home and that's something we can use!"

She sounded way too excited about the prospect. "Okay,

when you get that up and running, let me know, because I'm tired of chasing after Arkwright when he's in the middle of wrecking the city. I mean, none of you guys have even mentioned the damage from this round."

"Twenty-three dead, including the officers killed at Rosa Roja," Loredana said. "We have reports of hospitals inundated with the injured. SCPD has closed five crosstown streets. Several private sailing vessels sank in the harbor, as well, near one of the epicenters along the public docks."

"Great. Just great." I pointed at Alvarez. "And this guy's worried about optics while the city crumbles."

"Procyon Foundation will do what it can to help those afflicted by the disaster," he said. "And before you continue with your accusations, keep in mind you're not the only one with loved ones living in harm's way. Do what you have to do to stop Arkwright but keep it off the evening news for a change. If you have anything to report, I'll be in my office, using every last contact on my email list to keep the federal government out of our hair."

I shook my head as he left. "Seriously. When it comes time to put Arkwright down, I'd rather there *were* cameras ready, so everyone could see what it is we have to put up with."

"Not if it's going to incite further panic." Ramos held out the plastic bags. "Liz, could you have your tech give me a hand with these? I'm not officially on this investigation."

"You bet! Go on down. I'll have Narang help you out."

Ramos departed, nodding to Loredana on his way out, which left the three of us alone in Tracking. I gestured for the door. "I'd better get to the infirmary. Naos probably hasn't gotten any better, and Teget's down there, I assume."

"His injuries were minor, by comparison to others."

"You're talking about Dominic."

"He was never supposed to be part of this operation," Loredana said. "And yet you repeatedly drag him into danger."

"Me? You're the one who used him as our get out of jail free card when we were trapped at Syndax. When you were lost, Procyon figured out quickly that he was the best one to call when we needed fast transport."

"He has his own assignment with which to deal, and his involvement in San Camillo has set back his efforts." Loredana sighed. "Unfortunately, he's proven to be as stubborn as you and Wilhelmina."

"Comes with the operative territory, I guess." I tried a smile. "If it helps, I feel terrible about him getting stabbed and Ramos already told me it's my fault."

"Then perhaps a lesson can be learned."

"So, about Naos ..."

Loredana's gaze shifted away from my face to anywhere else. "His deterioration has accelerated. Doctor Becker is unable to find a solution."

My insides clenched. Now wasn't the time to break apart, no matter how much I felt like giving up and going home. "Okay. I'll—he and I will have to talk about that."

She touched my arm. "I'm sorry, Mercury. Watching a loved one slip out of grasp, in pain you cannot alleviate—I would never want you to go through it, especially having experienced it first-hand."

I nodded but couldn't think of any witty or deep responses. Not being able to remember the death of my parents was one thing. Fighting through the horror of Loredana vanishing, and Ramos with her, was bad enough. I doubted I could face the long, awful deterioration of a wasting disease.

We walked toward the infirmary, silent at first. I don't know which of us moved first, but our hands met, and we pulled in close to each other. Felt like a couple of high school kids trying out the whole dating thing.

"I told you I had to leave, both you and Procyon," she blurted.

"Yeah. I remember." As in, I couldn't make those cutting words stop replaying in my head.

"That may have been—a hasty decision."

"But you're still considering."

"I am. Dad has been persuasive, as usual. There is nothing that he believes he cannot get to go his way, once his will is applied."

"Sure sounded like you were willing to walk away from everything even before he showed up." At her upraised eyebrow, I added, "Something changed."

"This place and all its secrets, as much as you despise the latter, are vital. I was fooling myself to think I could simply walk away, as if I were a barista or a waiter, someone who could be readily replaced by the next applicant. I must finish my work here. That said, I do long for a place that has none of this—none of the death and darkness."

"I'm sorry I didn't go home with you. I figured you needed to get him out of Procyon before he figured out anything he shouldn't, and, well, who better to make you unafraid of being in your own living room than your dad, right?"

"It appears you had my best interests at heart." She smiled. "As you so often do, when you're not thinking of yourself."

My cheeks overheated. Glad no one else was hanging

around to see me go all, "Aw shucks."

The infirmary was a blur of bodies. Teget sat on a stool against a far wall, an ice pack pressed to his neck. He sported a busted lip and a swollen eye, which explained why he was ignoring everyone around him. Wilhelmina was in a chair behind Doc Arne's desk, knitting, while Garvey let one of the medical technicians bandage his forearm.

Doc Arne himself was huddled over a bed containing Dominic, who appeared to be sleeping. "The wound was deep but missed vital organs. I've cleaned it and stitched him up. He needs rest, which is something all of you need, and seeing as how he's the only one who's listening to me, I'd advise the rest to do the same. Just don't get yourself stabbed to obey your doctor's orders."

"He looks pretty good." I nudged Loredana. "For a guy who runs a mean superhero game, if quietly."

"Which I won't sign off on him doing. Not until he's healed."

"Of course, Doctor. I will see to it all his assignments are suspended." Loredana interlaced her fingers. "What of Naos?"

"He's another story." Doc Arne led us to the recovery room, which was now packed with way more medical equipment than I'd ever seen. White curtains shielded Naos from view. We had to wade through them like we were separating clouds.

Grandfather was dying.

I could tell it before Arne brought up the records on his tablet, and before he let out a deep, heavy sigh. "The infection has spread to all his vital organs. Even with the advance healing you people are gifted, his body can't fight it any longer. I've given him something for the pain. It's the best I can do. This kind of illness—I've never seen anything like it."

Grandfather's skin was pale, drawn tight over his bones. How could he go this badly downhill in mere hours? While I was fighting an insane battle against nightmare creatures—and my own cousin—Grandfather got rapidly sicker. I sat beside the bed. His fingers didn't respond when I grasped his hand. "Teget knows?"

"I told him as soon as everyone returned. He said his goodbyes." Arne cleared his throat. "You should, too."

No wonder Teget hadn't spoken when we arrived at the infirmary. I slumped in the chair. Listening to muffled sounds—Loredana and Doc Arne whispering. Didn't care what they said. The only thing that mattered was Grandfather's soft breathing, the irregular and shallow rise of his chest, the tinny beeps from the heart monitor.

An eyelid fluttered. "Mercury?"

"Hey. Grandfather." I squeezed his hand. He could muster only a little kid's grip. I couldn't see him well at all, hot tears fogging my vision. "About before …"

"I am truly sorry. For all … I did and didn't do." His eyes were unfocused and bloodshot. There was a purplish tinge, with black streaks at the edges. I pushed from my mind the memories of SCPD officers turning into corpse-fiends after they were attacked. "I failed you, as I failed Crux."

"You didn't fail anyone. We could get you back to Meda. To the healers."

"Many have already died because of my mistakes. I should never have left the protection of our relics …" He gasped. The monitor sounds jumped in pitch. "Mercury. Promise me … Promise me you and your brother will preserve the temple. The Hedron of Orbits must never return there."

"But it belongs in the temple. Locked up. Safe."

"Which it never will be, now that it lives again." He raised his head, which must have taken tremendous effort, because the muscles in his neck were as taut as bridge cables. His breath brushed my ear. "It hungers for this world. What Arkwright doesn't realize is, it will never be satisfied ... with being his weapon ..."

"Grandfather." Tears dripped on his sheets. Mine.

This wasn't fair. It was too soon. I'd barely gotten to know the guy. Hardly had the chance to know my true family. And I was standing around waiting for another one to die.

I might as well have been a toddler again, abandoned in Carlito's pizza parlor, wailing because there was no one left in my world.

A hand rested on my shoulder. I reached up, grabbed it, couldn't let go. I knew she'd be there.

The beeps grew farther apart and more infrequent. Naos' eyes rolled up, exposing black sclerae tinged purple.

Teget's voice carried in from the infirmary. I didn't know the language, but the song was beautiful, drifting to us like a leaf swirling in the bay breeze.

The heart monitor's beeps became a solid tone, for several seconds, until Doc Arne turned it off.

I reached over, and pressed Naos' eyelids shut.

And then I willed the pulsar stave to life, because of the cursed infection that wouldn't leave his body to rest after the soul made it's exit.

One more thing for which Arkwright was going to pay.

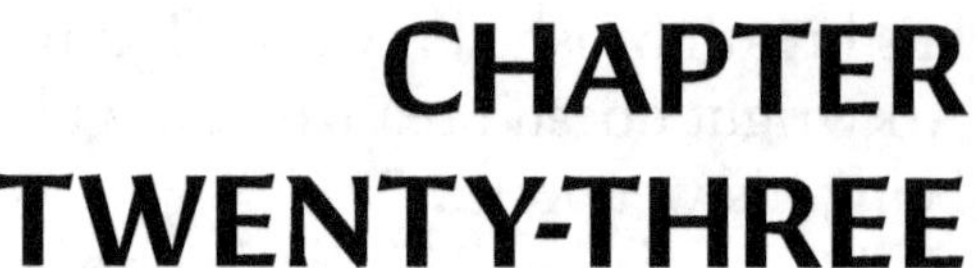

CHAPTER TWENTY-THREE

I didn't hear what people said to me. It was like I couldn't. Their condolences were muffled. My brain wouldn't accept them.

I drove Teget home. We didn't speak the entire drive. The rest of the afternoon and evening passed in utter silence. He dozed off on the couch, having skipped eating.

Good for him. Glad it was so easy to block out our shared tragedy. I resorted to draining every bottle in the refrigerator while I read the news on my tablet. Story after story about the second earthquake scrolled by. News organizations posted the sketchy facts they'd gathered. Bloggers ranted conspiracy theories, some of which were close to the truth. All of them mentioned me because, you know, when a guy with a magical staff shows up fighting the monsters everyone's been watching for in the dark, people take notice.

I didn't stagger to bed until the comments appeared begging me to help or castigating me for not doing enough. It was bad enough San Camillo continued to suffer catastrophes and nightmare beasts. They'd appointed me scapegoat and savior. Fix it! Stay away!

Screw them.

The night was devoid of sleep. Dreams tormented me, because one moment Loredana and I would be wrapped in each other's arms, and then next she'd be dead—shot, or stabbed, or a lifeless husk, or a twisted corpse-fiend reaching for my flesh. The scenario repeated with Ramos and Wilhelmina and Teget and Liz and even Dominic, minus the romantic parts, of course.

The last of them was Naos' corpse disintegrating under the harsh yellow-white glare of the pulsar stave's energy.

I burst from bed, unable to catch my breath, heart racing, body soaked with sweat. Sunlight lit the bedroom gold. Someone was pounding on the door. I ran a hand through my hair and squeezed my eyes shut. Wasn't going to vomit. Probably.

Soft voice. Then, Teget was in the doorway. He stared, his expression haggard, deep, dark circles under his eyes. Guess he didn't get any better night's sleep than I did. "Lieutenant Ramos is here to speak with you."

"Teget." I struggled into my pants and threw on a T-shirt that, while free of stains, smelled funky. One of the worst parts about being back on Earth after months in Meda was remembering to do laundry. Like I didn't have bigger problems. "It had to be done. He wouldn't have wanted to end up destroying lives."

Teget's eyes were bloodshot. "Do you think I do not know this? I made my peace with his death, Mercury. It is his life that torments me. You could not understand—you were gone, and the duty of training to protect the temple, to protect our people, our world, fell to me. Grandfather was my mentor, my family. He was my refuge in the storm. All he taught me … and then Crux. Grandfather's lies and cowardice compounded, leaving us to clean the mess."

"Crux made his choices, too. He didn't have to run off with the bad guys. He could have come back home, to try and make things right—"

"And Grandfather would have killed him!" Teget snapped. "He made an exception to the laws that guide us, and because of that exception people have died. How many more will die if we do not end this conflict?"

He started to leave. I caught him by the couch and seized his arm. "Don't go running off to do something stupid, okay? I'm the resident expert on that. We need a plan, so we can stop Arkwright and Crux—"

Teget broke free. He held the ax under my chin. I could feel the edges vibrating with power. "Do not presume to lecture me on reckless acts, Mercury. I will proceed with focus and insight, as I always do. And when I find that villainous pair, I will kill them while keeping all my wits about me. If you desire justice, you will do likewise."

He brushed past Ramos, who was waiting in the hallway. Ramos reached for his radio. "Do I need to issue a BOLO on him? His statement aside, the odds of him acting badly are high."

I sank onto the couch. "No. I'll handle him. Liz can track the tachyon emissions from the ax. Why not? She doesn't have enough to balance already."

Ramos shut the door and crossed to the kitchen. He started rinsing the empties I'd left scattered on counters. "How'd your self-counseling go last night?"

"Terribly."

"I'm shocked. This isn't the way to go about it."

"Yeah? Is this sermon time? Because I'm fresh out of caring."

"Too bad for you, I'm not." Ramos arranged the bottles in neat rows, then sat down next to me. "Do you know what kept me going, all those days and nights when I was prisoner?"

"I'm gonna go out on a giant-sized Meda tree limb and say your faith."

"Always. But on a more practical note, it was the clarity of understanding you would save us. Why?" He snorted. "No divine revelation. I was comforted by the knowledge of my soul's disposition, because I believe the promises of God. No, on that aspect, I had to go with my gut and my experience."

"What experience?"

"The experience of watching you win, no matter the odds. The experience of watching you put your life on the line, night after night, when the obstacles became insurmountable, and you kept going, kept fighting. That's how I knew you'd come back."

I couldn't look at anything but my bare toes on the wood floor.

"I know what it feels like, watching your grandfather die," he murmured. "You know a piece of your family's history has vanished, and you've moved up a notch. Then when your dad goes—you're it. You're the top generation, responsible for the legacy your name leaves. Point being, no matter the actions Naos took or didn't take, the legacy falls your shoulders. Yours, and Teget's. What you have to decide is how people will remember your name."

"They're scared of me," I said. "But they want me to fix everything."

Ramos stood, and as he did, I followed. Why? Can't say. Something about his presence demanded I be better.

"Then fix it. And make sure it's the bad guys who are afraid, because they should be."

My phone buzzed. Where? The kitchen? I followed the sound, but to no avail. I was about to knock over the bottles until I heard the fridge door open.

Ramos held out the phone, smirking.

Wow. It was ice cold. I was impressed the screen worked, albeit sluggishly.

A text from Loredana: <Please come over. I'm having a bit of a situation.>

<Emergency?> I typed.

<In Dad's mind, it always is.>

<Be right there. Faster if I could take the TARDIS.>

That earned me an eye-roll image, followed by an electronic kiss.

Nothing helps bolster a mood like Loredana Lark playing with emojis.

"Trouble?"

"Loredana's dad. He's—how can I put this? I hate him. And it's mutual."

Ramos grimaced. "When I met Olivia's dad, we progressed from handshake to fistfight in fifteen minutes."

"Wow. Okay, I'm winning, then."

"Don't worry about him. Call me if you need anything."

"Hey, Ramos?"

He paused, hand on the doorframe.

"Yesterday was Sunday, wasn't it? You probably had to blast out of church because of the earthquake."

"Not a problem, Mercury." He smiled. "The Lord doesn't frown on me playing hooky if I'm trying to save lives."

"Yeah, I figured. I mean—next time you're there, could

you put in a word for me? Since you're in with him."

"Doesn't have to be Sunday, but yes, I will. I have been, for a couple years now. And will you do me a favor?"

"Sure."

"Don't do anything stupid."

I snorted. Me? Stupid? I grabbed my car keys. I was on my way to meet the woman I loved while her irritating father was there, trying to convince her to leave the country, with my bloodthirsty brother out in the city while I was nursing a hangover and missing the one man I thought could be the replacement for my dead parents.

Stupid was almost guaranteed.

And I was about ready for some stupid.

I parked across East Sheridan from Loredana's condo. The morning was cold enough I zipped my jacket, watching as passing cars rattled leaves from the curbside trees. Weather was perfect, even if seemed grayer than usual, with clouds making for a damp sky.

Perfect was not what my conversation with Archie Lark was gonna be.

Which meant I was almost glad to find Serena Cyr leaning against her sedan, sipping on a coffee. She had two, both in paper cups from The Shattered Mug. Either she found the small chain of coffee shops as enticing as I did, or my drinking habits were the topic of a Homeland Security file.

"Good morning." She offered me a cup. "You look like you need one."

"As long as it isn't black." I sipped. "Ah. Right on. You found the optimal sugar content."

"Bowe likes them sweet, too."

"You brought the kid?" I rapped on the sedan window. Bowe glared at me, because I'd apparently interrupted a phone call. So, I rapped on the window again.

"Leave the man be. He's had a rough twenty-four hours. We all have." Serena frowned. "Though yours seems to have been worse."

"I lost someone." When was my chest gonna stop aching? Or was it permanent, like the way my throat closed off when I thought about Naos. "Close. Family."

"From the park?"

"Let's change the subject and get to why you're standing outside a place I just decided to come to half an hour ago, without telling DHS. Bugging phones, are we?"

"No. Surveillance. Ms. Lark's as much a person of interest as you are. Maybe more." Serena leaned closer, until her breath tickled my chin. "I thought I might catch you here, so I could update you without using official or even unofficial communications."

"Tell me what? I'm off Homeland's radar for good? Or I'm headed to prison?"

"Neither. We have a lead. I want you in on it."

"What kind of lead?"

"Our interrogation of Syndax employees and sifting through their computers has revealed several sites across the United States that were off the books. No payroll records, no budgets. Heck, we couldn't even find utility bills. But once we got some of Arkwright's true followers to talk, we pinpointed a few. One is here."

"Here. In San Camillo. Where?" I resisted the urge to toss the coffee and go tearing through downtown.

"Best to take you there."

"As what? Your guide?"

"As an extra weapon. As someone who's been inside a Syndax lab, too, and knows how to deal with whatever nasty surprises they could be hiding." Serena smiled. "If you've lost someone, I know you're itching for a rematch. What better way to hurt Arkwright than by cutting out his legs underneath him? These sites could be his network, his way of maintaining supplies and funding and support. I want them taken out. So do you."

It was obvious I didn't need much convincing. I was ready to sign on the dotted line when Loredana stormed down the front step of her condo. "What is she doing here?"

At first, I thought she was jealous, which was a ray of light through my mournful gloom. I mean, come on, how often does a beautiful woman get jealous of me having a secret meeting with another beautiful woman? I'll tell you. Never.

"She's not to be trusted," Loredana snapped. "No matter what she says."

"Hey, who says I trust her? She's a fed whose agency wants me locked up." I glanced at Serena. "No offense."

"None taken." Serena winked at Loredana. "From either of you."

Red bloomed on Loredana's neck and cheeks. "Do not think for a moment I underestimate you, Agent Cyr. Mercury, you must come with—"

"What is this rubbish?" Awesome. There was Archie, clad in sweater and slacks and tie, like an ex-military Mr. Rogers with a foul expression. That perpetual look of disapproval. "Ah. I might have known. Lori, here is your answer. Mark has someone lined up to take your place before you have even contemplated packing your bags."

The hurt on Loredana's face rankled off more than any

astral fiend's attempt at eating me could ever accomplish. I took one long sip of the coffee. And pried the lid off. "You're something else, Archie. Got a question for you."

"By all means. I would be happy to enlighten you as to the reasons my daughter should never see you again."

"Mine's more practical." I splashed the last half of the coffee onto the front of his sweater. "You got a good dry cleaner?"

"You twit!" Archie swiped at the mess with both hands.

"Dad, go inside before you embarrass us both," Loredana snapped.

"The only embarrassment here is your own." He balled his fists. "At having to watch your paramour being thrashed by his better."

The first swing was an easy block, but I was too mad to correct for the follow-up, because I tried to land my own wild punch. Archie's hand connected with my throat—only partially, thank goodness, because in theory a well-aimed strike like that could kill a guy.

"Sir!" Serena pushed between us, hand on her gun, coffee discarded on the pavement. What a waste. "This man is involved in a federal investigation. You'll leave him to us or face charges, citizen or not."

Archie's knuckles were red, his arms akimbo like he could throw another punch or two. But he loosened them up, then straightened his tie. "Do keep an eye on him, and away from my family, if you'd be so kind. Come along, Lori."

Loredana glared at him but followed.

"Hey." I got into her path halfway up the stairs. "I take it Daddy Dearest was what you needed help about."

"I needed you here to talk sense into him, to have my back as you did in my office the other night," Loredana said.

"Instead I see you consorting—"

"Hey! No consorting going on. Only talking."

Loredana grabbed my jacket collar. "I can't stop you from doing whatever you're about to do. Know this: she cannot be trusted."

"Which I don't. But if I can use what she knows to help us stop Arkwright, I'm going to."

"Fine." She sighed. "Then be careful."

She kissed me.

Left me standing with her door shut in my face like the very confused monster slayer I was.

"We're strange like that." Serena picked up the coffee cups and tossed them into a trash can.

"Who? Super-trained agents?"

"Women."

"I get that." I ran a hand through my hair. Bad idea. It smelled like coffee. Which, I guessed, was better than body odor. "Let's get out of here."

She climbed into the passenger seat, while I slid onto the back bench. "Site One."

"No backup?" Bowe started the engine. "'Cause that's a stupid idea."

"Yes, it is, but I want this under wraps, until we can confirm. Besides." Serena glanced over the back of the seat at me. "He's our backup."

Bowe watched me in the rearview mirror. I saluted with the pulsar stave. "I'm noting my disagreement in the report. And Hale? You owe me ten bucks."

"Me? What for?"

"I paid for the coffee," he muttered.

CHAPTER TWENTY-FOUR

Agent Bowe drove us out the northeast corner of the city, on the 311, heading into the Arbor Valley. Traffic was sporadic, headlights glowing like ghosts in the fog hanging to the hills. Serena cradled her phone, watching the tiny emblem of the sedan creep its way along the digital road.

"We're coming up on the private driveway in a half mile," she said.

"What's the name of the place?" I asked.

"None listed," Bowe said. "Our database geeks marked it 'Site One,' because it was the first one whose location they could confirm. Road's not labeled either."

That didn't surprise me. We passed a bunch of cutouts for dirt roads that lacked numbers and names. Probably they led to hiking trails, or fire lanes, or old cabins, not secret labs belonging to evil organizations headed by a villain from another dimension.

I stared out the window as Bowe put on the turn signal and left the highway. It'd be great if I could will the fog to dissipate, like I willed the pulsar stave to life every time I faced down an astral fiend. I kept seeing Naos, his breath faltering, the heart monitor and its awful insistent tone. Sunshine would have been great about then.

No such luck. We could have been in a Stephen King story, the way the mist shrouded the tops of the trees and made the rest of the forest beyond the first trunks disappear. I rooted for the morning sun to burn it all off, leaving happy pines and an even happier me.

Still nothing.

"Up ahead." Bowe steered the sedan over a gravel road rutted where washouts had stripped it to the dirt underneath. I would have spilled coffee if I'd had any left. "You see those tracks?"

"Fresh ones." Serena rolled her window down. The air was damp and heavy with the smell of soggy sap. The passing breeze caught strands of blond hair and pulled them in front of her face. "One set, maybe two overlapping."

"Call it in?"

"Not yet. Let's see what we've got. I want radio silence, so we don't scare anyone off."

The road wound around a couple hairpin turns, up a hillside, until it abruptly opened onto a clearing. Scratch that. It was a parking lot. Asphalt so new it looked like it had been drawn on a sheet of paper with Sharpie marker. The building on the other end of the lot was tucked among the trees, and equally new, if small—single story, concrete the color of pale eggshell except where it had been stained by the rain, thin windows of dark glass with a bronze tinge. It reminded me of the bunker the Rebels raided at the end of *The Return of the Jedi*.

That one blew up.

"If there was any other traffic, it's gone now." Bowe

parked us right outside the front door and killed the engine.

"I asked for a drone overflight." Serena sighed. "Goodness knows if the higher-ups actually listened this time."

Bowe opened the door. "You'd think with monsters on the rampage they'd be happy to oblige."

"If that's the case they'd have the assets circling downtown, not up here in the hills."

I stood back a few steps while Serena tapped the button on the box mounted to the right. I kept the pulsar stave handy, meaning, it was in my hand but unpowered. That way I could respond to a threat, should one arise, but if the place was staffed by regular techies, I'd rather they think it was a plain old metal stick.

Bowe waited all of five seconds after Serena's first buzz before pounding on the doorframe.

"If there was anyone home, I think they heard you," Serena say dryly.

"I'm being thorough." He leaned closer to the door. "Federal agents! Open up!"

A few more seconds ticked by. Serena gestured to the glass. "Okay, Mercury, you're up."

I let the pulsar stave's energy build until the glow seeped between my fingers, then bashed it dead center of the door's glass pane. Light shot out in a spiderweb pattern, from the point of impact clear to the frame. It shattered into a glittering pile at our feet.

The first thing I noticed? Lack of alarms. Somebody's security was slipshod.

The second? A stench. A sickly, burnt aroma. Melted plastics?

Serena and Bowe drew their guns. Bowe was first through

the door, with Serena a step behind and to his right. Their shoes crunched on glass. Made me wonder about glass repair businesses and how much they must be raking in thanks to me and my antics. Bowe swept his gun left, toward a wide-open work area of cubicles arrayed in two rows, their walls low enough I could peek in and see everyone's stations. Serena kept her back to the corridor wall on the right, which had two closed doors about thirty feet ahead. The way they moved, without words and only the slightest gestures, indicated they'd done this a lot.

After a few passes around the room, Bowe muttered, "Clear," but didn't put his gun away. They proceeded down the corridor, taking turns checking doors on either side. Both seemed satisfied once we reached the back of the building, which ended at a wall.

I was glad we didn't find any bodies.

Serena, though, was frowning as we returned to the main work area. "There's nothing here to indicate experimentation."

"No basement doors," Bowe said. "No closets, either, that might have a concealed passage."

I thumped the pulsar stave on the floor. "Doesn't sound hollow."

Serena holstered her gun. "Then let me at a terminal."

She activated a computer and clicked her way through menus. Whatever she was looking for wasn't there, because she resorted to pulling up the command prompt and forcing the computer to do stuff it obviously didn't like, judging by the alert screens that popped. She cleared those.

Meanwhile Bowe re-checked all the rooms. He poked his head out of one. "Make yourself useful, kid."

"Sure thing." I rolled my eyes. Why not use my

interdimensionally-powered weapon to bang on walls and floorboards?

Of course, I opted for the smarter method—looking for a floorplan. Which, unfortunately, this place lacked. It made sense. If my evil organization had secret labs, I wouldn't stock the interior with the layout schematics.

Which could mean they were stashed in the computers. "Hey, Serena?"

"Busy, Mercury." Serena stared at the screen like she was gonna fall in. She tapped on the keyboard, but it was a repetitive action, on the edge of the board, not inputting commands. "These databases aren't exactly open source."

"Big surprise. See if you can find a building layout stashed in there. If this place has a basement—"

A breeze ruffled blank sheets of paper on the desks. A poster—generic seascape—rippled where a thumbtack had gone missing. I craned my neck, peering over the cubicles, to the other end of the hall. "Bowe! If you're not too busy yourself back there, find the thermostat and dial down the AC!"

"HVAC's shut down," he said. "We're lucky the place still has the power turned on."

I frowned. If the vents were off, then what was moving the air?

My heart skipped as the first purple sparks skittered across the wall at the far side of the workspace, away from the cubicles. I forced the pulsar stave to life and separated its halves. "Guys? We've got incoming."

Serena's were wide. "Astral fiends?"

"If yes, then we don't want to tangle with them indoors." I grabbed her arm. She didn't budge. "Are you kidding me? This is the part where we get out of here!"

"Not yet." She snapped. "Buy me some time. If I can break into these databases—"

Bowe hurried down the corridor. "Did you say something about astral fiends?"

A long, jagged rip appeared in the far wall. Streaks of light shot from a dark center rimmed with purple waves. I positioned myself between it and the Homeland agents, ready to launch myself at the fiends, leaving Serena and Bowe time to escape—assuming Bowe could pry his boss away from the computer.

Instead of monsters, six men in combat fatigues, helmets, and facemasks fanned out into the room like they were the ones infiltrating an enemy establishment.

Man. I recognized them—their gear, their movements, even their H&K MP5 machine guns. Syndax soldiers. Guess the feds didn't have them as cleaned up as they thought.

"Federal agents! Drop your weapons!" I had to hand it to Bowe. He was facing six heavily armed guys, equipped with military-grade gear, and the first thing he did was try to arrest them.

They, of course, started shooting.

Bullets ripped through flimsy cubicle walls. Bits of fabric and plastic filled the air like a fresh snowfall. Bowe got off a few rounds but wisely hit the deck. Serena went with him, shouting something about the computers while drawing her gun.

Right. Stop the bad guys, without letting every hard drive in the place get blown away. Oh, and also, not die.

No sweat.

I rushed the trio on my side of the cubicles, their movements and even their bullets slowing to a crawl as the pulsar stave accelerated me with its familiar jolt. A handful of shots veered off course, shoved aside by the energy blazing from both halves of the weapon.

I melted the first guy's gun. Plastics and metal dripped over gloved hands but was still hot enough he cried out in pain as he hurried to strip them free. That gave me the opening to smash his facemask wide open.

Black eyes aglow with purple greeted me for a second before he collapsed.

Great. These jokers were hopped up on the tachyon enhancement Arkwright like to gift them with. That meant they were on par with me when it came to strength.

As if to reinforce that point, Soldier Number Two flung me against the wall.

The pulsar stave put a huge crack in the adjacent window. My head rang like a doorbell. But even with my vision gone shaky, I retained the wherewithal to fire a burst of energy from half the stave. No idea how much willpower I'd put behind it, until the flash of light threw Soldier Number Two into his nearby buddy.

The other three soldiers ignored our brawl, using the distraction to instead advance on Serena and Bowe. One stopped to reload, while the others gave him covering fire. I trained the pulsar stave his way, ready to drop him with a burst, when he suddenly shouted and disappeared from view.

Bowe popped up on my side of the cubicles, loading a new magazine into his pistol. When one of the two soldiers still standing happened to glance sideways, he put three shots into the man's throat, where there was no body armor to protect him.

Blood sprayed on his partner's facemask, He swiveled, aimed at us—

I was already diving headfirst.

We collided in a heap of arms and weapons, the pulsar stave burning away his gun. Heat singed the soldier's Kevlar and my shirt. The smell was awful. Really hoped the sickening stench wasn't my skin burning.

The guy was tough, though. He brought a combat knife out of nowhere, sweeping it toward my neck. I blocked the shot, the blade sloughing of where it struck the stave, which was great, but also meant I lost some of my concentration. This soldier pushed on the other half of the stave as hard as he could, bending my arm at such an angle muscles screamed. Then he headbutted me.

I staggered back, blood dripping from my nose, which I was pretty sure had broken. Don't noses break when they go *snap*? Tears stung my eyes.

The soldier let go of his weapons and drew a semi-auto pistol. I heard shots behind me, and grunts of pain, but had no idea how well Bowe was handling the Syndax guys behind me. I was more concerned about getting my brains blown out.

One chance. If I could summon enough power from the stave halves, maybe accelerate myself and bring them up so fast that—

Gunshots rang out to my right, near enough sounds went dull out that ear. Bullets tore into the soldier's shoulder and under his arm, penetrating his fatigues. He toppled left, into a lifeless heap. I stood staring at the wall, panting.

Serena advanced on my spot, aiming her weapon over my shoulder. "Are you okay?"

"Yeah. Yes." I nodded.

"Bowe?"

I glanced in his direction. Two more sounds, like meat hitting meat and probably bone, then Bowe straightened. He was breathing hard, shoulders heaving, blood on his right fist. His fingers curled around his pistol, but it was held like it had been used as a cudgel instead of a firearm. "Last one's down."

Wow. That went well.

Before we could ascertain who was dead and who could answer questions, the rip expanded. I'd forgotten it was still on the wall, swirling and storming, but it bulged into the room. First thing it did was drag loose staplers and pens into its vortex, then a Syndax soldier, the one I'd hit right off the bat.

"He's taking the bodies!" Serena cried. "Come on!"

She rushed the portal, but I put her in a hold, both halves of the pulsar stave deployed to prevent her passage. "No way!" I shouted. "Last time we did that, it was a trap!"

Serena struggled against my grip. She wasn't going anywhere. Of course, I guessed she wasn't putting up as much of a fight as she could. She knew I was right.

Bowe had the presence of mind to latch onto the man whose face he'd pummeled and hook another arm around a cubicle wall by punching through the fabric. I braced Serena and myself against him as the wind increased, dragging in the other four Syndax soldiers, dead and alive.

Then, with a whip-crack of thunder, the rip closed.

Papers fluttered to the floor. Pens rolled off desks. Serena and I sagged to the carpet. Bowe gave me a thumbs' up.

"Please tell me," I gasped, "That you got something."

Serena held up a thumb drive and grinned.

"Awesome." I closed my eyes and rested my head against a cubicle wall. "Coffee's on me."

CHAPTER TWENTY-FIVE

On the downside, the soldier Bowe clocked didn't survive his injuries. He was DOA at Procyon.

Which in itself was a troublesome situation, because when the Homeland sedan arrived with one battered DHS agent and one equally bruised monster slayer, driven by Serena and with a dead Syndax soldier for my passenger, Loredana would only admit two people.

Guess which two.

"You can't leave us sitting in the parking lot when we retrieved key evidence for this case and were nearly killed in the process!" Bowe snapped. "I oughta call in the cavalry right now and breach the front door of that drinking glass you call a headquarters!"

"We will be happy to share any pertinent information we ascertain from the delivery." Loredana was unruffled. Not a wrinkle in her clothes. The bay breeze didn't bother to mess with her hair. She stared at Bowe, her chin lifted, as Procyon lab techs retrieved the Syndax soldier's body from the car. "Since you saw fit to utilize a vigilante in your field operation, I shall choose to keep that information from your superiors, since I highly doubt they signed off on such a dubious venture."

Bowe snarled something under his breath, but Serena put a hand on his arm. "Easy, Hudson. Let's give these people their space. I'm sure they'll keep their word." She looked at me when she said that last part. "You have the thumb drive?"

"Yeah. Right here." I patted the pocket. "Thanks for that."

"It's the least I can do." Serena winked. "I have a whole set of hard drives to play with, after all. Rest up while I get Bowe some bandages."

They drove off, Bowe arguing something with Serena as she steered from the Procyon parking lot. I turned to Loredana and waggled the thumb drive. "So? Pretty good news for—"

"Not. Another. Word."

And one awkward elevator ride filled with frozen silence, we were at Tracking.

Wilhelmina was waiting for me at the door. "You left here in an awful huff this morning, didn't you? Glad to see you decided the climb up out of your funk."

"Nice. You remember the part where my grandfather died, right?" I winced at the words, mostly because my nose still throbbed even as it was healing at my rapid pace, but after getting thrashed by Syndax, my mood hadn't improved overall.

She hugged me. "'Course I do. That's why I'm here for you and with you. But there's work to be done. Naos knew it. He'd want you at your best. Must've had a boatload of faith in you."

"My best includes killing my cousin, apparently. That's

what Grandfather wanted. Correcting his mistakes." I patted her back. "Thanks. I need you on my side more than ever. If there's one thing I've figured out since I got back from Meda—and figured out painfully—is that I need allies. The more, the better."

"Sure bet Teget will be top of that list. He's your brother, after all, and the one who brought you home for the first time in your life."

"Yeah." I scratched the back of my neck. Awkward. "He'd be top my list, too, except that he's gone stupid and AWOL simultaneously. He thinks he can find Arkwright on his own without getting killed on this solo op."

"What if he succeeds?"

"Then I'll wait for Liz to point me in the right direction when the tachyon spike from his mad rampage throughout the city."

"Mercury?" Loredana crooked a finger.

I mock saluted. "On my way, ma'am." I winked at Wilhelmina. "Coming?"

"Wouldn't miss it, child."

Loredana touched my hand as I passed. I smiled back at her, grateful for the gesture. Whatever we were, it wasn't the normal I'd hoped for—at least, the normal we'd established with multiple dates and my profession of love. But the sternness was still there. She'd reacted poorly to—scratch that. She'd wanted to take Serena's head off, sure, and I'd assumed that was a professional rivalry. You know, Procyon vs Homeland. The anger she'd displayed, though, was a bit much.

"I've got Cyril running our data from the earthquakes through every comparison he could think of, which is a lot, because he can do thousands while we're scratching our noses." Liz spun slowly in her chair, a blue mug of coffee to her lips. "He's got some good news."

"I thought your buddies in the lab would find better news with that body." I leaned on her desk.

"Well, yeah, they will, but it's only been five or ten minutes." Liz wrinkled her nose. "So, I'll get to it as soon as Narang has something fun for us. But can I let Cyril talk or are you going to keep interrupting?"

"I'm not—"

"When the results came out, I was as surprised as he is." Liz stopped her rotation and tapped a panel on her screen. The map of San Camillo glowed, with epicenters from both earthquake attacks marked in red. That image slid left, as a second map appeared to the right, like a mirror image—though the more I examined it, the more I noted the different coastline. The harbor was longer, deeper, more sheltered. No familiar landscape. But the city did have red blotches similar to the ones on San Camillo's map. "I wanted similar tachyon readings and seismic indicators versus our attacks. Instead I got nearly identical matches."

"How identical?" Loredana asked.

"Within a couple percent."

I frowned. "That doesn't make sense. Why would Arkwright waste his time trying out the Hedron in another city? Weren't the tests here bad enough?"

"It's not just another city, Mercury. These recordings were taken by our Drake City labs." Liz grinned. "And here I thought we were the only ones with the fun stuff!"

Drake City. I saw a date and time stamp in the bottom right corner. Eastern Standard Time "Hang on. This is from when those terror attacks happened."

"Precisely." Loredana paced Tracking. "Authorities

labeled them as such, but our office indicated there may be more to the story."

I ran a quick Google search on my phone and waved it in front of their faces. "Yeah, you think? With Airfoil flying around? There's word out there another flying guy was involved."

"No way!" Liz's eyes widened. "Superheroes? And supervillains?"

"As if it weren't bad enough that we had our own." Wilhelmina sighed. "I tell you folks, whatever happened in Drake City, I thought the world was set to crumble."

"I don't suppose you witnessed the near-disaster firsthand," Loredana said,

"Oh, I told Mercury, I missed on the front row seat, but we felt the tremors. Heard all about it later."

I glanced between them. "This is good, right? If the same thing happened in Drake, we can combine intel and figure out how to stop Arkwright. I'll bet Homeland knows all about it, considering they know about *us*. I'll let Serena know—"

"No. I do not want Agent Cyr apprised of this situation."

"Come on, Loredana. This isn't time for a turf war. Not after she handed us a piece of the puzzle." I tossed the flash drive at Liz. "Catch."

"Oh! I've been waiting on this." She fumbled but kept it from hitting the floor. Her hands shook so badly it took her three tries to plug the drive into Cyril. "Ah! You guys did good. All kinds of Syndax goodies on here."

"What about a location? A potential hiding place? Perhaps you can cross-reference it with tachyon spikes abnormal when compared with the typical rip." Loredana was still watching me, like I was a prisoner contemplating an escape attempt from his cell.

"Sure, yeah, we can do that, and the sooner I run comparisons of all the coordinates against what we've recorded so far the better because I know Cyril's made some mental notes—well, the electronic kind—and once he's done that—"

I ushered Loredana from the room as Liz's rambling explanation devolved into a string of quiet murmurs. "What's your deal with Serena—I mean, Agent Cyr? She's been nothing but helpful. Even Bowe didn't try to slap cuffs on me. I'd call that an improvement."

Loredana folded her arms. She started to say something but bit her lip when Wilhelmina appeared.

"Don't clam up now," I said. "Once an operative, always an operative."

"Very well." Loredana brushed stray hairs from her face. "Unbelievable. The two of you are as stubborn as Dad. We've had preliminary results from the bomb fragment analysis. Lieutenant Ramos has confirmed, though we're still waiting for the more thorough tests, so we can be sure. The explosive was of a manufacture intended for military use."

I snickered. "Right. The Army's trying to blow me up? National Guard had their chance last spring."

"Not only the Army uses it, Mercury. So do several federal agencies. Such as Homeland Security, specifically the branch which deployed agents to San Camillo in the wake of our twin disasters."

"Seriously? You're pinning the bombing on DHS? They're after Arkwright, too!"

"And you. Don't let yourself be blinded by Agent Cyr's—attributes simply because she professes the same goals."

"I'm more convinced with her shooting a Syndax

mercenary in the head so he didn't kill me. Which is something I would've expected you to do."

Loredana's eyes narrowed. "Perhaps if you hadn't run off at her beck and call, you would not have been in such a predicament—one of your own making."

"Settle down, boys and girls." Wilhelmina pushed between us. She poked me in the chest. "You mind yourself around this lady. And girl, don't discount what he's witnessed. We could be dealing with rogue elements inside one federal agency."

"No kidding," I muttered. "Bowe would have loved to scrape pieces of me off the monastery walls."

"That's not ... Confound it." Loredana's heels went *pock-pock* on the tile floor as she paced again. "It would be best if I had Gemini explain. Please follow me."

Gemini. Dominic? Little harsh to go visit the stabbing victim when we were arguing about federal agents, but I was game for answers.

Turned out Dominic was doing significantly better, as in, he was out of bed and dressed. His steps across the infirmary ended with him clutching his side and shooting out the other hand to grab a table. Doc Arne tried to get him back to bed but Dominic waved him off. "I need to get back to work. I've left my wife and my architectural work for Procyon equally unattended for too long."

"Your schematics can wait, Dominic." Loredana touched Doc Arne's shoulder. "Could you give us all privacy, please?"

Arne muttered something about intrusions but left as requested. It was just the four of us. Loredana cleared her throat. "Let them see the deck, please."

The deck? Like, a patio? I knew Dominic was an architect, but with those Echo Watch armbands a major weapon in our arsenal, I'd assumed he'd had better things to do than design new outdoor structures for Procyon's HQ.

Dominic paled, even worse than from his injury. "You're certain. I trust your judgment, of course, but I don't know this guy."

"Gee, thanks." I rolled my eyes. "We were getting along pretty well."

"Getting along well? My job has been to transport you and to rescue you," he said. "Seems like I did all the work."

"Yeah? How many astral fiends did you put down?"

"Gentlemen." Loredana shot me a pleading look, then repeats, "The deck, Dominic."

He sighed and pulled a worn playing card box from his pocket. He opened the lid. "Which one?"

"Ten of diamonds, I believe."

Dominic fanned through the cards. Instead of classic art of the suites, or custom illustrations, there was a photo on the center of each one. People. Some were marked with black Sharpie—Xs on faces or check marks in the corner of the image. The swish of the cards seemed to cut the air in the silence around us, until he paused at one card—

Himself?

Dominic continued until he found the ten of diamonds.

"Hold up." I reached for the deck. "That was you."

"Yes. And no." Dominic turned the ten toward me.

It was Serena Cyr. Except—her hair was longer, straighter, tied in a ponytail. She was devoid of makeup. Somber. The collar of her clothes suggested a military uniform.

"You recall what Arkwright told us," Loredana said. "About how he was sent from a world like ours to take the place of his double here, which he did as a youth."

"Yeah. Which is crazy, but Serena seemed to believe it."

I held the sides of my head. "You're telling me, she was replaced, too?"

"It seems possible."

"I hadn't located the ten of diamonds yet," Dominic explained. "On her Earth, Cyr is an intelligence analyst in the Sierran forces."

"I'm going to pretend like that made sense and wait for you two to tell me what's next."

"What's next, is, we proceed with caution. As a high-level Homeland Security agent, we cannot simply follow Gemini's normal protocols."

I spread my arms.

"What kind of protocols?" Wilhelmina couldn't stop staring at the cards. She was probably wondering who else's face she'd see in there. Well, it wouldn't be mine. Wrong dimension.

"I capture the individuals and turn them over to the Home Guard on the other Earth." Dominic sagged into Doc Arne's chair. "You see now why I haven't mentioned it in casual conversation?"

"No worse than killing monsters for a living." I rubbed my face. "This is nuts. Okay, so I need to play it straight with Serena. With Cyr. If that is her real name."

"It is. She just may be a different Cyr."

"Sure. Because those are all people who have been replaced."

"Possibly." Dominic glanced at Loredana. "The question is, assuming she has been, why is she helping us?"

"I do not know. Commander Zein's project of replacement was long after the initial effort that deposited Arkwright here. The two may be unrelated." Loredana pointed at me. "But caution is the order of the day."

"Y'all folks are forgetting the bigger question: how do we stop these earthquakes from happening again?" Wilhelmina rapped on a metal table. "Mercury's already said he hasn't got the power for it."

"Hooray team," I muttered. "Seriously, though: she's not wrong. Between me and Teget and Dominic, we've barely been able to make Arkwright and Crux stumble. If we can't rely on Serena—and we don't know whether or not we can—we're gonna need bigger backup. Preferably, bigger backup with experience dealing with this kind of stuff."

"How do you propose—?" Loredana suddenly shook her head. "No. Absolutely not."

"What, you're reading minds again, Jean Grey?"

"I know you well enough to know when you're preparing to take a brash and inadvisable leap, Mercury. Your plan is out of the question, if one can indeed call it a plan."

"I'd like to know what it is, instead of you both being vague." Dominic frowned. "I'm wounded, but I'm not out of commission."

"That's the spirit. Because I'm gonna need your help again." I slapped him on the shoulder.

"How so?"

"Careful now," Wilhelmina murmured. "Try taking a few seconds to think this through before you make the leap, both of the figurative and literal type."

"Trust me, I am." I grinned. "I need Dominic for a fast trip, because we shouldn't waste time on a five-hour flight."

Dominic's frown deepened. "To—where?"

"Preposterous," Loredana snapped.

"Ignore her. Dominic, buddy, I need a portal to Drake City." I checked my watch. "The sooner, the better. We're going recruiting."

CHAPTER TWENTY-SIX

I really thought Loredana was going to call security and have Garvey lock me up. But, despite her evident exasperation, she didn't stand in our way.

"Our Drake City office hasn't shed any insight on the nature of this Airfoil individual," she said. "Whenever we do attempt surveillance, our methods are thwarted."

"Yeah?" We were in the middle of Tracking, where Liz was still muttering over Cyril the computer. Dominic had on a light jacket that concealed the Echo Watches on his wrist. He seemed drained, but there was a surprising firmness about his stance, like he was gonna force himself to get up and do this. The guy was growing on me. "Who was doing the thwarting?"

"Unknown at this juncture. Even our drones malfunctioned, despite having undergone inspections before we sent them out. Airfoil's speed is part of the issue."

"He seems fast."

"Drake City Office clocked him in excess of 300 miles per hour."

Yikes. "I guess I won't go running after him."

"How do you intend to make his acquaintance?"

I opened Twitter on my phone. "@Airfoil. Someone was nice enough to set up this and a couple other social media accounts. Fan-based. But I checked—he's responded live and in person to alerts the average Joe has put up there."

Loredana pursed her lips, either thinking what a great idea it was or determining if she could find a new boyfriend if I got myself killed or arrested.

Boyfriend? Was that really where we were going with this? My emotions on the matter were way more serious than those of a casual dating relationship. I kissed her.

She responded, hands pressed against my chest, which was great, because I thought for a moment she might shove me away.

"Do me a favor." I stepped next to Dominic. "Be here and not in England when I get back."

"I will endeavor to do so."

"And tell Archie I said 'hey.'" I grinned.

Loredana smirked. "One would think Dad is not quite ready for a third meeting between you two. He informed me you owe him a new sweater."

Dominic coughed into his hand. "If *you* two are done, I'd like to get going before I progress from second to third thoughts."

"Ready when you are, Gemini," I said.

He sighed and activated the Echo Watches.

Tracking disappeared in a blaze of blinding light and endless darkness, all wrapped into a smear. I squeezed my eyes shut, then experienced vertigo so bad I just knew I was gonna puke. So, I opened them and picked a point—something distant, anything other than trying to concentrate in the morass around us.

We staggered out of the portal into Dominic's loft apartment in Rampart. I squinted through the morning sunlight pouring in the windows and the glittering—snow? It was snowing out here?

"I forgot about the cold snap." Dominic pulled a phone from his pocket. "I wonder if Jess put Sammy inside."

"Fans of yours?"

"Wife and dog, respectively." Dominic texted. The answer came back quickly, his phone emitting a satisfied *ding*, and he smiled as broadly as any man I'd ever seen. Posture improved by a couple inches, too. I'd forgotten all about his wedding ring. "Are you ready for the next one?"

"Gimme a sec." I put both hands on my knees and bent over, breathing deeply. "Okay. I'm pretty sure my guts are gonna stay inside, so, let's roll."

"Hold on a moment." He crossed to a table and righted a photo that had tipped on its side. If the Middle Eastern woman it featured was his wife, it was no wonder he smiled like a big idiot when she texted him. "Okay. Brace yourself."

The Echo Watches glowed and spun, like they do every time, but the pieces of each band mingled into a single circle. A tiny dot of white popped into view, like someone's grabbed a star from the sky and dropped it into Dominic's living room, at the same size you'd see it in the sky.

The dot flashed out, filling a translucent sphere so thin I could have popped it with my finger. A scene appeared—thick forest, sloping gulley, a dry creek bed? There was an asphalt sliver in the distance.

Dominic gave me a push at the center of my back.

We stepped through.

Seemed like it should be a single step, sure, but I got stretched out and compressed all at once. There was a weird sensation, like I was a human rubber band, and the next thing I knew we were in that gulley, surrounded by trees that were mostly naked. Bet they wished they could use the last of their red and brown leaves for modesty's sake.

And then I threw up.

Urgh. I wiped the back of my hand across my mouth. "Nice trip. Terrible food service."

"If I'd given you a snack, you'd have thrown that up, too. This way."

It was a cool, misty New England day. A damp East Coast autumn. We climbed out of the gulley onto a pathway. It was the sliver of asphalt I'd seen from the other side. Devoid of people, at least, until a couple of teens in workout gear trotted around a bend a couple hundred yards away.

Dominic nudged me forward. We walked like two buddies out for a fall stroll, me taking in the sights, he on his phone—only Dominic wasn't checking social media. He was perusing a map.

The girls ran by, all leggings and tank tops, earbuds leaking music. Older than high school, I thought. "Hey. They had IDs on their phones, where they were clipped to their waists."

"We're on the campus of Gunnison State College. It's a decent arrival point—good cover, not a lot of foot traffic on this portion of the trail."

"You've been here before?"

"Twice. Loredana had me scouting for Airfoil, when he first started making headlines."

"Yeah? Seen anything interesting?"

Dominic glanced up from his phone. "He flew down Broad Street after bank robbers, shrugging off hits from a heavy machine gun, until he flipped their getaway truck upside down into Diamond Park."

Yow. "That's cool, I guess. Not too shabby."

"I'm detecting envy."

"How about you start detecting the flying superhero and find me somewhere good to eat, too."

"You're hungry?"

"Of course." I jerked a thumb over my shoulder. "Everything I had for breakfast landed back where we did."

"Okay." Dominic gagged. "Shut up and I'll get us to somewhere we can wait. Do you think the Twitter idea of yours will work?"

"No clue. But I have a backup plan." I found the @ Airfoil feed and composed a simple message: [@Airfoil we need to meet. Your favorite San Camillo monster slayer Mercury is in town.]

"You can't be serious." Dominic shook his head. "What good is that going to do? And why are you using your real name?"

"Are you kidding?" I flashed a crumpled business card in his face—solid black, with "Mercury" in silver letters.

"I withdraw the question. Well, if this is your grand idea, you'd better give him a location."

"What's the worst part of town?"

"Westerville."

"Okay, get us an Uber. Then find a burger place in Westerville."

"You want him to meet us there?"

"If we're going to try recruiting the resident superhero, we'd better make it worth his while."

I could see why Dominic answered so quickly when I asked

where the bad neighborhood was. Westerville was rundown. Like, it made Court Street look like the brand-newest Procyon affordable housing development. The trash bags huddled by the side of the street looked desperate to leap off the curb. The Uber driver did put the brakes on so we could get out, but man, if I hadn't been quick with the cash, I bet he'd have driven off sans pay.

The diner Dominic located delivered the goods, though—giant, greasy burgers accompanied by equally greasy fries. Run by a black family—Dad at the grill, Mom at the register taking people's money, twenty-something twins waiting tables. The Motown playing in the background was perfect, except when it alternated with country songs. I could have stayed there all day, eating and yakking with a friend.

Except we'd been in Drake City for almost as long as a flight would have taken.

"@Airfoil is getting us nowhere." Dominic sipped from a glass of soda.

"Yeah, I noticed, thanks." I blew out a breath. I'd tweeted twice more but didn't want to push my luck. Last thing I needed was to get banned. Especially since I made up a fake profile. "Are you planning to help?"

"I've texted the Procyon office. They don't have anything to report, other than an Airfoil sighting two days ago. Apparently, he stopped a smuggling operation at Newport, where the commercial docks are located."

"Yay for him." I spun my phone on the table.

"Loredana is going to want results, or want us back, soon."

"Also noticed." My phone buzzed. Speak of the angel? Nope, it was Ramos. I scooped it up. "Hey. No emergencies while I'm out of town."

"Don't worry, it's been quiet. No more tremors. No sightings of astral fiends."

"Why doesn't that make me feel better?"

"Probably because we both know Arkwright isn't sitting around waiting for you to come after him. Agent Cyr with Homeland passed us some good intel—a possible Syndax lab."

Glass shattered. Eight guys were gathered around a car on the side of the street, opposite the diner. It was a black Lexus. My bet? They drove up in the flashy neon-painted Honda and Camaro. "Watch yourself. Our last outing wasn't exactly unnoticed."

"Already there—or here, I should say. The feds are cooperating, letting us take a gander at the evidence." Ramos snickered. "What did you say to them? Do you have a blackmail file I should be worried about?"

"If I did, you wouldn't be in it."

"They also helped us track down your wayward sibling. Apparently, they've had him under surveillance since he left your apartment."

I rubbed my face. Great. Teget got himself captured. Again. "Please tell me he's at Procyon."

"That's a negative. Bradley has him in a holding cell at the precinct, under wraps. He's not happy about it, but he didn't put up a fight."

"Super. So, you're back on the case?"

"Not precisely. I asked Bradley to do me a favor. But we'd better head there as soon as you get back. They've got that ax of his in evidence."

Yikes. Loredana was going to throw a huge tantrum if she found out.

Hold up. Those guys? They dragged an older man and

woman out of the Lexus. Who drove that fancy a car in this neighborhood anyway? "Hey, I got to run."

"That's the other reason for my call. Loredana texted. She told me about your plan."

"And?"

His sigh rattled the phone's speaker. "Don't do anything—you."

"No promises. In fact, it's going to be opposite. Thanks." I hung up and tapped my phone on the table. "Hey, Dominic. You as bored as I am?"

"Hardly. I've been watching the proceedings outside." He squinted. "Is this your back-up plan? To wait until Airfoil shows up to foil a crime and then engage?"

"Nope." I tossed cash on the table. "I'm gonna commit a crime with a superpowered weapon to get his attention."

That must have floored him because I was halfway across the street, breathing in the cold, damp air laced with garbage stench before he caught up. "Mercury, this is a bad idea."

"Since you don't have any better, how about you hang back and shut up." I drew the stave. "You were stabbed, remember? I don't expect you to leap up and fight."

He was kind of limping, but he didn't slow his stride. "I'll be fine. Besides, I have an advantage you lack."

"Oh, yeah?"

"Ranged weapons." He smiled. "And patience."

"Take up improv if the whole Procyon operative thing doesn't pan out for you."

The gang was a poster for diversity—four black guys, two white, and two Hispanic. All of them wore similar style jackets, and red shirts. I snorted. "Hey! You guys ever watch *Star Trek*?"

The taller of the white kids, a redhead with spiky hair

and piercings, let go of the man he'd pulled from the car. "You say something to me?"

"Sure did." The couple clung to each other, apparently forgotten by the thugs now that Dominic and I were advancing on them. They were dressed in casual but classy clothes. License plate said New York. Ah. Lost out-of-towners. "How's about you leave these two alone and I continue your education in pop culture references?"

One of the black men slapped his bearded acquaintance on the chest. "Arturo, show these fools we don't like being interrupted."

Arturo was as tall as Agent Bowe and twice as wide, shiny bald. He had an extendable baton. No gun, so that was a plus.

I gestured. "You want this one, 'Gemini'?"

Dominic nodded. "Sure thing. Sir, put the weapon down."

"Don't sir me, cracker." His voice boomed across the street. "I'ma shove this so far up your—"

Dominic shot a burst of rippling yellow-white energy from his left wrist. It struck Arturo dead-center in his chest, tendrils enveloping his body, and he dropped sideways. He kicked and splashed a puddle, teeth clenched, eyes blinking and teared up.

"I don't like his attitude," Dominic said. "Or his mouth."

Red Spike Hair pulled a gun. So did a couple other of the kids—they really were kids, I realized, none of them older than twenty.

"Easy, fellas." I powered the stave. "Stay still and I won't have to do likewise. Or, you know, cut you in half."

The Lexus' tires squealed. Glad to see the couple had taken their cue and gotten out of Dodge.

"You best step off." The first black kid stepped over Arturo, a gun aimed sideways at our faces. We backed toward the Honda. "I don't know what you're tryna pull—"

"Yo, Derek, let's get going."

"Shut up, *Daniel.*" Derek sneered Red Spike Hair's name. "You can't math, huh? There's only two of them. And one ain't—"

"Isn't. You were gonna say, isn't carrying a gun." I leaned on the Honda's hood. "Yeah, but you haven't seen my toy yet."

"Tell you what—I'ma take that toy off your dead body."

"Maybe." I flipped the stave over, its length glowing like it was reflecting sunlight. Ah, good. A couple people in the diner had their cell phones aimed at us, like mini amateur paparazzi. "But you'll have to walk."

I drove the stave through the hood, into the Honda's engine block. Plastic sizzled and steamed. Metal turned orange as a campfire coal, dripping onto the pavement.

The thugs shouted their outrage in an overlapping chorus of some of the English-speaking world's most creative profanities, plus a few in *Español.*

And they threw themselves at us, just itching for a brawl.

Dominic backed away, the Echo Watches raised. "I really don't like you."

"Hey, when a plan works, it works."

I swung the stave.

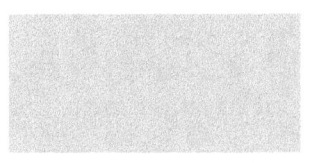

CHAPTER TWENTY-SEVEN

Derek was fast enough on the trigger to get off two shots, but they went wide, because he was shooting at a blur of lightning-colored energy blazing from the pulsar stave. And then I swiped off the barrel of his gun, leaving him with a trigger assembly and magazine connected to a melted mess.

I grabbed his collar and, letting the stave's power soak deeper into my body, flung him over my shoulder and onto the Honda's windshield.

It crumpled, like I'd dropped a rock onto sandpaper. He sagged, arms limp, head lolled against the windshield frame. Best part was his butt jammed against the steering wheel, holding him firmly in place and putting the car horn into continuous blare mode.

Dominic dropped two more of the guys with blasts from his armbands. Another kid came at him with a machete of all things. Dominic punched him and intercepted a blow with an Echo Watch. Sparks exploded.

The kid shielded his eyes, but he lashed out with a vicious backhand.

Dominic vanished in a burst of light that left my eyes watering and the kid howling in pain. He clutched his face, looking to any of us like the victim of the world's worst sunburn.

"Where'd he go? Where'd he *go?*" Daniel the punk shot at me, wildly, exploding windows on the Mustang.

I was already below his line of fire, skidding on the pavement. I rammed one half of the pulsar stave into his gut and threw the second.

It made a satisfying *thwack* when it hit a guy with a .38 in the nose.

I leapt over the heads of the other thugs, dodging bullets, and landed on Mustang's hood. I grinned at the ragtag gang as I ripped the covering open with the stave's slashing energies, ruining the engine of their second car.

There was flare of yellow, and Dominic appeared *behind* the gang. He blasted two with the Echo Watches.

The last two guys took off running down the road, dodging a city bus.

Dominic held his side, like he had a cramp. "That was … fun."

"You good?"

"I'm not bleeding through my stitches, so we'll say I am. But your backup plan wasn't successful, either."

I heard a rushing sound, like a windstorm barreling down an alley, and it was getting louder. "No, I think it worked just fine."

That would have been the place and time to say "Look, it's a bird!" But truthfully, I couldn't help staring in awe. And I'm not much for awe.

The figure swooped low over the buildings, a black and white streak with blue flashing on its edges. It—he angled his trajectory, reminding me of the videos of gunships lining up for a shot at the Taliban. Talk about a precision maneuver.

He aimed for the two men running and, even as I wondered what he had in mind, they rose from the street, treading thin air. They slowed and stopped, first flailing, then dangling immobile. They could have been wrapped in giant invisible spiderwebs.

Airfoil landed in the street a hundred feet from us. He twisted his wrist, fingers clenched. The two thugs hurtled left until they smacked sideways into a telephone pole. Airfoil then ripped a bumper from the Mustang, sending it hurtling over our heads. It wrapped the guys around the pole neatly as any Christmas present's ribbon, leaving them eight feet off the ground, kicking and shouting.

Dominic clenched his fists. "You realize he could view us as the dangers here. Look what he did to a couple punks with guns and knives."

"Sure. No problem. I got this." I actually *hadn't* considered that, because my focus was so singular. This guy had powers. Straight-up *powers*, that had nothing to do with a stick in his hand or fancy teleportation Taser armbands.

That was exactly what we needed in our fight against Arkwright.

I walked toward him, grinning, hand extended. "Hey, Airfoil? Mercury. Mercury Hale. I wanted to—"

Something lifted me off the street, flipping me end over end through the chilly air. For a panicked second, I thought I was gonna fly straight out of the atmosphere to become Earth's newest satellite. Instead, I bumped atop the closest apartment building, skidding on my pants four stories above where I just was.

Dominic landed two seconds after, right beside me.

"Stay put." Airfoil's voice was muffled behind a polarized blue-purple visor on a white helmet, but there was no question he demanded our obedience. "I'll deal with you two in a minute, after I clean up your mess."

And by clean up, he meant use his invisible powers to scoop the remaining thugs in their varying degrees of consciousness, then stuff them inside the two wrecked cars. He rose into the air, palms angled down. The roofs of the Honda and Mustang groaned, crunched, and flattened, until there was no way anyone could get out of either car without the Jaws of Life. Handy ready-made jail, I guess.

I scrambled upright and pulled Dominic alongside. "You okay?"

"Winded, and sore, but I'm managing." He scowled. "It doesn't help that I'm irritated."

"At me or him?"

"I don't feel I have to be that specific."

Air whipped around us. Something was holding us in place. I shoved forward, but I might as well have been pushing against a window no one could see.

Airfoil landed, boots balanced on the edge of the roof. "All right. State your business."

"That's no way for one superhero to treat another," I said. "After the help we just lent you."

"Help? You call stirring up a fight in a part of town I already have my hands full containing 'help'?"

"Those guys were hassling good people!"

"I'm sure they were. I've been watching their gang for a couple days now, hoping to catch them in the act." Airfoil stepped off the ledge, boots crunching loose asphalt as he neared us. "Instead I get word that two people with magical weapons are fighting them."

"What, are you afraid of competition?"

"The last person with abilities or weapons even close to yours caused damage we're still cleaning up," he said. "I'm not taking chances. Too many people died, and my city accumulated too many scars."

Sirens sounded up the street. Well, you couldn't fault Drake City's police response times. "Look, I really don't have time for this."

"Neither do I."

"Then let's talk, if you're done being a moron," I snapped. "I need your help. I didn't take a break fighting monsters just to slap some muggers and hope I get arrested—or whatever this is."

Airfoil tilted his helmet to one side. "You're really from San Camillo? Those stories circulating on the Internet—they said it was terrorism."

"Yeah. And what'd they do with the truth of what happened here?"

Airfoil glanced toward the oncoming sirens. Tiny blue and red lights flickered across his visor.

"That's what I thought. C'mon, man. I've seen the videos. I know what you went up against." Okay, not really, but I heard it was tough. Anything to get this guy on our side.

"Either way you consider it, I'd suggest we don't stand around up on this roof," Dominic said.

"That's the smartest thing I've heard either of you say so far." Airfoil squeezed his fingers into a fist. The invisible—stuff holding me tightened. I was not going anywhere. Until, that is, Airfoil floated off the roof and dragged the two of us skyward.

We hurtled up to the clouds, arcing north.

Flying. I was flying!

I hollered at the top of my lungs until my throat hurt.

Poor Dominic. He looked like he was ready to murder me.

We soared into the clouds, which soaked me, but I didn't care. I could have flown for hours. Finally, Airfoil dove toward the forested sides of the mountain—or big hill, I guess I should say. No one who's seen the Rockies or Sierra Nevadas would call that lump sticking up beside Drake City a mountain. We swooped between the trees, following a road to the summit. Mist obscured our arrival.

It also made our destination one out of a horror flick. Six rusted buildings were almost buried by the woods. There was a long rectangle, minus a roof, stripped to a skeleton of dark girders visible inside. Two sagging cubes had lost their doors and windows decades ago. But the three towers—those I admired. The looked like someone had forgotten to build the tops, after they'd put up octagonal structures three stories tall. Rust stains and flaking paint were the décor of the day. It would have been more impressive if not for the fact the place had suffered a bad fire, judging by the burns and soot.

Airfoil dropped us onto the nearest tower and landed at the edge. "This is a bit more private."

"I'll say." I put my hands on my hips and took in the view. Drake City was a train model town beneath us, stretching to a gray inlet. "Gotta admit—you know how to do a secret lair."

"I guess you could call it a former lair. The damage is extensive."

Dominic seemed to have forgotten he wanted to wring my neck, because he was peering over the edge of the tower, eyes wide. "That doesn't diminish the aesthetics of this place. It's a military design. A former radar station, isn't it?"

Airfoil nodded. "It dates to the 1950s. Only lasted a decade before it was abandoned and sold into private ownership."

"And it's yours?"

"I'm not technically the owner, but he's out of town and we have a ... partnership. I only use it in emergencies." He gestured at us. "You two qualify."

"If you building nerds are done, how's about we get to the important part?" I waved my hand. "First off, thanks for not squashing us flat, which I'm assuming you can do with your—super-powered hands."

"It's not the hands. You said you needed help. I'm listening, but let's move it along. I have to get back to work."

"Seriously? What are you, on your lunch break?"

I couldn't see his face but assumed from his sullen silence he was glaring at us.

"Fine. There's a bad guy in San Camillo. He's—" I looked at Dominic, who shook his head. "He's not from around here. And by that, I mean he's from a parallel dimension to ours. He's using an ancient artifact from my home dimension to drag life-sucking monsters from another dimension to flood the Earth, clean off the human filth. He's also reanimating dead bodies to use as conduits for his power and transfer that power into an army of mercenaries from two worlds. With me so far?"

Dominic sighed and shook his head.

Airfoil folded his arms. "That's—a crazy tale."

"All you have to do is start searching YouTube." I pulled out my phone. "There's videos all over the place. Instagram gets a new grainy photo of astral fiends every day, it seems."

"Astral fiends?"

"The life-sucking monsters. Size of an SUV, tentacles, spikes, stuff of nightmares." I showed him a picture I had saved in Recent Images.

"You carry around photographs of them?" Dominic regarded me as if I had a terminal illness.

"Sure. Don't judge too hard, considering you got that deck of cards in your pocket."

Airfoil's visor reflected the astral fiend image. "This kind of thing is faked on the Internet regularly."

"Fair enough. That's how Procyon keeps a lid on stuff, claiming the same thing. But you have to have heard the news. Seen the reports. We had the National Guard in town. Twice."

"And you still claim it's not terrorism."

"Why's this so hard for you to wrap your head around?" I gestured at our environs. "Look. We're standing atop your secret base. You can fly. Your powers make you as potent as Superman, though I gotta admit, I'm picking up a stern, Captain America vibe right now. I have no idea how much of your boss fight was true and how much was conspiracy theory, but it has to be at least close to as crazy as what we're dealing with."

He cocked his head to one side. "Supposing for a minute, I believe you, and that cancels out my appraisal of you two as possible threats. I'm usually all for a good story, but what makes you think I'm going to fly out of Drake City for that?"

"Because the earthquakes threatening San Camillo are man-made, and of the same kind as what struck Drake City this summer," Dominic said.

"You're serious?"

"Way too often." I spread my arms. "I don't have a lot

of time to negotiate this. Bottom line? We need someone powerful to stop this guy, and considering what I've heard and seen you do, nobody's gonna pack a bigger punch."

"And so far, all I've seen of you is your ability to inflict property damage."

I scowled. "Property damage? It was a little vigilante shout-out."

"I don't know about you, Mercury, but this is a calling I take seriously. You're right—I have heard of you, when reports of a vigilante operating in San Camillo started popping up. I thought it was more online embellishment. My best friend treated your appearance like his comic book fantasies come to life—like it legitimized my activities. Bottom line: Protecting Drake City rises above all other demands, family aside. It was worth me taking a stand against the very people who granted me these powers. My faith demanded I attempt the sacrifice. But that stand didn't come without consequences. I've got to remain here."

"Remain here?" My head was spinning. "I'm sorry, what? You can fly. At hundreds of miles an hour."

"That's right. But I've made an oath. I'm sworn to stay within an hour's distance of the city at all times."

I blinked.

"That must be a serious vow," Dominic offered.

"It's complex. My powers derive from a secret society and I've crossed them numerous times." He shrugged. "They're only begrudging in their permission to let me continue to operate as a superhero. But the way I see it, these powers, they're a gift from God more than they belong to any person or groups. I hope you understand."

"So, that's a 'no'?" I asked.

Airfoil nodded.

My insides went hot, then cold. It was too much of a letdown. Far from being angry with him, I was just disappointed. In a guy I thought would be the one to help us save the day. In Dominic, for standing around passive, waiting for us to decide the matter. In me, for being unable to convince Airfoil otherwise.

What were we gonna do now?

"Please." Hard to believe I spat it out. "Gemini and I have gone toe to toe with Arkwright. We can't do it on our own."

"I'm sorry." Airfoil's shoulders sagged. "I wish there was more I could do."

"Mercury, I don't think we're going to convince him." Dominic touched my shoulder. "It's true he would be a tremendous asset, but if he has prior obligations and a duty to his hometown."

"Are you serious? You've seen what he can do. How do you not want that kind of power on our side?" Even as I said it, I knew Dominic was right.

Airfoil pointed at me. "Do you have any idea how many crimes I've prevented in Drake City? Do you have a clue how many more I couldn't stop? I'm only one man. I can't be everywhere at once."

"Then be in San Camillo! This place got along fine without you for decades. I've got actual monsters and a killer earthquake relic trying to tear my city apart? Do you think they're gonna stop with the West Coast when they're through?"

"I'm sorry, Mercury. I've got responsibilities here."

"I … Forget it." I shook my head. "Come on, Dominic. On portal for our trip back home."

We turned from Airfoil, ready to leave our failure behind,

but found ourselves blocked by an invisible wall

"I don't think you get it."

Airfoil's voice prompted us to look back. He had his left hand outstretched, fingers splayed. "I caught you operating as vigilantes in Drake City. After the people I've dealt with—none of whom have good intentions—I'm not taking chances."

"What are you talking about?" I let my fingers graze the tip of the pulsar stave, which protruded from the edge of my jacket.

"I told you, I'll do what's necessary to protect this city and everyone in it. Homeland Security's been sniffing around, looking for me, especially after the Coast Guard disasters. I'd imagine they'd want to talk with you two."

"I think we should leave *now*," Dominic murmured.

"You think?" I smiled at Airfoil, and yeah, it was a fake smile, but I didn't want the guy doing anything stupid. "That's a bad idea, Airfoil."

"Sorry you feel that way." He rose into the air. "But I'm turning you two into the authorities."

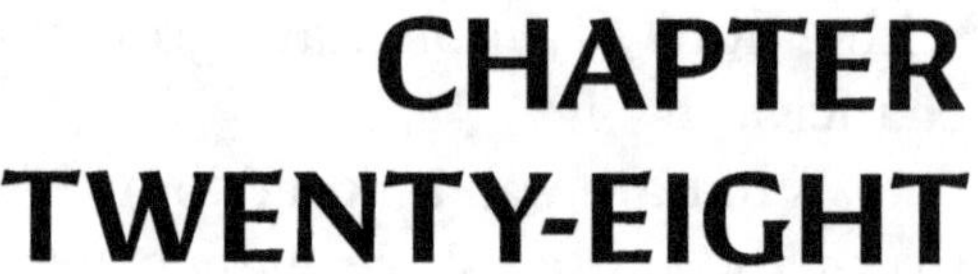

CHAPTER TWENTY-EIGHT

I hadn't come all this way and dealt with a bazillion obstacles for some monk in a leotard to turn me in to the cops. I willed the pulsar stave to life. "Don't do this, man."

Airfoil's hands clenched into fists. I could feel a pressure building in the air around us, a sudden shift in gravity. My footsteps were sluggish. "It'd be easier if you didn't resist. I don't want to hurt either of you."

"I second that," Dominic said.

Metal clanged in the distance. It clanked off the tower, below us, dragging and screeching the last several feet before it topped the side and rose next to Airfoil.

It was a staircase. Twenty feet long, torn free from who knew where.

Airfoil flung it at my face.

Seriously? Stairs?

After all I'd seen, everything I'd fought through, I wasn't about to let twenty feet of rusted metal knock me over.

I charged and cut through the oncoming tangle of mettle,

planting the pulsar stave in one half of them and catapulting myself toward Airfoil.

Didn't stop there. Even with gravity tightening around me, dragging my arms and legs through a morass I couldn't see, even as the pulsar stave blazed with its innate energies, I forced my way through the air, towards my opponent.

Toward the guy who should have been my ally.

I could tell Airfoil was having a tough time. He pivoted, trying to hold me back, but no matter how slow I got, the pulsar stave kept powering me forward, like it could read my determination.

I didn't want to hurt Airfoil any more than he wanted to hurt me, but with San Camillo hanging in the balance, I wasn't gonna spend my next few days—or years—in a cell.

And then I popped through Airfoil's barrier, like I'd burst an invisible window.

The sudden release caught me off guard and I came down at him too fast. Airfoil saw it, tried to back off.

Too late. The stave hit the bottom of his helmet on a vicious upward sweep.

The impact tore the helmet from his head, and he went with it, leaping backward off the edge of the tower.

Dominic activated his Echo Watches, both of them, one aimed at each of us, because apparently the poor guy couldn't figure out which one of us was being more unhinged.

I stood face to face with the man under the mask. He was probably mid- to late-thirties, weary lines around blue eyes, red hair ruffled by the wind. Other than the bright colors, he didn't have a memorable face. Could have hidden in a crowd.

Except he wasn't in a crowd. He was hovering in front of me, jaw clenched, probably wondering if he should use his powers to squash me like a bug. Literally.

And I'd just committed the superhero equivalent of kicking a guy in the crotch.

"That was my bad," I said. "But I told you we can't let ourselves be arrested."

"Airfoil, we're leaving." Dominic's tone was firm but there was no missing the hurriedness of his speech. "Mercury, stand down so we can get out of here."

Airfoil banked midair and held out a palm toward me. I braced myself for the gravitational smackdown I was about to receive and hoped Dominic was fast enough to, I don't know, drop me into a portal or something. I half expected to land on the couch at his Rampart loft.

But even though the air around me shuddered from the force of Airfoil's powers, the effect bypassed me completely.

Huh. How about that.

I swung at the edge of my reach, slashing the stave across Airfoil's chest.

He dropped to the roof, landing on a knee, hand bracing himself against the metal grating. He looked as astonished as I felt. "How did you do that?"

I teetered on the tower's rim. I'd mistimed my own landing. "Let me get back to you—"

Too late. Airfoil, the proverbial speeding bullet, slammed into me, arms encircling my chest and neck.

I've never been hit by a car, but it was as jarring as I'd imagined. Worse than getting blindsided by an astral fiend tentacle, sure, but at least it lacked the life-sucking component.

The tower receded as Airfoil plowed through the air. I gasped, scraping for every breath I could manage. The so-called superhero was trying to choke me. Or maybe knock me out.

I pressed the pulsar stave toward him, its energies crackling against his armor. He forced my arm away, but I pushed back, the two of us struggling for dominance in midair.

"Surrender." His voice rasped, the wind whipping the sound away from my ear. "I don't want to have to hurt you, but I will if you won't voluntarily—"

"Man, shut. Up." I twisted and threw a punch.

It missed, but it forced us off course. Airfoil veered toward the treetops, angling back among the ruined radar station.

His grip loosened, either because I was strong enough to force him off or because he was distracted. I'd take either.

A pulse of yellow-white light seared my vision. Where'd that come from?

The second shot caught Airfoil on the shoulder. He sneered and turned us again. There was Dominic, halfway down the tower's steps, brandishing the Echo Watches.

He fired again, but that time, the blasts splashed harmlessly a foot from me and Airfoil. They looked like they were dissipated, or redirected, or otherwise rendered harmless.

More importantly, Airfoil's grip loosened a fraction more.

I slammed the business end of the pulsar stave dead center on his chest, right where that big blue "AF" symbol stared me in the face.

We fell.

I'm not talking a smooth glide into an airline runway landing. I mean, we plummeted, on an awkward, tumbling arc. I might have done a bit more flailing than my aerodynamically inclined adversary.

We crashed through a stand of infant pines, which was great, because they were bendy. Not solid like the abandoned truck we hit next.

The saving grace was its cloth canopy had long ago rotted and its sides were flimsy. Still, we hit it hard enough to tip it off its wheels and knock it clean over.

I blinked away stars—and you'd think I was kidding, but the pulsar's stave had that effect on my vision. Airfoil was on his hands and knees. He staggered upright.

"You should've ... just said 'Yes'." I pulled myself up the side of the truck.

"How did you do that?" He lifted me the rest of the way, until my feet dangled above the wheels. "You shut off ... You negated my powers. No one can do that."

Maybe honesty was the best policy. "No idea. Tell me what you get your powers from and maybe we can negotiate."

Shoes scratched across the tarmac. Dominic sprinted toward us. He knelt at the corner of one of the buildings and tried another shot at Airfoil.

But he lunged sideways, dodging the energy blast. Fortunately, dodging meant Airfoil had to drop me, so I crumpled onto the asphalt again instead of getting body-slammed by the Echo Watch. The air sizzled over my head, though. I saw a YouTube video of a guy giving haircuts with fire and scissors. I bet it smelled like that. Toasted follicles.

The tarmac between us and Dominic ripped apart, like an invisible bulldozer had been turned loose. The jagged path zig-zagged toward the building at top speed, leaving Dominic next to no time to dive for cover—which he did, under the collapsing roof.

"Look out!" I leapt from the ground, stabbing toward Airfoil with the stave.

Too fast. The guy was just too fast. He could have been taking a page from my playbook, the way he zipped out of my path. Something grabbed my midsection and flung me aside. More of his powers, no doubt.

But those powers didn't make him invincible. The pulsar stave interrupted them. Dominic's Echo Watches knocked Airfoil out of the sky. So, we had options.

We. If Dominic was okay.

Airfoil got to the wreckage before I could. He lifted a forty-foot section of corrugated metal roof and flung it away from the building like you'd toss a napkin off a table.

"If he's dead, you're gonna have bigger problems than trying to take me to jail," I snapped.

"He has to be under here somewhere." Airfoil stuck out his palm toward me. "You stay put."

Stuck again, in a whole lot of nothing. This time, though, I was waiting for the stunt, and had the pulsar stave vertical in front of me, like a samurai posed with his sword. Gravity pulled at my legs, but I could move, a little at a time, faster with each step.

The pressure intensified around me. Had to hand to Airfoil—he fit the hero bill. He was sifting through rubble, trying to save the guy I brought to his city, who for all he knew could be a villain at worst or a determined troublemaker at best.

I wanted to dig Dominic out, too, but since Airfoil didn't seem amenable to a join effort, I was gonna have to continue the fight until neither of us was mobile—

Because, again, not going to jail.

He finally got the hint that I wasn't going to lay down

and surrender, because he stopped searching and applied all his power toward me. "Stay. Down."

Not likely.

The pulsar stave's energies flared, and I broke through the force field, hurtling like a jackrabbit from the starting gates. In a second, I was on him, delivering a blow that could have killed a regular person.

As it was, Airfoil marshaled his defenses and I felt like I'd struck a brick wall.

We flew apart, me landing on the collapsed wall, he halting midair after a somersault. Airfoil shot down from the sky, throwing up a halo of dirt and pine needles.

I swung and connected—with nothing. Again, with the nothing! His arms were up, the pulsar stave hovering six inches away. We maneuvered around each other, pressing for advantage, but he held me in place, and I wasn't about to budge.

I inched closer to his arms, and hopefully, to the stylized "A" symbol on his chest—which was about where I'd tagged him before, disabling his powers.

He was on the watch for it, though, because he punched me in the face.

Ow.

Didn't see that one coming, not with us relying on our amped-up abilities. It stunned me, threw me off balance. And it was his mistake, because it gave me the opening I needed to separate the stave's halves. One of them bounced off his armor's chest plate.

Airfoil staggered away. The thickening pressure vanished. I felt like I could sprint an entire marathon.

I tripped him up with the pulsar stave, dropping him onto his side. "One last time—back off."

His gloved fingers clenched, like he wanted to wring my neck with his powers, except he couldn't, not with the pulsar stave resting against his armor. It occurred to me I had no idea how I was gonna restrain him, and I really didn't want to knock him senseless—

A spray of pine needles and rocks hit me in the face. I flinched, managing to keep most of them from embedding in my eyeballs.

But his trick worked. A surge threw me across the tarmac. I spun out, dizzy, laying halfway to that stupid truck.

Airfoil strode toward me, maintaining a safe distance. Guess his powers came back pretty quickly once we weren't in contact.

"Come on." I winced. Something hurt, badly. "Last—chance ... to be reasonable."

He didn't give me a response other than to lift the truck over my head.

That was when, I think, I realized sparring with this particular guy had gone way beyond joining a brawl with Syndax soldiers or Kutsatuta warriors, even when they were amped up by tachyons.

Airfoil's fingers twitched. The truck shredded, its pieces streaming apart into strips of metal that he gathered around me. "Your next stop is Drake City Police Department, as soon as I get that stick from you."

Too many pieces for me to fend off. I knew it, even as I separated the pulsar staves and stood my ground. Well, maybe Ramos had some kind of pull with DCPD. Right?

More than likely, Loredana would have to bail me out. And Alvarez would love that.

The shockwave that followed forced me to shield my face. Airfoil's face was the perfect portrait of wide-eyed surprise, frozen in place as he dropped forward.

Dominic strode over him, fresh from a rapidly fading portal, the Echo Watches suffused with golden light and their pieces pulsing like embers in a fireplace.

"That was great."

"We never should have come here." Dominic had a few scratches on his face and hands, but otherwise looked in good shape for a guy who survived having a building fall apart on him. He was leaning to one side, hand on his ribs again.

"I'm not going to argue."

He blinked. "For once, you're being reasonable. Forget Airfoil. We'll find another way."

Dominic dialed up another portal for us. I glanced back. Our Drake City superhero was trying to get up, forcing himself to shake off the effects of Dominic's jacked-up Taser.

"We came here in good faith, asking for you to join us," he said to Airfoil. "Perhaps when you can have sympathy beyond your city limits, you'll really understand what it means to give up your life to save another. I know I had to."

He grabbed my shoulder and pulled me into the portal.

Find another way? Maybe.

But I hated leaving our best chance sprawled on that old tarmac while we headed home.

CHAPTER TWENTY-NINE

We made the transit to Rampart and then back to Procyon in total silence. Dominic wasn't a big talker, but the zero words were disconcerting.

As soon as the haze from the portal cleared, Liz grabbed my hand. It took me a couple blinks to reorient myself to the dim spaces and given how our exit from Drake City had just gone down, I was happy I didn't hit her with the pulsar stave.

"You guys are back already! That's great! I've been waiting forever it feels like, but I knew it couldn't take too long!" She grinned. "So, where is he?"

"Not with us, unfortunately." Dominic stowed the Echo Watches and limped out of Tracking without a backwards glance. "I need to see Doc Arne."

"Okay, yeah, we'll talk about it later!" I called after him.

Liz crossed her arms and squinted at me.

"What?"

"Come on. Lieutenant Ramos is waiting for us down in the lab."

"You called him in?"

"Of course! Between the bomb fragment and the wiring

and the dead Syndax individual, I had a lot of evidence to share with him."

My spirits momentarily buoyed, something I needed after getting tossed around by a flying superhero. "What about all those comparisons you had Cyril the computer running?"

"Shhh!" Liz ushered me from the room, towards the elevators. Where Dominic went, I hadn't the slightest idea, but given how the day had gone so far, I'd have guessed Alvarez's office. Nothing like running to the principal first thing. "Don't let Cyril hear you say that word."

"Computer?"

"He doesn't like it! Too machine-y. Then his processor will slow and there'll be a need for a reboot, and I'll have to restart all the tasks—"

"Liz, give me a break."

"I haven't found any connections so far but it's not my fault. The tachyon levels Ms. Lark wanted me to compare? They're weird."

"Define weird."

"Weird, like, the background levels are so elevated, anything other than a huge burst is lost amidst the noise. I'm not even sure I could pinpoint a rip if one showed up."

"Man." I ran my hand through my hair. "You mean if an astral fiend shows up tonight looking for a snack, we could be blind until it's too late?"

"Maybe. Cyril's working on it."

I really hoped Cyril was as good a computer as Liz made him—it out to be, but I wasn't gonna say it out loud. I'm not superstitious, but as deep in the mess as we were, I wasn't gonna take chances jinxing anything.

Narang the tech had several tables rearranged. The guy could multi-task. One container held the bomb fragment, which someone had broken down into tinier bits. The wires I'd found were stretched out in the second. The third box contained bits of clothing. It took me a minute to recognize the peculiar camouflage pattern as belonging to the Syndax soldier uniform.

Ramos was there, pacing among the tables. His limp was pronounced but there was no cane in sight. "Mercury. How was the errand to—?"

"Don't ask. We'll talk later."

"That bad." He shook his head. "I knew it was a bad idea."

"You could have told me ahead of time and saved the trip," I muttered.

"I could have. Would you have listened?"

I sighed. "Probably not."

Ramos gestured. "There you go. Listen to this, instead."

Liz joined Narang at the first table. "The bomb fragment was the easy part. Our database has thousands of records when it comes to military hardware."

"Even the illegal types?"

"Every weapon is made for a legitimate armed force," Narang said. "Whether or not it makes it into the hands of someone with bad intentions doesn't matter. Serial numbers, manufacturing methods, it's all there."

"Unless you're talking a home-grown device," Ramos noted.

"But even those use parts someone bought or stole from somewhere." Narang tapped the top of the container. "In this case, we know this is a countercharge."

Ramos stiffened. Okay, whatever that meant, it was bad, because he grabbed the edge of the table. "You're sure."

"Without a doubt. It's the type of explosive used by

law enforcement when they want to destroy another bomb quickly. I could go into details on the specific type, but the important part is it's in the inventory—"

"SCPD. Bomb disposal uses them in the exact manner you just said."

I stared at them. "You're serious? This bomb came from the police?"

"It wasn't even tampered with," Narang said. "I found a miniscule bit of residue on the casing that matches the composition of SCPD countercharges."

Ramos was doing a great job of being a functional mute, so I pressed on. "Same thing with the wiring?"

"Oh, that's where it gets interesting." Liz used giant tweezers to lift a strand. "This is a custom job. It was wired to what I'm pretty sure was a proximity detector—you know, a certain threshold of movement is crossed, and it sets off the explosive."

"Any luck matching that to anyone we know?"

"Not yet. But I can tell you whoever rigged it had some serious skills and you're lucky you used the pulsar stave to blast it from the wall. I'm pretty sure the overpressure would have killed you and Dominic."

"Overpressure."

"One of the two ways a bomb will get you—either shrapnel damage cutting through you or the shockwave causing internal damage."

"Sounds great." I rolled my eyes. "So, what've we got? A rogue cop?"

"A rogue cop with help." Ramos slapped the table.

"Easy. It could be stolen. It could be the manufacturer sold it to someone other than the local cops." I looked at Liz for confirmation. "Right?"

She shook her head.

"I appreciate that you're trying to make me feel better about this, Mercury, but it wouldn't be the first time I'd had to deal with corrupt officers in the department. It's not an easy thing, contemplating that someone you've worked with for years might be hiding the truth from you."

Tell me about it. I thought my entire world was gonna implode when the people I thought of as my extended family at Procyon—including Winston and Marigold Yen—confronted me with the secret that I wasn't from this world, or even from this dimension. In a way, I guess my world had imploded. But I'd survived.

"Okay, fine. We have to get to SCPD anyway, to bail my brother out." I elbowed Ramos. "Hey. Breathe. You want to go in guns blazing or subtle?"

"Subtle." Ramos exhaled. "If there is someone crooked on the force, someone conspiring with Arkwright, we don't want to alarm them."

"Sounds good to me. Liz, what about the uniform?"

"Right! The uniform. It's got traces of fecal contamination."

"Nasty."

"Yeah, very, but the point is, it's been in the sewers recently."

"You think he was downtown with Crux?"

"No ifs ands or buts about it, Mercury. Also, he was at the monastery, because the pollen grains are the same as those produced by the junipers on Lilac Ridge."

I grinned. "Two for two. But that only means one of Arkwright's flunkies was present with him. What's the big deal?"

She snorted. "Duh! The big deal is this little guy."

Narang swiped through images on a tablet. He held it up, showing us all the neon picture of—I didn't know what. Cells?

"It's a tiny piece of a microorganism common to the California coastline, but the greatest concentrations are in and around San Camillo Bay. It's not something that would hitch a ride on your shoes when you walk along the shore with your girlfriend after watching a movie or finishing dinner—for one to stick, you'd have to have prolonged contact."

Cue the lightbulb. "This guy was near the bay. A lot."

"A lot, as in, he could have set up shop in its vicinity," Ramos murmured.

Liz giggled. "Narrows down our search area, doesn't it? Bad part is, so far Cyril hasn't found any Syndax buildings on the waterfront—at least, none that were indicated in the files you and Homeland pulled from that secret office. He's still working on it. Meanwhile I'll send drones out—I mean, down. There's miles and miles of sewer to explore."

That sounded like the worst thing ever and I was really glad a bunch of robots were going to do it, instead of me.

Ramos nodded. "Mercury, let's go. We'll get Teget out of lockup and pass Bradley the word on what we've found."

"Yeah. Yeah, you're right. I'll meet you downstairs." I winked at Liz. "Nice job. You too, Narang."

They actually high-fived each other as we left.

"You do realize that having you show up at the precinct could tip off whoever's allied with Arkwright that we're onto them," Ramos said. "I don't like the idea of making that person skittish."

"Don't worry about it. My plan is to play dumb and get Teget out of jail. I'll let you handle the interrogating." I grinned. "If you need muscle, I'm your backup."

Ramos snorted. "I'd better call Olivia and tell her I won't be home for a while."

"It's got to be rough on you guys."

"What's that?"

I waved my hands. "All this. The Procyon quest. Arkwright and his assaults. She knows what's happened. It's not like she's hidden from the dangers you face."

Ramos had his phone out, ready to dial. Instead, he tapped it against his lips as he stared at the far wall. "She understands, more than I thought possible for someone outside the fight could. That's the thing about love, Mercury—when it's at its best, it doesn't falter, and it doesn't fear. I can't imagine what it felt like for her when I was trapped in Meda, even though she's told me in her own words. There's nothing to convey that sense of powerlessness. All I can do is honor what she sacrificed in my absence by saving as many lives as I can, and by coming home to her, safe."

He called Olivia, murmuring into his phone in Spanish as he headed to the elevator. I hung back by the door to the lab, my brain churning but unable to put words together in an answer to Ramos. Just when I thought the guy couldn't simultaneously drag me down to Earth and boost my confidence, there he went.

It reminded me I had someone to talk to.

I pulled up my list of contacts, thumb hovering over the button for composing a text message. There was a lot to tell Loredana. A lot to ask. But things were moving quickly along another track.

So, I started typing to Serena.

She wanted me to keep her in the loop? I'd oblige. With Airfoil out of the running for our cavalry, I had to look elsewhere. A federal agent who'd offered to put a bullet in Arkwright's forehead was top of my options list.

<Good news—lab thinks Arkwright base along bay.>

Serena answered in seconds. <Great! I'll task agents to expand the search.>

<How about the offices?>

<Hitting dead ends. Bowe's mad enough to eat our car.>

I chuckled. That'd be something I'd pay to see. <I'll let you know what else we find.>

<Thanks. Everything okay?>

Okay? Besides Loredana and Dominic warning me Serena could be an evil alternate version of herself? Oh, yeah, peachy. <Yep. No complaints yet. Good luck.>

"Mister Hale."

That would be Alvarez. He waited by the elevator, across from Ramos, hands on his hips. "I need to see you. In private."

Ramos was still on his call. He nodded to me and pointed down. Meet him at the car? Sure thing. I nodded back and watched as the elevator doors concealed him from me and Alvarez. "What's up, boss?"

"Things are progressing nicely?"

"From how I see them." I shrugged. "We've got some challenges but not for long."

"Agent Cyr from Homeland has been keeping me up to speed. I've sent Procyon Security to check various locations, under Mr. Garvey's command, at her behest."

I raised an eyebrow. Guess I wasn't the only one who Serena had taken for a walk to a sandwich shop. I wondered how much she knew from Alvarez compared to what I'd told her. "We're subcontracting to SCPD and the feds now?"

"Only temporarily, as she's indicated both departments

are pushed to their limits. Finding Arkwright has become a city-wide manhunt." Alvarez grimaced. "It's going to mean more overtime than the budget can hold, but the board of directors has assured me we can make do."

"Yeah, that's great, because, you know. Budget." How the guy could think about spreadsheets and finances at a time like this was beyond me. "My guess, though, is you didn't want to update me on fiscal situations."

"Not at all. You're astute, I'll give you that." He handed me a file folder.

It contained a single piece of paper. Somebody'd written a short, terse letter, and signed it with flowing, florid handwriting. "This the get out of jail free card I asked for?"

"No. This is Loredana Lark's resignation."

CHAPTER THIRTY

Alvarez had made minimal changes to his office since his predecessor. The giant oak desk was still the focus, and community service awards crowded a minibar. Except the minibar no longer stocked with a bazillion bottles of alcohol. Instead, there were so many bags of gourmet coffee packed shoulder to shoulder they resembled the offensive line of the San Camillo Comets.

Our fearless manager skipped the coffee maker and sat in a sleek chrome chair with black cushions. He set Loredana's letter in the middle of his desk, which was devoid of clutter. A computer monitor took up one corner, and a pair of framed photos faced away from me in the other. All other paperwork was filed in neat folders lining a shelf to his right.

"I was hoping you could shed some light on this situation," he said.

"Probably I could, but isn't this a Human Resources violation?"

"We're dispensing with strict adherence to policy, given that this is an emergency. Has Ms. Lark indicated to you she was going to resign?"

"Off and on since I brought her back. One minute she seems fine; the next, not so much."

"I wondered as much. She rejected the psych evaluation. Were it anyone else, I'd have fired her."

"No kidding." I made a face. "This is really none of my business."

"Again, if this were a normal work environment, I could be sued." Alvarez sighed. "As it is, I doubt the board will approve my handling of our in-house matters, not to mention our public visibility. Mr. Hale, it's apparent the two of you have some kind of relationship."

Some kind was right. "I won't argue."

"Then you'll understand why I came to you. She confides in you. Personal involvement aside, your professional partnership has seen Procyon Foundation's West Coast assets through times of tremendous trial."

"You're welcome."

"Dispense with the sarcasm, for two seconds, please." Alvarez tapped the paper on his desk. "This place? Loredana Lark ran it. I'm not one to speak ill of the dead—"

"But here goes," I muttered.

"Jack Jackson's stint as manager was—undistinguished. His loose style of operation is directly responsible, I believe, for the breaches in security Procyon headquarters experienced. If anyone else besides Loredana Lark had been in charge of Operations at the time, the results could have been catastrophic."

"As the guy who faced down a hole between dimensions that pulled monsters onto San Camillo's streets, I'd agree with that."

"Good. So, you see why I need you to convince her to remain."

"Right. I've already had this conversation with Loredana, several times. She's still in pain, mentally, and I get that. I've been trying to encourage her to do the right thing—which, obviously, I believe involves her staying here. Problem is, that's not up to me."

"It isn't up to her father, either."

I scowled. Suddenly I wished Alvarez would brew up some of his coffee, because the aroma drifting from the cabinet was driving me nuts. Of course, the mood I was in, I could have gone with whiskey in a tumbler courtesy of Jack Jackson's regime. "You've had the displeasure of meeting Archie Lark?"

"It's only rumors at this point."

"Oh, they're true."

"And you don't see eye to eye with him."

"Ask his dry cleaner about his sweater."

"I don't think I will. In all seriousness, he seems to have introduced the greatest doubt, and I'd like that to change. I'm open to suggestions."

"Yeah, me too." I rubbed the bridge of my nose. "Look, here's the deal—you're not gonna make Loredana do something she doesn't want to do. You'd be better off lifting a building with your bare hands, minus superpowers. Good news? She's prone to making the best decisions possible, after weighing all factors."

Alvarez pushed the paper to the left side of the desk. "That's reassuring."

"It should be. She's got to decide what she wants." And in more than just a professional capacity. The whole time I fed Alvarez those lines, making it sound like I was confident, the thoughts roiling inside my skull did a great job taking a detour and scooping out my guts. I felt like I'd gone a few days with the flu—hollowed.

"Good. Excellent." Alvarez stood. Well, that was quick. I mimicked him, assuming I was about to be dismissed. "I appreciate your input."

"And I appreciate your not kicking me out of Procyon, permanently." I offered my hand.

He smiled. We shook on it. "As much as your lack of impulse control dismays me, I can't deny you get things done around here. "*Buena suerte.*"

"Ditto." Now, if I could only deliver on my promises to him and everyone else, I'd be in really good shape.

First thing was first. Got to bail my brother out.

Ramos drove the Charger uptown in a way I was sure was gonna get us cited for speeding, except, you know, he was a cop. No need for flashing lights yet. He steered with one hand, a couple fingers drumming lightly.

I texted Loredana. <Alvarez showed me your letter. Talk?>

"What's she say?"

I rolled my eyes. "You mind not invading my privacy?"

"I assumed you were going to talk about it soon enough."

"You assumed wrong."

"When's her resignation effective?"

"Okay, A., not your business, and B. …" I make a face. "How'd you know about that?"

"Alvarez was putting the paper into his folder when the elevator doors opened. I read it. Upside down." Ramos shook his head. "I can't believe she'd back out now."

"We've been over this. She didn't come out of Meda as well as you did. And for what it's worth, I thought she was on the mend." I tapped my phone against my leg, waiting for an answer from Loredana. Could be she was still mad I threw coffee on her dad, ran off to a covert op with the Homeland Security chick she thought was an extradimensional infiltrator, then hopped to Drake City to recruit Airfoil to our cause. It was a decent list from which to pick.

"I know that. I'd have thought you'd have more success talking with her."

"You and Alvarez both, apparently. Why do you guys think she'll listen to me?"

"That's a dumb question, even for you." Ramos frowned. "You love each other."

Heat flushed my face. "I said it to her."

"Did you mean it?"

"Sure, I—"

"Don't 'sure' me." Ramos pressed jabbed two fingers into his chest. "Did you mean it? Here? And forget giving me a speech about not knowing. You know, or you don't."

I chewed on that in silence. "Yes. I know it."

"Good. And she loves you."

"But there's times when I wonder."

"Don't. I've seen it."

I blew out a breath. "Wish it were that easy."

"You two look at each other the same way Olivia and I still do." His voice was barely audible over the guitars strumming on the radio and the rumble of the Charger's engine as we accelerated out of a corner. "And because I know you, Mercury. You've been reckless, of course, but there's a reason for it, even if you won't admit it. You'll do anything for her."

I leaned back in the seat. "Does that make me an idiot?

Serious question."

"No. It makes you something you'll need to master if you're truly going to stick with Loredana—selfless."

"Pretty sure 'selfless' and 'reckless' only have their suffix in common."

"You think it's a joke, but the more you do for others, and less you do for you, you'll understand."

I flipped the phone over. The screen remained devoid of notifications. "Thanks for, uh, thinking I can handle this. All of this. You're on the short list. Like, only you and Wilhelmina. Everyone else has the idea that I'm creating a bigger mess."

"Even if you are, we know your heart's in it."

The phone buzzed. I grinned—until I saw the message was from Liz. <The shard from the playground! Tether must be active because it's floating from its container and Narang says tachyon bursts from its position are rising in frequency!>

I skipped the onerous task of typing a response and dialed her. "Liz! What's that all mean?"

"Hey! It means we can track it, which we're doing, from Tracking of course, but it's indistinct at this point. Give me a few minutes and I'll narrow a location."

"Nice work. Get Wilhelmina and—wait. Garvey's already out?"

"Searching town with a bunch of the rest of security, yeah, so I don't know if I can get him—"

"Never mind that." We parked in front of the Ninth Precinct and were headed up the steps. "Find Dominic. He and Wilhelmina can head for wherever this thing ends up. I'll get there with Ramos ASAP."

"You got it!"

"What is it?" Ramos asked as we squeezed past a pair

of patrol officers wrestling a handcuffed guy in ratty clothes through the front door. No need to repeat the words he was spraying across their faces.

"Maybe. The Hedron shard you found is acting up. If it makes a run for its owner, we may have to get out of here fast."

"We won't be long," Ramos muttered.

He quieted down and stormed past pretty much everyone who tried to get his attention, until were beyond the desk sergeant and the cubicles and the cacophony of people, phones, and keyboards of the bullpen. A couple of twists down short corridors put us in front of a line of cells, pasty-green paint flaking from the bars.

Teget lay on his back, eyes closed. "This is not how I envisioned my efforts ending."

"With you locked up? I would have guessed." I leaned on the bars. "Look, Teget—about before. Sorry I got bent out of shape."

"I am sorry. I was the fool." He rose. There was an urgency to each step, like he was a caged tiger ready to be let loose. "Hatred for our enemy consumed me, after what they did to Grandfather. The knowledge that Crux was one of the conspirators—someone of our own blood ..."

"Yeah. I know. We're even on the whole thing, I think." I nudged Ramos. "How's about you find the key?"

Bradley barged into the holding area, looking like he was ready to wrestle us both to the floor, with his sleeves rolled up and his tie askew. "What are you doing here?"

"It's still 'Lieutenant' even though I'm off the case, Detective." Ramos indicated the cell. "Time to let him out."

Bradley muttered profanities under his breath, but attacked the lock, keys jangling in the process. The cell door creaked open. Teget prowled out, circling us. "I require my weapon."

"The ax?" Bradley snorted. "Where's your permit?"

"Not really a thing where he comes from," I said. "Let's not make a big deal out of it, okay, Stan? Can I call you Stan?"

"No."

"Remember that the next time monsters come calling. I hear Rampart's pretty this time of year. Maybe we'll take an extended vacation, leave you the feds and the National Guard to shoot up the place when astral fiends get hungry."

Whatever Bradley had planned for a retort, Ramos interrupted with, "While we're in the locker, you can show us the blank spaces on the shelf where the missing countercharges were stored."

"Countercharges?" Bradley scowled. "For breaching?"

"And trying to blow me up," I added.

"You're nuts. What, you think SCPD was behind that bomb? We had our hands full cleaning up the mess you left in Rosa Roja Park!"

"Enough, Stan," Ramos snapped. "We know the charges came from here. I need security footage to prove it."

"Prove what? You think I'm going to let these suckers plow through our security video? You're crazy. No wonder the captain took you off the case."

Ramos pointed a finger under Bradley's nose. "This is beyond protocol, Detective. Beyond PR and captains and ranks and all the rest. This is life and death, for the whole city."

My phone went crazy, the buzzing a harsh tremor in the silence we'd lapsed into. I snatched it from my pocket and took the call. "Liz, I really have to call you back."

"No, you don't! You have to get out of there! The tachyon tether—its endpoint materialized. It's coming to the Ninth Precinct!"

An explosion rocked the building, shifting the floor so abruptly we all lost our footing. Concrete dust flooded the corridor. I heard cries and gunfire minded with a sickening *crunch*, with intermittent slashes of metal through flesh.

I willed the stave to life and hurtled the way we came, Teget running behind me. There was no time to check if Ramos and Bradley were injured. Besides, I heard them grousing and shouting orders into their radios.

"The charges?" Bradley gagged. I hoped Ramos wasn't choking a confession out of him. "S-stolen! Augh, this dust. Stolen a few days ago. Captain hushed it up. She didn't want the feds finding out, but they did somehow, even without the cameras. They were on the fritz during the time of theft."

I skidded on dust in the bullpen. Desks were tipped. Chairs were spun to the edges of the room. The cops were strewn across the floor, along with their papers, their coffee, and everything else not bolted down. The doors to storage lockup on the opposite wall were ripped off their hinges, crumpled like paper. As I stared, mouth hanging open, Arkwright clenched his fist, and those doors continued crumpling, until they were the size of basketballs.

He had the ax.

The Hedron floated ahead of him. A nauseating pressure built in my skull. Teget grasped the sides of his head.

Your end is beginning. It is my beginning.

That thing. I wish it'd shut up.

Arkwright held the ax aloft. It shone with power, because Arkwright was infused with the genetic code he'd absorbed from Marigold Yen—the same genetic code that allowed people in her bloodline to use the ax, the night's blade, and the pulsar stave, the code left on Earth by the original Medan warriors who'd first turned back the astral fiends millennia ago.

"Arkwright!" I coughed up dust. "Don't listen to it! The Hedron's got a mind of its own. You've got no idea what it's doing!"

The giggle that escaped from his lips chilled my insides worse than any foreboding proclamation. "Oh, Mercury," Marigold Yen's voice crooned. "It's sad you think you can end what's begun. The walls fell a long time ago. Every step you've taken has been at our direction. Finally, we will cleanse this world."

Your weakness is our strength, and, yes, we know how weak you are. Is there anyone who doesn't? The Whisperer's hideous overlap slithered between my thoughts. Shame. Self-hate. Sorrow. Guilt. He amplified all my pains. I was a failure. I saw it clearly. Why not stand back, while everything crumbled, because I'd been unable to stop them from the get-go.

Arkwright's eyes faded from brilliant purple to glistening black orbs, more of which erupted from his face. Tentacles sprouted, claws and fangs protruded, and with a ghastly ripping sound, he grew into his monstrous form. He hunched under the ceiling. The room seemed to flex with his breathing. "You're as much a close-minded fool as the old man," he murmured. "Casting aside family and friends for you own benefit."

"Enough of this!" Teget snarled. "Face us like a man!"

"If I weren't this powerful, I'd consider it, but not anymore." Arkwright's grin was a twisted exaggeration of his winning smile, displaying slavering fangs. "Excuse me while I destroy your home."

The Hedron lifted the ceiling, tearing tiles and warping the supports underneath, until daylight spilled through a gash that reached the upper floors and out the roof. Arkwright soared through his brand-new escape route.

I lunged for his leg.

But Teget tackled me.

There was a flash of light. Arkwright was gone. Like I'd imagined him.

I shoved Teget off. "What are you doing? I had him."

"No. He taunted you. Should I let my brother take his bait? Come."

Teget met up with Ramos and Bradley as more cops swarmed into the bullpen, reaching for fallen officers. Several guns were trained on us. "We'd better put out a BOLO," Bradley spat. "This guy could be anywhere."

"Not anywhere. Lieutenant Ramos, we need your vehicle." Teget's expression was sour. "I know where Arkwright can be found."

"How do you know—?" My chest ached. Arkwright said he was going to destroy my home. He couldn't get back to Meda. And who cared about my apartment? "Let's go, Ramos."

"Where to?"

I was already rushing from the precinct, dialing Liz as fast as I could without tripping down the steps. "Procyon. Arkwright's targeting headquarters."

CHAPTER THIRTY-ONE

It made perfect sense. Why hadn't he gone after Procyon Foundation itself before?

Maybe, like we'd all surmised, Arkwright hadn't mastered the Hedron to his satisfaction. If one could ever master a device that had independent thoughts and sounded like it wanted to murder humankind.

But he seemed way handier with it at the precinct. So, next stop, Procyon.

Imagine my surprise when Ramos hopped a curb and screeched the tires sideways across two handicapped parking spots, all to discover HQ was still in pristine shape. I don't even think the windows were smudged.

My panicked message to Liz, though, had the opposite effect. I meant it as, "Everyone look out!"

They interpreted it as, "All hands on deck."

Loredana was there, as was her father, hounding her footsteps as she hurried into Tower Three. Wilhelmina and Dominic were in the parking lot, apparently returning from one of the Procyon sedans, because she had her knitting bag—which I assumed contained her knitting needles and the improved Medan dagger—and Dominic hefted the portal gun over one shoulder. He'd changed back into his black garb, complete with mask.

There was also a horde of federal agents swarming the entrance to the parking lot, their SUVs and cars blocking the entrance after Ramos' car had made it through. Bowe towered over the rest of his people, barking orders that really did sound like a dog barking, from that distance.

"Hale." He said my name like it was top of the list of words he never wanted to hear come out of his kid's mouth. "This a fire drill? You get bored after not having any mercenary soldiers to slap around?"

"Hey!" Serena appeared from a cluster of agents. "None of that. We're on the same side."

"I'd feel better about that prospect if Bowe here hadn't tried to blow me and Dominic up. Real classy." My blood was pumping but I kept the anger locked down. Our proof was sketchy at best. I was hoping to goad Bowe into rash action. Ironic. "Bet that was the only way you saw to shut me down after you didn't get to lock me up."

"You're insane." Some of his FBI formed a blockade between us, but Bowe's head was six inches above theirs. "If I wanted you dead, I'd have a gun aimed center mass and I'd be face-to-face, like we are now!"

"Way better if you can blame it on dirty cops. What about it, Serena? Does he have munitions training?"

Serena looked puzzled. "He does. U.S. Army, Rangers."

"So?" Bowe's anger shifted toward her. "So do six other guys on this task force! That doesn't mean we've gone terrorist!"

"Everyone calm down and back away." Ramos eased me from Bowe. Which was fine. I'd gotten more info than

I'd expected. "These are serious accusations we're flinging around. We know the countercharges that were intended for two Procyon operatives originated from SCPD's Ninth Precinct. And DHS knew of the theft without word leaking out."

"You'd better double check for leaks," Bowe muttered.

"You and I need to talk," Serena said to him. "Mercury, you'd better focus on this apparent imminent threat—which is where, exactly?"

I blew out a breath. "I thought he was headed right here. Let me get up to Tracking and find out."

Bowe's agents ushered him toward the Homeland vehicles, with Serena marching behind them. As soon as she caught up with him, she lit into him with what looked like a superb reprimand. The guy started out arguing but ended up more like the kid in the principal's office.

I joined Wilhelmina and Dominic at the entrance to Tower Three, with Ramos bringing up the rear. "Sorry to rain on the parade, guys, but you missed Arkwright."

"Mm-hmm. Sounds like we weren't the only ones." Wilhelmina wagged a finger at my nose. "Dominic told me all about your trip, child. Sounds like you all should've sent me to do the talking."

"Well, turns out the guy operates with a set of strict and annoying rules. It didn't help he saw us as potential threats."

"I'm astonished," Dominic murmured.

"I get you didn't like my method of attracting attention, but you've got to admit, it worked," I said.

"Maybe, but there's no call for us to have made a new enemy." Wilhelmina smiled. "You do got that effect on folks."

She wasn't wrong.

Dominic held the door for us. He grimaced as he did so.

"Hey, you okay?"

"I've apparently aggravated my wound."

I thought his face looked paler. Upon closer inspection, Dominic seemed on the verge of puking.

"Well, take it easy. Just not so easy that we lose."

"Thanks," Dominic said dryly. "We were going to rendezvous with Garvey, but he has been off his radio since his team breached another Syndax facility north of here. The same goes for the rest of the security teams sent out to investigate."

"Alvarez said they were accompanying SCPD and Homeland units."

"They were, but our teams were kept separate. The manager didn't want the official responders learning more than was necessary about our capabilities."

"Smart." But I didn't like the idea of all our guys being out in the field, when we knew Arkwright could be on his way. That said, our villain was taking his sweet time.

We passed a lot of locked doors as we headed for Tracking. Narang intercepted me just outside the threshold. He held up an aluminum-sided briefcase.

"Unmarked bills or nuclear launch codes?" I asked.

"A change of clothing, Mercury. The fabricators worked double time ever since you turned it back over to our care."

Clothing? The suit? Awesome. "Give my regards to the tailor, even if it's a robot."

"Hey!" Liz beckoned from her desk. "Guys, you're gonna want to see this!"

"Quit teasing, Liz." I propped the briefcase against her desk. "What've we got?"

"A whole lot piled under nothing."

"You're gonna have to be more specific."

She waved her hands at her screens, which were full of so many graphs and charts and lines of numbers I thought she was playing the stock market. "Tachyon levels across San Camillo are at their highest we've recorded in decades, which is fascinating but doesn't do us any good because it makes it nearly impossible to pinpoint the Hedron's activity!"

"How about the shard?"

"It tried to break free of its container." She tapped a console panel and one screen flashed. It showed us the inside of the lab downstairs. The silver sliver banged against the walls of the clear box. No cracks in it, yet. "It's settled down now, poor thing."

Dominic leaned closer to the screen. "It doesn't appear settled. If anything, it's agitated."

"It is an abomination," Teget said. "We should destroy it."

"I'm all for that, but if it can show us where Arkwright is, we need to keep it in one piece. Nobody destroys it. Not yet." I glanced at Wilhelmina. "You were with Procyon back in the day. Ever see anything like this tachyon activity?"

"Nope. Then again, Tracking wasn't near as fancy as you kids have made it." Wilhelmina pursed her lips. "We ran through a nasty spell, in the late '80s, that made all the instruments haywire. Our Forecaster wasn't too happy, neither. Didn't seem like she got much sleep. All the commotion hereabouts? Same kind of chaos."

"Okay, good."

Ramos scowled. "How in heaven's name is that *good* news?"

"Relax, Ramos." I cracked open the suitcase. "If Procyon's seen this kind of thing before, that means we've got a better chance of surviving it, right?"

The suit shimmered under Tracking's lights. Good as new. Maybe better, judging by the thickness of the fabric and the way it resisted my attempts to pull its seams apart.

No one had answered me. I looked up at Liz, then Wilhelmina, and Dominic. "I said, 'Right?'"

Wilhelmina shrugged. Liz chewed her lip and became overly interested in her console.

Dominic set the portal gun down. "I can't speak to it. I'm new to all of this."

We were not a super confident bunch.

Loredana's heels announced her arrival a couple seconds before she strode into Tracking, with no more urgency than an executive prepared for her weekly staff meeting. Granted, she wasn't dressed like one. She had on her playtime clothes—and by playtime, I mean combat. Black T-shirt, Kevlar, gray fatigue pants. A ponytail swept her hair away from her face. She had a gray ballcap tucked under her arm like she was an officer reviewing the gathered troops and held a tablet in her hand. "What is our status, Elizabeth?"

"I've got Cyril parsing every bit of data we can gather from the drones but like I was just telling everyone I'm having a heck of a time getting through the increased background tachyon interference. The shard we collected that's down in the lab should help us once he makes his move."

Loredana pinned me to the wall with her gaze. That's what it felt like, though. "And you're certain of Arkwright's intentions? To attack this facility?"

"It's more of a hunch, but it makes sense, given that's he's got it out for me—and my family—in a big way." I didn't think she could read minds, but she'd better have been getting a "What do you mean you're resigning?" vibe from me. Of course, Ramos' heartfelt talk came back to me. About her. About love. If I really cared about her, I'd let her go, wouldn't I? Who was to say the best thing was her remaining at Procyon?

I wished we could have stayed the way we were—me getting the late-night call from her to go fight monsters, her enduring my lighthearted flirting with coy appreciation. Too many things had intervened. Funny how you can yearn to go back to the past, but you could never visit the future. If one thing had turned out different, we might not be standing where we were, at that moment. I might not have even found my way home.

"He has the ax," Teget said. "I carry the blame."

"It is disappointing, but not cause for despair," Loredana said. "One can hardly blame you for the headstrong steps that led to its abduction, given your family's predilection for extreme if misguided actions."

Wilhelmina would have snorted milk out her nose if she'd drunk any.

Teget seemed mollified, but I was more concerned with the *why*. "We should be asking what he plans to do with it, right? Maybe he needs it to jump start the Hedron? Power it up to full—I don't know, full power?"

"You're assuming he's the one who needs it," Ramos pointed out. "Crux is your cousin. And those weapons are linked to your lineage?"

"Yeah, and—oh." Hadn't thought of that. Judging by Teget's wince, neither had he. "It might be he wanted a weapons upgrade for his right-hand man. Or worse. Teget, can he get back to Meda? Because if he can, he can try breaking into the Atrium of the temple and steal the night's blade."

Combining the blade and the ax with the pulsar stave would solidify a permanent passage between Earth and the astral fiend-filled Interstice. But that didn't seem to be Arkwright's goal. His was more driven by revenge.

"I do not know," Teget murmured. "Grandfather would have the answer."

My heart clenched. Naos was beyond providing us wisdom, or anything else.

"I have news that should prove a relief." Loredana cleared her throat. "Serena Cyr is dead."

Dominic seemed to sag a bit, but I was confused as everyone in the room looked.

"She's downstairs," Ramos said.

Oh. Right. I massaged my forehead. "Not that Serena Cyr. These guys—they think she was replaced by a double from another dimension."

"From yours?"

"No. Arkwright's. Dominic and Loredana have a list of people who have probably replaced their doubles here. Or they're the doubles. I don't know." I sighed. "But now that's wrong?"

"It seems." Loredana opened a file on her table. "In addition to the deck, we knew an approximate date of arrival. A woman matching her description was found dead in a car accident not thirty-six hours after."

"She didn't have time, then." Dominic nodded. "Sierran agents need time to observe their targets, to ascertain details of their lives, before they can eliminate them and assume their places."

"You've got proof of that?" I asked. "Definitive?"

Loredana showed us the years-old newspaper article. Yep, there was Serena's face, grainy, but her. The paper was from somewhere north of Drake City, in rural New England.

"See?" I felt vindicated. Why shouldn't I? "The real Serena's standing outside, ready to put a bullet in Arkwright's face."

"I will feel most assured if and when she actually does so. Gemini?" Loredana handed Dominic a folded piece of paper. "You have new orders."

He scrunched his nose like he'd both stepped in and smelled something unpleasant. "I'm sorry, you—want me to leave?"

"This is a vital assignment. If Arkwright is marshalling his forces, we need to do likewise. I've already asked the manager to recall all our security personnel."

"Oh, did you get through to them?" Liz clapped her hands. "We were having comms problems."

"I've been assured Mr. Alvarez is addressing the matter." Loredana closed Dominic's hand over the note. "I can't stress it enough: carry out these instructions, as swiftly as you can. Do not worry over the particulars; I'll understand if you need to improvise."

Dominic withdrew and opened the note. His eyes went wide. Whatever it said, the message was enough. Ten seconds later, he vanished through the glare of his portable portal, leaving us all blinking and me wondering at his sudden determination.

"Very good." Loredana interlaced her fingers. "Lieutenant Ramos? SCPD units have arrived outside our security checkpoints. I believe they're debating jurisdiction with their Homeland Security colleagues."

Ramos grimaced. "I'd better get down there. If the captain sent Bradley, Bowe might get himself punched."

"Hey!" Liz yelped. "There's a buildup of tachyon

emissions at five—no, seven points! Like with the prior earthquakes. I'm mapping locations now."

Sure enough, red smudges blinked onto the main map.

"Better get those numbers out there, Ramos." I clapped his shoulder. "And grab yourself a big gun."

"We'll call for evacuations if we can and instruct those who can't to seek shelter." He returned the gesture by holding both of my arms. "*La paz del Seno sea siempre con vosotros.*"

It was suddenly hard to breathe for the lump in my throat as he hurried from Tracking, his sharp orders into his phone echoing in the hall.

"Are you prepared?" Teget held out his hand.

I knew what he wanted, without his having to ask. I activated the pulsar stave, watching as it shone with dangerous radiance. Yellow-white energies soaked the suit. I separated the stave and gave him half. "You know it. Too bad we don't have any giant trees to leap out of, because this might not be as fun."

He smiled, his expression very much like Naos'.

"Come on, honey." Wilhelmina looped her arm through the crook of Teget's. "These two have a lot to say before the fan gets hit with you-know-what. What say we take a stroll around our perimeter?"

"After you, my lady."

Which then left me alone with Loredana. Well, and Liz. And a couple other Tracking techies who were so hidden in the shadows, lit only by their clusters of screens, I'd forgotten about them. The clicking of keyboards and murmurs of jargon filled the room. Liz made a shooing motion with her hands.

I pulled Loredana out into the hall. "We need to talk."

"This is, as you would say, a terrible time."

"You know, I really don't care." I ran a hand through my hair. "I must be crazy, being in love with you, because I was perfectly willing to let you do whatever you wanted, for your happiness. Until I found out you went ahead and did it."

She held her hands behind her back. "You're referring to my letter of resignation."

"Yeah, that. Alvarez broke with protocol because he's worried. Has that sunk in? Alvarez! Broke rules!"

"I didn't expect you to comprehend."

"That's the problem—I get it. More than anyone else here." I gestured with both hands, as if I could hold all of Procyon in them. "You want out. I get it. But I was wrong about being able to handle it when the time came."

"What are you saying, Mercury?" She smiled. "It's unlike you to be so indirect."

I held out my hand. She took it. "Stay. With us. With me. I can't promise nothing will ever happen to either of us. That'd be stupid. I can promise that, no matter what, I'll always be there for you—always waiting, always searching, always. Or take me to England, if that's not enough. I'll pack."

She touched my cheek. "I can't ask you to do that. You love San Camillo so much, and I wouldn't take you from everyone who cares so deeply for you."

I snorted. "You mean the Fantastic Four I keep alienating?"

"You're an astute observer, Mercury Hale, but sometimes you can be as blind as a bat. Look around you. Ramos loves you like a son. Wilhelmina will always watch over you. Teget is drawn to his brother by affection and loyalty. Even Dominic, for all his disdain of your methods and your flamboyant nature, is willing to follow your lead. And that's the part of yourself you've never made amends with."

"I don't understand."

"Your ability to lead. In there, just now, I saw it. We are standing on the edge of events which most people cannot comprehend, and even if they could, would be driven to despair by their reality. And yet you—you are steadfast in your devotion. Which is one of the many reasons I love you, too."

No one had ever shown that much confidence in me. Except, perhaps, Ramos. But to hear it stated in so many words ...

Me. A leader. Not just the orphan who faced down threats in the dark, alone.

"Then get rid of the letter. Let Alvarez shred it. I'll burn it with the pulsar stave if I have to."

"The time for that discussion's long past, Hale." The refined, cold accent cut through our warm moment. Right. Archie Lark. I'd wondered where he'd gotten to, and apparently wherever it was, he'd found his way out. Maybe Doc Arne wouldn't miss a syringe of his favorite sedative if I swiped it from the infirmary. "I'll thank you very much to let my daughter be. Once your silly security drill is concluded, she's on the next flight to Heathrow, to return her home and to be with her family."

I stood nose to nose with him. Thought I could still smell coffee. "Sir, you're wrong. She is home. This is her family. The people who love her the most? We've been here the whole time. Think about that before you look so far down your nose at us you fall flat on your face."

"If you think that you—"

A siren sounded from the open door to Tracking. I'd

never heard that before. Judging by Loredana's open mouth and wide eyes, she hadn't either. It brought back memories of a PBS documentary on the Battle of the Blitz, complete with harrowing air raid klaxon. Red lights pulsed along the hallway.

A tremor built under foot.

"Here! It's here!" Liz grasped the door frame. "The epicenter of this quake is underneath us!"

A piece of information clicked into place inside the puzzle that was my brain. Sea life. Liz said the Syndax soldier had a kind of critter on his gear that was common to San Camillo Bay. "Arkwright. He's been here all along."

"The devil is all this?" Archie asked.

"Shut up, Dad," Loredana snapped. "Mercury—where?"

"Underneath. Arkwright's been hiding out right under Procyon the entire time." I felt sick. "That's what he meant by home—he made ours into his."

"We have to lock the facility down." Loredana punched a number on her phone.

Me? I stripped off my shirt and handed it to a properly startled Archie, who held like it was a rag I'd used to clean the staff lavatory. "Hand onto that, Dad. I've got to get changed."

After all, there was no time to find a phone booth.

CHAPTER THIRTY-TWO

Man, did it feel good to wear the suit again.

Not only did it channel the gathered energies of the pulsar stave into me with greater efficiency, making me feel like I could run around the curved walls of Procyon's exterior, it could also provide active camouflage, courtesy of the same powers. I touched a gloved hand to the nearest wall and watched it fade until my fingers were a wavy outline the same shade as the paint.

"Lori, darling, I suspect you had better educate me on this aspect of your community services." Archie hadn't blinked for the last thirty seconds, which must've been murder if he was wearing contacts.

"My apologies, Dad. I shall endeavor to do so while we make our way to the Historic Vault." She made for the emergency stairwell, near the elevator, because the shaking was intensifying and nobody in their right mind in California hopped into a box dangling from a steel cable when the Richter Scale started acting up. "Suffice it to say Procyon's primary ventures include managing extradimensional threats, though our community housing and support services are quite real."

"Yeah, you should see Alvarez's trophy collection," I said, voice echoing off the bare walls and concrete steps of the stairwell. "Except there's none up on the shelf about killing monsters."

"Mercury," Loredana warned.

"What? I enjoy my work."

We exited the stairwell onto the fourth floor and took the elevated walkway across to Tower Three. I could see herds of police cars, S.W.A.T. trucks, and Homeland vehicles all over our parking lot and the adjacent street. They'd cordoned off several blocks in either direction. It looked like civilians were getting moved out of the area, pronto. Procyon employees were streaming out, too, tiny figures hustled away by men in black body armor.

"What is taking so long?" Loredana held up her phone as we quick-marched over the walkway, heading, I assumed, for her office. "This is Ms. Lark. What is the delay? Evacuate all non-vital personnel. I called for a complete lockdown, not this half-hearted measure!"

The voice on the other end warbled apologetically. A series of reverberating *clangs* startled me. I thought the building was coming down, victim of the Hedron's quaking powers, but instead, I saw metal sheets protrude from the sides of Procyon's Three towers, twist, and slam sideways, until all three grew an armored exterior.

"Quickly, please."

"Yeah, hurrying, so don't—" I cut off my sentence when we passed the threshold into Tower One, because a barricade slammed down a whisper from my heels. "Oh."

"Yes. Fear not, I have access, so we'll be able to get into the vault."

Which was back in Tower Three. "So, did we come all this way for your purse?"

Any other woman probably would have slapped me, but Loredana being Loredana, she merely smiled sweetly and opened one of the many cabinets behind her desk—except that two cabinet doors were actually one disguised as a pair.

She had two rifles, two machine guns, and four pistols stored inside the concealed case.

"Ah." Archie smiled beneath his moustache. "That's my girl."

Loredana tucked the tablet into a backpack nestled at the bottom of the cabinet. It was already loaded with magazines, and by that I meant both the kind that hold ammunition as well as *Cosmopolitan* and *The Economist*. She selected the MP5 submachine gun and left the Uzi. The silver revolver and its holster wound up on her belt. "I have just the ticket for you, Dad."

She handed him the biggest rifle I'd ever seen. His expression became so beatific, he could have been the blond kid from *A Christmas Story*, cradling the Red Rider BB gun. "AWM 338, designation L115A3, bolt action, chambered for .338 Lapua Magnum. This will do quite nicely, Lori."

"When necessary, yes, however I'll loan you this for close-quarters." She reached for one of the semi-auto pistols.

"I'll not handle a bloody plastic pellet gun," he grumbled.

"Perish the thought. I still have your Browning." She loaded a magazine and gave it to him. "Regularly maintained. I prefer the revolver myself but—"

"My old service pistol. Thank you, darling." He kissed her on the forehead.

Despite or maybe because of the firepower being caressed, it was pretty touching to see father and daughter in a happy reunion. Granted, it would have made more sense to me if they were in front of a fireplace sipping Earl Grey, but hey, different strokes. "You're expecting trouble while we're locked inside?"

"I prefer being prepared." Loredana typed commands into her computer. The screened flashed. "The network purge protocols are in place. Good. Our data are being routed to off-site servers. They'll find nothing but blank hard drives should they try looking."

"Ah. Right." I tightened my grip on the stave. It hadn't occurred to me, with the walls shuddering and the floor shifting, that Arkwright's people could be trying to get into Procyon instead of just causing mayhem from underneath. "Better get to the Historic Vaults."

"What is your plan of action?" Archie followed us through the halls as we hurried back across the walkway to Tower Three. The sudden burst of daylight made me blink. The walkways weren't shielded. Why bother, since they were blocked off from the towers by the armored doorways Loredana could unlock? "This Historic Vault you mentioned—I assume it will be the target of whomever you intend me to shoot."

"Precisely that. It contains our most secret documents and long-hidden truths of Procyon's operations, dating to the 1840s and beyond."

"Well, now." Archie's moustache twitched, like it was itching to hop from his face and get downstairs faster than we could manage.

"Yeah, no kidding." I pointed to the parking lot below. "How many more people are we waiting to get out of here? The evacuation looks complete."

There were a ton of bodies milling about. Seemed like

civilians were moved across the street, and cars were few and far between on the nearby streets. I didn't see what I was looking for, though—a splash of brilliant pink.

"Tracking? This is Lark." Loredana paused by the door into tower three. "All is well?"

"We've picked up multiple tachyon spikes inside all three towers, small but intense readings." Liz's words trembled, and their velocity led me to believe it wasn't the increasing power of the earthquake that had them doing so. "A couple near your position."

"Be more precise, please."

"Fifty feet around the fourth floor and getting closer."

"Thank you, Elizabeth. If you haven't already, enact the data preservation protocols for your department and get clear."

"Umm, I've already sent everyone else out, but I have to complete Cyril's download. He's not completely transferrable to the servers and I figured you guys need someone up here watching over you."

I glanced skyward. "Any other day, I could break the glass and jump my way up the side of the tower to get her out, but the armor's gonna make that impossible."

Archie chambered a round in his pistol and leaned against the other side of the door. He had the rifle slung on a strap over his back. He ruminated on what I'd just said, mouth moving. Was he repeating my sentence to himself? "That's four floors. Do you fancy climbing?"

"Kinda meant a straight leap." Energies sparked from the pulsar stave. "You kids gonna open the door so we can start this party?"

Archie snorted. "Do try not to get shot. I'll gladly let you know if your services are required."

“Elizabeth, stay put. Mercury is on his way to retrieve you. I have to go.”

“Okay. They’re not here yet but I don’t know if the door will hold when they show up if they have anything other than guns because we’ve never tested the durability against the tachyon weapons.”

“Stand by.” Loredana ended the call. Her thumb hovered over an icon on her phone. “Ready?”

I nodded. Archie raised his pistol.

Loredana punched the button.

The door flung open, shooting straight into its ceiling recess. I zipped into the corridor, channeling the stave’s power into the suit and, thus, into my body, accelerating myself so I could hop-skip off the opposite wall.

It was four guys, not two—a pair of Syndax soldiers in their team camouflage, and a couple Kutsatuta. All four had the sinister glow of purple eyes bleeding through their visors and their metal facemasks, respectively.

I counted two automatic rifles and two swords among them.

Gunfire tracked me, though not expertly. The suit’s stealth attributes were active, turning me into a pastel smear along the wall. Probably looked like the floor was bleeding into it. Whatever you called it, they couldn’t get off good enough shots.

The Kutsatuta dudes, though, they could tell where I was headed.

I slid on my knees under the first swing of a sword and put the pulsar stave into his gut. The blast of yellow-white energy made a *crack* like a lightning bolt and threw him clear down the all until he slapped flat against the wall, three feet up, doing his best imitation of a bug against a windshield.

The other guy brought his sword in at a sideways angle, but I twisted around, blocking the slash with the stave. Sparks sprayed around us in true messy campfire fashion as we parried for advantage, him pressing me back toward a doorway where I couldn't maneuver, me keeping him between the guys with guns and my decidedly un-bulletproof self.

It was in those short first seconds that the gunmen finally noticed other people in the door to the elevated walkway, after my distraction's effectiveness had worn off.

Loredana opened fire from a kneeling position, the MP5 bucking against her grip as she put two bursts into the leftmost Syndax soldier. Archie's pistol barked three times, the sound almost lost among the hallway clamor. The second soldier flopped to the floor, his visor sporting bullet holes

My opponent noticed their demise in his peripheral vision—I caught the moment when his eyes flicked right—and that let me get clear of his onslaught. He repositioned, swinging wildly for what he hoped was gonna be the kill shot, but I let the stave fully charge until it blazed like the sun. This time when I blocked him, his blade sloughed off the hilt. One quick stab to his chest and he died, pinned against the wall, the purple and black swirl fading from his eyes until I was staring at a muted hazel not that different from my own.

"Bracing." Archie said. "We'd best keep moving."

"Agreed." Loredana brushed sweat from her brow. "Mercury, if you'd be so kind—"

"On my way up to Tracking. You guys be careful." I saluted Archie. "So, that means, don't let her die."

"Of course not." He scowled. "I may even refrain from shooting you if you surprise me with that ghost clothing."

"Good times, Dad."

We found the stairwell and parted ways. I headed up three floors, mindful of sounds, listening for bad guys even as Loredana's and Archie's footsteps faded. It helped that the suit was engineered to be physically stealthy as well as visually—my footfalls were virtually inaudible.

I'd passed the sixth floor when a shock rattled the whole structure, so severely I clocked my knee on a step. Grimacing against the pain, I heard shouting from above. Shouting, and metal banging against metal.

My phone buzzed. Liz. <They're outside the door hurry hurry!!!>

"Yeah, I know, I'm hurrying," I muttered.

I eased the door a crack. The windows to the infirmary were shattered. The lights were out. No sign of bodies, dead or otherwise. I hustled along the corridor. The floor rolled like it was surfing, so I rode with it. Swearing up ahead—in a language I didn't recognize, sure, but swearing was swearing, even if you're from another dimension.

Crux and two Kutsatuta were outside the door to Tracking. Crux took a few swings at the hinges of a thick metal door I'd never noticed before. Must be another security barrier. He swore again and then held the ax firmly. It took on a sickly-red sheen, mingled with its usual display of white light.

He jabbed it dead center of the door. The metal started melting, the surface bubbling as the damage spread outward. His buddies watched, their stances loose.

Move it!

I didn't go for stealth. I just barreled into their midst with as much force as I could muster, sending all three pinwheeling away from the door in different directions. One poor sucker wound up head and torso through the much flimsier walls across from Tracking. Crux and his other buddy sprawled on the tile, out of reach of the ax.

"Shouldn't leave your toys lying around, especially when they're stolen." I yanked the ax free and got an immediate surge as I pieced the stave together with its old friend. The half-stave-plus ax took on a low hum that resonated throughout my body.

With the two acting as one, I slashed through the door.

Immediately a blinding pulse nearly took my head off, but thankfully the aim was poor and the scream ahead of it gave me ample warning to dodge. "Liz! Liz, it's me!"

She edged from behind her computer, holding the portal gun. She had a small black bag clipped to her belt. Tears dripped from her cheeks. "Sorry! Sorry. I'm ready to go now that I've got Cyril backed up on a couple of external hard drives, but I thought those guys were going to kill me—!"

I hugged her until her breathing slowed from frantic. "Easy. Easy, I've got you. Come on."

She sniffled and wiped her eyes. It was hard to see her at all, really, because all the screens in Tracking were dark. Only a few lights flickered on hard drives scattered around the room. Liz's workstation was completely shut down. "I'm ready."

Good. 'Cause we were getting out of there.

We ran from Tracking, as Crux extended a hand toward me. "Mercury! You fool! You cannot stop us from taking what should be rightfully ours!"

I had a good, snappy comeback for that guy, but it was Liz who answered. "Maybe you should stop threatening people and pay more attention to the beeping sound."

Beeping?

I'd flung the door open to the stairwell when the explosion threw fire out the entryway to Tracking. Flame seared the opposite wall and scattered melted fragments across the floor. As if the earthquake wasn't bad enough.

"Come on!" I dragged Liz through the door and slammed it shut. A tap from the pulsar ax left the handle melted to the locking plate.

We took the stairs in a dizzying spin, not stopping for any of the sights or sounds or smells coming from the other floors. A great metallic *crash* from above gave me pause when we hit the third-floor landing, but I wasn't going back up to check it out. My guess? Crux wasn't stopped for long by my blockade.

"Since when does 'data preservation' mean 'blow up Tracking'?" I asked between breaths.

"Everything important was transferred to our servers," Liz huffed. "The destruction part was the safety option, to make sure nothing could be taken off our drives, and I wasn't going to leave it on a timer. I triggered it as soon as we got out of the room."

"That's reassuring." I hit the landing for the first floor at a run, boots sliding up to the door. I put my hand out as a barricade. "Stay behind me. Keep Cyril out of the line of fire."

Liz made sure the bag on her belt was between me and her, with Cyril's downloaded brains out of line of fire.

Not that my body would do a lot to stop a bunch of bullets.

Speaking of which, gunshots and clashing weapons echoed from beyond the door. I waited until footsteps went right by us then shoved it open, hard. The door collided with a body, and at that point I didn't care which one—Syndax or Kutsatuta, I'd take either.

It was the former. The kid was sprawled on the floor, moaning, with his helmet and visor askew. I smacked him a good one across the head.

The rest was under Teget's control.

He and Wilhelmina were back to back in the middle of the lobby, fending off two astral fiends. They shrieked their outrage at having lost several limbs, pressing in around their anticipated meals.

Loredana and Archie were in a far corner, laying down as much concentrated fire as they could. When Teget planted a devastating slash in a fiend's face and it reared up, flailing at the ceiling, Archie put two shots into its eyes with rapid succession using his rifle. That left Wilhelmina to finish it off, bucking bronco style.

I dove into the second one, the combined stave and ax ripping a jagged hole in its side and reducing the fiend to a quivering mass of blue goo that melted away.

"Mercury!" Teget grinned, his face and arms slathered in slime. He wiped as much off as he could, but didn't have to worry much, because it, too, was evaporating. "You retrieved the ax."

"Thanks to Liz and a very impatient Crux, the latter of whom got pretty sloppy with your weapon." I disconnected it from the stave and traded Teget for my half. Much better. I hated to keep the band broken up. "You guys seemed to have things under control."

"Since the Larks lent a hand, we've been doing just fine." Wilhelmina patted my arm. "Now what say we get into the Historic Vault?"

"Sounds good to me." I gestured to Loredana. "You're the boss, Boss. We're here to empty it? That's gonna take a while unless you've got a semi parked outside."

"No need." Loredana smiled. "We simply send it on its way."

The stairwell door blew open, its pieces littering the floor. Our happy gang of six froze as Crux exited, his body rippling with purple bolts, his eyes a soulless black.

"Then get moving." I put myself and the stave between everyone. Teget stood beside me. "We've got this."

CHAPTER THIRTY-THREE

Crux drew his black blade. It looked—bigger than before. Maybe a trick of the light?

With as bad as the floor was shaking, making all of us stagger, it didn't matter much, because landing a blow on the guy was near impossible.

A piece of the ceiling tile crashed into our midst, showering us with white dust. A couple overhead lights sparked. Broken glass crunched under foot.

"The walls are falling, both here and beyond," Crux snarled. "I yearn for the moment when your heart's blood is between my fingers."

I came at him again, but he blocked the pulsar stave seemingly without care. I spun into a support column, my vision and thoughts blurred.

The purple sparks entwined Crux's sword, and it grew a second blade from its hilt. He tore the weapon into two blades.

Great. Cloning swords.

Teget's battle cry reverberated throughout the lobby as he brought the ax crashing down on our cousin. His attack was wild, haphazard, a far cry from the cool, deliberate strategies of the guy I'd sparred alongside in Meda's forest.

"Such rage," Crux said. "Reserve it for your grandfather, the patron of lies."

"Grandfather is dead!" Teget snapped. "He died because of your treachery."

The revelation must've startled Crux, because he backed away from my brother. They circled each other, weapons ready, while I inched up the column. I imagined I could feel my body knitting the damaged cells back together. Not fast enough. Get. Up.

"Is this true? He is ... dead." Crux ran his hand through his hair, a gesture that was jarringly familiar. "I had hoped he would live to see my achievements."

"Achievements? You defiled Meda and its temple, ransacked what he held most sacred, and brought the living dead who infected his body with the filth no amount of healing could scour." Teget twirled his ax. "And he left me his purpose—to end your life, as he should have done years ago, when he made the mistake of showing mercy."

"On that we can agree, Cousin." Crux nodded. "Leaving me alive led to this moment. You have only Naos to thank for the death and destruction that has come to this world and yours in its wake."

Teget cried out and struck. Crux slapped away the attack with his swords, whirling them in an expert ballet of Medan steel. With each blow they exchanged, I could feel the room change—the air pressure, the temperature, the smell. Static electricity rippled across my arms.

Teget's passion wasn't working in his favor. Put simply, he was getting stomped. Crux backed him into a corner, battering away with his dual swords, until Teget had nowhere to run. He dodged a double strike and brought the ax into the floor. A blinding sunburst forced Crux to shield his eyes and gave Teget the opening he needed to somersault over his opponent's head to safety.

But Crux spun, and with a backhanded slash, caught Teget across the spine.

I was already moving to intercept, staggering across a tile floor that felt more like quicksand than a solid surface, and thought my heart was gonna snap in two when Teget was stabbed. There was little blood, however, and I realized the blade had sliced into the leather armor Teget wore over his tunic.

He hit the tiles hard enough to crack them. Teget curled on his side, writhing, teeth clenched. I reached him and rolled him over. Black tendrils snaked from the long, jagged cut, sizzling his leather like it was steak on a grille, grasping for the bloody gash underneath.

I lit the pulsar stave and cut the vest free. A good burst of energy from the stave burnt it to a foul-smelling crisp.

"Pity. I would have had him experience the same agony as Naos." Crux prowled towards us. He sidestepped a light fixture that shattered on the floor, narrowly missing his stupid helmetless head.

"You're a barrel of laughs, you know that?" I snapped. "No wonder you and Arkwright get along."

"We 'get along,' as you put it, because he is not a weakling," Crux snapped. "He is not a man who tells you one thing and does the other, concealing a dagger in the left whilst praising with the right. He is stronger than Naos, than my father, than everyone else who has failed to do what should have been done long ago—free the relics from their dusty sepulcher in the temple Atrium for the glory of our people."

"Our people die if you destroy everything."

"We need not destroy all, Mercury. Only enough, to prevent this world from ever becoming a threat. And the more astral fiends can be bled from the Interstice onto Earth, the fewer will endanger Meda."

"You're a world-class moron, you know that? Arkwright isn't running the show. Every time he takes a sip of the Interstice Kool-Aid he's receiving his orders from the Whisperer and his fanatic, Marigold Yen! They want the Interstice to flood *all* worlds with evil! What's gonna be left then?"

"I will take the word of the man who showed me purpose over the traitorous seed of Naos." Crux brandished his sword.

"Don't mock the seed, Crux," I sneered. "Or have you not figured out a how a mirror works?"

Crux bellowed and brought his swords down on us. I raised the stave, which I'd been quietly let simmer until it was ready to leap from my hands for all the energy it had reined in.

And Teget, the stubborn mule, brought the ax up alongside me.

Our weapons met with the swords in a thunderclap that sent a hurricane throughout the lobby. A visible shockwave undulated out from us, battering the walls and ceiling, shattering the rest of the lights, cracking pillars, rippling tile like it was crusted sand.

I dragged Crux through the windstorm with one arm, using the other to fend off the swirling needles of dust and broken tile. A terrible groan echoed overhead, and I made the mistake of glancing back to make sure Crux wasn't coming after us.

He wasn't, because the lobby ceiling was collapsing.

Huge swathes of tile rained down, joined by supports and whatever else was in the crawlspace, like big, snaking HVAC ducts. Crux disappeared in the shower of debris.

I banged open the door to the stairwell as the cloud rushed in around us.

The roar of the collapse continued, until the ongoing rumble of the earthquake took its places. Teget grimaced as we took the steps as quickly as we could manage. "Give me but a few minutes with the ax and I will be rightly healed, brother."

"Maybe I'll find you a comfy couch and a six-pack while I'm at it," I murmured. "We're not out of this mess yet."

If anything, we'd traded one mess for another.

The thick metal doors to the Historic Vault on Tower Three's basement were cracked open, having rolled along their tracks set in the floor. Archie Lark was in the middle of moving the clerk's desk toward the stairwell door when he saw us stumble into the vestibule. "By George! I thought you blokes had bought the proverbial farm."

"Hate to disappoint, Archie, but I'm too stubborn." I helped Teget into a chair. "Check the desk. Should be a First-Aid kit the bottom drawer. Procyon protocol."

Archie had it out and was tending to Teget's wound before I could explain what I wanted done. Even though the guy was determined to convince his daughter she should leave the only life she'd known for a long time, I couldn't deny his skill.

Loredana, Liz, and Wilhelmina were busy rearranging boxes inside the vault. And there were rows upon rows of them, all shapes and sizes. They were taking the newer plastic and glass containers and shoving them into place by the older and rattier boxes at the back. The musty paper smell was stronger than ever.

"Mercury! You're okay!" Liz aimed a handheld device at me. Or maybe past me, because she frowned over its screen and added, "The spikes are continuing their increase. If this keeps up the towers won't last much longer."

"I am well aware of the seismic threat, Elizabeth, thank you." Loredana rammed a glass box onto an upper shelf. She brushed a smudge from her cheek. "We're nearly done. Wilhelmina, if you'd be so kind—"

"Smooth your skirts out, missy." Wilhelmina put her shoulder against a cart laden with a half dozen bankers' boxes, each one bulging with paper. "Have to say, I'm envious you kids get to play around with your electronic records. I remember how many floppy drives it took to store our data back in the day."

I gently pushed Liz's device from my face, which is when I recognized it as the modified tachyon tracker. Handy. "What's our status?"

"I believe that is my line." Loredana smirked. "The vault is nearly ready for transfer. But here. I want you to take personal charge of this."

She handed me the shard of the Hedron.

Slippery thing didn't want to remain in my grip. It pressed against my hand, until I transferred it into one of the suit's pockets and sealed it tight. Even then, it did its best to wriggle free, which was more than disconcerting. "If you're waiting for someone to come get the files, I think the armored sides of the building are going to be a problem."

"It is far from a problem." Loredana uncovered a fuse box panel just inside the door. Except there was a computer screen and keypad underneath, instead of, well, fuses.

A fresh round of tremors shook us as she tried to type commands. Liz caught Wilhelmina before she could topple. I heard a crash and a sharp, "Bollocks!" from the vestibule. I held to a shelf I hoped was anchored and steadied Loredana with the other arm, so she could enter whatever code she had in mind.

The opposite wall of the vault, lined only with shelves that were now empty, detached from its moorings and trundled twenty feet away. A gaping rectangular hole dropped probably another thirty feet onto—tracks? Like a subway?

"Step clear of the vault." Loredana directed us out, our motley crew clinging to each other as the walls shuddered all around us.

The back of the vault broke free and rolled along concealed tracks to that newly opened hole, then started its descent. I heard the squeal of metal on metal—train wheels. Sounded the same as San Camillo's trolley system. Before I could ask where Procyon had got its hand on a subterranean tramway, the ceiling opened up, and black and silver crate after black and silver crate dropped into the gap.

"Sensitive projects from the lab," Loredana explained. "Rerouted here via the 'dumbwaiter,' as Elizabeth calls it."

"Let me guess—Procyon's had that longer than it's had Wi-Fi."

Loredana smiled. "A tad."

"Where does this all go?"

"An undisclosed secure location, which is hopefully undamaged by the tremors."

I fell to my knees, catching her in the process, as the latest seismic wave hit. "I think we're way beyond 'tremors,'

Loredana. I take it this is our way out, too."

"Indeed. Assuming the rail has remained undamaged."

"Only one way to find out."

The thirty-foot drop led down a dingy tunnel lined with concrete, though I could make out brick beneath where the newer covering had chipped away. The only illumination was from a few scattered bulbs, flicking yellow behind wire mesh.

I helped Wilhelmina onto the railway car, nothing more than a flatbed with raised sides. The vault boxes and extra containers from the lab fit snugly. Liz went next, squeaking, her eyes pinched shut, as she clambered down the same ladder inset into the wall.

I went back up for Loredana. Archie assisted Teget, one arm slung over the other's shoulder. "This poor lad's taken a beating," Archie said. "I've patched him as best as I can manage, given the circumstances."

"Looks good to me."

Teget insisted on taking the ladder on his own. "I am neither invalid nor elderly."

As soon as he was down, I turned to Loredana. The quake was at its peak, sending constant streams of dust from all corners of the vault. I could hear rocks cracking below. "All aboard."

"I am sorry about how things have turned out." She kissed me.

"Tell you what. When this is done, Carlito's. I'll listen, and you let me know your final decision." I glanced at Archie. "Yours, not his."

"Agreed."

She was halfway down the ladder when Wilhelmina's shout sent a spike of adrenaline through my body. "Mercury!

We got company!"

I leapt down the hole, landing in a crouch atop the vault's contents.

It wasn't any old company. Arkwright walked toward us, dead center of the tracks, the Hedron hovering over his left shoulder, the tunnel squirming under its gravitational pressures.

Arkwright issued no challenge, no warning. He merely took the Hedron between his fingers and the whole world collapsed.

Archie shouted as a tremendous roar rushed down through the hole. Loredana called his name, and she started back up the ladder.

"It's coming down!" Liz shouted. "The whole building!"

I jumped halfway up the ladder and grabbed Loredana by the waist. "My turn to apologize."

I threw her down to the train car.

Teget leapt beside me, and I had enough time to glimpse Loredana's astonished and pained expression as the car hurtled away—north, the opposite direction from Arkwright.

Archie was pinned under a collapsed shelving unit. He shouldered against the bent shelves, swearing, his face red as his hair had been in his youth. Didn't seem as if his legs were badly damaged, since they were kicking and straining.

The ceiling was cracked. A support beam broke through, crashing to the floor. The lights stuttered and died, and the orange emergency beacons a second after they activated.

"Get clear, lad!" Archie bellowed. "You have to get Lori and the others to safety!"

"Already done, so shut up and hold still unless you want to become an amputee!" The pulsar stave blazed in the pitch black, its brilliance more comforting than it had ever been.

I slashed at the heavy shelving unit, cutting pieces free, mindful not to put the energy blade through Archie.

Teget used the ax as a lever, heaving a portion of the shelving that I'd cut off out of the way. Archie scurried out.

The room shook so violently none of us could walk. We crawled toward the tunnel.

The roar overhead intensified, drowning out all other sounds. Some would say it sounded like the end of the world. I'd already seen that—astral fiends flooding Earth through an open portal. This was worse. It overwhelmed my senses. Teget's and Archie's words were lost. Crawl. Just a bit farther …

I dragged them through the opening.

My body bounced off the sides like a careening pinball. Darkness engulfed me.

I blacked out before I hit the ground.

Falling forever.

CHAPTER THIRTY-FOUR

I walked on a beach. White sands, white cliffs, emerald grass rippling along the top. The sky was cobalt, the sun a golden disc, the few clouds white cotton.

Loredana held my hand. She kicked sand with bare toes. "Isn't it lovely?"

"Yeah. I always thought England was rain. And pubs."

She laughed. "I'd be delighted to find you a pub, though there's no rain in the forecast."

Forecast.

Another woman walked toward us—lithe, with chestnut hair, chocolate eyes, wearing a black dress that the summer breeze whipped around her legs. Marigold Yen.

Her appearance didn't surprise me. I didn't have the pulsar stave.

She did.

She wielded the stave, the ax, and the night's blade, in their configuration as the only weapon that could breach the barrier between the Earth and the Interstice permanently. Astral fiends broke from the sand behind her, an unending army whose ranks were bolstered by the corpse-fiends shambling out of the water. Syndax soldiers rappelled down the white cliffs.

Marigold's eyes glowed purple. Her voice was not her own. "Mercury Hale. Your failure's been a blessing to us," *the Whisperer said through her mouth.* "I am so glad you're here, for the end of it all."

Instead of being terrified, screaming in horror, I kissed Loredana, and beckoned with both arms. Ramos was at my right hand, his crucifix glimmering against his chest where his shirt buttons were undone. Teget rose from the sand to my left, and Dominic, too. Airfoil burst from behind a cloud.

"It isn't over," I said. "I won't let it be over. I'll die first."

"Which is too bad." *Marigold-Whisperer's form distorted, expanded, grew into the monster frame of Arkwright.* "Because I'd rather you realized you were always on the wrong side."

And then I saw me, Mercury Hale, with pale, black-veined skin and violet eyes, take the weapon.

A slap brought me into real life.

Which sucked, because real life hurt a lot.

Catalog: searing pain in the left shoulder; throbbing jaw; hot liquid—probably blood—on the face, aching head; bruises all over. More blood from more cuts. But, hey, not crushed to death! Which, at that moment, I kinda wished I had been.

"Good, you're awake." Arkwright chuckled. "And yes, I did smack you to make sure. I wouldn't have you miss out on the spectacle."

Great. Him. And to top it off, it was raining. I tried opening my eyes, which resulted in a big bright blur.

Arkwright must have been the silhouette smeared with colors right in front. The drizzle washed the blood from my vision, which I appreciated, because my hands were bound behind my back.

"Mercury." Teget's voice was slurred, either because my head was still a mess, or he was. I turned my head right. He looked the latter. Bruises, blood, clothes ripped.

Huh. My suit was more intact than I'd anticipated.

"We're okay for now," I murmured. "Stay with me."

"Twit." That was Archie. He was on my left. Which made two things happen at the same time—relief flooded every inch of my body, and I rolled my eyes. "Okay, you say. This is a sight less than 'okay,' Hale."

"Relax. I've been a prisoner before." And we had a bit of an advantage. There was a mix of Syndax soldiers and Kutsatuta mercenaries guarding us, but they weren't paying us much attention. Their gazes were fixed on Arkwright, who was walking to the end of the pier outside Procyon, his form reverted to that of a confident, cocky business executive.

Which meant the three of us were lined up on the public walkway. It would provide a stunning view of the bay, the boats, the rising waves.

They were rising *way* up. Like, approaching, tidal wave heights.

"Okay, he says," Archie muttered. "God help us all."

I looked up.

The waters of San Camillo bay were pooling a thousand feet above us, at the end of a column hundreds of feet wide being drawn from what should have been a calm surface, not a churning, inverted whirlpool. The pool in the air had to be hundreds of yards across, already bigger than the entire Procyon property—heck, the entire half dozen blocks around—and was rapidly spreading, like someone was pouring the bay out but in reverse.

And it was raining. Which meant whatever was holding it aloft had … leaks.

My heart hammered. If all that water fell, everything would be crushed.

"You see? I wasn't exaggerating the power of the Hedron of Orbits." Arkwright's voice boomed. He'd stopped in the middle of the pier and faced us. He let go of the Hedron, which didn't affect the bay's siphoning. Arkwright drew the pulsar stave with one hand and Teget's ax with the other. "This is how my world ended. How it went off the rails from the same path yours was on—a catastrophic asteroid impact, resulting in tsunamis than wrecked the Pacific Coast. Millions dead. Millions more dispossessed, then abandoned by their government. I dug you out of the grave because you needed to see, to understand, that if I couldn't bring light into the darkness of my world, I'd turn your world into *mine.*"

He wasn't kidding. The Syndax guards grabbed me by the shoulders and forced me to turn. There were Loredana, Liz, Wilhelmina, and Ramos, lined up about fifty feet behind us. Corpse-fiends formed a wall around them, blocking their escape to the SCPD and Homeland Security. I spotted Bowe, glaring as usual, rifle ready but no idea how to use it. Garvey was there, two, with a couple dozen of the Procyon security forces who'd managed to get back to headquarters.

Except, there was no headquarters.

Procyon's three ivory towers were gone. A trio of stumps stood in their place—piles of rubble, that was all, with crumpled skeletons of twisted steel protruding from their corpses. Astral fiends crawled over the broken concrete, slithering out of crevasses and appearing from rips that sprouted around the property. They were keeping the gathered law enforcement from taking action, or from leaving.

The airborne pond approached lake size. And I was out of ideas.

Arkwright had our weapons. Had our friends. What was I gonna do to stop them? I cursed under my breath. Loredana's sending Dominic on some stupid errand was looking, well, stupider by the second.

"This is how it will end," Arkwright said. "And I can't think of a better beginning. Once I scour San Camillo from the coast, the rest of the world will see what the Hedron is capable of. They'll know the Interstice has come. All the lies they've been fed will shrivel in the light of the truth—that the Interstice is going to flood Earth. Those who die in the deluge will be the lucky ones. Everyone else will be enslaved or become food for the astral fiends."

"You're out of your mind," I snapped. "And I'm tired of your posturing. All this 'I'm ending the world' nonsense. Hiding behind your floating toy. You want a fight? Put it down and cut me loose. I'll fight you."

"With the precious pulsar stave, you mean. Not a chance." Arkwright chuckled. "I'm not an idiot, Mercury. I know what you value most. Family."

Kutsatuta approached from our right. Teget sucked in a breath.

They had Crux.

The men threw him onto the pavement, right in front of us. He moaned, unable to rise. As badly as his right leg was twisted, I was surprised when he got onto a knee without assistance.

"This man here, he was my hope. I needed a second, a lieutenant I could trust." Arkwright swung the stave idly, even as he held the ax firm in the other hand. "Ask any of my employees—the former ones of Syndax Multinational, of course, not these brothers who are one with me through the power of the Interstice. I expect excellence. Crux, as it turned out, was never anything but a nuisance."

He pinned Crux to the ground with the ax's blades. Crux gasped as they cut into his chest.

Teget tried to get onto his feet. A Syndax rifle stock crumpled him in place.

"What did you expect, Crux? That'd trust you with everything? That you'd stand beside me while everyone perished and that would somehow redeem you?" Arkwright shook his head and sighed. "You betrayed your family. True, they'd cast you out, but instead of crawling back for their forgiveness, you took the devastating knowledge they'd given and turned it against them."

He bent low. "I never needed you to lead with me. Because I always had that spot reserved for her."

Serena Cyr walked out of the midst of the corpse-fiends, unharmed.

They let her pass as easily as if she were one of them, without so much as a scratch. She smiled that easygoing, bold smile that had brought me into her confidence. Bowe looked like he was going to faint.

"You're kidding." I sneered at Serena. "All that talk about how you hated Arkwright? What, that was an act? Gemini was right—you're from Arkwright's world."

"Wrong again, Mercury." She traced a finger along my jaw. "His Earth did send Serena Cyr to replace me. Arkwright killed her before she could do it."

"Serena's always been a close friend. We never let family know, of course, because her parents always found me arrogant." Arkwright shrugged. "Go figure."

Serena wrapped her arm around his waist and rewarded him with a passionate kiss. "Now, thanks to you and your Procyon colleagues, we have all your secrets. They'll be disseminated to the world when San Camillo is crushed. How do you think people will react, when they learn your organization has hidden a terrible threat all these years? What do you think the other governments will do? It'll be chaos and riot and war. Which will make our conquest so much easier, in my opinion."

"And that, Crux, is why your services are no longer needed." Arkwright pressed down on the ax. "At least, not after this."

"No! Please!" Crux choked. "I turned my back on everything to serve you! I gave you the Hedron of Orbits! These are my kin, as the perfect sacrifice for you!"

"For which I'm grateful. But, seriously, Crux, you should have known if I could never trust Mercury and Teget, I couldn't very well trust anyone related to him. Take solace knowing you'll do some good for me, one last time."

He thrust down with the ax.

I cried out, wordless, anguished, not sure what I was so upset about. Maybe it was the way Crux pleaded for his life, recognizing the evil he'd done. Maybe it was watching yet another member of my family—no matter how lost—die.

Crux sagged, his head lolling back, eyes sad, unseeing hazel. Purple sparks surged from his body. The ax absorbed them. They spiraled into Arkwright, swirling into the stave and back again, until he let out a triumphant cry.

I strained against the guards, but I couldn't break free.

Not without the pulsar stave. No matter how hard I pushed.

Something jabbed my side.

The shard from the Hedron. It was still in my pocket.

Use it.

Use—what? The shard?

Destroy your bindings. Fight. End Arkwright.

That was the Hedron's iron tones again. I could feel the shard moving, its sharp end cutting its way out of my pocket. It traveled around my back, under the suit, until it was by my bound hands. The shard slowly poked through a seam in the suit. I touched icy cold metal with my fingers.

It was insane. If the Hedron thought I was going to be grateful, it had another thing coming.

Arkwright waved at Crux's body. A couple Kutsatuta rolled it into the bay, where it joined the current streaming toward the column in the sky. The water level was way under low tide, exposing the mucky bottom of the bay. Rotted shipwrecks poked up from the mud. Fish flopped around, bodies making tiny wet slaps.

Even though Crux had spent the entire time I'd known of his existence plotting and trying to kill me, I was sick with the knowledge he'd been discarded by the man he'd admired as casually as I'd throw a Katsaros Deli sandwich wrapper into a trash can.

"This one." Arkwright considered Archie Lark. "This one was not who I requested. But the similarities are uncanny. Loredana Lark is your daughter, I take it? Good. You'll do, once you join the ranks of the living Interstice."

He indicated the horde of corpse-fiends.

"You'll not touch him." Loredana could have been a schoolteacher admonishing a naughty child who'd been caught tossing ice chunks in the middle of a snowball fight.

"So help me, I will kill you myself."

"Any other time, I'd take that threat seriously. Given the numerical advantage—and the fact that you're fourth in line after I obliterate these three—I'll take it under advisement." Arkwright used the ax to lift Archie's chin. A wisp of smoke drifted up from where the blade, still shimmering with its pent-up power, scorched Archie's chin. "I bet you wish you'd stayed at home."

A lightning bolt hit the inside of my head, igniting a part of my brain I'd apparently been too stupid to use up to this point. Stayed at home …

Archie spat in his face.

Arkwright smirked. He wiped the spit from his cheek.

"Hey! Don't." I scooted on my knees. That earned me a hit from one of the gun-toting goons, a nice sharp blow to the kidneys. "Urgh. Thanks, I didn't need that organ. Look, Arkwright—all this mess, it's a waste of your time and energy."

"Oh? You'd interfere again? After ruining my chance at taking the night's blade and returning to the dimension from which I came? Look how that turned out."

"We all make mistakes. You more than others. But it isn't too late." I struggled upright, lurching onto my feet. I felt the guards adjust their stand behind me. Arkwright waved them off. "I can get you home."

Loredana snapped, "Mercury! Do not—"

"Shut up." I didn't dare look at her. That was gonna cost me later. No time for her to interrupt, though. "Seriously, Arkwright. You've gone about this the wrong way. I have, too. We never should have been fighting, not when I know the way back for you."

Arkwright seemed puzzled. "You're—offering to take me

home? To my Earth?"

"Sure. Why not? We all get what we want. This Earth stays intact. You go back to your buddies. And if there's to be another attempt at opening the Interstice, well, we can cross that proverbial bridge when we come to it."

"Careful." Serena was at his side. She had her pistol trained on my face. Even with the leftover energies from the pulsar stave trickling from the suit into my skin, I doubted I could dodge a bullet at that close range, especially if I couldn't break free of my captors' grip. "We've come too far."

"Hold on." Arkwright grabbed the front of my shirt. "How? The portal in Cavill Cemetery … It didn't lead where I needed, not without modification."

"That's because you've got the wrong one." He'd moved me just right. I stood in front of Teget, his face at eye level with my hands.

Which were using the Hedron shard to cut through my bonds.

Hurry. You can change the outcome. Stop him. Free me.

Free you is right, Hedron, so I could lock your creepy self right back up in the temple's Atrium. "Gemini. The guy who helped in Procyon's fight. The one who partnered with me, so I could chase you."

Arkwright's eyes widened. "The man in the breach."

"Bingo." I grinned. "What do you say? Let's give it a try. Loredana can give him a call."

"Bring Lark over here," he snapped.

"Wait." Serena touched Arkwright's arm. "The risk is too great."

"I understand, but—I can't stay here forever. Not like this." Arkwright kissed her cheek. "It's worth attempting.

And if it fails, we can still crush this world."

Loredana's temper had cooled, which was actually worse, because if she could have, I'm sure she would have frozen me in a block of ice the second they brought her up in front of us. A Kutsatuta warrior produced her cell phone. She swiped it open and tapped a single key.

"That's it?" I asked.

"Indeed. Gemini should arrive shortly." Her mouth was pressed shut, but her eyes—seemed like she was begging for an answer.

Really hoped I had one.

The tell-tale flash and swirl of Dominic's exit portal pushed everyone nearer the walkway. He was materializing between our people and the corpse-fiends. I could see SCPD officers adjusting their stand beyond that, hunkered beside squad cars.

Ramos caught my eye. He shrugged.

I shook my head. *Wait a sec.*

Dominic stepped free of the portal. It remained a large, pulsing sphere—and grew, slowly, expanding to twice or three times its normal size. He took one look at the situation and did exactly what I'd hoped he would.

He blasted a cluster of Syndax soldiers with the Echo Watches.

I pulled my bindings apart. They cut into my wrists, sure, but they'd been weakened enough by the shard I snapped free. I lunged for the pulsar stave.

Serena's gun went off.

But she was already falling, because Teget had launched himself at her feet.

I grappled with Arkwright. Guy was strong as three of me, but I got my hands on the stave and yanked half of it free.

Flashes from the Echo Watches lit up the air, sending Syndax and Kutsatuta warriors alike onto the pavement. Archie Lark pulled his legs through his arms and put a Syndax soldier into a chokehold until the guy sputtered his last breath. Loredana did the same maneuver, leaving her hands in front—so she could pick up Serena's gun, which came spinning across the asphalt, courtesy of Teget's kick.

"All units, engage!" Ramos cried out.

The explosion of gunfire shattered the relative silence. Astral fiends shrieked as they descended into the midst of their corpse-fiend buddies, the hideous army turning on the gathered law enforcement forces.

I activated my half of the stave and swung, cutting off Arkwright's arm.

He bellowed, an awful, reverberating noise. I stomped on the severed limb and pulled the other part of the stave free, so they could be rejoined, then struck hard.

He blocked it with the ax, holding us in stalemate. His eyes blazed violet. Tentacles sprouted from his ruined elbow, and his mouth sprouted fangs. "Betrayal everywhere!"

"I learned from the best," I snapped.

That's when about forty guys poured out of Dominic's portal and things got *really* insane.

CHAPTER THIRTY-FIVE

They were soldiers, every last one clad in an unfamiliar assortment of camouflage. Mottled gray and tan? Like an ugly version of urban camo. Their guns were weird, too, like someone dropped an AK-47 and an M-16 into Photoshop in the world's sloppiest mashup.

But they had American flags on their shoulders, so, bonus.

"Fan out! Suppressive fire!" The young black man in charge led the platoons toward the corpse-fiends, shredding their ranks. "Watch the squids on the left flank!"

Eight men reoriented, shooting into the astral fiends as they slithered down the rubble pile that had been Procyon headquarters. The portal dissipated, leaving them ensconced in our battle.

I remembered Arkwright in time to stop the ax inches from my face. Heat singed my eyebrows.

"I don't believe this," he snarled. "You bring the Home Guard down on me? Is that your idea of a joke? Never mind—at least I know you're telling the truth. Once I kill you, I can get back to my Earth without your help."

"Let's skip to the part where we beat you down and revisit that question then." I planted a foot on his chest and backflipped off, sending him tumbling along the pier. I landed in a crouch, brandishing the pulsar stave.

He raked clawed hands along the pier, ripping the planks to splinters. Tentacles stabbed deep between the wood, anchoring him, and then launched Arkwright with the force of a cannonball.

I dodged, but, too slow. His swipe with the ax slid along the stave, throwing off a shower of sparks, and threw me back onto the pavement. I wound up at Loredana's feet.

"Stay down, please." She emptied an entire magazine of bullets at Arkwright, striking him center mass with most of the shots.

"No problem." I rolled aside, brought the stave up, ready to blast away—

Arkwright slammed the ax into the parking lot. The shockwave knocked us over. Thankfully, Loredana's legs weren't bound.

Where was Dominic? He was firing the Echo Watch among the corpse-fiends, taking out a couple with each shot. The way he spun through them was impressive. I wanted to ask him what else he had in mind, but when a pair of astral fiends hurtled toward him, he vanished into a new portal.

Arkwright kicked me aside and caught Teget by the throat as my brother came after him—wielding the Hedron's shard. Teget must have used it to cut himself free, because his slashed bindings dangled from his wrist. Arkwright poised the ax over Loredana's face. "Best to keep you two near while I kill your favorite woman."

A soldier appeared next to her. "Release your prisoner and relinquish the weapon, please."

She—what?

"Impossible." Arkwright's arm sagged.

The soldier removed her helmet and visor. The hair was cut shorter, and secured tightly in a bun, and the face was missing most of its signature makeup, but there was no mistaking the rest—the freckles, the nose, the gleaming green eyes.

I was staring at Loredana Lark—who was holding a rifle at Arkwright, while she protected Loredana Lark.

That was the opening Teget needed to swing his legs up, wrap them around Arkwright's neck, and flip him over onto his back with a brutal *crunch*.

And he swiped the ax from Arkwright's grip in the process.

Arkwright roared, an inhuman sound that gave even the astral fiends pause. He leapt into the air, hovering, as purple lightning shot from his hands and legs and—wait. Where was he channeling that from?

Oh. A blinding stream of light connected him to the Hedron, which he must have left on autopilot, because the water showed no signs of slowing its rush into the sky.

Teget helped me to my feet. "This is our moment, Mercury. Together, we avenge Grandfather."

"Ramos said vengeance isn't ours to deal out." I rolled a crick out of my neck. "But I'll give it a try anyway."

"If you gentlemen are quite ready to continue, I shall return to the ranks of the Home Guard." Soldier Loredana nodded at our Loredana and trotted into the battlefield strewn across the parking lot.

I jerked a thumb. "You gonna comment on—whoever that was?"

Loredana smirked. "When there's a better moment."

Archie Lark hunkered behind a concrete barrier at the edge of the lot. Ramos was with him, Liz shielded by their bodies as she worked the portal gun. "Get down there and stop him!" Ramos shouted. "We can hold out here as long as that army can keep up their fire!"

"Yeah, working on it!" I gestured upward. "Might want to dial up your buddies at the National Guard!"

Ramos waved his phone at me, then stuffed it into his shirt pocket as he and Archie fired into the mass of corpse-fiends. They were putting them down pretty well, as were the cops and Homeland agents clustered around their vehicles. And Wilhelmina? She leaped up the back of an astral fiend, slicing its back open with the Medan dagger. Liz let loose a brilliant beam from the portal gun, which let Wilhelmina force the fiend back into the Interstice.

We were holding our own. But I knew cops were dying. Some uniformed officers rose as tattered, burnt versions of their alive selves, ready to join the shambling corpse-fiends.

"All right, Arkwright." I strode down the dock toward our main baddie, who hovered six feet up. "Let's you and me dance."

"Let us all put your terror to an end," Teget said.

Arkwright sneered. His body had completed its metamorphosis to its monstrous form, complete with the glistening black scales that tore through his clothing. "You're too late. The Hedron can't be stopped. And I don't need your pathetic weapons to fight you anymore."

He dove at us, and our trio collided in a clamor of metal versus—whatever his scales and claws were made up. It felt like we were going toe to toe with the entire Interstice compressed into one body. Each of his blows drove us to our knees, or pressed us to the edge of the pier, while our slashes didn't do much more than leave jagged scratches in his armor.

Swirling wind caught my attention. Dominic was back, emerging from his portal at a run, and headed right for us.

"Good!" Arkwright snarled. "More of you to kill! I'll remove his limbs one by one and use his devices to get to my world while yours is crushed beneath—"

A white blur streaked out of the portal, right before it closed. It hit Arkwright broadside, severing the connection he'd established with the Hedron.

Arkwright tumbled end over end, never hitting the ground. He finally stabilized next to the Hedron. Tentacles lashed the air.

Airfoil settled to the ground in front of us.

Dominic trotted up beside me, panting, and still leaning on his injured side. "Sorry about the delay. I had several errands to run."

"No kidding." I gawked. "How did you get him to show up?"

"I appealed to good Christian decency and the love for one's neighbor." Dominic smiled.

I blinked.

"Also, unlike you, Mercury, this guy isn't unbearable." If Airfoil was smiling, I couldn't tell. "So, where can I be of the most help? Or maybe, where can I do the most damage?"

I eyeballed Arkwright. He was advancing on us again. But there was a tremendous battle behind us, so ... "I haven't seen one word on the Internet about you using your powers to kill a person, even in self-defense."

"I did. Once. Never again, if I can help it."

"Then channel some of that aggression towards the things that aren't people." I pointed.

Airfoil pivoted in midair and zipped across the sky toward the astral fiends and the corpse-fiends. I wondered if Teget and I should provide him back-up. We were, after all, the only chumps besides Wilhelmina who could use superhuman abilities against the monsters.

But he swooped toward the nearest astral fiend, a thirty-foot beast that lashed skyward with spike-studded tentacles. Airfoil wove between them, right hand outstretched.

The fiend let out a pitiful wail. It crumpled in on itself, like someone was wadding up a scrap of paper, until it was a viscous mass of hide and blue-black ooze a couple feet across. Then, with an audible, squishy *pop*, it imploded.

"Impressive," Teget murmured.

Even more impressive when he thinned their ranks even further, allowing the SCPD to corral and cut down the remaining astral fiends. Airfoil spun after a herd of corpse-fiends that were drawn to Ramos' and Archie's position by their gunfire. Archie was dropping one after the other with shots to the head; Ramos, too, but with more misses. They were still outnumbered twenty to one.

Airfoil made a quick pass that mashed the undead into black smears on the pavement, with crushed bone protruding.

"Wow," Dominic said.

I was, uncharacteristically, mute. Arkwright was my target.

He came back for Teget and me on a rampage, tearing chunks of the pier for missiles. I leapt over one, launched myself off a second, and brought the stave down on his big ugly mutated face.

His neck snapped around, at an angle I was pretty sure should have killed him, but he wrenched it to the front without the slightest indication I'd done any damage. Claws raked the pulsar stave, pressing me toward the pier.

Teget slashed at him with the ax, landing strikes on the armored scales that had sprouted across his body. Arkwright put up with the abuse for a while, until he backhanded Teget, flipping him into the water.

Check that. Into the bay, which had barely a lake remaining. Teget hit the mud below and slid against a sunken sailboat.

A shout carried through the tumult of the battle. Ramos. He was pointing at San Camillo's skyline.

At first, I thought he wanted me to see Airfoil, who was turning astral fiends into mush and landing punishing attacks against the corpse-fiends. Nope. Black specks on the horizon grew bigger. A rumble trailed them.

Jets. As in, jet fighters.

I beat Arkwright back with a frenzied flurry of blows I hoped would be enough to keep him occupied. If the National Guard could land a cluster bomb on his chest, I hoped that would be enough to take him out.

The specks became miniature images of F-16s. The pair banked to the north, angling for the shoreline.

"Have fun with them!" I vaulted over Arkwright, his claws dragging along my boots but failing to draw blood. I landed ankle deep in muck. Man. That was a smell I could have done without.

The fighters raced toward us. I could make out individual missiles dangling from their wings.

Insignificant.

The Hedron broke apart. A third of it shot into the air, beneath the sprawling canopy of water covering San Camillo. The fighters skirted the underbelly, too, right on target.

Until they came apart.

No explosion. Large chunks broke off, then clouds of smaller bits, and finally a spray of glittering particles. One second, two heavily armed warbirds were headed our way with bombs to obliterate the enemy. The next, two streaks littered the sky, until the breeze scattered their elements.

The rain washed the particles out of the air.

Dominic wasn't waiting for the tide to change in our favor again. He advanced on Arkwright, firing bursts from the Echo Watches. When Arkwright charged him, he vanished into a portal—and reappeared five seconds and six feet behind him.

"Come on!" I hurtled onto the pier, Teget trailing me, and we caught Arkwright in a three-way assault. Our weapons battered him, forcing him to his knees. He slowed his retaliation until he was teetering, gasping for breath.

"It's over, Arkwright." I held the stave above his head. I was ready to take it off at the neck, and with every face I saw—everyone who'd died—I itched to get it done.

"Home." Arkwright coughed a viscous slime. "You said you could send me there."

"You seek banishment?" Teget growled. "Death should be your only escape."

"He isn't just a monster." Dominic had the Watches trained on Arkwright, forming the third point of our triangle around him. "This is a man corrupted by his own evil desires."

"And a bunch of awful outside sources," I muttered. "He'd be better off in the Interstice."

"No! Don't send me there." Arkwright's hideous expression carried something I'd never seen before—anguish? He grabbed my suit, not to attack, but—beg. He was pleading. He was terrified. "The Whisperer. Marigold.

They'd kill me. I'd be subsumed by them and not remain … me."

I glanced at Teget. He was seething, shoulders rising and falling with his heavy breath, but he wasn't killing, so that was good. Dominic? He waited. For what?

For me. They were waiting for me to make a decision.

Airfoil alighted. "Those—things are all dead. The police have the enemy combatants handled, too, though it's getting tricky to figure out who's on whose side and from where. And this is the guy behind it all?"

I nodded. "Our prisoner."

"Let me end this." Arkwright bowed his head. "She's gone. Left me. What does it matter what I do now? Give me a way home."

She? Yeah, he was right. There was no sign of Serena. Not among the straggling Kutsatuta and Syndax soldiers who weren't already dead.

But I was more worried about that third of Hedron that was descending into the rest of the artifact.

"You surrender, I'll see what I can do."

Arkwright looked up. His face reverted, slowly, to its human features. "Yes. I can."

The air crinkled around us. Airfoil? What was he using his powers for?"

But he was frozen in place. So was Dominic, and Teget. They strained against an invisible wall. I was stuck, too, mired in … nothing.

And that nothing was crushing Arkwright where he knelt.

He screamed, his voice warped as his larynx crumbled. His body contorted, limbs, mangled, until it came apart in a spray of endless particles.

A blast of purple energy exploded from his sides,

obliterating the ghastly remains. One stream struck the Hedron, causing it to accelerate into a spin, the air throbbing. The other hit Teget, flinging him toward the tower wreckage.

"No!" I shouted.

Ramos was up and running in that direction, before I could think about asking for help.

"Mercury?" Airfoil managed a shaky step forward. "What did you do?"

"Me? You executed him!" But I knew it was a stupid response even as I said it.

He was weak. He failed me, like biological forms always do. It is time to carry out his goals. I will complete them. Then I will have the power. Maintain it. Wield it. Shape worlds. Bring the Interstice here, so I will spread power and remove all biologicals of inconsequence.

It killed him. Like it destroyed the fighters.

The Hedron of Orbits floated toward us, and we were stuck inside its shell of—whatever was holding us in place. How fast would it kill us? What would it feel like to have my body torn apart, molecule by molecule?

We were helpless.

Unless ...

The stave was a hunk of metal. Dead. Airfoil flexed his fingers, but nothing seemed to happen. Domini's Echo Watches maintained their glow.

"Turn him," I grunted.

Whether or not Airfoil understood me, I couldn't tell. He couldn't move his head, and his return grunt was vague. I heard soles scrape wood. Dominic's arms raised, but he looked befuddled, like he lacked control over them.

You three biologicals contain great power. I will consume it from your sources, then from your bodies, then—

Dominic blasted the Hedron.

We stumbled free, the pressure around us released. The Hedron was intact, sadly, but we weren't stuck. And better yet, the pulsar stave hummed to life again.

"Works better if you shut up," I sneered.

The Hedron had no snappy comeback, but it didn't need it.

The drizzle turned into a deluge.

CHAPTER THIRTY-SIX

We were all seriously screwed.

"Hey!" I shook Airfoil's armored shoulder. "How much can you lift?"

"He pushed a container ship through the air," Dominic said.

Airfoil shook his head. "I don't know what my limits are, unless I test them."

"I need you to counteract whatever the Hedron's doing, while we try to stop it." I gestured with the stave. "Come on, Gemini."

"Wait." Airfoil rose a few feet off the pier. "You want me to hold the water up? Off the city?"

"I want you to push back, no matter what happens." There were still hundreds of people around Procyon's ruins. They'd all die if the Hedron of Orbits let the bay fall—and that didn't count the tens of thousands more in San Camillo, because the hovering body of water stretched dozens of blocks. "Buy us all the time you can."

He nodded. "Will do. Signal if anything changes."

I glared at the Hedron. "Trust me, you'll know."

Dominic followed me down the pier, his steps wary. The air was thick with humidity. Rain pelted us. It clinked on the stave, a beautiful ringing sound that would have relaxed me if I didn't know the source of the rain was millions of tons of water hanging over my head. The downpour soaked even the supersuit. I slid the mask back. It wasn't doing any good to keep me dry, and right then, I wasn't worried about identity issues, not with Procyon's cat out of the proverbial bag.

"How do we stop it?" Dominic's arms were loose at his side, presumably so he could blast the relic.

"Not the slightest idea. But I'm betting we can try to control it."

"We?"

"Look. There's a long backstory, but Cliff's Notes version—I'm Medan. Our people can use the artifacts from the temple, because of our bloodline." I tapped one of the Echo Watches with the stave. "You were never in the temple, but there's a statue there that's missing its hands and whatever was attached to the wrists."

His eyes widened. "These came from Meda?"

"Makes as much sense as every other crazy thing. Besides, Loredana got all tight-lipped when we hit that part of the tour." I glanced behind us. Loredana was on the bayside walk, she and Archie, helping Liz and Ramos bring Teget down from the rubble. He limped but didn't look much worse for wear. Well, aside from the bruises and cuts and scrapes he'd accumulated.

Speaking of which, my body ached. As in, if I took a nap I'd probably never wake up. But I couldn't stop now. Not even take a breather so the stave could let my otherworldly body heal up.

"Mercury." Dominic gestured at the Hedron. "If you're

correct, we should be able to control the Hedron—or at the very least, give it instruction. New commands."

"I hope."

Our gang brought Teget to us. "Take it." He held out the ax, his arm trembling. "You may need its strength."

"Looks like you need it more." I touched his shoulder. "Sit this one out."

A gushing sound overwhelmed the torrential rains, like a waterfall had suddenly formed—and it had. Two blocks north, a stream twenty feet across poured straight down from the Hedron's suspended lake. It crashed through the roof of an apartment complex, bursting windows and crumbling walls. Cars flipped onto their sides.

Airfoil swept in from the east, his hands outstretched. The fountain reversed, spraying sideways in all directions. It forced him out of its path, but his powers were sufficient to end the massive leak.

I took the ax. "Don't worry. I'll get it back to you in one piece."

Teget sagged against Ramos. "See that you do."

"Hey." Ramos reached for my arm. "Be careful. *Vaya con Dios.*"

"Thanks. You guys had better clear out."

Loredana shook her head. "Absolutely not. Without team providing backup—"

"You'll all be a bunch of squishy targets." I poked Archie in the chest. "Get her and everyone else out of here."

"Understood." Archie pulled her aside. "Come along, Lori."

She shook him off. "Mercury, don't be daft."

"That's my default setting today." I kissed her like I'd never get another chance.

Once we'd parted, she frowned, but backed away with the rest of our entourage.

"Don't get hurt!" Liz hugged me about the neck. The tachyon tracker bumped the base of my skull. "The readings I've been gathering indicate there's an instability at the Hedron's core, but I don't understand why it's able to hold together so if you can find a way to disrupt it with directed tachyon bursts you might be able—"

"We'll give it a go." I gestured. "Let's go, Gemini."

"God have mercy," Dominic murmured.

The Hedron of Orbits waited patiently for us, without launching an attack like it had on the National Guard planes, or smushing our bodies like it had with Arkwright. Why should it bother lashing out? We were walking straight towards it, like a couple of idiots.

You will suffice. Take his place. Let me feed on your power and complete the task.

"Yeah, that's not the plan." I touched its surface with one hand.

The surge lit up every cell in my body. Forget flying like Airfoil or holding a lake aloft. I was already cupping San Camillo Bay in my palm. I could see for miles beyond the pier—the mucky and drained basin of the bay, the traffic clogging the city's streets as people tried to escape, National Guard soldiers and vehicles ringing the outskirts, aircraft steering clear of the great sprawling swirl of water looming over my hometown.

I could feel power working against the Hedron's—against ours. Airfoil's. It was enough to hold back the deluge, to prevent the gravitational field from collapsing.

Crush him. Exert your will.

I could do that. Easily. I gave a push. Just a nudge.

Another breach opened, letting a gusher pound down on a deserted intersection. It tore chunks of pavement.

Piece of cake.

Wait. What was I doing?

Dominic's hand joined mine. He sucked in a breath, and in that instant, my mind—touched his. My already jumbled thoughts mashed against his. The gorgeous woman from his photos—Jess. What would become of her if I died? I mean, become of Loredana. Teget. Ramos. Curt. Curt? I didn't know anyone with that name. But I did. Dominic did.

Stop. The Hedron's silent order cut off our contact. *Continue your work.*

Too late. Dominic had already mentally slapped me back onto the right path. No one else was gonna die because of this thing. Arkwright would be its last victim, and rightly so, because even though I'd extended him a way out, he'd been too far gone.

I saw the giant lake in the air. I pressed at its edges. Nothing.

Do not attempt to reverse the process. I will not allow it. You are inconsequential.

Maybe I was. But it wasn't just about me. It never should have been. Dominic stood beside me, his eyes aglow with a clean but awful silver brilliance. And Airfoil circled us, using his powers to hold back the crushing tide.

I was inconsequential. *We*, on the other hand ...

I found the barrier in my mind that kept me from Dominic. Sensed his thoughts on the other side. *Push back. Find Airfoil's mind.*

It was there, on the underside of the water. I pushed the same direction he was. Felt Dominic doing the same.

The waters moved. A couple feet at a time, slowly,

agonizingly lurching toward the bay.

No. Treachery.

A cold spike impaled my chest. I gasped, expecting twisted metal protruding from a bloody gash and broken ribs sticking out, but when I looked down, there was nothing. The Hedron came apart, releasing that third portion it had sent against the fighters. It shot up toward Airfoil.

The core! I remembered Liz's warning about a tachyon burst. This thing was vulnerable. *Dominic!*

I jammed the stave-ax combo into the center and willed it to life with every ounce of my being. Dominic thrust a free hand into the same opening, the Echo Watches both spinning to life.

Purple bolts tinged with black exploded in all directions. They angled off of us, avoiding a golden sheen around our skin—and where that had come from, I didn't have the slightest idea. But I kept pushing at the waters, urging them back into the bay. The first echoes of their thunder as they began pooling in their proper home reached my ears. The rains slackened.

Come on, I thought. *Keep moving. Don't quit.*

A grating scream cut my thoughts apart. *Relinquish!*

Not a chance.

All of a sudden, Ramos' murmured prayers in Spanish filtered into my head. Were they ones he'd said before? Could I hear them now? Didn't matter.

The beams of energy tore chunks off the pier, whipping them through the air, and picked up shattered bits of boat hull long buried in the harbor. All the detritus the Hedron could get its hands on went spinning in a cyclone that slashed through the waters pouring back down into San Camillo's harbor.

I will scour you from the Earth.

Why was this thing not dead yet? I couldn't force the pulsar stave to dump more energy into the Hedron's core. Dominic was ready to collapse at any second. Even Airfoil was in danger of being swallowed up by the rushing waters and the debris tornado.

We had nothing left at our disposal.

Hang on.

The shard.

It was in my other pocket, where I'd stashed it during the brawl, and it kept trying to find a way out of the sealed compartment. I left the stave stuck in the Hedron's core and yanked the fragment free,

A new sensation rippled over me. Fear. But I was already scared out of my brain. Dominic? Airfoil?

No. This was a primal panic. Whatever the shard represented, the Hedron didn't want it anywhere near itself. Especially not the core.

But the waters were heaped over the bay, roaring down, a titanic waterfall sending up an impenetrable spray. The entirety was almost past the harbor walkway.

Almost …

A huge, rotten board slapped Dominic from out of nowhere. He dropped into the muck below, now swirling with muddy currents.

The Hedron began to close.

Ready or not.

I jammed the shard deep into the Hedron's core, the raw energy scalding my hand, and then gave the pulsar stave one last shove.

The dying scream was gonna tear my mind apart. I could feel it. And I could see into the Interstice—the astral fiends swarming, the pipeline to the other Earth, the portal to Meda, innumerable lands and realms beyond and all the life there was—so much life!

You're not going anywhere near it, I ordered the Hedron.

It shattered like glass. Its remnants smoldered and died like sparks escaping a fire, lost in the swirl of debris.

Finally.

Gone.

Airfoil dove down, his landing more a stagger-step than a touchdown. "You did it! Where's the other one?"

"Down here!" I vaulted the side of the pier and wound up to my waist in the foul, churning muck. I tried to ignore the huge wall of water plowing down into the bay's basin, getting closer and deeper with each second.

There. Dominic's head was, mercifully, above water. He floated on its surface. I scooped him up, Airfoil and me each taking an arm.

Then the pier disintegrated. Tons of wood pilings broke apart, joining the cyclone, and came careening into us. I let go of Airfoil and kicked off him into the water as a huge beam slashed between us. He shot off, Dominic dangling in his grasp, and disappeared over the lip of the walkway.

And the beam dropped on me.

It pinned me to the slope of the shoreline, a crushing, nauseating pain that would not let up. I thought I'd pass out. Kind of wished I could. But the agony was unforgiving.

Water rushed over my head.

In an instant, I was drowning. No time to catch my breath. The pressure unrelenting. I could only see a glassy blur. Debris pelted me from all sides.

Airfoil. He was overhead, somewhere, a white flash here and there lost an instant behind the bits and pieces that were dropping from the sky.

I wasn't gonna die down there. Not after all this.

But I was, if I didn't get free.

I couldn't push it off or worm from underneath. I hacked at the beam with the ax's blades, but it was too thick. Switched to the energy-blade end of the pulsar stave. No luck.

Blackness pressed in on the sides of my sight.

One way out.

I twisted the stave-ax one last time. Its energies fizzled as my consciousness started to bleed away. Soon it'd be useless, because I'd be knocked out.

So, I cut.

The intense heat was as bad as the pain of the crushed limb. I ignored it, clawed my way through the water, wondering if I'd bleed to death or suffocate first—

My hand broke the surface. Warm, damp air.

An invisible force scooped me out of the water.

I alighted on the sodden ground, in a puddle, coughing up half the harbor. Airfoil landed next to me, crouching, a gloved hand cradling my head. "Easy. Hang on."

More voices.

"His leg ..."

"Get some pressure on it!"

" ...Partially cauterized ..."

" ...Too much blood ..."

None of it made sense. But I heard everyone talking, so they were alive. Tears warmed my eyes. My heart was happy, even if it was slowing. Probably too much.

"Hey. Hey." I reached out. Too weak. Couldn't even hold air. "Wait."

Was that for me or them? Or something else?

Fingers found mine. Loredana's face filled my view, eyes red-rimmed, hair soaked. "I'm here, Mercury. I'm here with you."

"Always?"

"Yes." Her voice broke. "Always."

"Okay. That's good." My heart felt better—and worse. And funny. Too fast, too slow. A terrible beat. The missing leg didn't matter. It was a dream. See? Pain was already gone. Then sound. Then sight.

I was that little kid again, in Carlito's pizzeria. Sobbing. My parents were gone.

Until Mom and Dad came through the door.

Huh. They hadn't left me after all. But Loredana and Ramos were outside the window, with a bunch of other people crowded in their wake, saying something. Pleading.

I found my Mom's fingers and smiled.

CHAPTER THIRTY-SEVEN

Loredana Lark

Three days after

All calls from Alvarez remain on my phone, unanswered, texts unacknowledged.

There is no other communication from Procyon. It doesn't exist. The heart has been torn from the body. No doubt there are emails flying around the ether, as the branch offices struggle to comprehend the magnitude of the disaster.

Our headquarters is demolished. The Historic Vault? Mostly intact.

Security personnel located the train at its endpoint. Several boxes were missing, no doubt in the hands of Serena Cyr.

There was no way to stop her. She was waiting for us at the end, as Procyon collapsed into the tunnel. But she must have fled during the battle, unable to take all that she wanted.

This day I remember to eat before noon. Toast and jam.

An orange. I sit on the couch, reading the newspaper. There they are—astral fiends, in broad daylight, for all the world to see. Speculation runs rampant throughout the special edition. Homeland Security says it is pursuing the threats.

Indeed.

A fist hammers on the door. "Lori? Open up."

Dad. Of course. I clear my throat. "It's unlocked." The words seem strange. Likely because I haven't spoken with anyone in days.

The door opens. Dad. The smell of coffee laced with hazelnut follows him inside. He smiles, brassy and bold as ever, but he stands off from the couch a few meters, as if there's a wall between us.

Perhaps there is.

"You shouldn't be here. Alone. It isn't right." He approached, steps wary. Does he expect an attack? Why should he? Dad fought alongside us.

Mercury saved him.

He saved all of us.

I blink back tears. I accept the coffee. "Thank you."

"Tastes much better when one doesn't have to wring it from one's sweater." He chuckles, but the sound dies quickly. He clears his throat, identical to how I did moments ago. "We need to talk."

"It seems we are."

"Don't be like that, Lori." Dad sits on the arm of the couch, near my purse.

I pull it closer.

He cranes his neck. My phone's perched next to the purse. "Been remembering?"

Yes. The wallpaper image is of Mercury, from our date at Saito on Sky. Our one and only date, really. The Procyon gala in Rampart hardly counted. Though in an instant, I'm back dancing with him, the scent of his aftershave lingering in the room when the memory fades. "Always."

"Stubborn lad," Dad grunts. "But brave. I'm not ashamed to say I misjudged him."

Of course you did. We all did.

"I have the tickets. I'm leaving tonight. Your Manager Alvarez has already cleared me to return to England—as if I need that pillock to grant me permission to travel. I do, however, understand the need for keeping certain events classified."

"Yes, I concur."

"I have two tickets."

I nod.

"Does that mean you're coming?"

I would have. Weeks ago. When Mercury pulled me from the Medan dungeon, from the torture Arkwright inflicted, and I couldn't forgive him for taking so long—so very long—to find me. I thought I would never heal. But it took time. Time, it turns out, that was in short supply. "No, it does not."

Dad sighs. "You're not making any bloody sense."

"Of course I am. My duties here are not ended. They may never be. This isn't a job, Dad, nor is it a term of service. This is a calling. This is destiny. My life is forever intertwined with Procyon. That truth extends beyond the boundaries of this dimension, as you no doubt saw for yourself."

He grimaces and sips his coffee. His expression becomes unfocused, eyes staring off into a space far away from my living room. "Yes, clearly. Tell me, that young woman who intervened …?"

"She was me. Only, not of here."

"Blimey." Dad took a longer sip of his coffee. "All the more reason to get you back home, as far away from this nonsense as possible. I won't have you hurt."

"That isn't your decision to make. I've made mine." I rise from the couch and kiss him on the forehead. "Thank you for everything, Dad."

"Well, when I took off from Heathrow, you can be sure I didn't think I'd end my time taking up arms." He snorts. "And certainly not against monsters. You've a fine team to work with, Lori. I know you won't let them down. Just as you've not let me down."

We embrace, tears warm on each other's shoulders. He smiles. "I love you, darling."

"I love you, too."

He's gone, whistling as he heads down the hall. I curl up the couch. It's half past ten. I have half an hour.

The phone goes off. This time, it's Wilhelmina. *Ramos and I are coming to get you. Don't even think about staying home, child.*

I tap the phone against my chin. I have considered it. But only in a moment of selfishness, the egocentrism everyone experiences at one time or another.

I dig into the purse and come up with a pair of sapphire earrings, one immaculate, one still bearing grime in its tiny recesses. There's also an ornament—a miniature of the blue T.A.R.D.I.S. phone booth from my favorite television program. The marker on the bottom is worn, but "Star Wars Forever" is still readable. I press it to my chest.

<Ready and waiting,> I text back.

The message app fades and Mercury's face is there again, grinning at me.

Soon. Finally.

CHAPTER THIRTY-EIGHT

Lt. Gabriel Ramos

Two weeks after

He the source, the ending He, of the things that have been ..."

The songs lift to the sanctuary ceiling. With two hundred other voices at top volume, mine's a drop in the bucket. But I belt out the tune anyway. Always do.

" ...And that future years shall see ... Evermore and evermore!"

Olivia grasps my hand. I circle an arm around her shoulders. The kids are pressed in close—Camilla and Lucina side by side, sharing a hymnal, Alejandro at my right elbow, maintaining that middle-school teen distance while glancing up every couple seconds to make sure I notice how well he's singing. Hector is at the altar, dousing the candles. He bows and makes his way down the aisle, tall and proud. He gives me a wink.

Could be Mercury doing the same.

I stay behind as everyone files out for chatter and refreshments. Sunday school in fifteen minutes. Plenty of time for this. I find the kneeler and flip it down. Pain shoots through my right leg as I descend. Not that I'm one to complain.

There's eight others praying—couples and widows, even Greg, the homeless man with the shock-white beard who never misses a service. He helped me sweep the walk this morning before the rest of the congregation arrived.

I don't know what to say. My thoughts drift to everything that's gone down. Those memories become a tidal wave. Poor imagery, too. My heart races. Palms sweat. Throat dries up. All that water …

Saint Peter speaks of being drowned to new life. Standing on San Camillo Bay, watching a second Flood threaten our city, I have to admit, I thought I'd lose hope. I was one, cold, awful doubt away from giving up.

Not him. Not Mercury.

The footsteps shuffle, trying for respectful silence, but I hear them well before the body squeezes into the pew. The wooden bench creaks under his weight. Detective Stan Bradley shifts, apparently unsure of how to respond.

"I'm surprised you haven't shown up at my door," I say.

"Captain didn't want anyone going near you." He shrugs. "Can't blame her. We took losses, L.T. Bad ones."

"I know, Stan. I was there."

"Yeah. That was the problem. Everywhere you been, this—stuff happens. And you're right in the thick, even when you're ordered to stay out of it."

"Is this a resignation request, then? Because you won't get it." I shake my head. "The things I've seen—that we've now *all* seen—convinced me a long time ago that sometimes

I was going to have to break procedure. Work around the law."

"Even outside it?"

"If it means saving lives, perhaps. That's what you never understood about Mercury. He didn't care for red tape."

Bradley snorts.

"Think what you will, but when it came down to it, he had the lives of others on his heart. He wanted to put a stop to the evil that the police and City Hall and even Homeland Security in their infinite wisdom couldn't figure a way to end. And he did."

"Yeah. It's been quiet." Bradley fumbles with his fingers. "No monster sightings. Anything that was down at the waterfront just, I don't know, evaporated. Can't even get near it now, what with Homeland cordoning it off. 'Cause they're the ones who were knee-deep in it with Procyon."

"No substantial ties to Procyon, though."

"Sure. Right. And my momma's the next Aretha Franklin. C'mon, L.T. You know Procyon had something to do with the monsters. It's all over the news!"

"From an unsubstantiated source. Odds are, that source is Serena Cyr."

"Our BOLO was a flop. No one's seen or heard anything. And whatever cooperation we were getting from Homeland fizzed. That Agent Bowe's about as helpful as a junkyard dog and half as nice."

I can't help chuckling. "As much fun as it is to talk shop, Stan, why are you bringing all this up?"

"Captain's putting me on a new task force. One in charge of keeping an eye on—the strange stuff. The stuff you keep wanting to chase after, screw the rules."

"I'm sure you'll do a fine job."

"She's putting you in charge, L.T." He's barely above a whisper, his voice so subdued I have to lean in to catch the rest. "City Hall's not happy with the way things went, especially since SCPD keeps getting bloodied and doesn't seem to have a handle on the monsters. Relying on vigilantes and the likes. Word is, the mayor leaned on the commissioner and he had the captain's head dropped into her lap."

"*Que lastima.*" That's uncharitable of me, heavy on sarcasm. She's only trying to do her job. But she won't open her eyes to the truth. She's in the dark—or in this case, refuses to see the dark, which is what I've tried to stand against. "I take it this is an order."

"Nope. Friendly request." Stan smirks. "But you'd better believe there's a couple emails for you from the mayor and the commissioner by the time you come in tomorrow."

"Nice way to let me know my suspension is over."

"Don't worry about it." He slaps my shoulder and stands. "There's a whole bunch of us that IA been grilling. You just got off the easiest because you're the only one who came off being kidnapped. I'll see you."

"Thanks, Stan." I shake his hand.

Soon as he's gone, I crack open my Bible to the Gospel of Saint John. Finding the fifteenth chapter is simple—I've dog-eared it enough the corner's in danger of tearing off.

"This is my commandment, that you love one another as I have loved you. Greater love has no one than this, that someone lay down his life for his friends."

This is what I hold dear. It is what I'm called to do. When the terrifying threatens San Camillo, I have to step up. But it's more than just a city at stake—it's the people. The lives. The loved ones. So, I can do no less than follow the example set before me, as a believer, a husband, a father, an officer of the law, a friend. It's worth risking everything.

I never would have guessed it would have been Mercury who'd reminded me.

CHAPTER THIRTY-NINE

Mercury Hale

Three weeks after

Twenty-two days.

It was that long before they let me go home. Because, you know, I had to learn to walk again.

Don't get me wrong—Doc Arne was great. Sure, he groused the entire time and made Nurse Rachet seem like a coddling grandmother, but I noticed out of the corner of my eye when he smiled the first time I made it to the end of the rail without falling.

It hurt. Badly. There were long, sleepless nights when I figured I was gonna put the pulsar stave clean through the center of my face, because I couldn't take the insane sensation my leg was cramping, or full of hot needles, or itching like ants were eating it.

Except that half wasn't there.

It was the people who made it better. Like Teget, who stayed in the building for a solid week before he went back to Meda to check up on things. Even then, he came back every few days, courtesy of Dominic's Echo Watch portals.

Teget stood in front of me on that last day, arms folded. "Faster."

"Yeah, thanks, I'm working on it." The steps were excruciating. I would have wiped sweat off my forehead, but my hands were busy making sure I didn't fall.

"Let go."

I snarled but did as demanded. I could walk, sure, but it wasn't pretty, and it wasn't fun. I stumbled.

Doc Arne hustled over.

"Nope. Hold up." I wavered, swayed, then steadied. I slowly reached down and upped the volume on my phone, which was hooked to the single bud dangling from my ear. Aerosmith, of course.

"Walk This Way." Ramos shook his head and chuckled. He was leaning against the wall, near enough he could read the title, upside down, where it was clipped to my shorts. "If nothing else, the doctor has to be impressed with your attitude."

"I think he loves my attitude." I grinned at Arne and shuffled a few more steps.

"If the patient would concentrate on recovery and progress instead of being an insufferable idiot, I'd be happier," he muttered.

"Whatever, Arne. Stay put so I can hobble over and give you a hug." Almost the end. A few more steps. It felt like a thousand.

"Move. You cannot lose your footing with an astral fiend prepared to devour your life," Teget said. "Push onward."

"Thanks for the pep talk." I gasped the last few feet. Teget caught my hand as I stepped off the mat.

"Well done." He clapped my arm. "Well done indeed."

I grinned. "How's that for progress, Doc?"

"You're lucky your body has healed as well as it has. We'll chalk that up to your—special genetics." Arne shook his head. "I'll get the forms finished so you can be on your way."

Man. You'd think I'd run over his cat. I rolled my eyes at him as he left the room. Didn't let it bother me. I slumped onto a bench and removed the prosthetic leg. Pretty sweet rig. Titanium, with a custom printed plastic shell—black, speckled with stars. I rubbed at the place where my knee had been, now a bone that ended in sewn flesh. Doc Arne was right. The wound was barely perceptible. Guess the pulsar stave's energies burning it closed had helped. I'd still almost bled to death.

"You've got visitors," Ramos said.

No kidding. Alvarez, Garvey, and Wilhelmina made an odd entourage. Liz barreled into the room, her tablet held in outstretched hand like she was gonna stab me with it. Teget caught her in a defensive grip, spun her sideways, arresting her momentum. She blushed. "Oh! Sorry. No harm meant. I wanted to show Mercury the specs for what I have in mind for a permanent replacement but it's way too soon to fabricate because I'm still coming up with some of the servos—"

"Don't worry about the guard dog, Liz." I accepted the tablet and swiped through image after image. It was some Iron Man-level augmentation. "This is … Wow."

She clapped, a gesture made more difficult by Teget's restraining hold. "I knew you'd like it! We'll get started on it once the new lab's better outfitted."

"Yeah? You get your stuff back?"

"We've retrieved most of the prototypes." Alvarez shied away from the door and every surface that could be touched. His eyes flicked to every surface on which a patient could sit. "She's correct. The Procyon site is being cleared of debris as we speak. There's a new plan in the works, but until we get permission to rebuild, we've had to lease space elsewhere in San Camillo. Fortunately, Procyon Foundation has several holdings. Unnamed holdings."

"I might be a while getting back into the office, at any rate." I rubbed the stump.

Alvarez looked like he was gonna hurl. "There's no rush. From what I understand, tachyon breaches have been negligible."

"And I've given the ones that ain't a proper look." Wilhelmina prodded him with her cane. "As if you've forgotten."

"Well, I'm glad to see you're doing well. There's no need to re-evaluate your operative status until the extent of your injury—or recovery—is evaluated." Alvarez was pale and sweaty. "Welcome back to Procyon."

Garvey had to slide out of the way to make room. He chuckled. "Sorry about that, Mr. Hale. Mr. Alvarez isn't a fan of hospitals."

"I had no idea." I shook my head. "Thanks for filling in for me, Wilhelmina."

"Ain't been no filling to do, child." She patted my knee. "Best you rest yourself up in case real trouble rears its head. Me? I'll mind the store—and the occasional hoodlum who gets out of line around Court Street."

"Garvey's going to drive you home," Ramos said. "I'll come with you two."

"Police escort? Outstanding." I refitted the prosthetic and

stood, with Teget holding my arm. "How about you? Want to celebrate by cracking open a couple of beers?"

"I would be delighted, Mercury, but for a short time. Your friend Gemini is due to return me to Meda. I must speak with the wardens of the temple. Change is coming to our people. I believe Grandfather would wish I played a role in it."

"If not lead it. You'll do fine." I elbowed him. "Hey. I say so, and since I'm the older brother, what I say goes, right?"

Teget snickered.

Dominic knocked on the door frame. "Can we talk to you for a minute, in private?"

"Sure." We? I glanced at Ramos. "I'll meet you guys at the car."

Ramos nodded and helped usher everyone out. That left me alone on the bench, with Dominic guarding the entrance.

"Thanks." Dominic brought in another guy, this one dressed in a casual polo shirt and khakis. Nothing out of the ordinary about him—fit, like he exercised a lot, not bad looking, but I probably would have walked by him on the street had he been mixed into a crowd. Took me a second, but I recognized the red hair and blue eyes.

Airfoil, sans helmet.

"Brandon Tusk." He offered his hand.

We shook. "You were awesome," I blurted. "Solid grip, there. What's your day job? Cop? Bouncer?"

Red flushed his neck and cheeks. "Technical services. Librarian."

"You're kidding."

Brandon shook his head.

I pointed at Dominic and then him. "Architect and librarian. Am I the only guy who doesn't have a life outside the crazy?"

Dominic chuckled. Then he winced, hand pressed to his side like he had a muscle cramp. Still healing, after all these weeks. "Back to your first statement—yes, we were all awesome. That's why we're here."

"You invited him? What, does he want my autograph?" I winked.

"Not exactly." Brandon closed the door to the room and leaned against it. Nope, nothing suspicious about that. "I came and introduced myself. Revealing my secret identity was worth the risk, considering the fact that you guys had already done so, without hesitation. I wanted to propose we—"

"Permanent team-up?" I clapped my hands. "Let's do it. Speed dial all around."

"This isn't a joke."

"Who says I'm joking? Hey, pick up your phone. It's gonna be blowing up with stories about what people saw—me in my suit putting the smack down, Airfoil holding a lake over the city, and a shadowy guy appearing out of nowhere to help save the day. Guys, come on—we saved a *city*, from two mercenary squads, an army of the undead and their slimy, tentacled cousins, not to mention the deranged killer relic that murdered its partner. We'd be stupid not to put the band back together the next time something catastrophic happens."

Brandon shared a look with Dominic. "I told you he'd be enthusiastic," Dominic said, grinning. "It isn't how I would have summarized our proposal, but it'll suffice."

"You bet it'll suffice." I stood up. "Look, I was used to doing this gig solo. That's was fine when it was me versus a monster once a month. Now? I'd be an idiot to try juggling everything on my own. Anytime the danger gets serious—as in, super serious—we should have each other's backs. We're the only ones on Earth with these gifts, so far as we know." I tapped Brandon on the chest. A spike of pure cold lanced up my arm and through my body. My teeth chattered. "And whatever yours is, I got a pretty good idea what it does."

Brandon hesitated, but soon produced a medallion dangling on a chain. "These are secret to the rest of the world."

"Yeah, but you saw the Hedron, right? You know it didn't come from here."

"I suspected as much. The Hedron's pieces, as Dominic described them, shared similar characteristics." He seemed troubled. "There's an organization that's going to be upset, to put it mildly, if they find out."

"If they don't already have their own secrets like Procyon does." I shook my head. "Don't worry about it. I'm not gonna."

There was a knock on the door. Doc Arne poked his head in. "If you're done with your fan club, Mercury, we're ready."

"Me, too." I grabbed a cane leaning against the wall. Did I mention that I got a cane? Black walnut with a brass top and tip. Not practical, but give me a break, I cut my own leg off. Screw practical. "Let's go, boys. Party's at my place."

It was a tight squeeze. As Wilhelmina and Teget could attest, my apartment's not meant for big crowds. Of course, even a dozen people make a huge gathering. Lots of bodies elbowing past each other, a warm room made even warmer by said bodies, with beer and wine and a sampler of everything off the menu from Katsaros Deli. It smelled great and sounded better.

Wouldn't trade the memory for any other.

Ramos exchanged stories about crime in San Camillo versus Drake City with Brandon, who presented himself to everyone as a "friend of Dominic's." Which was fine. His work was more street level and frequent, so he deserved anonymity for his safety and that of his loved ones. I heard metal clank. Apparently Teget was holding an impromptu sparring session, albeit in slow motion, with Wilhelmina. Liz and Dominic were comparing notes about their immigrant families. Garvey was chatting at the door with Isaiah, my neighbor from down the hall, because Isaiah had been nice enough to hold onto my mail and dropped by with it A.) as a courtesy, B.) to good-naturedly grump about the music, and C.) get himself a cold one from the fridge.

No Doc Arne or Alvarez in the mix, but I had text messages from them advising me of their absence.

That wasn't the text that made everything else mute. It was Loredana's, telling me she'd see me at Carlito's in half an hour.

Ramos found me off in a corner by the kitchen window. "Everything okay?"

"It'll be more than okay if you got what I asked you to pick up while I was in the hospital and essentially Doc's prisoner."

He handed me a small paper bag. I peeked inside at the black box.

My heart accelerated.

"Hey." He clinked a beer bottle with mine. "A word of advice—speak from your heart. That's all she wants to hear."

"Yeah. Yeah, I'll do that."

"Good luck and Godspeed, son." We hugged. A good, manly, hug, that left us both blinking. Must have been dust.

"Thanks for everything. I'll need it."

Because I'd never been more scared.

Carlito's.

Twenty-Second and DeLeon. Every time I walked through the door, I was that little boy. The owner offered me all the soda I could drink until someone from Child Protective Services could come schlep me off into the system.

I stood outside the door on my prosthetic leg and its flesh and blood partner, leaning heavily on the cane.

What is she going to see? The valiant wounded warrior? Or a cripple who is less than a man? A disappointment. An invalid, in need of coddling

That was more than my own insecurities talking. There was no mistaking the insidious, cool tones.

Whisperer. I snarled the word inside my head. *Jealous, much?*

You think you've won.

Sure looks like it. I'm sorry, how many of your lackeys are dead? And where are you? Still stuck in the Interstice.

His voice faded, replaced with bubbling laughter. *"Mercury … your destiny isn't complete, and neither is mine. You'll see, soon enough, when the light amasses anew."*

Sorry, Marigold. You're the one walking in darkness. It's way too late for you to come back.

Heed our warning.

Screw. You. I shoved the door open. Bells jingled.

The aroma of sauce and salt rolled over me. White tile floors. Olive-green walls. Black and white photos of celebrities who've visited, most prominently Ray Liotta and Idris Elba, who were paired in a place of prominence above the front counter between the huge menu boards. The radio station was tuned to the '50s classics. No jukebox, though. I spotted the young dark-haired gal behind the counter changing the playlist on her phone.

Then I spotted Loredana.

She wore a blue blouse and black skirt and sported the earrings—the ones I'd used to track her down in another dimension. A pizza sat on the table already. Pepperoni and sausage, half with olives. I wouldn't be touching that half.

But I wasn't hungry, and it had nothing to do with the party, because I'd fasted since leaving the hospital. It wasn't doctor's orders.

"Okay." I stood by the edge of the table. "This is weird."

"How so?" She had her hands folded on her lap. They were fidgeting with the strap of her purse.

"It used to be I could count on you as my handler, someone who'd fix problems that got way out of hand, or who gave me the green light to go kill monsters," I said. "Then I could count on you as a confidante. Someone to talk with about all this stuff we couldn't tell anyone else. Then things got—complex. But at the same time, they weren't complex, because they were simpler than anything had ever been in my life. That's when I figured out that I loved you."

She smiled. "I understand what you mean, Mercury, and that's why I'm staying. Because this work, with Procyon—with you—is my life. And I love you, too."

"That's great." I grinned. Tried not to bounce on my heels and look like a complete goofball, because I was already well on my way. "I wondered. You hadn't said anything when you came to visit me, and I knew your dad had left a while back, so I hoped—"

"Mercury." She touched the hand I was using to prop against the table.

"Yeah, okay." I blew out a breath. "Bear with me for this next part."

I set the cane down in my seat. Kneeling with a prosthetic leg is tricky, and painful, but I did it anyway. I was gonna do this right even if my other leg came off.

Loredana's eyes went wide.

"Loredana Lark." I dug the black box out of my pocket. Dropped it, of course. I picked it up and cracked the lid.

A slim, silver band with a ruby in the center. Pretty cheap. I forced down the chagrin of not being able to put enough cash together for something extravagant and was just thankful I'd remembered the name and address of the store I'd found months ago.

It was an antiques shop a block from here, where I'd saved the owner, an old lady, from being robbed and stabbed. She'd paid me in silver coins.

I'd cashed those in elsewhere and given Ramos the money to pick up the ring.

Loredana's eyes were filled with tears. "Please continue."

Right. "Will you marry me?"

Carlito's had gone silent. I think the girl had shut off the music. Murmurs carried over from other tables. Pretty sure I felt the flash from cell phone cameras.

Loredana nodded, over and over, her hands to her mouth, until she finally said, "Yes. Yes, of course I will."

She kissed me as I slid the ring onto her finger, her hands holding my face. The restaurant erupted in cheers and whistles. I was crying, she was crying, heck, everyone was crying. The waitress brought over our check with a crumpled assortment of bills on it, blubbering about how the staff and some diners had paid for our meal.

I ignored the hoopla. Loredana was what mattered. She and our friends, our loved ones—our weird family of misfits and heroes. I'd lost mine from almost before I could remember. This replacement bunch that fate or God had cobbled together? They made me proud.

Whispers aside, I was ready to face whatever came our way.

And when the time came, I'd take the fight into the Interstice itself.

Mercury's adventures continue...

Stay tuned

www.steverzasa.com

www.ingramcontent.com/pod-product-compliance
Lightning Source LLC
Chambersburg PA
CBHW071736110726
47908CB00006B/1609

* 9 7 8 1 7 3 3 5 8 5 1 2 5 *